The Hous

Book 1 of The Dimensional ——— Series

By: Bonnie K.T. Dillabough

Cover art by Richard McKenzie

DimensionalAllianceHeadquarters.com

Copyright 2019 – All rights reserved

Acknowledgements:

At age five I was already a bookaholic. My mother, Donna Gail Tussey (Webster), introduced me to that magical place, called a library before kindergarten. The kindergarten teacher said, in my presence, that she was at a loss as to what to teach me, since I was reading at a first grade level at the time. My grandmother, Anita H. Tussey, continued to encourage me to read and also to engage my creative mind to write and to notice my surroundings in detail. Then followed many great teachers who inspired and encouraged me to read and write and explore my world.

When, after raising six amazing children, with my awesome husband of (now) 46 years, I am a
grandmother of 17 awesome grandchildren and a great grandson. I am only just now, finally, writing the novels I have been told for so many years I was destined to write. I was 65 years old at my first book signing.

That being said, I want to give credit to another group who have been my cheerleaders in making this happen. My sweet husband, my children and grandchildren, Richard G. Lowe (who helped me get the ball rolling), Mercedes Lackey (for her inspiration and advice) and my beta readers as follows:

Delia D. Michael, Jennifer Dillabough, Aurora Jay, George S. Dillabough, Tymara Michael, Tyler Michael, Luz Rives, Kitty Connell, Annette Foster, Cindy Jones Erickson, Lynnette Dillabough, Maria Gurriere, Caleb Michael, Patricia Burke, Angela Bryner, Maureen Burrows Briscoe, Shelah Dow, Jacob Michael, Scott McKenzie, Richard McKenzie and George C. Dillabough.

Contents:
Chapter 1: The Tiny Key 5
Chapter 2: Deliveries 14
Chapter 3: Thinking Outside the Box 20
Chapter 4: The Hike 27
Chapter 5: The Gatekeeper 37
Chapter 6: Arrangements 48
Chapter 7: Skylark 57
Chapter 8: Pushing the Limits 67
Chapter 9: Beginnings and Endings 76
Chapter 10: In the Loop 81
Chapter 11: Daddy's Little Girl 92
Chapter 12: Assignment 99
Chapter 13: Under Fire 106
Chapter 14: The Alliance 116
Chapter 15: Besties 124
Chapter 16: Dilemma 133
Chapter 17: The Honey Trap 142
Chapter 18: Interesting Times 152
Chapter 19: Revelations 161
Chapter 20: Pick Up the Pace 170
Chapter 21: Cloak and Dagger 174
Chapter 22: Queen of the Groga 185
Chapter 23: A Shot in the Dark 194
Chapter 24: Seeking Sneaky Sam 200
Chapter 25: Shedding Light 212
Chapter 26: Q&A 225
Chapter 27: The Lair 231
Chapter 28: Out of Small Things… 242

Chapter 29: Into the Swamp	251
Chapter 30: The Dissembler	257
Chapter 31: The Devil in the Details	265
Chapter 32: Out of the Frying Pan	276
Chapter 33: Out-sneaking The Sneak	297
Chapter 34: When All Else Fails	316
Chapter 35: The Road Less Travelled	331
Chapter 36: Where's the White Rabbit?	346
Chapter 37: Debriefings	364
Chapter 38: Full Circle	372

Chapter 1: The Tiny Key

"Here are the keys to the estate," the grim-faced attorney said, handing her a small key-ring. "Front door, back door, garage and storage shed in the back. You can take up residence whenever you are ready. My secretary will have the deed documents for you on your way out."

He extended his hand and she shook it solemnly. As she returned through the outer office and retrieved the documents from the trim, well-dressed secretary, she realized she must look a bit dazed, but that was to be expected.

"Wow," she thought, shaking her head in disbelief.

As she fished for her car keys in her bag, her hand brushed the lavender envelope with the unfamiliar hand of her Aunt Elizabeth, known as "Lizzie" by the family. The note, inscribed in green ink, had been short and inscrutable. "Don't forget to feed the cat and check the mantle for the rest... Regards, Lizzie"

What "the rest" was, she had no idea, but her aunt's will had been very clear about some things. The cat came with the estate and she would lose the property if she neglected or removed the cat. Jenny had never had a cat or any pet, for that matter, so she was a little bemused by this information.

The whole thing was just so very bizarre. She had met her Aunt Lizzie only twice before. Once, when she was 10 and had won an award for an essay, she had submitted to a national writing contest, entitled: "Why Aliens Must Exist". The second time was at her college graduation where she had given the Valedictorian speech for her class.

Lizzie had been "an odd one" according to her dad. She was her dad's great aunt on his mother's side and, despite her advancing age had been an avid traveler. It was unclear how she had made her living, but she had no children, nor had she ever married. Why, of all her cousins, Jenny had been chosen to receive all her belongings, including the house and cat, at her death, Jenny had no idea.

She tried to picture the dark grey wool beret that had perched upon her aunt's silvery hair and the funny way she had of cocking her head to listen to what was being said. She always seemed to be smiling about a private joke that only she could understand, and her dark eyes seemed to miss nothing.

Jenny sighed. It seemed that she would soon know much more about her, as everything Lizzie had owned had been packed into the large storage shed behind her house, per her instructions in her will, so that Jenny would have no trouble moving her own things into the roomy two-bedroom home in the Los Angeles foothills. Jenny had never actually been there, but the attorney had described it as part of the reading of the will.

Jenny shook her head. It was all still very unreal to her, but now she was beginning to feel some excitement. Her friends had helped her pack up her little studio apartment the night before into the moving van. She had not had the luxury to take her time as she had less than a week before the next month's rent would be due for her apartment and she didn't want to spend the money if she didn't have to.

She skipped the freeway as it was much quicker to avoid that snail's pace by going the back streets and putting up with some traffic lights. So, it came as almost a surprise when she realized she was nearly there. When she reached the twisty figure-eight road, she consulted her GPS and began to watch for the address coming closer and closer. Four blocks… Three blocks… Two blocks… Finally, her GPS said, "Arrive at destination on the right." She double-checked the address: 888 Infinity Loop. Yes, this was the place. She pulled into the driveway in front of the garage door.

She didn't know what she had expected, but it wasn't this hacienda style home with a white stucco wall enclosing a small garden in front with a large wrought iron gate under an archway of bougainvillea. The terra cotta roof tiles set off the white stucco and the yucca and pampas grass plants that framed each side of the red brick step leading onto a small porch. She sat there for a moment, just taking it all in.

This was her house. Her home. She had the papers in her glove box, signed, sealed and delivered. She glanced around the neighborhood. The houses were spaced well apart with generous breezeways between homes. Across the street was a large home, similar to her house, with what appeared to be a large workshop of some kind down a long driveway. Based on the nice cars parked in the driveways in either direction, this was a well-to-do neighborhood. The landscaping was well cared for and the hacienda theme was similar in every direction that she could see.

The sound of a car pulling up behind her in the driveway pulled her out of her reverie with a start. Behind her was the little red Smart Car driven by her best friend, Sam.

"Hey, new homeowner, are you ready to move in?" she called, her green eyes sparkling. Sam had burnished curly auburn hair cut short to her head. She was taller than many men and her freckles just seemed to enhance those brilliant green eyes dancing with mischief.

Jenny grinned. "I suppose so. The movers will be here in about 15 minutes. Wanna take a look around?"

As they went through the wrought iron gate into the front garden, Jenny noticed bougainvillea was also trained over the lattice archway framing the porch. Huge aloe vera plants played sentinel around the edge of the walkway. There was no lawn, but a rock garden like nothing she had seen before. Rocks from small boulder size to marble size in a range of colors that she didn't expect covered the ground. Flat steppingstones formed the walkway that led from the gate to the porch.

As she approached the door, which matched the roof tiles, and reached for the handle, she inserted the key into the lock and, taking a calming breath and looking at her friend with an anticipatory grin, she turned the key.

The large brightly sunlit entryway led to a living room with white stucco walls, a window seat framed by a huge picture window looking out onto the front garden and a fireplace with a wooden mantle. And there, to Jenny's surprise, was another lavender envelope with a small lump in it, labeled in the hand she recognized now as Lizzie's. It simply said, "For Jenny".

She opened the envelope and out fell a short note and a very small ornate key on a gold chain, such as you might use for a jewelry box. The bow of the key was decorated with interlocked circles that almost seemed to disappear into the center of the circle. Sam's raised eyebrows encouraged her, and she read the note aloud: "Dear Jenny. Wear this until you find a use for it. You won't be sorry. I have great expectations for your next adventures. Love, Aunt Lizzie."

Jenny handed the necklace to Sam, who examined it carefully. "Nice," she said, "Would you like me to fasten it for you?" Jenny turned her back to Sam who gently fastened the tiny chain behind her. The weight of the small key was feather light on her neck. Jenny didn't wear jewelry much, but it was a momentous day, and this seemed an appropriate way to celebrate.

Sam let out a breath. "This is why I love hanging out with you, Jenn. You make life interesting. What do you think she meant by 'adventures'?"

Jenny shook her head. "I have absolutely no idea. I think we should postpone the treasure hunt until we have some furniture in here, though, don't you think? Let's see what else this place has in store, so I can decide where I need to put everything."

They moved from the living room into the dining room, which showed French doors looking out into a back-yard patio with a large, brightly colored, striped awning and many potted plants. From there they examined the kitchen with old-fashioned enamel appliances lots of cupboards and counter space and a large window over the double sinks that also looked out into the back-yard.

"This place has some real potential," breathed Sam, her eyes sparkling. "We could have some pretty amazing parties here."

Jenny grinned back. "I like the quiet, but I suppose we can do a house-warming…a SMALL one," she said wagging a finger at her friend. "No big blow-outs here. I haven't met the neighbors, and this doesn't seem like that kind of a neighborhood."

Sam sighed. "I guess you're right," she said, shaking her head. "But that patio looks like it would make a great place for it."

A knock on the door interrupted their plans and they went to greet the movers. Three muscular men in t-shirts that proclaimed them to be "College Guys – Movin' and Shakin'" stood in the door.

Jenny had labeled the boxes before they went into the truck with the various rooms and she and Sam supervised the unloading. Everything but Jenny's computer equipment had been packed into the moving van, as Jenny preferred to keep her tech close, in order to pack, move and unpack it herself. So, once the desk had been installed in the room she designated as "the office", she and Sam pulled her equipment out of her little blue SUV and, while the movers continued moving the rest of the boxes and furniture into her house, "My house," she thought continuing to grin, she set up her equipment.

She had been surprised to discover that this older home was well wired for all of her needs, including high speed internet. The cable company had come in the day before to turn it on, at the attorney's request.

It wouldn't have been a big deal, but Jenny made her living as a paid blogger for several online companies. She had stumbled into freelance blogging while still in college and it had paid for her education, her little apartment and her car payment, not to mention all of the expenses of living in Los Angeles.

By the time she had everything assembled on her desk and all the connections handled, the movers were on their way out the door. It was odd to see her things, most still in boxes, in the bright room with its deep red tiled floor.

Shaking her head at the seeming unreality of it all, Jenny wandered into the kitchen where Sam was stowing things from a cooler into the refrigerator. "Lunch?" Sam asked.

They made up some sandwiches and sat out on the patio, taking in the warmth of this sunny spring day and watching the butterflies swooping and fluttering over the meandering herb garden.

"I still don't believe it," said Jenny as she and Sam cleared their lunch away. "I am at a loss as to why Aunt Lizzie decided to give this all to me."

"Well, it all looks pretty real to me," laughed Sam. "I have to run, though. Unlike you, I have a 'real job'. Are you going to be alright?"

The whole "real job" thing was a standing joke with her and Sam, as most of Jenny's relatives (including her parents) didn't approve of her choice of vocation. It didn't much matter that Jenny often wrote 10 hours or more a day for several days at a time. And it didn't seem to matter that she was making a fairly good living at it. Sam, on the other hand, worked at a local television station as tech support, post production and crewing in the studio.

"No, I'm good. I definitely have plenty to do." And she looked around at all the unpacked boxes.

When Sam pulled out of the drive, Jenny stood there at the gate for a few moments, still very much in wonder at her new circumstances. She looked up and down the quiet street, noting that nothing seemed to be stirring besides the birds burbling cheerfully to one another.

Back inside she busied herself with unpacking her books into the shelves in the living room. The doorbell rang, and she answered the door only to find a short, salt-and-pepper-haired man of middle years with a short mustache smiling at her, a huge black tabby cat in his arms.

"Hey there, neighbor!" he said, his blue eyes twinkling. "I'm Bob Reid, from across the street. I'm here to deliver Tidbit," gesturing with a nod of his head at the big black cat.

The cat! Jenny had completely forgotten about the cat. "Hi Bob. I'm Jenny Japhet. Come on in. Did you know my aunt then?"

"Lizzie was an amazing lady," and his voice was soft and concerned. "She'll be greatly missed."

"I didn't know her all that well. I'm as surprised as anyone that she left all this to me."

"Lizzie never did anything without a really good reason," Bob replied. "I'm sure you must have some very interesting qualities for her to have singled you out."

He put the cat down who rubbed himself sinuously around Bob's ankles. "As I said, this is Tidbit, your aunt's most faithful companion. I'll bring over his food, his dishes and his bed in a bit. He's fairly friendly for a cat and not very demanding. I'm sure you'll be good friends. If there's anything at all you need while you're getting settled in, let me know. I'm usually in my workshop."

The cat didn't follow him out as he left but curled up in the window seat that looked out onto the front garden. As the sunlight hit him, she could see the black on black stripes of his fur and he looked up at her with large amber eyes as if expecting something. Jenny patted him tentatively on the head. "Tidbit, eh? Looks like you grew into a big chunk instead. I didn't know housecats got this big." Tidbit merely stared up at her, his expression inscrutable.

Jenn spent the rest of the day putting things to rights, humming unconsciously as she put her things away, made her bed and arranged her kitchen. Bob stopped by a few hours later with Tidbit's things.

"No litter box?" she asked as he set the box down.

"Doesn't use one," Bob replied. "He's mostly an outdoor cat. He'll ask to be let out when the need arises, and he likes to stay out at night. Think he goes out hunting. About the only time he stays inside at night is when it's raining…so, very seldom, the drought being what it is."

"He's got a cat bed, but mostly he likes to hang out on the window seat, watching the birds. He's missed his place since Lizzie passed. I'm sure he's glad to be back."

Bob gave the cat a thorough scratch of his ears and under his chin. Tidbit purred loudly, closing his eyes, his head nodding slowly side to side.

"I've never had a pet before," Jenny began. "I really have no idea how to care for him."

"Tidbit, doesn't seem to need much looking after. Keep his water bowl filled and food in his bowl and he'll pretty much take care of the rest. Cats are good that way. You'll soon get used to one another; I'll warrant."

Jenny nodded, unsure of what to say. Bob nodded at the door. "I've got to get back to work," he said. "By the way, what do you do?"

"I'm a blogger," she said, tensing herself for the usual negative comments she was so used to.

"Really? What do you blog about?"

"Various things. I'm a ghost-writer. I write blogs for companies online, so you'll never see my name attached to any of them. Companies pay me to put out interesting content to attract the right kind of buyers and clients," she said, surprised that his face showed a real interest in what she was saying.

"Hmm. I guess that means you work out of your home? This should be a great place to do what you do. I have a workshop behind my house. I guess you might call me a tinkerer. Invented a few useful gadgets a few years back that set me up pretty well. Now I follow my thinker," he said, pointing to his head. "I'm usually either in the workshop or puttering in the garden out back."

He headed out the door with, "So don't be a stranger, if you need anything."

Jenny turned to Tidbit. "O.K., Mr. Tidbit. I guess it's just you and me. I don't know a lot about cats. I guess it's time I learned, right?" The tip of Tidbit's tail twitched as if to say, "I'm good with it," and he turned his big head, looking out the window, his ears swiveling as he watched the sparrows in the bougainvillea outside.

Jenny considered what to do next. In anticipation for the move she had gotten ahead on her writing assignments and had a couple days to work on organizing her new space and getting to explore her environment. But where to start?

The living room was much larger than her tiny apartment and her furniture looked a little sparse for the size of the room, but she set about assembling her bookshelves along one wall and once the cushy armchair with the old fashioned stand lamp was positioned in the corner facing the entry way and her couch had been graced with her mother's afghan and throw pillows, it started to feel a little more like home.

She took in the fireplace and the empty space over the mantle. It needed a large painting or a big mirror, she decided, but that would have to wait.

After sorting out the living room, so she would have a place to welcome a guest, she worked her way through the bedroom and kitchen and by the time she had finished it was very dark outside. She had let Tidbit out for the night and finally decided it was time to head to bed.

As she prepared for bed, she went to remove the necklace with the tiny gold key, which she had quite forgotten about until that moment. It wouldn't come off! She searched the chain several times for the tiny clasp, checking in the bathroom mirror and the clasp was just gone. How could that be? "I'm probably just tired," she told herself. "It won't hurt to wear it to bed. I'll figure it out in the morning." And with that, she fluffed her pillow, turned out the light and went to sleep in her very own house.

Chapter 2: Deliveries

In her dreams she was wandering through her house, looking for something. She wasn't sure what it was, but it was vital and just why she couldn't say. Her house seemed to be huge, acres and acres of rooms and furnishings and doors that sometimes would not open. When she awoke it was disconcerting to be in her cozy small bedroom once again.

Despite her disorientation she got up and went through her morning routine. She paused in front of the bathroom mirror when she finished brushing her teeth. "Well, look at you. You don't look like an 'heiress'," she chuckled at her image. "As a matter of fact, you look pretty average, as people go."

She looked at herself critically, as women are wont to do. Her ash blonde hair was really curly and hung below her shoulders in the back, but mostly, like this morning, she wore it either braided or in a ponytail or a knot on the back of her neck. Her deep blue eyes were nearly violet and large for her face. She always thought her nose was too big and her ears and mouth were too small. She didn't have any excess weight on her, but there was only one word for her body. She was "curvy" like her mom.

She didn't have the usual "California" tan, because she spent much of every day in front of a computer screen, but she did like to run and hike. She would have liked to spend more time on the beach, but there was a price of being good at her job. All of those enticing advertisements you see online about working from home showed someone with a laptop on a chaise lounge poolside. The reality was that computing outside was one of those urban myths. It really didn't work all that well, even in sunny California.

She dressed hurriedly and rushed into the bright kitchen, prepared her green shake and headed into her office to check emails and get ready for the day. In her email inbox was an email with the subject line: From Lizzie.

Puzzled, she opened the email. In it, was a photo of Aunt Lizzie, seemingly not all that long ago, and a tall black man. Aunt Lizzie would have been considered a tall woman, but next to this man, wearing colorful robes in oranges, yellows, browns and reds she almost looked petite.

He was built almost square, broad shoulders and muscled arms, much like many weightlifters she had seen photos of. His broad forehead blended into the bald shiny head. The sunlight glinted off of his head as if it had been polished. His face was solemn, but Lizzie looked elated, as if she had won a marathon or the lottery. She had never looked as ancient as her age would have implied, probably due to her mischievous attitude, and, as usual her eyes crinkled with laughter, her mouth in a wide grin that showed all of her white teeth.

Jenny didn't recognize Lizzie's surroundings, but it was almost like one of those safari photos you see on travel pages. You almost expected there to be a Land Rover behind them and jungle foliage. Instead, they were in front of a large green building with odd architecture, all curves instead of angles.

Lizzie wore the same grey beret Jenny always associated with her aunt and around her neck was…THE KEY! The same delicate gold chain held the pendant just above the neckline of her V-necked t-shirt. Jenny raised her hand to the little gold key around her own neck, remembering, all of a sudden, her attempts to take it off the night before.

It was hard to tell where Lizzie and this large, somewhat forbidding stranger were standing, but in Lizzie's hand there was what appeared to be a map. "X marks the spot," chortled Jenny, now wondering if her aunt had been into treasure-hunting. She knew so little about her and this photo with no caption and no clue as to what it represented was tantalizing, but she felt no wiser.

She heard a yowl at the French doors in the dining room and got up to let Tidbit in. He waited patiently and wound himself around her ankles as he entered. "Good morning, Tidbit," she greeted him with a grin. It seemed that Tidbit was willing to accept her for now. "Hungry?"

His answering mrrrr trilled at her as he led the way into the kitchen and stood expectantly by his bowls. "Hey, kitty, do you know anything about this key?" she asked conversationally as she filled his bowl with what she recognized as one of the more expensive brands of cat food.

Tidbit was non-committal, however and set to eating his food almost daintily.

"Time to take a look around, I think. Are you coming or are you ready for a nap after 'catting around' all night?"

Tidbit looked up at her, blinking, his black furry face unreadable as ever, ears pointed forward.

"Fine. Bon Appetit."

She headed out the French doors into the morning sunlight and as she stood on the cement of the shaded patio she looked around at the large yard before her.

To her right, behind the small garage was the storage building. The white wooden siding and red roof tiles was a perfect match for the house. It was large, easily large enough to hold several cars and appeared to be two stories, from where she stood. There were no windows. A red door with a matching frame was the only opening she could see. She had the key on her key ring but didn't want to spend however long it would take inventorying Lizzie's possessions.

Before her was a lovely herb garden, featuring a small trickling waterfall that fell tinkling into a small pool where decorative koi swam lazily, glinting in the sun. "I wonder if I'm supposed to be feeding them too?" she asked herself, filing that question to ask Bob, when she got a chance.

By the koi pond were two wrought iron chairs with colorful cushions and a small glass table topped with a brightly colored patio umbrella. It appeared this might have been one of Aunt Lizzie's favorite spots as there were worn spots in the grass before each of the chairs, worn by the feet of Lizzie and past visitors.

Did the large man in the photo come to visit here and would she meet him? She giggled as she thought of that rather large man perched on one of those chairs, sipping herb tea and eating cookies with her aunt.

To her left the large variegated herb garden continued with such an amazing variety of herbs that she realized that this yard would take some caring for and wondered how it had stayed so neat as much traveling as her aunt had done.

Tidbit had wandered out to stand beside her on the patio and turned his large lamp-like eyes on her, cocking his head slightly, almost dog-like in his curiosity. "Interesting place we've got here, kitty cat," she remarked.

She turned and wandered back into the house and her hand strayed back to her neck. "Very interesting indeed," she sighed.

The morning passed quietly, just her and Tidbit. She had plenty of time to think, continuing to unpack boxes, hoping she could get it all done by the end of the day, so she had a clear mind when she started back to work. She didn't expect Sam to pop by as she had a parasailing lesson that day after work, so she was surprised when her front doorbell rang just before lunchtime.

It was a tall young man with black curly hair and a rake in his hand. "Just checking in before I head back to the garden," he said with a lop-sided grin. "I'm Ted and I have been caring for this garden for the last few years for Miss Lizzie. You must be Jenny. Lizzie's paid me a year in advance, so you don't owe me anything. I just didn't want you to see a stranger in your backyard and call the cops."

He said all of this in a big rush, his words sort of tumbling out of his mouth, and a bit of a flush to his pale freckled skin. He held out his free hand and Jenny took it and shook it. It was rough and callused.

"Well that explains that," she said. "You wouldn't happen to know anything about the fish?"

As it turns out, Ted did know about the fish. He explained that the koi were part of an aquaponic system where the plants around the pond fed the fish and the waste from the fish fed the plants. It was a self-sustaining system and would require very little maintenance, all of which was covered under Ted's contract. He pointed out that the plants edging the pond were strawberries and would soon be blooming and producing berries "so sweet they make sugar seem sour" as he said.

After he showed her around the garden, pointing out the various herbs in the garden, many of which she was unfamiliar with and their traditional uses, he shooed her back into the house, saying, "I've got this. I'll give you a holler before I go."

Jenny made up her lunch in her cool classic kitchen and took it into the living room, setting her plate on the little table beside her cushy armchair and pulled out a mystery book featuring a reporter who solved mysteries with a couple of Siamese cats that she had been meaning to read. She only got a few bites into her meal and a few pages into the book, however, when the bell rang again.

It was Bob. He had rung the bell with his elbow, evidently, as his arms were full of a stack of boxes that appeared to be heavy.

"Sorry," he panted as he set down the boxes with a thud on the dining room table. "I was supposed to give you these the first day and I plumb forgot. These were Lizzie's and she wanted you to have them, but she didn't want them put into the storage shed, in case you didn't get a chance to poke around in there for awhile."

"What are they?"

"No idea, Jenny. Lizzie just told me to hang onto them until you got the house…"

"Wait a minute. What do you mean? Are you saying she knew she was dying?"

"Didn't they tell you? Didn't anyone tell you?" Bob shook his head in disbelief. "She had an inoperable tumor. By the time they realized it, it was too late. She only had weeks to live. While she was dying, I wondered why no one came to see her."

Jenny was stunned. She hadn't known. This had all been such a shock. An aunt she hadn't known, but by reputation and those two brief meetings, and who had been so generous, but she had only found out she was dead after the fact. How sad that she had to die without family around her. Why hadn't she reached out?

Bob saw her shock and gestured to the couch beside him. "She spent her last weeks preparing this all for you. I guess I thought you two had been close."

"I didn't know her. Nothing about her really, except she used to travel a lot, that she was unmarried and that she was dad's oldest aunt."

"Well, judging by the weight of these boxes, they've got papers in them, or maybe rocks," Bob said, handing her yet another sealed lavender envelope. "This was supposed to go with it."

He got up, sticking his hands into his jean pockets and rocking on his feet. "Gotta get back to work," he murmured, ducking his head. "Let me know if you need anything."

Jenny thanked him, still somewhat numb, and saw him out the door. As she turned back to the dining room, there was Tidbit, sitting on a dining room chair, looking at her as only a cat can do. "What do you think, Tidbit? I wish you could talk. I'll bet you know a whole lot more than what you're saying, don't you?"

She fingered the seal on the lavender envelope, wondering if she really wanted to read what was inside. With a deep sigh she put her finger under the corner of the seal and pulled it open.

The note in the now familiar green ink read: "Jenny. I know this is all pretty overwhelming for you right now, but I want you to know that you will understand soon. The boxes have a lot of documents that may come in handy at some point and hopefully will answer some questions as they come up. Bob is a good guy and he can be trusted, if you need anything. Box number 1 is where you should start. The others will come in handy and are also numbered. The manila envelope on top should be your first stop. Don't forget to feed the cat. Love, Lizzie"

Chapter 3: Thinking Outside the Box

Jenny lowered herself almost unconsciously into the dining room chair, eyeing the 3 boxes warily. "What do you think, Tidbit? Do we open up Pandora's box?"

Tidbit had sidled up beside her looking calmly into her eyes. The very tip of his tail twitched, but he didn't mrrrr back at her.

"Well, you're no help," she muttered.

She pulled the tape off of the top of the first box and pulled open the top. As promised, there on the top of a pile of file folders was a large, thick manila envelope. There was no writing on the outside, but she opened it as instructed. Out of the envelope fell another sheet of lavender paper attached to something that looked somewhat like a passport, but it was different than passports she had seen. The cover, instead of dark blue, was a yellow gold. And, surprisingly, there, just inside the cover was a picture of Jenny which looked like one of her college photos, but she didn't remember posing for it.

She didn't recognize the language or even the characters of the printing inside it, so she stopped to read the note attached to it. "You'll be needing this. Put it somewhere safe, where you can get to it easily and quickly. It isn't time yet for me to explain all of this, but you will understand in time.

The other documents in this box are some old photos, like the one you got in an email I had scheduled to send to you to get your attention. I have set up an auto-responder with additional messages you will receive from time to time. I want you to know I'm not playing games with you or trying to be mysterious, but what has been set before you needs to be done in order.

Unless I have misjudged you, you will not only be up to it, but I think what comes next will enrich your life and give you so much more than you can imagine.

One last thing. The next mail you receive will give you the details of a special account I have set up for you at my bank. There should be enough in there for you to live on for the next few years. After that, you won't need it. You might want to consider taking a leave of absence from your current duties very soon.

Love, Lizzie"

Jenny sat there dumbfounded and perplexed. What in the world did all of this mean? What in the world had she gotten herself into? She opened the "passport" again, staring at herself beaming up from the photograph on the first page. Other than the writing on the facing page, the rest of the little book appeared to be blank. It didn't have a country seal on it that she recognized. The symbol on the front cover was an 8 on its side, the symbol for…infinity.

"Whoa," Jenny breathed. "Whoa, whoa, whoa…"

She realized she was fingering the little gold key at her neck. What was this all about? How in the world had she gotten involved in what was beginning to feel like an adventure she hadn't volunteered for? Who was her aunt anyway? What she didn't know about her aunt now seemed to be a lot more important than ever before.

How in the world could she go to her agency and tell them she would be taking a "leave of absence" and what exactly did her aunt want her to do instead? Her head spun with questions and uncertainty. Evidently this "gift horse" had some serious strings attached.

Her eyes strayed to the contents of the box. Several large old-fashioned picture albums and large hard-backed books that looked like old accounting books or journals practically filled the box. She gingerly pulled one of the albums out. It was very old and as she opened it, black and white photos of people she didn't know filled the pages. She turned them idly. They were labeled with some names she actually recognized.

Her father had been a family history enthusiast and she knew a lot more about her ancestry than she had thought she would have researched on her own volition. Her dad used to tell her stories about her grandparents and great grandparents that dated clear back to pioneers in covered wagons and handcarts, who had pushed their way across the territories of North America and settled new places that eventually became the western states.

The people in these old yellowed and bespeckled photos stared out at her without a smile among them. Women in long dresses with aprons and men in white cotton shirts and dark trousers held up by suspenders peered out from the past at her. As she thumbed through carefully, for fear of tearing the fragile pages, the photos began to change, they were clearer, although still in black and white. Names were carefully inked in a cursive hand she didn't recognize. The ink was fading, but legible and as she got closer to the end of the album more and more familiar faces appeared.

As the photos crept forward in time, she recognized the wedding photos of her grandparents, copies of which hung in the dining room of her parent's house. And then, faintly colored photos of her dad and mom as small children. There was a photo of her dad taken at a family reunion, his parents were in the photo, and among the large family, what looked like a much younger Lizzie.

He and his aunt had never been close, but he had always spoken of her with a twinkle in his eyes. "You never knew what Lizzie would be up to next," he would say, his eyes focused on something only he could see. "When she wasn't in the library, she was corresponding with several pen pals around the world and writing in her little notebooks. She must have had dozens of them. And always fiddling with things until they did what she wanted them to do. She had the travelling bug for sure, never knew where we would get a postcard from next."

That was the most she knew of her aunt, however, and now what she didn't know made her wonder again, just exactly what was going to happen next.

She put down the album just as the doorbell rang again.

"Now what?" she grumbled.

A short, stocky older man with piercing blue eyes squinting under a plain black ball cap stood at the door with a large grey great dane at his side. He stabbed his thumb at his chest. "Elias Mensch. I'm next door. This is Cinder," he said nodding his head at the dog.

"Hi, I'm Jenny..." she began, but he cut her off.

"Postman must be new," he said. "I think these are yours."

He thrust a handful of letters at her and nearly didn't wait for her to reach for them until he began to turn back down the steppingstone walk. "I'll make sure he knows where you are," he said over his shoulder. And he stalked off down the walk.

The dog, Cinder, however still stood and stared at her. He could have been made of stone. Jenny had never seen a dog this big and his glare seemed menacing, although he did not growl. In the meantime, Tidbit had appeared at the doorway as well, stropping her ankles. As he did so, he made the most eerie sound. It wasn't a meow or even a growl. It went from a deep mrrrr, ascending to a high pitch and down again. Cinder's eyes widened, and he took a step back, never taking his eyes off of the cat.

Tidbit stepped gracefully forward like a leopard Jenny had once seen in a jungle documentary. His front quarters were low, his tail twitched like a flicking finger. One step forward. Cinder backed up one step. Another step. Cinder backed again one careful step. Was that a whimper from the big grey dog? The mirrored action of the dog and the cat was almost a dance. For every slow forward stalking step Tidbit would take, Cinder would back up one step, constantly keeping wary eye contact with the cat, almost as if mesmerized.

As they reached the wrought iron gate, Cinder suddenly turned tail and ran full out with Tidbit in hot pursuit until they were out of sight. "Looks like you've got this well in hand, Tidbit," she murmured to herself, shaking her head. "Curiouser and curiouser."

She sorted through the pile of three letters. One was marked "resident". One was obviously from her mom, covered in little heart stickers. And there was one thicker envelope from a bank.

She dropped into her reading chair with another sigh. She opened her mom's letter first. The letter went on and on about her mom's new Zumba group and the many goings-on of her siblings and concluded with:

"I'm glad to hear you're settling into your new 'digs'. Your dad says this is typical Lizzie, to spring something like this on someone. I am sure you are as surprised as the rest of us, but you should know that, although many thought your aunt was a bit 'dotty', she was a nice person. I always liked her, as much as I ever saw of her.

Dad and I may come down to visit in a few weeks. I've never been to her house before. It will be good to catch up and you can show us around. We got you a little house-warming present and we'll bring it with us when we come. Love, Mom"

Jenny grinned. Her mom always had such a positive take on things. She knew her parents were unused to the idea of someone working from home and being their own boss, but although they hadn't approved of it, they hadn't once discouraged her from doing her best at her chosen profession. Jenny thought they may have been a little disappointed that her writing career had left few traces. As a ghostwriter, she seldom got public credit for her work and that didn't leave much in the way of bragging rights.

She then hefted the thick envelope from the unknown bank. This must be the bank her aunt had told her about in her last missive. Inside the envelope was a debit card with her name on it and the details of her account with all the usual legalese. If her aunt hadn't mentioned it specifically, she would have been suspicious. She had received cards like this in the mail that had turned out to be fraudulent.

She goggled at the amount in the account. Lizzie's note had said something about the money sustaining her for a few years, but, considering her own spending habits, she calculated that she could live very well on this for many years to come, especially since her housing was rent free.

This reminded her of the boxes sitting on her dining room table. What were all of those photo albums really about and why had Lizzie kept them separate from the other things left to her in the storage building? She felt like she needed time to catch her breath. All of this was happening so quickly. She remembered fantasizing as a kid about fairy godmothers and all, but in no way did she ever expect anything like this. And it was beginning to feel like this was about way more than just an estate from a "dotty" old aunt.

In the meantime, she heard Tidbit meowing loudly from the back yard. "Business taken care of?" she asked him, letting him in. He peered up at her with his big golden eyes for a moment and, after drinking daintily from his water bowl, he hopped up gracefully to his place on the window seat, curled up and closed his eyes.

She wandered back over to the dining room table. Surveying the first box, she decided to thumb through the remaining albums later. She was surprised to see that the light was already fading, the colors in the sky beyond the backyard fence diluted like watercolors and she realized she hadn't even thought about supper. She fixed herself a sandwich and took her plate into the office and ate while she considered what to say to her agency. She had never considered changing her vocation and she couldn't help but feel like Aunt Lizzie was taking a lot for granted.

True, she had provided a beautiful house and a substantial nest egg. Not to mention a cat, of all things. But the rest of this was so bizarre it set her to wondering if this was some elaborate joke. Again, she touched the key at her neck, which, despite her ongoing efforts to find the catch, she had been unable to remove. What was up with the little key? She had searched the house pretty thoroughly to discover some mysterious box that it might open. At first, she had been sure it went to a security box or jewelry box, but there had been nothing.

She didn't mind the cat. Tidbit was his own "person" and most of the time she didn't even know he was there. Occasionally he would strop her ankles with a rumbling purr or butt her hand to be petted, but mostly he had his own business either outside or contemplating the front garden from his perch on the window seat in the front room.

But what exactly **had** she gotten herself into? She passed the boxes in the dining room on her way to take her plate to the kitchen. And these boxes? A puzzle for tomorrow. WAIT! Not tomorrow. Tomorrow was her weekly meeting with her hiking club. They were going to hike Topanga Canyon, on one of her favorite trails. The nearly 10 years of drought had taken its toll, thinning the trees, lowering the water levels and yet it was still one of the most beautiful hikes in her area.

This meant she needed to set out her gear before bed, as it meant getting up at 4 a.m., if she was going to make the meeting at the trailhead. So, she washed up and as she walked past the dining room table she noticed the little passport, or so she had begun to think of it, sitting on the lid of one of the unopened boxes. She grabbed it to put into her wallet and headed off to get her things together and get to bed.

That night she dreamt she was walking in an unfamiliar forest. Up ahead of her were Aunt Lizzie and the large black man moving purposefully ahead at a quick pace. The trail ahead of her was clear, but try as she might, she couldn't quite catch up to them, even though they didn't seem to be more than a couple hundred feet ahead of her. For some reason she knew she shouldn't call out to them, but she also knew, as one often does in a dream, that it was somehow important not to lose their trail.

Chapter 4: The Hike

Her alarm broke her out of sleep and she remembered that it was hike day. She jumped out of bed, dressed in her hiking clothes, good hiking boots and her hat. The little gold key hanging around her neck felt so incongruous with her cotton shirt and jeans, her sweatshirt tied around her waist and her favorite ball cap. But there was nothing to be done for it.

She grabbed her backpack after eating a quick bowl of cereal, but as she was heading out the door, her backpack slung on her back, Tidbit showed up. He was mewling at her somewhat piteously, something he had not done before.

"What's up, kitty?" she asked him. "Are you hungry? There's food out for you in the kitchen."

Tidbit butted his head against her legs, still mewling. It was as if he wanted to push her in a certain direction. She checked her watch. She had a little bit of time. He was so pitiful that she couldn't leave him without finding out what was wrong. He continued to butt his big head against her leg. "O.K. ... Let's see what you need," she capitulated, somewhat amused at this new trick of her cat.

Tidbit seemed to understand that she would follow him and began to walk through the hall between the dining room and the bedrooms. Halfway down the hall he stopped in front of a closet. Wait! A closet? There were no closets in the hallway of her house. She was sure she would have noticed it before. The door was painted the same as the rest of the walls, for sure, but still. It was a door; it was an obvious door. The brass handle definitely gave it away, she thought wryly. How in the world could she have possibly missed it?

Tidbit was looking up at her expectantly. It appeared he wanted her to open the door. She shifted her knapsack, eyeing the cat with renewed confusion. "Is there something in here that you need?" she asked him, one hand on her hip. Tidbit mewled again, cocking his head as if to say, "What are you waiting for?"

Jenny reached for the handle and suddenly the little key on her neck warmed, not uncomfortably, but it definitely was growing warm to the touch, more than was accounted for by her body heat.

She pulled the door open and, to her astonishment, it wasn't a closet at all. It was a room that could not possibly be accounted for. She stepped into the room in amazement. It was like a little office. There were shelves full of books and various unusual pieces of statuary, large and small, on the tops of those shelves. A small, plain office desk with an antique wooden swivel chair behind it stood at the back wall and a large something that looked like some sort of clock sat at one end of the desk.

The clock didn't have numbers on it and there were multiple hands pointing to icons which had no meaning to Jenny. This windowless room was not, in and of itself, terribly out of the ordinary except for the undeniable fact that it couldn't possibly exist. There was absolutely no room for it in the floorplan of the house. And there, on the opposite wall of this impossible room was another door!

She turned to Tidbit who was purring his big rumbling purr, obviously happy to be in this room. She noticed that next to the desk, on the floor, was a comfortable looking cat bed that looked very much lived in.

"OK, cat. What is this all about?" Her mind was racing and, although she knew she would get no answers from the cat, she couldn't help herself. Tidbit launched himself up onto the red cushion on the wooden desk chair and looked expectantly at the desk. Sure enough, there on the desk was another lavender envelope with her name on it in green ink.

She shooed him from the chair and sat down, her mind racing. She opened the envelope with a certain trepidation. What could this possibly have to do with her and how could this room even be here? She remembered from her childhood one Christmas when her parents had sent her on a treasure hunt with little clues hidden all over the house. The final stop had been a shiny new blue bicycle with a huge red bow on the handlebars. This was beginning to feel like that, but she was pretty sure there was no toy at the end of this trail.

"Speaking of trails," she said aloud, thinking that her hiking group wouldn't wait long for her, if she got there late. They would expect her to catch up. There was little to no cell signal where they hiked, so she couldn't even send them a text. "I really don't have time for this." Nevertheless, she pulled out 2 sheets of lavender paper. The note said:

"Jenny. This is an important day. When you read this, you would have been guided to the door and the key on your neck would have granted you access. As you have experienced, this key need not be inserted into the door. It is like a pass. I can't explain the technology to you, except to say that it is of ancient date and it works well to keep those out who should not have access to this room and all it contains.

Yes, I know this appears impossible. And no, you aren't dreaming, hallucinating or losing your marbles. This cozy little room is a dimensional portal. The physics of it is beyond anything on our world. It isn't a time tunnel or a wormhole. It isn't magic, although it certainly feels like it. Having said that, you should know that a lot of what you will experience in and through this room will definitely feel like magic, as our folklore would describe it.

Very little of what you think you know is as factual as it is presented to be by scientists. A lot of things you are used to counting on will prove to be unhelpful. However, you have a bright and inquisitive mind. You also have your mother's fierce independence and your father's knack of solving puzzles. It's one of the reasons you are such an amazing writer. (Yes, I have been following you online for a long time.)

So, now that the portal has accepted you, there are steps you must take. First, make sure you have your passport. (*I knew it was a passport! How did I know that, Jenny wondered?*) Second, take the cat with you. This is important. Lastly, be nice to The Gatekeeper. (*Gatekeeper?*)

I expect great things from you.

Love, Lizzie"

Jenny sank back into the chair. She wanted to scratch her head. What in the world or out of it was actually happening here? She looked down at Tidbit who had made himself quite comfortable in his white wicker bed with a great red cushion in it. "What does this have to do with you? And what's behind that other door?" Tidbit looked up at her, unblinking golden eyes staring solemnly into hers. His ears had swiveled forward in what looked like a question.

All thoughts of the hike had fled from her mind. She hadn't even noticed that the backpack was still slung on her back as she leaned back. Tidbit stood in his bed and stretched a long luxurious stretch, his hindquarters high in the air, his tail tucked under his body and his shoulders low on the floor. Then, tail held high with a little crook in the end like a little flag, he sauntered over to the door on the other side of the room and turned to look at Jenny expectantly.

"I take it I'm supposed to go through that door?" Jenny said shaking her head. "I guess I'm up to rummaging through another room. The guys will have to go on without me."

Shaking her head that she was even considering this, she reached for the door handle and opened the door.

It didn't lead into another room. Rather it was a long hallway…a very long hallway. She actually couldn't seem to see the end of it. The hallway was wide, covered in a dark grass-green carpet and lined with doors on either side, somewhat like a large hotel. She couldn't see the end of the hallway, as it bended slightly to the right. She gawked for a moment, once again looking to Tidbit for a clue as to what to do next. He went and stood, waiting, before a green door, the first on the right.

Jenny sighed and reached once again for a handle, wondering what kind of maze she had found herself in. This was all so impossible. She opened the door and…

…the warm breeze smelled of something akin to lilacs with a slight difference, more tangy than sweet. Before her stretched a long black sand beach, but unlike anything she remembered seeing. "I don't think we're in Kansas, er, California anymore, Toto, I mean, Tidbit." As she turned to look at the cat she gasped. There, behind her on what appeared to be a porch of a small hut, was not her cat, but the immense black man in the photo her aunt had sent her.

"Who are you and what have you done with my cat?" she demanded.

"I am Tarafau Bane," he replied calmly in a deep, resonant voice. There was a slight sing song cadence that felt foreign, but nothing she could put her finger on. "I *am* your cat, Jenny Japhet."

"You're my..." Jenny breathed.

"Your cat is me." He said, showing large white teeth in a grin. Fangs. He had fangs. Not just eyeteeth, but fangs, if not as exaggerated as a fantasy vampire. They were longer and thinner than a normal person. "I cannot assume my favorite form in your dimension. But I like being a cat. Very amusing."

Jenny stared at him, completely undone. Her aunt had told her in that letter that this was not a dream or a hallucination, but she was having a hard time believing it at the moment. "I'm still in my bed," she thought. "In a moment I'll wake up and the cat will still be a cat and I can go on my hike."

He stood there his muscled arms folded confidently across his broad chest. He was dressed in a flowing robe in colors and patterns that seemed to be a cross between traditional African and Polynesian patterns. The bright colors contrasted well with his almost blue black skin, coincidentally (?) nearly the identical colors of Tidbit's dark fur. His eyes twinkled, and the corners of his large amber eyes were wrinkled in amusement.

"You're my cat. You are Tidbit? How is that possible?"

"I am a Daringi. Our people are shape-changers. I am "The Guide". It is my job to get you safely where you need to be and guide your footsteps as we bring order to the shape of things in the dimensions. For now, I must take you to The Gatekeeper. She will explain."

He paused, waiting expectantly for her to comment. She shook her head; she had no reply for any of this.

"First you must be scanned, of course," he continued, obviously by the tilt of his head and his wide grin, amused by her reaction. "It's ok," he continued. "It won't hurt you and it is necessary."

Scanned? She looked around for some kind of equipment such as you would expect at an airport terminal or a federal building. She saw nothing but sand, the rolling surf ahead of her and some trees, similar to palm trees, but with red-orange leaves. However, moving up the beach, something was flying towards them. There were two of them and they resembled nothing so much as dragonflies, but their wingspan was around 3 feet across.

She looked at Tarafau, but he didn't seem concerned. "Ah. Here they are."

"What are those things? Shouldn't we run or something?"

"Those are the scanners. We call them gem eyes. They won't harm you. Just stand still."

The huge bugs, she couldn't think of them as anything else, pulled up in front of them, hovered in front of them both, each vibrating slightly due to the rapid movement of their wings which were moving so fast as to be nearly invisible. They started at just above their heads and slowly descended to almost ground level. Then they whirled and sped off back the way they had come.

"All done. You pass. Now we can go meet The Gatekeeper."

"OK, Tarafau, or Tidbit, or whoever you are. What's going on here?"

Tarafau smiled his catlike smile. She could almost see his ears pointed forward…wait…. His ears were pointed, but not like Spock or any elves she had seen depicted. The points were on the lobes of his ears. This was definitely not from any dream she had ever had. She hadn't noticed this in the photograph of Tarafau and her aunt, more than likely because she just wasn't looking for it.

"Come, let us not keep The Gatekeeper waiting," was all he said, gesturing with a broad hand toward the red palm trees that lined the beach. "It isn't far, and it's a pleasant walk."

She shrugged. At least she was set up for a good walk. She realized she was still wearing her backpack and had her binoculars hung around her neck. She hadn't counted on a hike like *this*, however. The black sandy beach had a sparkling quality to it and stretched up and down the coastline as far as she could see in both directions. She stepped off of the porch into the light of the pale yellow sun. The sand was fine enough that as they walked their footprints filled back in quickly behind them.

As they grew closer to the trees, she noticed there was a soft musical sound floating toward them over the low murmur of the gentle surf that lapped the shore. It was not instrumental but came from voices in the trees. She looked up and realized that there were small creatures of some kind perched on the wide stems of the red palm fronds. Bright blue eyes peered at her from pale green furry faces. They reminded her somewhat of a tamarin marmoset she had once seen in a documentary about exotic species. These had long dark green mustaches that extended onto their chests and white circles around their eyes, which made their blue eyes stand out in their dark green faces. They were crooning softly and harmonizing in a nearly hypnotic song that was both soft and yet seemed to fill her up from the inside.

"What are those?" she asked Tarafau.

"Those are Linklings. Their song changes when they sense danger, but mostly they sing to the sky and *this* song is one of welcome. They are not fierce or ferocious, but they are faithful and brave little creatures. They live along the shoreline and keep watch."

"Watch for what?" Jenny asked. "They're beautiful and this beach seems a peaceful place, so what am I missing?"

"You must meet The Gatekeeper. She has the answers you seek."

The path they had been following through the trees finally emerged into a place that reminded her of some of the scenes from tapestries of medieval Europe. Around a large market square, full of colorful booths with many goods she did not recognize, were brightly colored houses whose walls tended toward rounded archways and very few hard angles. Even the windows were mostly round or oval, framed in wood like large, elegant portholes.

People milled around the square, some peering into what must have been shop windows or stopping to peruse the goods at a particular booth. There was something strange about it, however. Behind her she could still hear the soft hooting song of the linklings, and she realized, despite the bustling foot traffic, there were no human voices at all. Nods and smiles and body language were the only level of communication she could discern. It was so extremely odd. If she had not been able to still hear the Linklings, and the soft breeze through the palm tree grove behind her, she would have thought she had lost her hearing.

Tarafau was scanning the crowd without the slightest indication he had noticed anything unusual.

"Is this some kind of religious thing? A vow of silence or something?" she whispered to Tarafau, fearing lest she violate some local custom by speaking aloud.

"Oh, no, not at all. It will all be made clear when we meet The Gatekeeper," he asserted in a normal tone of voice and, gesturing encouragingly for her to follow, led down the main thoroughfare, smiling and nodding to the people they passed. None of them seemed to notice anything unusual about him or her, for that matter, with her ball cap and backpack and hiking shoes, although she couldn't have been more differently dressed than the folks around her.

For one thing, she was dressed in jeans and a casual cotton shirt, not to mention her hiking gear. The people she passed, however, were dressed in brightly colored clothing, like something out of a Dr. Seuss picture book. The women wore breeches, like the men, but with touches of embroidery on the collars and cuffs of their loose-fitting smocked blouses. With few exceptions women's hair (mostly brunettes, she noticed) hung loose and long, often hanging to their knees behind them.

The men also wore their hair long, but braided in a single plait, the braids hanging over one shoulder or the other. Like the Linklings, she noticed their eyes tended toward blue, and occasionally green. Their faces were long and most of them, including the men were in the range of 5 to 5-1/2 feet tall. Most of them were carrying net bags, filled with what appeared to be their purchases of the day.

Tarafau strode among them, appearing giant-like and yet, not even the children, silent like their parents, appeared to be threatened by his presence. In contrast, Jenny couldn't help but wonder how these people would have been treated in one of the cities from home.

The streets of the town were clean, and boxes of exotic bright flowers lined the avenue. The silence continued, which was eerie, but she didn't feel at all threatened, so she walked along beside

Tarafau and kept her thoughts to herself until she could get him alone or until she met The Gatekeeper to get her dozens of questions answered.

The square was dominated by a green building, larger than the rest and styled in the same way, more curves than angles. She realized suddenly that this was probably the same building she had seen in the photo of Lizzie and Tarafau. The large elaborately carved double doors opened as they approached, like the automated doors from home. She realized as they went through, however, that there were actually two people holding them open and beaming at them. They were dressed alike in the same forest green as the building and Jenny assumed it was some kind of uniform.

Tarafau gestured to an alcove to the right of the door. There were shelves lining the wall by the door, with dozens of pairs of shoes. Tarafau removed his shoes and motioned for her to do the same. As she removed her hiking boots, something occurred to her.

"Tarafau, where did your clothes come from? As a cat you had no clothes."

"It is a part of the gift, Jenny. Whatever clothing we are wearing when we transform to another form is adapted, such as the fur on the cat. It is part of the energy exchange. In some way we do not fully understand, the molecules in the clothing are part of the matter that makes fur or scales or the like."

Scales? Then Jenny noticed that Tarafau also wore a small pendant on a gold chain around his neck. It wasn't a key, but a stylized infinity symbol. She wanted to ask him about it, but she didn't want to wait another moment to talk to The Gatekeeper, who evidently had the answers she needed.

The man and woman in green uniforms looked at them with interest. Silently, they looked expectantly at them. Tarafau looked into their eyes. They nodded and gestured toward a flight of stairs that led around the curved lobby. The floor was carpeted with a pattern of red and gold leaves on a dark green background. There were tables with vases of flowers and cushioned benches around the edges. The curving stairs led up to a kind of balcony that looked over the high ceilinged room. Round windows high up the front wall let in streams of light and in the ceiling was what appeared to be a type of chandelier with balloon-like globes.

They walked up the stairs, the soft padded carpet seeming to caress their stockinged feet. Jenny thought fleetingly that it was a good thing she didn't have any holes in her socks and then blushed slightly at the thought of walking in this elegant place with holes in her socks.

At the top of the stairs on the balcony was another carved door, but smaller than the huge doors at the entrance. As they approached the door she noticed there was no handle, but the door let out a soft chiming sound. After a short pause the door opened but there was no one holding the door open this time. Tarafau led the way into the room and Jenny followed with just a little trepidation. This "Gatekeeper" was the key to all her questions. Finally.

Chapter 5: The Gatekeeper

Jenny couldn't help it. She gaped. The large room was kind of like entering an egg. The curved walls flowed upward to a large globe in the ceiling which exuded a bright light that illuminated the colors in the room in a way that they popped out. It was furnished similar to the offices of executives in office buildings at home. There were no windows, but where windows might have been were ovals that appeared to be glass that glowed softly, occasionally shifting in the color spectrum independent of one another.

Shelves lined the walls with many interesting things that were mostly unidentifiable to her. However, all of this was taken in with one quick glance around the room, for in the center of the room, dressed similarly to all of the townspeople was a woman. The difference was that the colors she wore were subtler, not necessarily pastel, but muted colors of green, gold and brown. Her brown hair was long, as what appeared to be the common style, but it was held back with a headband of the same green as her loose, smocked blouse.

Her eyes were an intense green and her smile was welcoming. She said nothing but held out both hands to Jenny as she almost glided across the room to stand before her. Jenny hesitantly held her hands out as well, as seemed to be expected. The woman grasped her hands firmly, still smiling warmly. Her eyes twinkled with some hidden mirth and, still not speaking, she reached one hand to Jenny's little necklace. She touched the key with one long manicured finger.

"*Welcome, Jenny.*" Jenny heard this, but the woman's mouth had never moved. "*Now you can converse with us. I am Miriha. I am The Gatekeeper. When you wish to speak to me, think my name and then what you want to say. Try it now.*"

Jenny marveled but followed the instructions. "*Miriha, how is this done?*"

"*It is mind-speak. It is how we communicate. We can, vocalize when we wish, mostly to sing, but we prefer this way for everyday conversation. It is more accurate, and it is calming. We communicate concepts, not really words, exactly. Therefore, the meaning is always clear and truthful.*"

"Can you read my mind?" Jenny asked with some concern.

"Not at all. This is why you think my name first. It creates the connection between you and the person you are speaking to. You can do a general broadcast to a group if you don't think the name first. For instance, Tarafau cannot hear our conversation currently." Her green eyes twinkled mischievously. *"As far as he is concerned, we are exchanging disgraceful secrets about him."*

"Tarafau, can you hear me?" Jenny queried.

"I can now hear you, Jenny." Tarafau replied turning his amber eyes on her. *"Miriha, we are here to align Jenny's key to the gateways and to explain to her the tasks that Lizzie left her."*

At last, Jenny thought, I'm going to get some answers.

Miriha gestured to some comfortable chairs. *"Let us sit,"* she said. *"And we will talk."*

They seated themselves and the lights on the wall shifted to forest colors, as if they sat in a grove of trees. The bright light at the top of the egg-shaped room dimmed slightly.

Jenny's head swam. What questions to ask first? Miriha looked at her expectantly.

"I know almost nothing about what Aunt Lizzie was involved in or what she expects me to do." She started, trying to organize her thoughts. *"I guess maybe the first question is: Where am I and how did I get here?"*

"Your home is a portal or 'gate' to many places. Each door in your hallway leads to a different dimension. You will notice that they are represented by different colors and symbols on each door representing the place they will take you. These physical representations are, of course, an illusion generated by the gateway to communicate with you. The doors do not exist as a solid form nor do they have any reality. A person without the key cannot see them. The door in your hallway was never "built" into the physicality of your house. It exists only as a concept in your mind to allow you to locate the gateway."

Jenny considered this. It sounded very much like the magic in her favorite fantasy books and she said so.

"Ah, magic. Well, you could consider it that way, if you prefer, but there is nothing magical about it. Matter is more flexible than you may think. The science of your world is evolving rapidly, but there are many misunderstandings of the order of things and you tend to think of matter in terms of relative solidity. Matter, time and space all have many more dimensions than we suspect, I think.

In any case, the portals are ancient in origin. You have several on your Earth. Once we fully activate your key, you will have access to all of them. The passport you carry will identify you as a "Guardian" and, regardless of local politics, you have what your people might call "diplomatic immunity".

Anyone but you will see the passport as whatever document they are used to seeing. Your papers will always be in order. You cannot access the gates on your own planet directly. You must come through our gateways here to do that. Therefore, from time to time you will be travelling by conventional means. Lizzie has VIP accounts with most of the major airlines and hotels on your planet, so this should be no inconvenience."

"You said dimension, not planet. What does that mean?" asked Jenny. *"I thought I had been transported to another planet."*

"Oh, you are definitely on another planet, Jenny. This is Lanatrix, but we are not in your galaxy or even your universe. The portal is not a 'transporter' as portrayed in the legends of earth, but it is a doorway to alternate dimensions. It is not a time travel device either. Rather it simply allows you access to places that would otherwise be impossible for you with your current level of science."

"But why? I'm not sure why they even exist and why they would be connected to Earth at all."

"Your aunt was right about you, Jenny. You are a thinker with a curious turn of mind. The gateways aren't of our construction and their origins are lost to us, but they have been discovered over time, mostly by accident, and as time progressed and people started realizing the implications of the potential havoc that could be caused and the potential advantages of the gates, eventually, over thousands

of centuries, a coalition formed of a 'Gatekeeper', 'Guides' and 'Guardians' whose mission is to allow the dimensions to live safely together and to prevent potential invasions or harmful interactions by those with ill intent.

The Gatekeeper, Guides such as Tarafau, and Guardians are carefully chosen as beings with integrity, the ability to handle difficult things and make decisions that impact billions of worlds in dimensions we have as yet been unable to count."

Jenny sat back in her chair, realizing that she had been perched on the edge of it. "*And how am I involved in all of this? And what do you expect me to do?*"

"*If you accept, you will become a Guardian. This will require you to travel occasionally to other dimensions as you are called to help with issues that may arise. You will associate with your fellow Guardians on a great council on a regular basis to learn of developments and issues in the council and you will further your education about the science involved.*

You will be given technology that will allow you to interact with other planets in your universe, at a certain point in your training, as you will become the representative of all beings therein. It will be your job to keep track of anything that would threaten the Dimensional Alliance."

Jenny's eyes widened, and she realized her hands were shaking. "*Me? Why me?*"

Miriha's eyes crinkled in amusement. "*I am not laughing at you, Jenny, but you must know that this is the exact question your aunt asked me so many years ago. She was about your age when she came to us. I imagine she left you her journals?*"

Jenny's mind went to the yet unopened boxes on her dining room table so very far away and nodded. Had that been only yesterday?

And she looked more carefully at Miriha. She looked to be about the same age as her mom. How could she have known her aunt when she was her age?

Miriha continued. "*You will find great instruction in reading her journals. I encourage you to focus on them when you can. I understand this is a lot to take in at the moment and for now, most of what I can tell you are generalities. If you choose to accept this position, you will receive instructions and guidance from the tech I will give you."*

"And what happens if I refuse?" she asked.

"If that were to happen, your memories would be altered, and arrangements would be made to deactivate the portal. Your key would disappear, and you would no longer be able to see it or access it. Your house would just be a house and the cat would just be a cat, replaced by a common feline of Earth. You would live your life out in your house, doing what you have always done. The funds in your bank account would remain for you to use as you choose, and the inheritance would continue as if nothing had happened. Your aunt's boxes of journals and photos would be removed as well as all traces of communication from her that mentioned anything about the portal. You would have no idea about any of this and you would live your life as before.

I doubt Lizzie would have recommended you, however, if you had not been an ideal candidate."

Jenny quieted her breathing and realized she had been gripping the plush arms of her chair in order to calm the shaking.

Suddenly Tarafau spoke up in her mind. *"Jenny, I have observed you to be a responsible person, intelligent, kind and you adapt well to surprising circumstances. I am sure I would miss you if you decided not to accept, but you should know that this is entirely your choice. I have something for you."*

He reached into a pocket of his robe and pulled out…

…a lavender envelope.

Jenny couldn't help it. She rolled her eyes and chuckled. *"Another one?"*

She unsealed the envelope and opened the note in her aunt's precise lettering. "Jenny," it began, "You are now in the presence of The Gatekeeper. Miriha is a kind and an amazing being. The offer she has made to you has many responsibilities. It also has many compensations. As she has already told you, you have a choice to make. I want to suggest to you that you take the opportunity and the potential risk it implies. At any point, should you decide this is not for you, you can go to Miriha and she will reverse you and all memory of portals and dimensions will be removed and you can go about your life.

But I want you to know that in all the time I have been a Guardian, even when things were difficult, I have never regretted choosing to be a part of the Dimensional Alliance. As I have kept track of you over the years, when I was on Earth, I have been so impressed with you: your steadiness, your curiosity and your strong desire to be actively engaged in something worthwhile. How I was able to do that will be revealed when you are ready.

This is important, in ways I cannot clearly express to you at this time. Please, consider taking the post. I feel strongly that you will not only not regret it, but it will enrich your life and give you the power to do many good things that will affect billions of beings you will likely never meet.

Love, Lizzie"

Jenny thought back on her life. She had been comfortable with her choices, following her passion for writing and her interests in science and nature. She had, however, considered herself more as a reporter of life rather than someone who had "adventures". She liked her clients and enjoyed her routine of writing and hanging out with her friends.

Her little apartment had been in a nice part of town and she didn't really want for anything, although she didn't have much in the way of luxuries. A quiet life. A safe life. And it didn't have to change. She could go on that way in a beautiful home in a nice neighborhood. She wouldn't realize that there was a portal in her house. (Would it still be in her house?). She would be able to afford to live very well, with no rent to pay. And with her writing income, she wouldn't have to touch the money in Lizzie's account except for emergencies or the occasional splurge.

"Aunt Lizzie had been doing this for a very long time, hadn't she?" she said at last.

Miriha smiled, reminiscing. "*Indeed. As I said before, she was about your age when the key was passed to her by one of her university professors. She was very skeptical about the whole thing, but Tarafau helped her see the value of what we do. Lizzie has made a large impact for so many over the years. We will miss her.*"

This last thought held a wistful sadness. This method of thought speaking was more than mere words. The actual intent of the speaker came across so clearly that there was no mistaking exactly what they meant, and their feelings were attached to the thought.

Jenny looked at Tarafau. "*You knew my aunt well. Why did she do what she did?*" Jenny meant so much more than just being an interdimensional ambassador. "*Why did she choose me? How did she even know I could do this? What made her think this is something I could even succeed at?*"

Tarafau looked seriously into her eyes. His amber eyes were piercing, yet kind, and his face was solemn. "*Your aunt was one of the most joyous, kind, and intelligent beings I have had the pleasure of knowing in my lifetime. She cared deeply for peace and justice and was anxiously engaged in doing her part to keep the cosmos in balance.*

I won't lie to you. This work is intense and can be dangerous, but it is also very satisfying, and you will see and do things that even your fertile imagination cannot yet picture. It will mean you won't see a lot of your friends and family, and like your aunt, you will be more of a family legend than anything. But every action you take will be a protection to them and every other Earthling you know, not to mention all living beings on planets in galaxies your kind have yet to discover.

You are feeling inadequate at the moment. You've had no training and you had your life set the way you wished it. This will be a sacrifice on your part, but I promise you it will be worth it. And, as your guide, I will be with you every step of the way. Should you choose to join us, you will be thoroughly trained in all skills you will need to do your part."

His thoughts came to her mind forcefully and there was no doubt he was sincere.

"*And my friends? Won't they notice I'm not around much? Won't it cause them to be suspicious?*"

Miriha nodded. "*We have taken all that into account. Remember, we have been doing this for a very long time. Your cover story is that you have been hired by a large travel firm to do a series of documentary guides and that it will require you to travel extensively. This is not a lie. You will be recording your travels for us and you will be traveling to places you can't begin to imagine. You will even go many places on your Earth you may not realize exist. There are other agents on Earth with whom you will consult from time to time and one of them will be your trainer while you are learning what you must know to function in your position.*"

Jenny felt that her mind was going to explode with the influx of thoughts, ideas and possibilities. As a young person she had always known she would be a writer. She had imagined herself writing impressive, popular novels or great scholarly works. Her instructors had always told her to "Write what you know." Admittedly, most of what she wrote at this time was all researchable online. Very little of it actually had anything to do with personal experience. This was her opportunity to experience things that would light her imagination and help her to make a difference as well.

"*All right, so, if I find, down the road, that I no longer want to do this or find that I can't what happens then?*"

"*Your life and mind will be purged of anything having to do with the portals and you will be given a good cover story and the necessary memories to support it. This doesn't happen often, but we have the technology to do it.*"

"*So why don't you just implant the suggestions in my mind to make me do it and by-pass the whole 'choice' thing?*"

"*That would contradict everything we stand for. It would violate one of our primary directives. Only Evil ever uses force to accomplish their goals. We will not compromise this, and we would never use the technology available to us in this manner.*"

Jenny decided. "*I'll do it. When do we start?*"

"*Give me your passport,*" Miriha said, holding out her hand.

Jenny slid her wallet out of her backpack and removed the little gold book. "My golden ticket?" she thought wryly.

"Now give me your left hand."

Jenny held out her left hand and before she could wonder what would happen next, Miriha poked her finger with a needle that appeared from Miriha's pocket. She gasped, but Miriha held her finger firmly and pressed it on the first page of the passport.

The blood stained the page and then disappeared as the page filled with characters, first unrecognizable and then they squirmed and became English. It outlined her name, her address (with the appendage "Earth" after "United States of America") and then an updated photo of her formed above the writing.

"*Wow, you could have warned me,*" Jenny gasped.

Miriha dabbed at the puncture with a piece of gauze. "*Hold that there for a moment. You had said you would do it and I saw no need to hesitate.*"

She handed the passport back and said, "*This is an important document, if a little archaic. It is infused with your genetic code now and cannot be forged or impersonated by anyone. You must keep it with you at all times and to facilitate that...*"

She pulled out what looked like a black sports bracelet with a gold and burnt orange logo on it. She proceeded to insert the passport into a horizontal slit in the bracelet. The 3x5 inch passport slid into it as if it were smaller than the slit and disappeared. "*Another dimensional portal. This will hold an amazing cache of things of various sizes, somewhat like your backpack, but it has no weight, because the things in the bracelet actually exist in a different dimensional space.*

There is no actual space in the bracelet. They are just like the doors. They simply appear to be this shape because you see them this way. Other beings will see them as something different and someone who cannot see gateways will not notice you have anything more than one of those rubber bracelets that are so popular on your world.

It also has a beacon you can invoke that will allow us to know where you are. In addition, the room inside has equipment you will need as you travel, from tents to food to tech of various kinds. To open it you say, 'transport' and tell it what you need. Try it now."

Jenny started to do this, but hesitated. "*Do I say it out loud or mind-speak?*"

Miriha grinned. "*You are as smart as Lizzie told us you were. You could say it out loud as often and loudly as you wish, and nothing would happen. This is a 'Miniature Dimensional Portal" device. The MDP is attuned to only your mind and Tarafau's. Only you or he can activate it. We give both of you access so that if you were incapacitated, Tarafau could still get the things you need and activate the beacon.*"

Jenny took a deep breath. "*Transport passport.*"

The passport appeared on the floor in front of her. She picked it up and examined it with increased awe. "Coolbeans!" she exclaimed aloud. Miriha and Tarafau both grinned.

"*To replace it you need only touch the bracelet to it, and it will return to its place in the dimensional room. In your training we will familiarize you with the resources that are already contained in the MDP. For now, would you like to put your backpack in there?*"

Jenny grinned. She touched the bracelet to the strap of her backpack and it kind of shriveled and slid into the bracelet as the passport had done. "*Wow. Are there any limitations to what I can put in there?*"

"*We have yet to find any,*" Miriha replied, "*but there are probably some things that would be somewhat impractical to do. You'll learn more about the capabilities of your MDP in your training.*"

"*So, when do I start?*" The possibilities of this new opportunity were beginning to excite her. She was anxious to get started.

"*You will need to return and make the arrangements your aunt will have sent to you in an email. Follow her instructions exactly. Something else you should know. This is no time portal. The same amount of time will have passed on Earth as has passed since you came here. I know of no actual applications of time travel among the dimensions, for reasons you will begin to appreciate as you proceed.*

Once you have made all your arrangements, invoke your bracelet with my name. It will notify me, and we will then schedule your first training."

Miriha held out both hands as she had when they had first entered the room. *"Blessings of The Creator of All Things on you, Jenny. We will see you again soon."*

This was clearly a dismissal. *"Thank you, Miriha. I will get everything done and see you again soon."*

Chapter 6: Arrangements

Jenny had almost expected everything to look different when she got home. It was all still there, all her things, the boxes on the dining room table. It was dusk when they returned, Tarafau was now Tidbit again, but Jenny saw him with new eyes.

Jenny found she could still mindspeak with Tidbit, even in his cat form. Here on Earth (Jenny found it odd to think of her home that way), she could still communicate clearly with him.

"*You will be able to speak with any of the other Guardians who have been given the gift.*" Tidbit said, his ears perked forward and his amber eyes nearly glowing in the half light. "*Your key and your passport have been activated now. You will be able to sense portals by the warming of your key against your skin. And the portals will be able to sense you and will show themselves to you. The key can also serve as a warning device under certain circumstances. It rarely happens, but you should be aware.*"

The boxes still sat on the dining room table and although they held a new fascination for her, Jenny knew the boxes would have to wait until tomorrow. It had been a long day and she needed to check her email for the missive from Lizzie with her instructions. She knew she was going to have to make arrangements for someone to take over her workload at the freelancer's agency and many similar things. She also realized she hadn't had a single thing to eat since about 4:30 am.

And then it occurred to her. What will I tell my friends? I'll need to get my cover story straight, if I'm going to pull this off. Her heart tugged a bit at the idea of deceiving her friends, especially Sam. "*It's like I'm some kind of super-hero, secret identity and all, only without the spandex,*" she thought towards Tidbit.

"*Your mythological super-heroes may have their 'secret identities'*" Tidbit replied, a sardonic tone to his thought, "*but you were always who you are. You just have an added dimension that your friends are not ready for. Lizzie actually enjoyed it.*"

Lizzie. How she now wished she had known her better. So far, everyone she had met who knew her seemed to really like her. Jenny had a suspicion that she would have felt the same, if they had had any opportunity to spend any time together. Which reminded her that she still wanted to find out how Lizzie had kept such strong tabs on her. She was beginning to feel like it was some kind of dimensional tech she had yet to be exposed to.

Jenny filled up her water bottle and Tidbit's food and water bowl, made herself a sandwich and a small salad and headed for her office. Her mind was still spinning, and she wasn't sure if she would even taste the meal she had made for herself.

Sure enough, she ate mechanically as she sorted through the day's email. Along with a few spam messages, some communications with clients and an email from the freelancer's co-op, was an email from Lizzie, subject line: "Arrangements".

She was surprised the list of action items was so short:

1. Contact the bank and set up all utilities payments and other bills on auto-pay.
2. Study your cover story and the accompanying info pack before discussing any of this with your friends or family. We have included business cards and the calls to the number on the card will go to voicemail.
3. Your gold passport will function as United States Passport. It will allow you to cross any national border, except in time of war. Keep it in your MDP and don't even take the bracelet off to shower. No one can take it from you unless you give it willingly. It is waterproof, shockproof and there is nothing we know of that can damage it.
4. Create an autoresponder sequence that will send occasional emails to friends and family, in case you may be gone for longer than expected.
5. Touch your cellphone to the key. It will upload an app that will allow you some new communications options outside the capability of current networks.
6. When you have completed all of these steps, let Miriha know. If you have any questions, Tidbit will be happy to help."

She closed the email: "Love, Lizzie"

Jenny chewed thoughtfully on the big bite of salad she had unconsciously put into her mouth. For a professional writer, she sure was having trouble finding words big enough to describe the churning of her mind right now. Amazing? Overused. "Awesome?" Too trite. "Enormous?" Too general. "Supercalifragilisticexpialidocious?" Closer, but, no. No prizes here.

She mechanically deleted the spam messages and replied to the client's emails. Tomorrow she would begin to tidy up all of her projects and talk to the writing co-op manager to inform her of her "new job". In the meantime…

…But what would happen in the meantime would have to wait for later, as the doorbell broke her reverie.

Sam stood on the porch, in her hiking clothes, one hand on her hip.

"We missed you on the hike today. Were you sick?"

Now it began…

"Actually, I've been really busy. I have a new job and I had to do orientation and get all the paperwork done."

"A new job? I didn't know you'd even applied for something new. I thought you liked free-lancing."

"I was contacted by a head-hunter, privately. They made me an offer I couldn't afford to refuse."

"Wow. That's my Jenny. I knew you'd be famous someday."

"Well not today," Jenny replied, sagging a little with relief that Sam didn't appear to be suspicious at the sudden turn of events. "It's a private gig. Very hush-hush. My name probably won't be made public, as usual, but it pays well, and the bennies are pretty good. Plus, I'll be travelling a lot."

Sam reached out with a ready hug. "Sounds like a blast. Maybe some time you can take me along. Every super-hero needs a side-kick, don'tcha know."

Jenny was startled. Her friend's use of the word "super-hero" was way too close to the mark.

"Well, all the more reason to throw a house-warming party. Now you have two things to celebrate." Sam's eyes twinkled. "And as your bestie, I get to make all the arrangements."

Jenny opened her mouth to speak, but Sam waved her away. "No arguments. I promise to keep it small. Maybe just the hiking club? We can barbeque, and the guys can bring their guitars. Whaddya think?"

Jenny sighed, "All right, but it'll have to be soon. As soon as my passport is processed, I'll be leaving for training."

"So what you're saying is that we finally have time to hang out in your new pad and you'll be gallivanting off into the blue yonder someplace. Well, if that's how it is, I'll have to get as much friend time in as I can."

So, they sat in her living room and chatted and laughed and Sam told her about the hike and showed off her photos of the group against the beautiful canyon scenery. By the time they had wound down, it was late and after hugs and another chuckle about Jenny's new status, Sam left. She put Tidbit out with an admonition to be safe, at which Tidbit sent her a mental "evil laugh" and left, his tail waving like a banner behind him.

She didn't remember dreaming, but when she awoke, she could tell by the tumble of blankets that her sleep had been pretty restless. The sun spilled like handfuls of gold into her room. A new day and so much to do. It was a Sunday, a day she reserved for quiet restful activities. She dressed and went to church, as she had every Sunday since she was very young. She tried to focus on the service, but her mind kept wandering to the boxes on the dining room table. What would she find in boxes 2 and 3?

She pulled up to her house on Infinity Loop and noticed Bob out mowing his lawn. She parked in the driveway. He waved back at her as she grinned and waved. She wondered how much he actually knew about her aunt and her adventures and how she could find out without tipping him to the fact that she was now in what could be considered "the family business".

Tidbit was curled up in the shade of the bougainvillea that climbed over the archway over the wrought iron gate. When he saw her, he stretched as only cats can do from his front paws to his tail, then sauntered over and stropped her ankles.

It seemed only yesterday she had met Tidbit, but in the short week and a half since she first stepped in the door of her house so much had happened that it was beginning to feel like she had always lived here and Tidbit had always been her companion. And yet, what did she really know about him?

"Have a good night?" she thought to him, considering how convenient it was to be able to communicate directly.

"Passing fair. The neighborhood is quiet, and Cinder has been cowering in his backyard unless he's on a leash, so I am content."

Jenny chuckled. It appeared this conflict between the big dog and Tidbit was a *thing,* and she wasn't going to get in the middle of it, figuratively or literally.

In her kitchen, as she prepared her breakfast, her mind went to the boxes. "This is as good a time as any to see what's in there. Can't do any of the business tasks until tomorrow," she thought.

Tidbit had curled up in his usual sunny spot on the window seat and she sat her sandwich and salad on the table next to the 2nd box. She opened the lid and found what appeared to be a stack of journals. On the top of the stack was a lavender envelope.

She grinned. She wondered if her aunt had really liked lavender or if this stationary set had simply been on sale somewhere.

"Dear Jenny:" it read.

"By now you have met The Gatekeeper. Miriha is a great mentor and resource. She will see you get where you need to be. I expect the fact that you are reading this now means you have accepted the charge to become a Guardian.

I want you to know that despite the fact there have been times I wished for easier solutions to some of the challenges involved, I have never regretted making the decision to do this. What we do makes a difference, as you will begin to see as you progress through your training.

I hope you and Tidbit are getting along. Be sure to always address him, even in your mind, as Tidbit when you are on Earth. The name Tarafau has some significance in a dimensional sense and there are those who would like to find him in his Earth form. That being said, there is more to him than appears, as you will discover.

These journals are a resource for you. They are numbered to make them easy to reference and I have tried to make them clear. You will notice the last one is not up to date. The reason for this is that the journals continue in electronic format on the tablet included in the 3rd box. This tablet may be a bit different than those you are used to, but you will get the hang of it quickly enough. Keep it in your MDP for ease of access.

And that's all for now. The 3rd box contains some equipment that I have found useful. Put the entire box into your MDP. You will want it during your training.

Love, Lizzie"

Jenny decided to skip reading the journals for now. She sealed the 2nd box, tapped it and the 1st box with her wristband and the box shriveled and passed into the wristband. It was odd, she felt like her arm should weigh many pounds by now, but it still felt like a light plastic wristband. Shaking her head, she opened the 3rd box.

There was no note on top of this box, but it contained a number of things, some of which did not seem out of the ordinary and some of which she could not identify. She recognized the tablet at once, however and removed it.

It resembled any one of a number of generic tablets. The screen appeared to be about 8 inches tall and it was black. But try as she might, she could see no buttons along it's edges, nor were there any ports for attaching earphones a usb or a charging device. She felt along the edges, not trusting her sight, and there was nothing. "OK, Tidbit," she thought to the cat with a frown, "how do we open up this cute little piece of tech?"

"Touch your key," Tidbit replied, opening one amber eye lazily.

Jenny reached up to her throat and touched the tiny key. The screen on the tablet flickered to life. The icons on the screen seemed clear enough and she touched the one that looked like a small book.

Aunt Lizzie's smiling face looked up at her. She appeared much older than Jenny had ever seen her and her face was pale, not tanned as in the photo of her and Tarafau. "Oh, there you are!" Lizzie looked straight into her eyes. It didn't seem to be normal video, feeling almost three dimensional. The screen was indeed flat, but it looked as if she could reach in and touch the little key around Lizzie's neck.

"It's great to be able to reach out to you this way. In this journal you will find many helpful resources, as well as an abridged version of my story and how I got started in all of this. Reading this between now and when you start your training may help you get through it easier than I did. However, I don't intend to tell you all of the specifics. Some things must be experienced to be understood.

In this box I have included some of my favorite tools and tech. You needn't sort through all of them at this time but be sure and store them in the MDP. You'll want all of it at one time or another as you go along.

Any questions?"

Jenny shook her head at this. What? Questions? Lizzie had paused, her head cocked slightly as if waiting for a reply.

"What are you?" was the first thing that came to Jenny's lips.

LizzyAI laughed a warm chuckle deep in her chest. "No, I'm not back from the dead. This is me, but not me. I created an AI assistant for you and figured it would be more fun this way. I may not always have the answers you seek, but I know a lot. Most of what I know is referenced in the journals. Just invoke me by saying my name and I will answer."

"Cool..." was all that Jenny could think to say. "What else is on this tablet?"

"You'll find a number of apps that are very helpful, weather, time schemes for different worlds, historical information as you go on new assignments, political briefings and so forth. Oh yes, and Candy

Crush," she added mischievously. "You may find yourself doing more waiting than you'd like, sometimes."

Jenny shook her head. This was all too much. But her aunt's warm and humorous nature had a soothing effect. Between Tidbit and LizzieAI, she wouldn't really be alone in this. She began to feel like this was going to be doable after all.

"What kind of assignments?" was the next logical question.

"In the beginning, it will mostly be meet and greet. You'll need to get to know the other Guardians, otherwise known as 'agents'. You'll be introduced to the first several 'friendly' dimensions and, at some point, you may end up doing some undercover work. You aren't exactly a spy, but there are some of the cultures we don't know nearly enough about and not all are members of the Alliance. The rest they'll tell you at your mission briefings, since things tend to change quickly in the Dimensional Alliance."

"Is there anything you left off of my to-do list?"

"I don't think so. Just get it all done as quickly as you can and get in touch with Miriha. That and don't forget to feed the cat." The corners of her eyes crinkled with silent laughter. "He gets grumpy when he's hungry. Not that he needs the cat food, really. Tidbit is a mighty hunter."

Tidbit opened his eyes to slits. "*A cat can eat just so many pigeons*," was all he said, but the tone was sardonic.

Jenny laughed.

LizzieAI then spoke up. "I'm supposed to tell you that from now on, you just need to say, 'Lizzie', to initialize the tablet. The initial connection to the key has already been made."

"How do I charge it? There are no access ports."

"The tablet is self-charging. It's Dimensional Alliance technology. It actually uses the electrical charge in your body to charge. And not to worry, it won't drain your body's battery," she added with a grin. "This tech is not as bulky as ours is. This tablet, with all its applications takes a fraction of the system resources of Earth tech with many multiples of capability and storage."

"Awesome," Jenny breathed.

"And I am also to caution you that this tech must not fall into the hands of anyone on your Earth not authorized by the Dimensional Council. It contains applications that your planet and dimensional culture are not ready for, at this time. It will come, but like the MDP, there are too many ways it could affect your culture in a way that will be detrimental. Experience has shown us that each culture must progress at their own pace. When new tech is introduced out of sequence, even the simplest things can wreak unexpected consequences.

Speaking of which, you need time to assimilate all of this. I suggest enjoying the rest of your day. You have a lot to do tomorrow."

The tablet went black and Jenny didn't attempt to turn it back on. Assimilate? She felt like a grain of sand in a centrifuge. Her mind was spinning so fast that she wasn't even entirely sure what she was thinking.

She realized she had finished her meal and had not tasted a single bit of it. She decided she would take Lizzie's advice. "*Good plan,*" injected Tidbit. "*You should take a nap.*" And, taking his own advice, he curled up in a big fuzzy ball with his tail curled over his eyes and went to sleep.

Chapter 7: Skylark

The next 4 weeks developed a kind of rhythm. Mornings she breakfasted with Tidbit and began reading Lizzie's journals. Lizzie had begun journaling as a very young girl and the depictions of school and home life of the 1930's was entertaining and somewhat sobering. The wars and financial and political upheaval of the time was distressing and yet, she felt inspired by the way her family had stuck together and made it through.

True to her word, Sam had thrown her a house-warming party with their hiking buddies. It had been fun playing hostess, but she couldn't help but wonder how often she would be able to interact with her friends in the future. She was aware that friends did have a tendency to drift over time, but her heart was somewhat wistful as she bid them good-bye at the end of the evening.

Each day was all about tidying up her own life: Tying up loose ends for her clients, arranging finances and settling into the house. Sam would come over to chat several times a week and she went hiking with her hiking club. Tidbit had advised her to keep as normal a schedule as she would have if she wasn't launching herself as a Guardian. She would be gone a lot, but her cover story would make that expected. So, while she was home, it would be important to keep good relations with her neighbors.

She had informed Bob about her "new assignment" and that she would be "in and out" a lot. He just grinned and said something about, "It must run in the family." Evidently Lizzie's unpredictability had been well known in the neighborhood and they just thought it an interesting quirk. They knew that she had gotten rid of her old car years ago and only used taxis or rented limos to get around, unless she rode with Bob to the L.A. Farmer's Market or the grocery store.

There were no new boxes, but as it turned out, there didn't need to be. She had totally forgotten about the big shed in the back yard and one day when she finally unlocked the door, she took a step inside and realized there was much more in there than she would have thought possible. It was like a small museum.

Besides all of Lizzie's old furniture which had been mostly very good quality antiques, there were artifacts (Jenny could think of no other way to describe them) of such a variety as to be a bit overwhelming.

There even appeared to be a section dedicated to safari-type supplies as well as a wall with a door In it that split the building into two sections. Jenny had just stood there for a very long moment, then backed out and closed and locked the door. She had no time to catalog all of this and she suspected, that if she asked the LizzieAI, she would discover it had already been very accurately sorted, listed and described in a document somewhere.

The one thing she had learned about her aunt was that, although she appeared to be this somewhat scattered and eccentric old lady, she had been extremely well organized and surprisingly tech savvy. Considering that she had lived in a time when both horses and cars had co-existed on city streets, she had stayed on top of new tech in a way that most of her peers had not.

So, the time passed until she had made all of the arrangements on the list and, although she didn't think there was any way she could have said she was ready regardless of how much time she had been given to prepare, she was as ready as she could be.

Lizzie had advised her not to pack a lot of things, as most of the things she would need would be provided for her at the training facility or were already stored in her MDP. If she had wanted to, she could have packed half of her household in the wristband, but it made sense to wait and see what would actually be needed, so she packed a few different outfits, her toiletries, her tablet and her documents. Tidbit assured her that his needs would also be adequately provided for and so it was that she walked through the portal once more and entered the hallway of doors.

Miriha had indicated that she was to come to Lanatrix first, so she took a deep breath and went back through the door.

She and Tarafau were greeted on the beach by the gem eyes who did their odd little bobbing dance in front of each of them. It appeared to be early morning here. The Linklings crooned to them as they passed through the trees on the way to the village.

Since it was early in the morning, in the village square the various merchants bustled about, preparing their stalls for the customers of the day. Here and there an occasional early customer perused goods or haggled silently, but for the most part it appeared that the townsfolk were still making their morning preparations for the day.

In no time, she and Tarafau found themselves being welcomed by the chiming of Miriha's automated door.

Miriha welcomed her warmly, her hands outstretched. "*I am so excited for you, Jenny,*" she said, her bright eyes gleaming. "*This very day you will begin a journey that will surprise, delight and amaze you. Let me introduce you to Lova.*" She turned and gestured a woman forward. Lova was tall and it seemed obvious that she wasn't "from around here". Her blond, nearly transparent hair was cut very short. Large bluish-grey eyes lit her face, and she was muscular. Her light brown tunic came to her knees where it met breeches (were they leather?) of the same wood tones. Laced up to her calves, moccasin-type boots completed the outfit. Her only adornment was the tiny gold key necklace that peeked out of her shirt collar.

She extended her hand to Jenny who shook it solemnly. "*I will be your instructor, Jenny. Your aunt has recommended you highly.*" She gave Jenny and appraising look, noticing her hiking attire. "*I see you came prepared to work. This bodes well.*"

She nodded at Tarafau. "*We've made your usual accommodations, Tarafau,*" she said briefly. There seemed to be some subtext to this statement, but it obviously had something to do with the fact that these two knew each other from before.

Jenny realized that she hadn't even noticed that at no time had any of them vocalized anything. Mindspeak was becoming commonplace to her already. It never ceased to amaze Jenny how easily people could adapt to new circumstances when they were accepted by a group as normal.

Miriha didn't ask any of them to sit. She simply gestured to a door set into an alcove on the wall opposite the door they had entered. "*I look forward to hearing of your progress,*" was all she said, once more holding both hands out to Jenny. Jenny grasped them with a smile, and with a look at Tarafau, headed through yet another door.

Many years later, when Jenny thought of travel, she wouldn't think of any kind of vehicle, but of a door, but for now, this method of getting from place to place was still amazing to her. They stepped through the door which opened under a lattice archway covered in climbing roses, to a glade of very tall, apparently very old, aspen trees. At one end of the grove past a large field of wildflowers, was what appeared to be a huge two story wooden lodge with carved shutters on large windows that glittered in the morning light.

"Where are we?" she asked Lova.

"We are in the mountains of Sweden on Earth. We call our home Sanglarka. It means 'skylark'. We all use mindspeech here as good practice in our other travels and a convenience, since most of the native languages of the Earth Guardians are not English. This is the first step of your training and we find it best to begin in familiar surroundings, hence this first training ground is in your home dimension. In the next stage you will be travelling to the major touch points in the dimensions, but for now you need a place that will allow you to focus on your training. This place was designed with some very special options to be sure we can prepare you for what lies ahead, not that we can prepare you for every eventuality, but you won't go out into the dimensions unequipped to deal with most situations.

Some things you can only learn by experience and there will be some things you will encounter that will be new to all of us. The dimensions are vast and infinite. None of us will explore them all in our lifetimes, but we are doing our best." And at this her mouth quirked in a rueful grin.

Jenny grinned back at her. She had met an older lady while she had been in college who reminded her of Lova. She had gone by her last name, Hibbs, and had been an army veteran. Jenny had always suspected Hibbs had been a drill instructor. She was business-like in all of her communications and, although not unkind, had applied herself to every task with a single-minded enthusiasm, belied only by the intensity of her steely gaze that seemed to take in every mistake and flaw. She had seemed to have radar where slacking was concerned.

Jenny turned to Tidbit, wait…not Tidbit, Tarafau. "*Wait a minute, I thought you said we were on Earth? How is Tarafau in this form? Isn't it a rule that he is always Tidbit on Earth?*"

Lova smiled and Tarafau grinned. "*As I said, we make special arrangements for Tarafau while training here. This area is shielded in a way that allows Tarafau to take on his humanoid form. Only in Sanglarka can he do this, not counting exceptional circumstances.*"

Jenny couldn't help but wonder what "exceptional circumstances" would entail as Lova led the way into the lodge. As they moved into the entryway, Jenny could see a large great room with a fireplace large enough to cook an ox and blonde wood furniture with brown cushions. Here and there she noticed landscape paintings and little conversation areas circling low round tables. Lova gesture towards the curved wooden stairs.

Over the balustrade she could see that the back wall of the lodge was all glass doors flanked by what looked to be shutters that could be closed if the weather got nasty. The view through those windows was breathtaking. From the valley they nestled in she could see the surrounding mountains, their snowy peaks reflecting the bright sunlight as if they were strewn with diamonds. Lova helped Jenny find her room on the second floor. It was as rustic as the lodge implied. The room was generous (for some reason she had been picturing a monk's cell) and the large picture window looked out over the grove.

From this vantage she could see a path that led to what appeared to be a large lake through the large picture windows. In front of one window was a plain wooden desk. On the desk was a large book that looked new with a lavender envelope on it.

Lova noticed her surprised start. "*Yes, Lizzie wanted to welcome you here as well. You can read her message in privacy in a bit.*" She cocked her head. "*You will find many of her influences in various places as you travel. This was her room while she was here.*"

The bed, in the center of the room was spread with a colorful quilt and two rather comfy looking pillows. All in all, about what one would expect in an inexpensive bed and breakfast.

"*The bath is through here*," Lova said, indicating a door beside the bed. "*By the way, all doors in this lodge are just doors,*" with a wink, "*except the portal room, which I will show you tomorrow. Tarafau has the room next to yours.*"

She then led them downstairs to the great room. The large stone fireplace was laid with wood, but not lighted. She could easily picture herself with a cup of hot cocoa and a book, watching the snow fall through the windows on either side of the fireplace. A large, blond, polished wood table with a dozen rustic matching wood chairs sat on one side of the room beside a door that led into a roomy, white-tiled, professional looking kitchen.

"*We can stock any particular food you may prefer here, or you can sample some of our Swedish dishes. I recommend you get used to eating unusual food. It is considered impolite to turn your nose up at the delicacies offered to you in other dimensions, with the exception of those places in which their available food is not safe for human consumption.*"

She then led them to a corner room which turned out to be a large workout facility with a sauna, hot tub and an indoor pool. The pool was small, about 18 feet long and 10 feet wide, but deep enough to stand up in with water up to one's chest.

"*I expect you to make daily use of these facilities. The pool is what is known as an 'endless pool'. It generates a steady current that you can swim against, basically like a treadmill for swimmers. It wouldn't be a Swedish facility without a sauna, of course. Since it is summer, we won't be able to do snow baths, regrettably, but this time of year allows us to do much longer training as the sun is up most of the time.*

When you left, it was morning, but it is already bedtime here. It may take you awhile to adjust, but this is something else you must get used to. You will have to adjust your body clock quickly each time you port. You will be learning some techniques that will help you with that.

As a matter of fact, we will start your first lesson now."

Lova led her into the workout room and gestured to some mats on the floor. She sat on the mat, lowering herself to the ground in a graceful movement. She motioned for Jenny and Tarafau to sit on the mat in front of her.

Jenny had taken a few yoga classes in college, but she didn't give herself high marks for her grace this time. She settled to the floor beside Tarafau and waited.

Lova folded her hands, positioning them on her breastbone. *"I will walk you through an exercise you will repeat first thing in the morning and last thing before bed every day from now on, wherever you are.*

The purpose is to focus your energy in a way that will allow you to control your bodily responses to your environment. It will utilize a 'keyword' that will allow you to invoke this high level of focus at any time, once you become proficient at this exercise. The first several times you try it, you will not reach maximum effectiveness, but your ability will grow over time."

The exercise involved specialized types of breathing, timing the breaths at precisely staggered intervals while focusing on tightening some muscles while relaxing others at the same time. It seemed like it should have been simple but isolating the different muscles and making them each do different things while concentrating on the staggered, precisely counted out breathing patterns was more challenging than she could have imagined.

At the end of the hour she had finally mastered the simplest combination, but she couldn't help but compare her progress to the effortless performance of the other two.

"We will do the basic exercise one more time. This time you must do the exercise and with every exhale you will use a keyword. The keyword must contain 2 syllables and must be significant enough to you to come easily to your mind in crisis."

Jenny had already decided to also use "Lizzie" as her keyword for the exercise. This was the passkey to open the LizzieAI on her tablet and when things heated up, as it seemed they were likely to do, Lizzie's name would be the first thing on her mind.

They ran through the exercise a final time. Jenny was surprised how adding even this one simple element increased the difficulty.

"*Don't be too hard on yourself, Jenny,*" Tarafau said, noticing her small frown as they rose from their mats. "*I would be embarrassed to tell you how long it took me to learn this. It will require some effort on your part, but Lova is a good instructor. She will see to it that before you are certified, you will be able to do this without even thinking.*"

"*Now, we must go to bed. I know you think you might not sleep, but you may be surprised. We will arise very early. You need not set an alarm. I promise you that you will awake on time.*"

The intonation of that final thought was one of amusement and Jenny suspected that she was in for a lot of potentially not-so-pleasant surprises, for her experience told her that what was amusing for the perpetrator of a joke seldom was as much fun for the person on the receiving end.

When she closed the door to her room her eyes were immediately drawn to the lavender envelope on the book on the desk. The now familiar hand was somehow comforting to her. This aunt was becoming a friend, or so it seemed.

"Dear Jenny:

Well, you've made it this far and by now you are probably of two minds. On the one hand all of this is strange and perhaps even a little frightening. And you would be unusual indeed if this was not so. This goes beyond simple unfamiliarity and it will be more so as time goes on. But, unless I seriously misjudged you, you will stand up to it and enjoy the adventure.

On the other hand, it's all very exciting and your natural curiosity is pulling you forward. You can be enthusiastic at times, and that will work for you as you progress. Please know that I did not choose you lightly and I have been watching you for a very long time. You have more in you than you imagine. Don't shortchange yourself.

This book is a small gift, but something I have found helpful. There are pens in the drawer. Take the time to document your journey. There will be times when things will be somewhat overwhelming, and this may allow you to organize your thoughts.

Love, Lizzie"

Jenny opened the leather bound journal. Blank pages. To her, as a writer, blank pages represented potential. As Lizzie had said, there were pens and pencils in the desk drawer. She pulled one out and began to write…

…In her dream an emergency fire drill bell was clanging over and over again. She sat up, startled to realize that she could still hear it. Was the lodge on fire? The moment she sat up and was conscious of it, however, it stopped, and she realized she had not heard it with her ears, but in her head. She sniffed the air cautiously, just to be sure, and, realizing she didn't smell smoke, she jumped out of bed, put on her workout clothes and headed downstairs.

She had only written for a half hour the evening before and had been asleep the moment her head hit the pillow. She felt rested and ready, at least she hoped so, for whatever they would throw at her today.

Tarafau was already there. His bright colored robes had been replaced by what appeared to be a karate Gi, only instead of the traditional white, it was a soft forest green, belted with a dark green sash instead of the traditional "obi". She felt a little shabby in her dark grey sweats.

Lova was dressed as the day before in what Jenny thought of as a pathfinder outfit. With the exception of the fringe, her clothes were very similar to those worn by the American frontiersmen and some of the native American tribes.

"Before we eat, we will do our draga breathing. This will be your routine every morning. Following breakfast, we will run. After our run, we will study. Then lunch. Then limbering and balance. Then study. Then supper. In the evenings you will pursue your choice of creative exercise and then you will journal. Just previous to bedtime you will once more do your draga breathing. Some of the physical exercise will vary from day to day, but the first week we will use this routine."

She led the way into the workout room. Jenny noticed, as she focused this time, that she fell into the basic exercise fairly easily. *"Remember your keyword,"* Lova reminded her. Adding the keyword, she then proceeded to the more complex forms. She was still struggling with them, but she persisted, determined to master every skill presented to her. She ended her session with the basic pattern which felt better.

Breakfast consisted of cracker-like "crisp bread" of dark rye, hard-boiled eggs and mild yellow cheese to lay on the bread and a large glass of milk. *"I would offer you coffee,"* Lova said, *"but the caffeine will give you an artificial burst of energy that will deflate fairly quickly with what we will be doing today."*

"I don't drink coffee," Jenny agreed. *"I could never foster a taste for it."*

"Be sure to eat all of your meals. We won't overload you, but you will need the energy today. I have also prepared a small snack pack for you. Nuts and dried berries. I think you call it 'trail mix' in The States."

When breakfast was nearly done a short wizened man with white wild spiky hair that stuck out in all directions and big violet eyes bounced into the room. He was dressed in a long tunic of soft green tones that reminded Jenny of a pattern of summer leaves. He seemed unable to stay still for more than a moment, not exactly fidgeting but rather standing on the balls of his feet as if ready to spring into a run at any moment.

"Lova, all is in readiness." His mental voice was soft and nearly a bass, which was surprising in such a small man. He glanced at Jenny then nodded to her, *"Welcome to Sanglarka, Guardian. I am Arvid."* He then returned his attention to Lova. *"Will you be needing the packs today?"*

"Not today, Arvid. We'll save that for tomorrow. We'll be running the course, though. The usual precautions."

Precautions? Jenny wasn't sure she liked the sound of that.

Chapter 8: Pushing the Limits

Jenny wiped sweat from her forehead with the small towel she kept tucked into her belt.

She had always been active, and she loved being outdoors. Sanglarka was as beautiful as its name and her run took her on a path around one end of the lake and through the woods. There were stations along the path at which she was to pause and do the exercises indicated on a raised wooden plaque; squats, jumping jacks, pushups and sit-ups as well as different stretching exercises.

After a week of this routine she found she was making better time and feeling less tired, but it was still quite a workout. The 5 mile course included varied terrain, sometimes sloping up and sometimes down. There were logs in the path she was supposed to jump over and even a small creek she was to cross over on a twelve foot long log.

Looking back, she was beginning to realize this was a lot more like military basic training, without all the shouting. Her physical training was intense. In addition to the daily obstacle course, she swam for an hour every day in the evening before heading gratefully up to her room to bathe, journal, do her draga breathing and sleep. She arose at 5 a.m. every morning and started the routine all over again.

Her instructors varied. Arvid was so full of energy that sometimes Jenny felt he would burn himself up. He only ever stood still when they were tracking. He had taken her deep into the woods and taught her not only how to follow the tracks she saw of various animals in the area, but how to use the draga breathing to become so still that even a rabbit or deer wouldn't notice them.

Lova taught her to memorize her surroundings as well as passages of text quickly and often tested her memory about exercises they had done days ago. Jenny's training as a writer came in handy here, as she had been taught to notice small details.

She had continued her lessons with LizzieAI on that part of her schedule and she was beginning to understand the tiniest fraction of how big this all was and that her training could take years to complete. Lova had explained to her that this was only the first section of her training. That she would have the opportunity to meet each of the Guardians at their own gates and each of them would have something to teach her. After this stage, Tarafau, as her Guide, would teach her more about the capabilities of her tech and her gateroom.

Today, after lunch they would be learning something new, she was told. She couldn't help but wonder what it was. As she headed into the lodge, she saw Arvid, whistling happily as he toted a bundle of what looked like long sticks into the workout room.

Tarafau was waiting for her at the dining table. He handed her a large glass of water. He quirked a dark eyebrow at her, "*You're making better and better time. I've got a snack for you.*" He indicated a plate of cheese and apple slices. "*Lova says you can take it into the study with you. You'll need the extra fuel.*"

That sounded a bit ominous, Jenny thought. She grabbed the plate and headed for the study. This was a room with large windows with many shelves and books, a few large desks and a smaller fireplace than the great room. Before the fireplace on a large braided rug were three overstuffed chairs with a small table by each. On the table by the chair she thought of as hers, was her tablet.

This was her study time with the tablet. LizzieAI was her instructor for this part of the schedule.

"Lizzie, it's study time," she intoned to the tablet. It responded with a glowing screen featuring Lizzie's smiling face.

"Good morning, Jenny. How was your run?" Jenny never ceased to be surprised at how realistic this representation was. She knew, of course, that the Lizzie on the tablet was just a very cleverly programmed artificial intelligence, but it often felt so real that she had to remind herself that this wasn't a voice chat with a real person. However, it gave her a very connected feeling to her aunt.

"I cut nearly 30 seconds off of my time." She found that even though she knew LizzieAI wasn't real, she couldn't help responding as if she were. "I'm not sore in the morning anymore and I haven't fallen into the creek for a couple days now. What are we discussing today?"

"Today we will learn about the gateways. So far you have learned the basics about your tech and how it works. Now we will talk about why the gateways are important and you will start to learn about your mission and what it entails."

"Finally," Jenny thought with a grin.

"The gateways have always been. And you may have already guessed that those doorways aren't really the gates. They are a visual representation of a very complex branch of physics that is still beyond me. The simple explanation is that these dimensional pathways allow us to move between dimensions without a spacecraft or other technology. It is only in the past couple hundred years or so that the Dimensional Alliance Council has seen fit to allow Earthlings to take part in dimensional missions. Up until that time we weren't ready, and we are still considered not much more than trainees by most beings in the Alliance.

Over time you will continue to learn more about the 'politics' of it all, but for now, let's just say that our status is small, along with a few other newly accredited dimensional representatives from dimensions other than our own.

It is both simpler and more complex than you might think. The gates allow us to move between dimensions. Each dimension has its own universe and its own physical laws and political systems. The gates do not allow us to travel between planetary systems, only between dimensional way stations. Once in a dimension, you would visit other planets in their systems only if they have adequate space travel. Which is why we don't currently represent any planet but our own in this universe. We will eventually begin adding others, but unless we are approached by a much more technically advanced culture than our own, it's just us Earthlings.

We don't know why any particular planet is chosen, or seems to be chosen, as a dimensional portal for their particular universe. Some cultures at a gateway are very advanced and some aren't. The Earth portals have been active, seemingly, from the earliest beginnings of the planet. Many of our myths and legends stem from accidental incursions into other dimensions or by beings from other dimensions stumbling onto an Earth gate.

As you continue to learn, you will begin to notice strong hints in fairy tales and believe-it-or-not phenomenon on our planet that strongly indicate gate usage from someone unwittingly triggering a gate or beings from other dimensions discovering our gates through accident or intentional exploration.

Your key is intentionally tuned to gateway entrances, but from time to time over the centuries, it appears that certain weather patterns and magnetic and gravitational combinations have also given random access to gates, which may be how they were discovered in the first place.

However, over the past couple of centuries, we have secured all the gates we are aware of on our planet. There are possibilities there may be some in the deepest depths of our oceans or within caves or glacial fissures we have not yet discovered, but each of the gates we know about have a Guardian assigned.

You have met The Gatekeeper. It is her job to help the Guardians find and secure gates as well as keeping tabs on the known dimensions who are either already part of the Dimensional Alliance Council or who are developing to a point that they may be considered for membership. A large part of her job is overseeing the effort to be sure the gate system is secure, as well as assisting in the choice for new Guardians and their training.

The Dimensional Alliance Council is the ruling body who deal with issues between and within different dimensions and try to keep a balance between the needs and rights of the dimensions we know about. You should understand that, as far as we know, there are an infinite number of dimensions.

Note that these are not 'alternative time-lines' where you might find yourself living a completely different life in a duplicate universe. I am not sure whether or not that exists. This is also not time travel. Some of our Earth scientists might refer to it as a 'multiverse'. Regardless what you call it, it is as real as anything we know.

As in any body of 'people', (Let us call them 'beings', as many of them are not humanoid.) there are disagreements about how to deal with inter-dimensional conflicts and what, if any responsibilities the other dimensions who are aware of the gateways have to dimensions which are in danger or which may be failing.

The beings on the Alliance Council are as varied as any large council, such as congress or the United Nations, and do not all agree on all things. One of the things that has been agreed upon is that the representatives of each dimension should have a say and they must learn to understand the issues before they are allowed to do so.

Mind speech is how we address the issue of interdimensional communication. Since there are many different kinds of "speech", mind to mind communication is pretty much universally accurate and prevents misunderstanding, which, as you can imagine, is vital.

One of the things you will do a lot is to travel between several dimensions to learn their cultures and from time to time you will be assigned to aid the Council with issues that an Earthling may have a better chance to resolve. In this way you become an ambassador for our dimension.

It is true that Earth does not yet have space flight capability and it may seem ironic that one puny planet represents the entire universe as little as we know it. Nevertheless, because each dimension has only one gateway planet, ours is the only gate planet in our universe and we must make decisions based on our best knowledge.

Fortunately, you will not be alone in this. There are a dozen Guardians on the planet, and you will get to know each of them over the coming year. There are also many Guardians in each dimension. Over time, as you are assigned, you will get to know many, but never all of them."

Jenny munched contemplatively on an apple slice.

"So why have I been chosen? I'm just a 'twenty-something' with a college degree and nearly no life experience. How can they trust me not to blow up the multiverse or something?"

"This is one of the reasons you were chosen, Jenny. You are no 'flibbertigibbet'. You have a bright mind, you're a responsible person and you care about what happens. As a writer, you notice things other people might not. As a lover of nature, you are serious about preserving things that are important.

I promise you that you will be trained to prepare you for what is to come, but you must know that no amount of education and experience will qualify you for this work. This is something so new and different that we find it is better to start with someone without any fixed agenda or strong habits that make them inflexible and unteachable."

Jenny noticed the time and realized she needed to get to her limbering and balance training.

She closed the tablet, picked up her plate and took it to the kitchen where she cleaned it and put it in the drainer. It seemed strange doing such mundane tasks when something huge seemed to loom over the horizon of her life. The great heroes in the stories she was so fond of never seemed to do dishes or wash clothes.

Balance and limbering training had been a fun break in the routine, as it was a combination of stretching and yoga exercises along with things like walking a gymnast's balance beam and performing various tasks on it as well as using a balance board, a round board covered in a rubber-like substance that sat on a half ball. Each of these things was designed to give her grace and the ability to cope with difficult physical tasks. Jenny liked the challenges and looked forward to working out with Tarafau and even Miriha. Admittedly she had acquired a few bumps and bruises, but she knew she was just beginning. Tarafau teased her with a wicked grin about her clumsiness, but even he admitted she was improving.

However, Jenny did find herself wondering from time to time what she could possibly be assigned to that would require all of this physical training. She had assumed from Lizzie's gate office that most of her time was about welcoming people through the gates and doing paperwork. She was quickly being disabused of that notion.

The workout room reminded Jenny of a cross between a dance studio, a dojo and a gymnastic floor. Half of the floor was covered in a large padded mat and on the wall on one side was a floor to ceiling mirror with a barre at about hand height. The opposite wall featured tall windows that let in the bright sunlight that infused the house throughout most of every day in the Nordic summer.

As she entered the workout room, she noticed a basket of long sticks standing just off of the mat. Beside it stood Arvid. He bounced cheerfully on the balls of his feet. His wild, unkempt white hair was the only thing about him that was not neat and precise. He wore his usual leaf-patterned green tunic and breeches, but he was barefooted. His feet were wide and a bit larger than you would expect on such a short fellow. And, as usual, his face was plastered with that grin that said there was something very amusing about the world and he was in on the prank.

"*I will be your instructor today,*" he said in his deep soft voice.

Tarafau stood by the side of the mat, also barefooted. Jenny took the hint and removed the slippers she usually wore in the house. "*What are the sticks for? Are we building something?*"

Arvid gave a bark of a laugh. "*You will encounter a number of situations in your travels. At some point you may need to defend yourself. The gates do not allow weapons to be transported through them, not even something as simple as pepper spray or a knife. Every gate has scanners of one type or another. Therefore, for your protection, all Guardians learn three types of defense; hand to hand, mental protection and this…*"

He pulled a stick out of the basket, held it parallel with the floor and tossed it to her. She managed to catch it and held it as he had, in both hands, palms down in front of her. It was about as tall as she was, just thick enough for her to get her hands around it and surprisingly light.

"*This is your 'staff'. All Guardians carry one. In some cultures, you will encounter, they consider this part of your 'power'. Some consider it a staff of office. Actually, it is just a stick unless you know how to use it properly. In Earth cultures, it is called a quarterstaff, a Bo, a Marotte or a Gun, depending on which martial art they ascribe to.*

I have no expectations that you will become a master of the staff in the short time we will have you here for training, but today we will get you started, and you will continue to work out with Tarafau daily until you can beat him. At that point, we will consider you have mastered it, although it is a lifetime pursuit."

"*I'm sorry,*" Jenny broke in, "*but what good is a stick, really, when it comes to defending myself from someone bigger and stronger than I am?*"

Arvid smiled. "*Allow us to demonstrate.*"

Tarafau casually reached for a staff that had been leaning on the wall next to him. Arvid grabbed a staff from the basket. He and Arvid centered themselves on the mat facing one another about 10 feet apart. It was like David and Goliath. Arvid was no taller than Jenny and Tarafau was well over 6 feet tall, square built and muscular. Arvid was also solidly built but seemed no match for someone of Tarafau's height and girth.

Suddenly, Tarafau charged with a roar like an angry lion, swinging his staff one-handed at Arvid's head. Jenny was sure they were going to have to rush Arvid to the hospital. At what appeared to be the last fraction of a second, Arvid, almost casually, swung his staff up to meet it with a loud, "CRACK!"

With no pause, Arvid swiveled, swinging his staff low at Tarafau's shins. Tarafau surprised Jenny with his agile leap above the staff's low arc and then blocked a follow up blow that swept up from below toward his chest.

"Clack! Clack! Clack! Clack! Clack!" There seemed to be no space between blows. It appeared to be a choreographed dance between two expert dance partners. Neither seemed to have an advantage and neither was giving any quarter. They leapt and turned and swung around one another. The rhythm of it was like the beating of a heart, one blow following another only pausing as they circled facing one another, looking for an opening for the next flurry of blows.

Finally, in a rapid and furious exchange, Arvid swung his staff in an upward arc directly at Tarafau's throat. It stopped abruptly nearly touching the Adam's apple. Tarafau lowered his staff and bowed his head. Both were panting with exertion and sweating.

Both then bowed respectfully to one another. "*You almost had me, my friend,*" Arvid grinned.

"*Someday,*" Tarafau replied grimacing. "*Maybe someday.*"

"*Does that answer your question?*" Arvid asked, smiling at Jenny. Jenny nodded numbly. "*Then let us begin.*"

Chapter 9: Beginnings and Endings

Tarafau pulled the elastic bandage tight around her ribs and Jenny gritted her teeth. She would not complain. She was determined not to give in to the pain.

"I've crossed that log 50 times and there was never a turtle on it before. I wasn't looking at my feet. I was looking ahead, thinking about LizzieAI's last lesson and wondering what surprises Miriha has for me today."

Tarafau merely nodded. She expected him to chide her for not paying attention. His silence irritated her.

"Quit being so inscrutable, you…" she groped for words and they failed her. *"You, CAT, you!"*

She thought she saw one corner of his mouth almost twitch into a hidden smile.

"Do you think this is funny?"

"No, Jenny," he finally said. *"Not funny at all. I'll get some ice for that."*

As he left from the dining area into the kitchen, his hand over his mouth, she ground her teeth. She had stopped counting bruises over the last few weeks. Between her daily runs, her quarterstaff workouts with Tarafau, gleefully overseen by Arvid, and the increase in complexity of her balance and limbering exercises, she never felt anything but challenged and even though she was in better shape than she had ever been, she still felt clumsy and slow compared to Tarafau, Arvid and even Lova.

Lova often came into the workout area during her exercises and even joined in more often than not. She was lithe, quick and incredibly skilled at everything from tumbling to battling with the staff. From time to time the four of them would pair up two on two and the rhythmic "clack, clack, clack" was starting to invade Jenny's dreams at night.

On the one hand, she felt like she was making progress, albeit slower than she would have liked. On the other hand, she felt like she would never measure up to the tasks ahead of her. She had really skated through her years in school, never really feeling challenged, even in her physics and advance math courses. She just seemed to "get it" when a new concept was presented to her. She had watched her classmates struggle and she had a hard time understanding why.

She had undertaken to do some tutoring at the urging of some of her professors, but found she wasn't very good at it. Evidently there was an art to simplifying complex concepts at the level at which most of her fellow students navigated. She felt sympathy and she didn't judge them, not really, but relating to them was a struggle.

But this! For the first time in her life she began to empathize with her fellow students. Every day brought a new concept and there was so much to learn.

Lova strode into the dining room, a small leather satchel under her arm. "*Working hard, I see*," she commented, one eyebrow raised slightly. *Well, it's about time for your break, anyway.*"

"*Break? It's study time.*"

"*Ah, yes, well, actually, after Tarafau gets you iced up, he'll be packing whatever you need to take back with you.*"

Jenny's face fell. Had she failed? Were they giving up on her? Had her clumsiness finally made them decide she wasn't up to the task?

Lova seemed to notice Jenny's confusion. "*Oh dear, Jenny. I see I'm not communicating clearly. You need to go home and spend some time there, to keep up your cover story. Your training isn't finished, and you will be returning here from time to time, but you have made enough progress that we'll start sending you through some gateways now to start meeting your fellow Guardians.*

While you're home, you can take some time to heal..." She looked pointedly at Jenny's bandaged ribs. "*And it will also give you time to absorb what you've learned so far. Please continue your physical conditioning and your training with Lizzie. Tarafau will also continue to help you. You can stop in here at any point to use the facilities by going through the Lanatrix gateway. Or at any time, if you need help, you are always welcome here. After all, it isn't like it is a long commute..."* She grinned, and Jenny grinned back with a sigh of relief.

Tarafau returned with the ice pack and headed up the stairs.

Lova, handed Jenny the satchel. *"This is your traveling kit. Of course, you could keep the individual items loose in your MDP, but for organizational purposes, this little kit will make it much easier to get out your emergency supplies. In here you will find first aid supplies, which Tarafau will teach you to use."*

Jenny interrupted. *"I am first aid certified,"* she said.

"Ah," Lova replied. *"I think you will find that beyond standard first aid, we have added a few things you may not expect and that may come in handy. You will need to be instructed in their use and know they are available. I won't go into this now, but just know they are there.*

In addition, we have included some special emergency rations we developed for the use of the Guardians. They aren't exactly lembas, but they work in a similar way. There is also a backup beacon that will let us know, under most circumstances, if you need emergency assistance and the MDP isn't connecting. There are some dimensions that have a vibration that blocks this beacon, but it works the majority of the time." The wry twist of her lips said volumes about what she thought of the beacons only working "the majority of the time", but she moved on.

"There's a compartment for your tablet in here and your passport. I suggest when you go through the gateways that you carry the satchel outside your MDP, so it can be easily scanned. Strictly speaking, the other dimensional beings are aware of the MDP's, but they don't generally search them. The satchel is another sign you are a Guardian. Speaking of which, I'll be right back."

She left Jenny to contemplate her words. Why was it that it seemed like everything just kind of dragged on and then when things finally seemed to be happening it was uncomfortably quick?

Before Jenny could ruminate on this for long enough to come to any conclusions, Lova was back. In her hand were two quarterstaffs.

One was plain and unadorned, like the practice staffs they normally used. The other one was shod on either end with engraved steel caps. On close examination she realized a stylized "J" was part of the design along with a small globe that appeared to be Earth on one end and a representation of the Sun on the other.

"This marks you as a Guardian," she indicated the shod staff. *"The other is for practice. Keep them in your MDP when you are not using them. Always carry your staff outside the MDP when you go through a gateway."*

Jenny took the staves with a little wince for her sore ribs and tapped the MDP to them. They shriveled, folding in on themselves and fading into the MDP.

"I've been wanting to ask. I know there were already some things in the MDP when it was given to me. I've put a few things in it myself, but how do I know what's in there?"

"You can simply think the word "peek" and you will be shown a mental image of your inventory, as if it was stored in a warehouse. In this mental image, you can walk through your inventory and even virtually pick items up and examine them. Try it now."

Jenny obediently thought, *"Peek."*

Like some kind of transparent overlay of the scene before her, she saw a large warehouse-like room with shelves somewhat like some of the big "box stores" in her town. The majority of the shelves were bare and some of the items she didn't recognize. Her satchel was there, her tablet, what looked like a pantry, her staffs, a tent and camping supplies and a number of boxes, including the 3 boxes Lizzie had left her.

She found that by thinking of the contents of a box or bag, she could peer into the contents of the boxes as well. Too bad the storage shed at home wasn't this easy to explore, she thought wryly.

"While you are home, you should be seen by people who know you. You might want to visit family and friends, for instance. It will be important later for you to be considered a part of your community and for you to be seen coming and going.

We will contact you in a couple weeks about your next steps. Continue your studies with the LizzieAI and keep up your physical conditioning.

You will find a gym behind the purple door in the dimensional hallway that you can use anytime, if you don't want to take the time to come here. It has all the facilities you are used to. Since Tarafau is Tidbit on Earth, you will need to use it when you want to work out with Tarafau. However, do your running in your neighborhood, so they get used to seeing you.

Any questions?"

Jenny thought a moment. *"Does this mean I'll be getting an assignment soon? I can't say I feel ready for that, yet."*

"You are more ready than you know and yet, you will never be completely ready," Lova said with a small grimace. *"The thing is, it all changes from day to day. Just when we think we have a handle on it, something new comes up. It's all right to be a little confused at this point. This is one of those things that you have to experience yourself.*

Your next stage of training will take place in the headquarters for the Dimensional Alliance Council. You'll understand a lot more at that point."

Jenny nodded without any real understanding as Tarafau entered the room with her travel bag.

Lova and Jenny stood and Lova reached out both hands. *"I'd give you a good-bye hug, but I don't know if your ribs could handle it right now. If you need anything, you have my cell number. Just text me."*

Jenny had to laugh even if it made her grab at her sore ribs. All of a sudden texting seemed a little primitive. *"Will do. Come on Tarafau. Let's go home."*

Chapter 10: In the Loop

Jenny was not surprised when she returned from her run the next morning to see Bob waving for her to stop to chat.

"Long time no see, neighbor!" he grinned as she slowed and stopped. He held some trimming shears in his hand and appeared to be trimming the large sage bushes under his windows. A half-filled basket of clippings stood on the ground behind him.

"I've been training for that new job I told you about. I'll be continuing my training online for a bit. Didja miss me?"

"Yeah and so did the mailman. I've got quite a pile of mail for you." Bob had volunteered to check her mail for her while she was gone.

"I can't imagine why. I'll bet most of it is just junk mail."

"I'll let you be the judge of that. Who did you get to take care of Tidbit? I didn't see him around and you didn't ask me to check on him while you were gone."

"Actually, my new job allows Tidbit to travel with me. Great company, cool bennies. Travel is paid for and health benefits as well. I'm learning a lot and I get to write, so it's all good."

"Yeah, Lizzie never left home without her cat, either. I knew you two would hit it off."

Jenny saw a small red car coming down the street. "That'll be Sam," she said. "Drop in later for lunch and we can sort the junk out of that mail together."

Bob chuckled and waved at Sam as she pulled past and into Jenny's driveway.

"Hey, you!" Sam said as she got out of her car. "I got your text last night. Did you have a good flight?"

Jenny's insides gave a little squirm. This was the part she wouldn't enjoy, she realized. Regardless of her other faults, she had always been an honest person. Her "cover story" was a lie, any way she framed it, but both Miriha and Lova had made it clear that every Guardian had the duty to keep the gateways secret. Earthlings weren't ready for instantaneous travel to the unknown dimensions. They had all they could do with preparing for possible space travel.

"You know, jet lag and all of that. Looks like I'll be spending most of my time travelling, but the benefits are good, and we always wanted to see the world, right?"

Jenny and Sam had met in their college days. Sam had started one semester behind her, but before she knew it, she had been ahead of her in just about everything. By the time they had spent a semester getting to know one another, they had gotten a little apartment together just off campus. People seldom saw one without the other, unless they were in different classes.

Today she was dressed in jeans and a t-shirt, ready for a casual day of hanging out. Her job at the news desk of the local television station meant dressing professionally every day, so on her days off, she had to "let it loose", as she said.

"I've got some lemonade in the fridge," Jenny said. "Let's take it out on the patio."

They settled down at the little table with its colorful umbrella. "Such a nice garden," Sam said with a sigh. "And a cute gardener guy too. I hear he came with the estate."

Jenny's eyebrows shot up. "You've been talking with Ted?"

"I dropped by from time to time while you were gone, just to check on things," Sam shrugged. "You said you'd be gone for awhile and I thought someone should be keeping an eye on the house. You're not exactly in my neighborhood anymore, but I thought it was the least I could do for my best friend." She sighed again. "I missed you so much. The hiking club has been asking about you. They want to know if you'll still want to hike with all of the travelling you'll be doing with your job."

Sam wasn't kidding about them not being in the same neighborhood anymore. With L.A. traffic, it was about a 30-45 minute drive from Sam's place to here.

"Well, thank you, Sam. Bob has been keeping an eye on things, picking up my mail and watching out for anything suspicious for me.

I've missed you too. And as far as the hiking club is concerned, don't we have another hike coming up this week?"

"Will you be here?" Sam asked hopefully.

"I expect to. I understand I may be called away unexpectedly from time to time, but I should be staying here for awhile. My training has gotten to the point that I can do it online. I guess there is paperwork as well. A lot of my work is research and writing, as usual."

Jenny could tell that Sam would have liked for her to say more on the subject, but she didn't push. They spent the morning with Sam telling her about the hijinks of one of the cameramen at her studio and the last hike they had taken near Griffith Park Observatory. "Tough one, that. Not a flat stretch the entire hike, but the view was worth it."

Tidbit wandered into the yard, his black tail held high, streaming behind him as if leading a parade. He seemed to be watching the butterflies dancing over the herb garden, but Jenny could tell he was more interested in Sam. He sauntered over to be petted, purring with happiness when Sam reached out to scratch under his chin and behind his ears.

"So how are you and the cat getting along? I seem to remember you really aren't a pet person."

"Tidbit and I get on well enough. He's pretty low maintenance as pets go. A small price to pay for all of this," and she gestured around the garden with a flourish.

Tidbit sent a disgruntled unformed thought in her direction and she chuckled inwardly.

"So, if you want out of your running clothes, I'll sit here with the cat and enjoy the butterflies. Then maybe you and I can go do something."

Jenny agreed. By the time she had her shower and changed into jeans and a t-shirt, she was ready to do something fun with her friend, but she remembered she had invited Bob over for lunch and junk mail.

"Do you mind doing it a bit later?" she asked after ringing him on her cell phone. "Sam and I are thinking about gallivanting today. Should be back about supper time. Will that work for you?"

Bob agreed and she went outside to find her friend looking pensively into the koi pond.

"There's something very calming about big fish like this," she said, dabbling one finger in the water. One of the koi noticed it and swam up to nibble on Sam's fingernail. Then, looking up at Jenny she asked. "Are we ready?"

They took off in Sam's little red car and had plenty of time to talk, moving at a snail's pace along the I-5 towards the Pacific Coast Highway. Jenny loved that drive down the coast. They stopped in at a little seafood place for lunch. There were long silences, as are comfortable between old friends, but they also laughed at the very old surfer guys hanging out on balconies in the sun and reminisced about college days.

"So, where'd they send you for training?" Sam asked, out of the blue, when the silence had stretched for several minutes. "You didn't say much about the company you're working for."

Jenny went into the spiel she had memorized while she was in training about an international company that needed on-the-ground researchers who could dig out information and then could write it up in reports for their investors and for marketing purposes. Sam quirked an eyebrow.

"Sounds a bit mysterious," was all she said.

"Yeah, I have a non-disclosure agreement. Not allowed to even name the company or tell any of their trade secrets. That's pretty common when you're ghost-writing, though. You know I almost never get my name published with my work."

As they headed home, they chatted about this and that, but Jenny realized that this "job" could easily disconnect her from friends and family. She could see why part of her assignment was to re-connect. And lie. The cover story had enough truth in it to be believable. Lova had explained that you had to keep things simple. "The less you have to remember, the better."

Jenny understood the need for secrecy but something inside her rebelled at lying to friends and family. She was committed to do her best for the Dimensional Alliance, but this part of her duties was weighing on her mind like a lead hat.

After checking out the little shops in the beach towns on the PCH and strolling along the beach, Sam drove her home, still chatting about this and that. When Sam pulled into the driveway on Infinity Loop, she got out to give Jenny a hug. "See you tomorrow after work? I want to take advantage of you while you're here."

"Sure," Jenny agreed.

Tidbit was waiting somewhat impatiently on the porch, the tip of his tail twitching. He followed Jenny into the house.

"Your friend is a little snoopy," he remarked. "Poking around."

"What are you talking about?"

"She made a full circuit around the shed while you were getting dressed. Then she went into the kitchen and opened every cupboard and drawer, as if she was looking for something."

"She was probably looking for something to go with the lemonade," Jenny scoffed. And the shed is an interesting building. Sam is always up for a good mystery."

Tidbit just stared up at her, his amber eyes nearly glowing in the faint light from the porch.

"Hey neighbor!" Jenny turned and saw Bob striding across the street with a small box of mail in his hand. "Have a nice jaunt?"

"You can put those on the dining room table," Jenny said as they walked through the front door. "And yes, I always have a great day hanging out with Sam."

"She seems a little," he paused, searching for a word, "enthusiastic. Quite a ball of energy. She dropped in on your place a few times a week while you were gone, and we had some conversations. She wanted to know what I know about what you're doing, and I told her, that I really didn't know much. She even offered to hold your mail for you."

"Yeah, that's Sam. Always up to something, especially if it looks like there might be adventure involved. It's why she works for a television station. She's always on top of everything going on in the area. But why she would want to hold onto my mail, considering you live across the street, I have no idea."

"She probably didn't trust me not to snoop," Bob said arching his eyebrows and narrowing his eyes. "I have shifty eyes, see. Once I put on a suit for a job interview and a lady in a parking lot told me I look like a spy or someone from the mob." His shoulders shook with mirth at Jenny's giggle.

"I sorted out the obvious junk, Jenny, but there are a lot of things from various companies I wasn't sure about. Might make the sorting a little easier."

"I thought we might order in some Chinese food," Jenny said. "You know the people in this neighborhood pretty well and I was wondering about my neighbors."

They settled in, he on the couch and Jenny in her "reading" chair. Bob was a wiry man, but muscular. Obviously much of what he "tinkered" with required a certain amount of strength. His brown eyes twinkled as he regaled Jenny with tales of her two neighbors on either side.

"You've already met Elias and Cinder," he said. "I think they invented the word curmudgeon just for him. He's an army veteran from the Vietnam war days. He's pretty crusty, that one, all points and edges, but Lizzie had him wrapped around her little finger. He took her death pretty hard. As far as I can tell, he's got no family other than his dog and Lizzie was kind to him.

You've probably noticed that Cinder and Tidbit have a running feud. The dog is as much of a grouch as his master, but really a big baby and mostly harmless."

Jenny nodded. She made a note to herself to be less quick to judge based on first impressions. She had dealt with a professor like Elias before and although he terrified her and her classmates, it turned out that as the year progressed, she found him to be intelligent, perceptive and that his exterior brusqueness stemmed from a clear focus on his goals. His students tended to score high on their exams, because of the clear expectations he had of them.

"Now, Miss Longtree, is a completely different batch of cookies," he continued. "She's been out east lecturing at one of the big colleges. She teaches ethics and is well known in academic and political circles for being outspoken and passionate about preserving and increasing the integrity of political systems. But when she's home, she writes, putters around in her garden and builds amazing animated kites that she flies in kiting competitions all over the world.

I think you and she will get along well, if you're ever both around long enough at the same time to get acquainted."

Bob leaned back in his chair. "Me, I putter around in my workshop. You haven't met my bird, Ignatius, yet. He's my workshop buddy and he makes for a great alarm system. My son, Cleo, pops in and out from time to time. He's attending Berkley, majoring in robotics. Kinda takes after his dad, I guess." Bob's face softened. "Or at least his mom always said so. My wife and Lizzie were good friends, you know. Nattered together like a couple of songbirds sitting on a powerline. My wife passed about two years ago. Complications of a lung infection. Lizzie got me through it though."

Jenny wasn't sure what to say. "I didn't know, Bob. I'm sorry. I wish I had really been able to get to know my aunt. From what I hear, from those who knew her, she was an amazing person."

Bob smiled, shaking his head. "Ah, Lizzie was definitely one of a kind. But don't let all of us fans fool you. She could be hard as rock and cold as ice when she chose to. There are a lot of folks who think they can prey on older folks like her. But more than one have discovered that more often than not the reason they got to be so old in the first place is because they use their brains for more than to keep their ears apart.

She and Tidbit were always a good match, I thought. Tidbit wouldn't be afraid of a mountain lion. I wouldn't want to mess with those two, if they teamed up, for sure."

Jenny was enjoying letting Bob ramble on. He was animated, gesturing often with his big calloused hands. Being around him was comfortable.

"So, what do you putter on, in that workshop of yours?" Jenny asked. "Hotrods or nuclear fission?"

Bob laughed. "Nothing so typical. You'll have to come over and see. It's hard to explain. I was an engineer for years and once you get your hands into creating new things, it's hard to stop. I have worked on a few projects for Lizzie, in the past. I imagine you'll find them when you get around to sorting through the shed out back. Lizzie was a collector, for sure. She admired clever gadgets and I was never quite sure what I'd find her playing with on any given day."

"Speaking of workshops, I really should get back to mine. Did you get anything useful in that stack of mail, I wonder?"

Jenny looked at the small box full of mail. True to his word, Bob had removed all the ad flyers and there were no letters addressed to "resident" in there. She sorted through the business stuff, laying it aside for later, and found a letter decorated with little panda bear stickers. From her mom. "My mom has always decorated her letters with cute stickers, since I left home for college," she said to Bob, somewhat embarrassed.

The postmark indicated the letter had only been mailed a few days ago.

"Dear Jenny:

Your dad and I will be headed up the coast next week to attend a genealogy convention and we thought to drop in to visit on Friday. Will that work for you?

We miss you and we want to see you in your new home. I might even be able to persuade your dad to make his famous deep dish pizza, if you'd like. What do you say? Send me a text.

Love, Mom"

The short note was surrounded by more frolicking panda bears with little hearts and flowers.

Jenny couldn't help but grin. That was her mom all over. There was nothing elegant about her. Her mop of dark brown curls tended to be untidy and she was round instead of slender. But Jenny had to admit that her mom had the market cornered on cuteness.

Her dad was tall and skinny, and he adored her mom like a schoolboy with a crush. They were the world's cutest couple, in Jenny's opinion.

"You'll like my parents," Jenny said to Bob, who was standing, preparing to leave. "My dad is famous for his home made deep dish pizza. You should come over for supper. And dad would love a tour of your workshop. He'll talk your ear off, though.

My mom is just a cute, sweet bookworm with a penchant for anything sparkly that isn't a rare gem. She doesn't approve of how precious gems are mined, so she prefers crystals and cleverly created glass items. And dad says that's ok with him. A lot easier on his budget." Jenny laughed.

Bob smiled. "I'll look forward to meeting them. And now I'll be off. Have fun with your mail."

Jenny rolled her eyes. "Looks like that was the only 'fun' in *this* pile. See you tomorrow."

Jenny carried the stack of mail into her office as Bob saw himself out. She sat down in front of her computer. It almost felt alien to her. While she had been in training, she had taken to writing in longhand in the leather bound journal Lizzie had given her. The only tech she had spent any time with was LizzieAI and that was more like talking with a friend than interacting with an electronic device. The laptop sitting on her desk reminded her of how much her life had changed.

Nevertheless, she checked her email, sorted out the spam and went through the newsletters she subscribed to. There was nothing earth-shaking there.

Tidbit mewled at the back doors. "*I guess I don't really have to do this*," he thought to her. "*But if someone was around and I forgot, they might catch on to the fact that you and I are communicating 'unnaturally'. It's time for our workout.*"

Jenny realized she had really lost track of time between her conversations with Sam and Bob. She and Tidbit headed for the gate room. There she went through the second door and saw the door next to the door she used to visit Miriha, the purple door described by Lova.

The door opened to a large space patterned after the gym in Sanglarka. The familiar grey floor mats appeared to have been well used, if not exactly shabby. In one corner stood a basket of quarterstaffs. The balance equipment was all there and through the door on the far end she was sure she would see the workout pool.

Tidbit was now Tarafau, dressed in his muted green Gi. Jenny had asked him why green, when all of the Gi she had ever seen were white. Tarafau had simply shrugged. "White makes you a target. This color blends into many backgrounds."

Tarafau wasn't exactly a chatterbox, but he was a good listener and nearly always made sense when he did speak. He seemed to be of the school of thought that, when speaking, 'less is more'.

They dropped to the mat to do their draga breathing. By now, Jenny found the exercise soothing and energizing at the same time. She had learned that this breathing technique had other benefits as well. She had graduated from doing it seated to applying it even when she was moving, such as when she went on her run.

She found that intentional breathing made a huge difference in her performance. When she did it seated, it cleared her mind and allowed her to concentrate more fully on whatever she was doing at the time. And when she was in pain, she could use the breathing much like women did in labor. The focused breathing helped her to distance herself from pain to a certain extent.

The quarterstaff sessions were getting more and more challenging. They had gone from carefully choreographed block and parry drills to adding a freeform fight at the end of each lesson, applying the tactics she had learned.

Tarafau was a patient instructor, but he had no problem tweaking her when she messed up. This sometimes took the form of a "light tap" of Tarafau's staff and "*Let's try that again.*"

Jenny was amazed at Tarafau's control of the staff. She knew, as strong as he was, that he could land powerful blows to an opponent, but he never gave her more than a few bruises, no matter how furious the flurry of blows had been leading up to that "light tap".

"Ow!" she exclaimed, rubbing her shin. She needed to think less, react more, she realized.

Tarafau just said, "*Again*."

Chapter 11: Daddy's Little Girl

Friday morning Jenny answered the bell and there they stood. Her mom rushed to give her a warm hug and her dad grabbed them both, making what her dad had always called a "Jenny sandwich". It was good to see them, although she admitted to herself, she was a little (no, a lot) nervous, knowing she would have to be very good at her cover story. Neither of her parents were thick or slow on the uptake.

When she was a kid, she was sure her mom and dad must have some kind of crystal ball, the way they always seemed to know what she was up to.

Technically, everything in her cover story was true. She was working for a very large entity with deep pockets with which she had a strict non-disclosure agreement. It did involve a lot of travel and she was writing about it. Of course, that was leaving out the part about dimensional portals, quarterstaff fighting and that her mentor just happened to be a shape-changer.

"So, give us the grand tour!" her dad said. His eyes crinkled. "We're not getting any younger, you know." With a wink he entered the living room and did a slow turn. "That fireplace needs a painting. Have you talked to your Uncle Bill? He just did a gallery show in Seattle last month."

"You know dad, I think it needs something too. I've just been too busy to think about it. Great idea. I'll give Uncle Bill a call."

Her mom noticed the crocheted throw on the couch and her eyes went warm. She loved to crochet and loved giving her projects away and seeing them used. The warm colors of the afghan were just the right accent for this room.

"I get a lot of compliments on that, Mom. It goes perfectly with the dark floor tiles, don't you think?"

She took them through the house and noticed for the first time that she could see the door to the gateway room. She felt a sharp swell of panic until she realized that her parents' eyes seemed to slip right past it. She had expected it to be invisible when others were in the house, but she had thought that would mean she wouldn't be able to see it either.

Dad loved the little kitchen. Of the two of her parents, he was the one who loved to cook. Her mom was a great cook, but her dad was the one who loved doing it. "I've got the ingredients for our pizza in a cooler in the car. I'll go get it," he enthused. "Be right back."

In the meantime, she led her mom out onto the patio. Tidbit was there, basking in the sun and watching the butterflies. "What a beautiful cat!" Upon hearing this, Tidbit sauntered over for some ear scratching, so mom could tell him how beautiful he was. Jenny sent him a mental, "*Pretty kitty.*" He sent back a mental smirk.

She could hear her dad puttering around in the kitchen through the open French doors. "So, tell me all about this new job of yours. Are you still free-lancing as well?"

"No, I finished out my contracts and those clients were passed to some others in the co-op. This job will be taking most of my time and I won't be around much as it involves travelling a lot."

"Looks like you didn't just inherit your aunt's place," mom mused. "Lizzie had the 'travel-bug' too. That woman was nearly never home. Does this job pay a salary and benefits or is it another pay-as-they-go thing?"

Jenny's mouth pursed for a moment. Her parents were of the generation that believed in settling down with a company in a career and building security by being good at your job and working hard until those retirement benefits kicked in. Her dad was of the opinion that Jenny was "flying by the seat of your pants" and that she needed more stability.

"It's a salaried position with good benefits," Jenny was relieved to be able to reply truthfully. "Lots of travelling and lots of writing."

"It sounds perfect! Send us lots of photos, will you?"

Photos! Oh no! Jenny's thoughts raced. How was she going to send photos of her in foreign places? It isn't like she would be taking selfies with Tarafau on her inter-dimensional forays.

"I'll try to remember, mom," she replied dutifully.

Tidbit broke into her thoughts and it startled her slightly. *"You can keep that promise. I'll show you a cool trick later that you'll like a lot."*

It was amazing to her how insightful he was. He seemed to sense her moods and her needs already, even though they had only been together for weeks instead of years.

Her dad came out into the garden, gazing around. He walked over to the koi pond and watched the fish doing their sinuous watery dance, golden scales sparkling in the sunlight.

"Are those strawberries?" He reached down to part the leaves and sure enough, there were little green strawberries peeking out from between them. "Nice set up. I've seen aquaponics projects on a much larger scale, but this is really nice. Lizzie always did have good taste. And I notice you have a fully stocked herb garden here. Will you be doing anything with them?"

"I have a gardener, Ted, who was hired by Aunt Lizzie to take care of all of this." Her wave took in the garden. "As well as the front yard. But I hadn't really thought much about what to do with them."

"I have a good herbology book at home I'll lend to you. Lizzie was really up on all of that. She was an old-fashioned girl, that Lizzie," he said with a fond smile.

Jenny thought that her dad would have been shocked to know that Lizzie had used out-of-this-world tech, traveled inter-dimensionally and could fight with a quarterstaff like a warrior.

"So, about this job of yours…" Dad began, but Mom cut him off. "She just told me. It's a salaried position with benefits." She emphasized the word **benefits** with a satisfied smile.

"Well then, moving up in the world in more than just your digs." He looked as satisfied as Tidbit did after putting Cinder in his place. "We always knew you'd get there. I'll bet it feels good, knowing you'll not miss a paycheck, eh?"

Jenny just barely restrained herself from rolling her eyes. Quickly she changed the subject.

"Tell me about this convention, Dad."

Her dad launched into an enthusiastic description of the speakers, the vendors and the various events that took up a good half hour, her mom inserting an occasional comment, but mostly letting him roll on.

"I'm hungry," he said suddenly, finally rolling to a stop in his narrative. "I'm going to get started on that pizza." He rubbed his hands together in anticipation and went into the house, leaving Jenny and her mom to enjoy the beautiful sunny day.

Mom caught her up on the antics of her siblings, her nieces and nephews and the neighbors she had grown up with. They talked about options for personalizing Jenny's new space and just general "girl-talk". Jenny enjoyed watching her mom's animated face.

Her mom was a curvy lady, not exactly fat, but rounded. Her dad called her "comfortable", something that always got a wry look. She was one of the most optimistic people Jenny had ever met. Sometimes folks took that as meaning she was unaware of the bad things going on in the world, but Jenny knew better. Mom had had her share of trials and sorrow, but she never let it pull her down for long. It was one of the things she admired about her.

Her dad, on the other hand, was practical and a trifle cynical about the world. He had a strong work ethic built by a strict up-bringing and 20 years military service. He often saw the world as "us against them", and yet he had a mischievous sense of humor and mom knew how to take him down a peg or two when he went overboard.

The smells of his "secret sauce" were wafting out into the garden. He came out with a plate of sandwiches and the pitcher of lemonade Jenny had made for the occasion.

"Sauce is simmering and the dough is rising. Thought we should have a little something to tide us over," he said, setting the plate down on the little table. He got himself a lawn chair from next to the koi pond and sat down with a satisfied sigh.

"Do you mind if I invite my neighbor, Bob, for supper? I've raved about your pizza and he'd like to meet you both," Jenny asked before her dad could get started on a new topic.

"We'd love to," her mom replied enthusiastically. "Give him a call."

Tidbit wandered over and sat staring up at her dad. "Oh, your aunt's cat, what was your name? Little Britches or some such?" The end of Tidbit's tail twitched.

"It's Tidbit, Dad," Jenny laughed.

She texted Bob to come over for supper and when it would be ready. He replied in the affirmative.

They passed the time, nibbling on sandwiches and chatting about nothing consequential. Her dad told some funny stories about his own travels in the military and her mom listened with amused patience. Jenny knew she had heard all of these stories many times before. And she and their family had all traveled with him. Like all "army brats" Jenny had not had much of a chance to put down any roots anywhere. And it looked like that wasn't going to change much.

When the last crumbs were gone, they headed back into the house, which, by this time, smelled like a fine Italian restaurant. Dad had always said that the secret to his pizza was his sauce, made from scratch and simmered for hours.

In the living room, Dad pulled a little thumb drive out of his pocket and handed it to her. "I thought you'd like a copy of our family history," he said, gesturing as if he could see down the ancestral path, far beyond. "There's the pedigree, some of it going back as far as the beginning of the Roman empire, and several family journals. Even one of your Aunt Lizzie's when she was a girl. Thought you might enjoy that, since you never had a chance to get to know her."

Jenny threw her arms around her dad. "Thanks, Dad. What an awesome gift!"

"Speaking of gifts..." her mom said. "I'll be right back."

She went out to the car and came back with a box.

"I made this when we found out about you moving into Lizzie's house. Thought it would make it feel more like your own."

Jenny opened the box carefully and inside was a beautiful door wreath with sage and seashells and little birds. She knew her mom made these every year as a fundraiser for their local food bank, but never thought to be the recipient of one.

"It's beautiful, Mom. It's just perfect."

Her heart warmed to the kind acceptance of her parents. She admitted to herself that she had been somewhat apprehensive about this visit, but so far it had been a big boost for her.

Her dad helped her mount the wreath on her front door. It gave it a very welcoming look, she thought and definitely put her own stamp on the place. Every time she saw it from now on, she would remember how loved she was.

The doorbell rang about suppertime. It was Bob. Jenny introduced him to her parents and he and her dad shook hands with enthusiasm. It turned out Bob was also a veteran and he and her dad reminisced about military life and her dad told him stories, some of them embarrassing, about Jenny's teen years.

They chatted and ate her dad's amazing pizza. She always thought she exaggerated the taste in her mind until she tasted it again. It was definitely heaven on a plate. Bob enthused about it and then told them he needed to get back to his project in his workshop, but that he looked forward to spending time with them again, the next time they were in town.

"Good to see you have good neighbors," her mom remarked, when he had gone, and her dad nodded approvingly. They cleared the table together, still laughing and chatting about nothing important. It was great.

"Well, we have to head out," dad said as he helped her clean up the last of the dishes. "There's enough leftover pizza for a good lunch for you tomorrow. We've got to get to our motel up the coast before bedtime. I want you to know we're proud of you. And just because you're all grown up, remember, you'll always be daddy's little girl."

Jenny nodded. It had been a long standing joke. As Jenny had grown into teen-hood, she had always corrected him about not being a little girl. But it had become a running joke with them by the time she had gone away to college. They made another "Jenny sandwich" and she waved until their little green sedan disappeared around the bend in the loop.

As she went back through the door hung with her mother's wreath and into the house which still smelled yummy, she mused that the visit had exceeded her expectations. This just might work out after all.

Chapter 12: Assignment

Jenny had scarce turned around when she felt her key warm. She immediately checked her cell phone. One of the apps Miriha had added to her phone was interdimensional texting and sure enough, there was a message inside the app for her. "Report." Was all it said.

The app had been designed to only respond to someone wearing an authorized key. Anyone else would see a crossword puzzle game app icon, which would actually take them to a crossword puzzle game.

Jenn looked up to see Tidbit staring at her from the window seat. "*Get your gear,*" he thought to her. "*And don't forget to trigger your auto-responders.*"

Jenny obediently went to her computer, keyed in the code to her personal email and messaging AI and then gathered her things, knowing she would appear to be responding to friends and family in a normal way, while she was in other dimensions.

She grabbed her official staff of office, grabbed her satchel out of the MDP, per her instructions, and left a text to Bob that she might be away for awhile, and could he please collect her mail?

She opened the door to the impossible little gate office room with Tidbit at her heels. She remembered that no one had given her an exact amount of time till her first assignment, but she had thought it would be a little longer. She hadn't even been home two weeks. And she just realized that she had told her hike club she would be going on the hike. Looks like she was going to miss it again, so she left a text for Sam to please send her regrets.

When they went through the door to The Gatekeeper's dimension, she realized something wasn't quite right. First, there were no gem eyes speeding across the sand to scan them. Secondly, an odd keening was coming from the trees that surrounded the path to the village.

Tarafau frowned. "*It's the Linklings. I've only heard them do that once before and it wasn't good. Put your satchel back into the MDP and keep your staff handy.*"

Jenny was surprised at Tarafau's grim tone. "What would cause the gem eyes not to show up?" she wondered aloud.

They entered the shaded path. Linklings stood on their branches, their mustaches bristling, and their bodies completely erect in a posture of extreme alert. The sound was wrenching, like the wail of police sirens.

They emerged to complete devastation. The market square was empty of human life and the booths were collapsed or burning, goods spread across the ground as if discarded carelessly by some giant hand. Shop windows were smashed, and here and there buildings burned without anyone rushing to put out the fires.

"Where is everyone? What has happened here?"

Tarafau shook his head in answer to Jenny's questions. They peered around through the smoky air, still not a single person in evidence. As they rushed to the Gatekeeper's building, the large carved double doors hung off their hinges, splintered and broken as if by a battering ram.

Tarafau went ahead into the building his quarterstaff in readiness. No one greeted them there. The only light was from the high windows. They called for someone, anyone who might be here, but their voices echoed into the silence.

They climbed the curved staircase, which was strewn with rubble, evidently out of the ceiling, and the balustrade was missing in a few places. Hugging the wall, they got to the top without incident. The door to The Gatekeeper's office was intact, but there was evidence of someone trying to break it down and it didn't open automatically as before.

Tarafau's big fist pounded on the door. "Miriha, are you there? Are you all right?" he bellowed.

There was no handle on the door, but a small sound behind the door alerted them that something was going on in there. It sounded a lot like a moan.

"Stand back," growled Tarafau. He took a few steps back himself and launched himself at the door, his big booted foot impacting it not a bit.

"Wait," said Jenny as he prepared to try again, this time with his shoulder.

She "peeked" into the MDP and did a mental search for a tool they could use. And there it was. She pulled a large crowbar out and handed it to Tarafau. "Maybe you just need a little leverage," she said almost sheepishly.

For a moment Tarafau stared at the big metal bar in his hand, shook his head and placed the prying end under the edge of the door. He heaved it upward and there was a large cracking sound, almost like a rifle report.

The door swung open to reveal a darkened room, the floor covered with what appeared to be broken chunks of the ceiling. The only light came from holes in the egg shaped ceiling. And on that rubble strewn floor lay…

"Miriha!" Jenny shouted, at the same time that Tarafau demanded, "*What happened here?*" For just a moment, Jenny was afraid there would be no answer. Miriha lifted her head with an effort.

Her eyes were blackened and there was a cut on her forehead. "*They're back*," she said, her mental sending voice not more than a whisper and her brows furrowed with the effort. "*They didn't get through to the portal room, but they told me that my people would be returned 'mostly unharmed' when I come to my senses and give them the key.*" This statement seemed to have used up all of her strength.

"*Who's back?* Jenny asked, sick to her stomach. In all of her life, she had never encountered anything like this. The destruction of that beautiful village with it's peaceful and kind people. Women and children! And now Miriha lay before them on the floor of what had been the beautifully appointed Gatekeeper's office. Violence had never been a part of Jenny's life, even though her father had been a soldier.

He never talked about the time he had spent in battle. On career day at school he had simply talked about defending his country, not about shooting people or seeing people die. And he certainly never harmed helpless innocents, although she knew it sometimes happened. It shocked her to her core now that anyone could be so cruel and callous.

Tarafau lifted Miriha gently and placed her on a couch near the entrance to the gateroom. Miriha groaned as he moved her, even as careful as he was trying to be. It never ceased to amaze her how graceful and gentle this big man could be.

Jenny examined her carefully, employing first aid skills she had never thought to actually use. It appeared that her collar bone and both arms were broken, and her body was covered in bruises. Jenny knew there were likely other injuries she couldn't see. It appeared that rubble from the ceiling had struck her in several places.

Miriha didn't answer her, closing her eyes wearily. It was Tarafau who finally said, *"The Groga."* He said it in a flat voice that suddenly sounded tired and defeated. *"I thought the Council had been hasty in assuming they would stay defeated. I regret being right about this."*

Miriha's breathing had become shallower. As broken as she was, Jenny suspected there must be some internal bleeding. *"What can we do for her?"* she asked, setting the Groga aside for the moment.

Tarafau shook his head. *"The healers in the town were taken with the rest and I'm afraid if we move her again it will kill her. I don't have the skill, do you?"*

Jenny had to admit she didn't. She so desperately wanted to do something. She suddenly realized Miriha was trying to say something.

"Take the key." As she said these words the little key around Miriha's neck developed a clasp that didn't appear to be there before. "So that's how they do it," Jenny thought. Jenny unfastened the tiny key from Miriha's neck.

"Touch it to your key," Miriha gasped, as if it took all of her strength to utter these few words.

Jenny did so and as the key touched hers, it vanished. Jenny gave out a startled "Oh!" and Miriha sighed and was still.

Tarafau stroked her hair with tears streaming down his cheeks. "Give Lizzie my love," he whispered, nearly choking on his words. "We will take it from here."

He stood and turned to Jenny. *"The Groga are a radical group from a dimension called Mefluance. Not all of the beings in Mefluance are evil, but the Groga definitely fit that description without exception. They raided the dimensions like the sea pirates of old Earth history. The Dimensional Alliance has been fighting them for hundreds of years. About 50 years ago, The Council believed they had eradicated the threat. Obviously, they were mistaken.*

They have no mercy and no ethics. They take what they wish and delight in destruction, pain and torture. There was a man, here on your Earth, who is infamous for the number of people he had slain and the destruction he caused. Imagine if he had been given access to the portals."

Jenny cringed at the thought of someone like Hitler able to march through the dimensions inflicting terror and pain.

The big man looked so fierce as he spat these final words that Jenny was reminded of Tidbit backing that huge dog step by careful step down her driveway. She shuddered.

"So, what happened to the key and what do we do next?" Jenny asked, fearful of the answer.

"We have to get to The Council. Miriha just gave you access to the entire gateway network. This will be reflected in the gate room inside your home. You now have access to not only the full dimensional gate system, but all of the earth gates as well. You have become, by default, The Gatekeeper."

Jenny's harsh intake of breath made him look up from examining his hands.

"Me? Shouldn't this pass to someone who has completed their training?" she asked hopefully.

Tarafau regarded her soberly, once again catlike in that golden stare. *"It doesn't work that way. Traditionally the key is passed to someone more experienced, it is true, but regardless, when it is passed, the recipient cannot pass it to another except when their body is failing, or they are dead and then only if the recipient is already a Guardian.*

You have been given a great responsibility. But we will go to the council. They have dealt with unusual transfers of Gatekeepers in the past. For now, the gates, on this planet, in this dimension will seal when we depart. Only the Council will be able to reinstate them. We need to leave."

"But what about Miriha?"

Tarafau looked troubled, then his face cleared. *"I will seal her into the gate room, a fitting tomb for such a hero."* He put words to action, lifting Miriha tenderly once again. Jenny stood before the gateway to open the door.

Tarafau gently placed the body on the floor of the passageway. *"Rest and rise,"* he said. Then he did something strange. He placed his hand on Miriha's diaphragm and pressed gently. A last puff of air escaped from her lips. Tarafau reached out with his large hand as if catching that last breath, clenched it into a fist and placed it on his heart.

"My honor. I will avenge your death and restore your people, dear one. This I swear."

Rising he turned to Jenny. *"We must go."*

He moved through the door to the gate office. *"Tell it to seal,"* he instructed her grimly. Jenny sent a thought to the door. "*Seal*," she commanded, and the door glowed and disappeared as if it had never been there.

"No one can enter that again without your express command." Tarafau rumbled with barely concealed emotion. He moved toward the outer door, but something made Jenny stop and look around one last time. On the desk was a small figurine nearly glowing in the part light. She grabbed it and put it into her MDP. "I won't forget you, Miriha," she said blinking tears from her eyes. "I will not fail you." She imitated Tarafau's gesture, with her fist to her heart and followed Tarafau out the door.

As they navigated the rubble strewn streets of the beautiful little village, Jenny gave in to tears. She had no clue what she could do about any of this. She was barely trained in the absolute basics of her calling. She hadn't even met the other Guardians on Earth, much less the members of The Dimensional Alliance Council. She was nobody, a thought that had never occurred to her before now.

This was all too much. Then something even more disturbing came to her. *"Can these Groga get access to Earth?"* she asked, nearly panicking as she thought about the destruction that lay all about them as they approached the path to the beach where the Inklings had gone completely silent. This was even more eerie than their plaintive siren-like cries of earlier.

Tarafau shook his head. *"I really don't know. The gates to your dimension are relatively new, in the scheme of things, and have only had active, trained Guardians for a couple centuries. It is hard to say how they got access to the portals here."* He looked up. The branches above them were deserted.

"They will have migrated to a populated area up the coast, assuming the Groga haven't decimated the rest of this planet already. But we have no time to investigate," he continued, shrugging his broad shoulders. *"We must get you to The Council right away."*

They walked down the beach in silence, feeling the weight of these events and what they might mean like blocks of stone on their shoulders. As they passed through the gate, Jenny thought, *"Goodbye, Miriha. Rest and rise. Seal."*

Chapter 13: Under Fire

It was surreal to step from her gateroom through the gate office and into her quiet house. She realized she was trembling. Tidbit looked up at her. *"You've already made arrangements, but we may not be back here for a long time. Consider what you will take with you and get it into the MDP as quickly as you can.*

Also, use the app on your cell to send out an alert to all the other Guardians on Earth. Your new status as the Gatekeeper will have added them to your 'contacts list'. They will see your message on their cells as an official message."

"What should I tell them?" Jenny asked, her stomach still roiling.

"Tell them that Miriha's portal has fallen and her key was transferred to you under emergency circumstances. Tell them…" he paused and made that odd sound he had made when attacking Cinder. *"Tell them that Miriha is dead and the Gatekeeper village is destroyed. Let them know that The Council will be in touch as we know more."*

"Won't the others be resistant to taking orders from someone like me? I'm only a trainee, after all."

The cat gave a querulous "mrrrreow" and Tidbit replied, *"They know how this works. As long as you don't try to appear to be something you're not, they'll be willing to work with you. And besides, they know you have me."* This last was said as if it was a long-standing joke.

Jenny sent a brief message, per Tidbit's instructions, and bustled through her house, which had already been put to rights when she thought she would be getting her first assignment. She had been so excited. Was it really only hours ago?

She had already taken most of what she would need. She looked longingly around at her lovely little house. Her aunt had done what she was doing for many years. Had she felt as Jenny felt now? She knew she would possibly not return for quite awhile. Bob would get her mail and Ted would tend the garden. All would seem normal and quiet on Infinity Loop.

Or would it? Tarafau had been somewhat evasive about the potential of these attackers finding their way to Earth. She tried to picture this beautiful little street ravaged and the people, her neighbors, dead, dying or taken who knows where to be enslaved and tortured. Her heart raced as rapidly as her thoughts.

She paused before the door that no one could see but herself. With one more backward glance, she entered with Tidbit at her heels.

"*The yellow door,*" Tidbit directed her.

She turned the handle and stepped out onto a promontory overlooking a valley with a fairly large city cuddled into green fields. Two suns hung high in the nearly violet sky. In this case, instead of the portal being disguised as some kind of building, the door just stood on its frame, seemingly built onto nothing besides the cement block on which they stood. About six inches in front of them appeared to be a curtain of liquid glass. It hung unsupported in front of them. Jenny looked at Tarafau

He nodded toward the shimmering curtain and walked through. Jenny followed. Only the slightest tingle tickled her from head to foot as she stepped through. *"Scanner?"*

"Yes, it is different at every gateway. None of them are harmful and most have been in place for longer than we know."

Taking a deep breath and stepping down she turned to Tarafau. *"Well?"* she inquired. *"What now?"*

"Come with me," Tarafau said, taking the lead down a curving path that led around to a gentler slope down the hill. As they rounded the bend the city came into sight. From their vantage point Jenny could see that, unlike Miriha's little village, this was definitely a city and an extremely modern one. Tall glass buildings, reminiscent of New York City, as portrayed in superhero books, soared above wide streets, and wheel-less vehicles went along their way. There were no traffic lights, but the traffic flowed smoothly along the broad avenues.

They walked about 2 miles before they encountered the fringe of the forest and the edge of the city itself.

The valley seemed very earthlike. Trees with green leaves, birds (albeit no breed she recognized) and sounds around the path that might have been some small creatures, made it feel familiar, like one of her hikes with her hiking club. White clouds scudded across the violet sky. After what they had just witnessed, it seemed so normal. Like having a nightmare and waking up in your bed at home, safe and secure.

Jenny wished that this had been only a nightmare. She was glad for the calming effect of the forest on either side of the path. She had always felt an affinity for ancient trees, and these were huge, even compared to the Sequoias at home.

At the end of the path they encountered two "beings". They had a mostly humanoid shape, but their skin was very pale, and they had a third eye in their forehead. As Jenny and Tarafau approached, Jenny realized they must look pretty grim. One of the beings held up a long-fingered hand with claws rather than nails. "*Guardian, we greet thee,*" he sent in mindspeech. "*Tarafau, my friend, what is amiss? I sense you are troubled.*"

Tarafau stepped forward, placing his right hand on the guard's shoulder. "*Alas, my friend, we are here to warn the council. The Gatekeeper is dead, and her gate city decimated. Her people have been carried off. Jenny,* (Tarafau nodded his head toward her) *is now The Gatekeeper. She must consult with the council at once.*"

The guards were open-mouthed. "*Right away. Come,*" the first one agreed.

They escorted Tarafau and Jenny to a car with no wheels. It hovered about a foot above the ground. They motioned for Jenny and Tarafau to step in and seat themselves. When she did, she noticed two things. One, there was no steering wheel and two, there were no safety belts. Both of these things made her a bit nervous. However, Tarafau seemed unconcerned.

The little two seated vehicle was roomier than it looked, accommodating Tarafau's large frame with no problem. The guard said to Tarafau before he closed the door, "*Hama and I need to stay here until our replacements arrive. I'll see you at your suites in the council building."* Then, apparently to the car, he said, *"Council Chamber. Priority One."*

As he closed the door, the little vehicle smoothly rose an additional 6 inches or so, making a faint humming sound and moved forward onto the broad avenue before them. The street was lined with trees, younger than their forest cousins, by the look of it. Hover cars like the one they sat in hummed along through the streets. The little cars smoothly avoided one another, despite the lack of traffic lights, never coming close enough to do any harm, but it made Jenny nervous, nevertheless.

Jenny knew there were experiments with self-driving cars being conducted in different places on Earth, but they hadn't caught on, yet. They probably wouldn't be practical until the human element was removed completely. But people loved their cars and loved to drive them. Jenny wasn't sure they would ever all be convinced to change.

It all seemed so peaceful here. As they hummed along in the little car, she began to notice people walking along the boulevard. Well, maybe, as Tarafau had said, "beings" was a better word, as few of them actually looked more than marginally human and many of them bore no resemblance at all.

Tarafau, seeing her consternation, told her, *"As the official gathering place of the Dimensional Alliance Council, we have beings from all through the dimensions. You'll notice some of these beings wear a small pack on their backs. Not all of them can survive in an oxygen rich atmosphere. All Guardians are equipped with a pack that coincides with their species and planetary breathing requirements. Those who live and work here are all dedicated to the continued peace among dimensions. There are disagreements, to be sure, but none you will meet here will harm you."*

Jenny just nodded. It was all so much to take in. She had imagined going to The Council many times during her training, but she hadn't imagined being the bearer of really bad news. She had thought she would be coming as a humble trainee, not worth being noticed. Now she would be thrown into the middle of all of it, with only her initial training, the LizzieAI and Tarafau. Surely the council would take one look at her and tell her to go home and they would take it from here, passing the title of Gatekeeper on to someone much more qualified.

"*Did you know those guards?*" Jenny asked, hopeful that this would divert her from her current train of thought.

"*Yes, we've served together before, long before I was paired with Lizzie.*"

Long before? Once again Jenny wondered, how old was Tarafau? Lizzie had been her own age when she had begun as a guardian, but that was over 60 years ago. Jenny kept that thought to herself, not sure if Tarafau would be offended by queries about his age.

The little vehicle finally pulled up in front of a huge multi-storied building which appeared to be hewn whole out of granite. Small colored flecks of shiny minerals shone in the polished stone surface. Beings were coming and going through the twelve foot tall double doors, flanked by two more guards.

The car doors opened automatically and Tarafau unfolded himself, greeting the guards with a nod. "*We're on our way to the council chambers to inform the council of ill news, I'm afraid,*" Tarafau said to the guard. "*Will you let them know we are coming?*"

"*And the young human woman?*"

"*She is a Guardian and the new Gatekeeper. More than that I cannot say, for now. Assuredly all will be made clear when the council comes to a decision about it.*"

The guard nodded, and his face went blank for a moment. "*They will see you now. Go up to the arboretum.*"

Tarafau led Jenny through the now open doors into a lobby area. It was huge. It reminded her of a modern version of a cathedral. Stained glass windows or something like it streamed colors onto the white marble floor. They stopped in front of what appeared to be large elevators. Indeed, the doors slid open and, except that it was about twelve feet tall and as wide, it was so similar to an Earth elevator, that Jenny blinked in surprise.

Catching her bemused expression, Tarafau said dryly, "*Some designs just work.*"

He spoke aloud to the elevator. "Arboretum."

Unlike elevators Jenny was used to, there was no sensation of movement and no "elevator music". A soft ding after mere seconds was the only indication they had stopped. "Arboretum," intoned a soft voice. Jenny had gotten so used to mindspeak that she gave a start at the voice.

The doors slid open to a brightly lit room that seemed to be made of glass. Small birds twittered in the foliage high above. The arboretum appeared to be a casual space, although breath-takingly beautiful. Here and there chairs, perches and, what appeared to be long padded lounges, but way out of proportion for any humanoid shape she had ever encountered, were scattered among trees in planters and various exotic flowers and shrubbery.

Tarafau led the way around a waterfall that poured over large rocks from what seemed to be the end of a small river. "*This building is heated and cooled with water,*" Tarafau explained. "*It is an interactive system. The water is pulled from the bottom of the fountain pool and recirculated through plumbing in the walls. It is heated with passive solar energy and when they need it cool, a reflective covering slides over it. The covering also generates power.*"

Jenny was taking all of this in as fast as she could, but she now felt anxious. How would these advanced beings feel about a young girl, barely out of school, becoming The Gatekeeper?

As they turned the corner, she realized that this area was about twice the size of the average university auditorium. The difference was in the variety of seating arrangements. All seats faced a raised dais. On the dais were seated three beings. One was a dragon! It's brilliant blue-green hide glistened in the golden light of the arboretum. Huge emerald eyes were focused on her and Tarafau as they approached, narrowing to slits. Next to the dragon was a tall, slender, birdlike creature. The feathers (or was it fur?) reminded her of the coloring of a sun conure, brilliant oranges, yellows and reds. Barely visible on a raised chair was a tiny little bearded man short like a dwarf and with a face much like the gnomes out of stories (without the funny red hat).

The "gnome" stood, bowing slightly. "*Tarafau, I understand you have dire tidings for this council.*" The other beings gathered before the dais stirred in reaction. But, unlike an earth gathering, the crowd was silent.

Tarafau nodded. "*Chief Councilor, I wish to present to you, Jenny Japhet of Gateway Earth. She is the Guardian heir of Lizzie Japhet and the Gateway heir of Miriha.*"

The crowd stirred again.

The councilor furrowed his brows. "*There is dire news in this pronouncement, friend, Tarafau. We knew, of course of the passing of Lizzie, but what of Miriha?*"

Tarafau bowed his head for a moment before he continued. "*She is dead, Chief Councilor, at the hand of the Groga.*" An audible intake of breath was heard throughout the council hall. Some were shaking their heads in disbelief. "*The entire Gateway village has been abducted and the village destroyed. Miriha lived long enough to pass the key to Jenny. That network is now sealed and has been transferred to Earth.*"

Arching his eyebrows, the Chief Counselor turned to Jenny. "*I hear you have received the basic Guardian training and you were to begin your apprenticeship soon. I won't lie to you. That you have been given this task so soon in your training is concerning, Jenny.*

There is nothing we can do to reverse the process. The Gatekeeper key can only be transferred at death, extreme illness or mental instability. This post is ancient, its origins lost in the eons of time. This has been thrust upon you untimely, but I have learned that there is a pattern to the multiverse.

From here on, the choices you make will be critical. Do you accept this?"

Jenny nodded, swallowing, bereft of speech, mental or otherwise.

"*Tarafau do you accept the assignment to be The Guide to The Gatekeeper?*"

Tarafau put his fist to his heart. It echoed the gesture he had made with Miriha's final breath and Jenny could see that his pledge was as much to Miriha as it was to her. "*I so pledge,*" was all he said.

"*There is much you must learn, Gatekeeper, and you have little time. Tarafau, please escort Jenny to the guest suites. There you may refresh yourselves and rest until tomorrow morning, at which time we will begin.*"

The Chief Councilor peered over their heads at the assembly. "*We will adjourn until tomorrow at this time, when we will decide on a plan of action. If the Groga are raiding again, we must seek for a more permanent solution. This is a strike at our heart, and we will not let it lie.*" With that, he retreated to the back of the dais to consult with the other two councilors.

Tarafau led Jenny from the hall. Faces, and what she guessed were faces, followed her as she walked, trembling, down the aisle between the seats, past the waterfall and into the elevator. No one approached them, but the stares that followed them as they passed sent shivers down her back. As the elevator doors closed behind them, Jenny realized she had never felt so small and insignificant in her life. She felt like a very small bug under a magnifying glass. She was overwhelmed to the point of numbness. She followed Tarafau mechanically out of the elevator and down a long hall. He stopped at a door. "*Touch your key,*" he instructed.

She did so, and the door opened. "*This door will only open for The Gatekeeper and her registered attendants. These are her permanent suites at Alliance headquarters*." He waved her in ahead of him.

The spacious living suite was tastefully furnished. It included 2 bedrooms, a well-appointed bath and a tiny kitchen. The living area opened out to a balcony, over-looking the city below. Jenny sunk down into a soft armchair.

"*Tarafau, what just happened?*" she asked, her voice shaking. "*What am I supposed to do? I have only just begun my training and now I have the entire Gateway network to be responsible for? How does that work? How do I explain people coming and going all the time? Does this mean I'll be stuck in the reception area all the time doing*

113

paperwork?" She realized this last was said in a whining tone. She realized it sounded petty and selfish. and she felt embarrassed.

Tarafau heard the frustration and despair in her voice, but simply said, "*All will be made clear, Jenny. There is much more to the Gatekeeper role than greeting new Guardians, I promise you. If anything, you will be spending more time away from your house. The access gateway will be placed so that none will be seen entering or leaving.*

But that is all for later. For now, you must eat and rest. I ordered some food for us and a healer is on his way to check on us. He will have something to soothe and replenish you and to help you get the rest you will need to take on the tasks of tomorrow."

Jenny didn't want to think about tomorrow. She didn't want to think about today. With everything that had happened and the potential for disaster, her thoughts just wouldn't focus.

The food arrived followed soon by the healers. They were very slender, with a bluish cast to their skin, they were nearly as tall as Tarafau. As far as Jenny could tell they were completely hairless. Large grey eyes were wide in oval faces, but they had no apparent ears or nose. Their mouths were lipless slits. Had Jenny not seen all of the different beings in the council chamber already and knew they weren't a threat; she would have been more than a little shocked.

"*I am Alla and this is Ira,*" one sent, pointing to the other. "*We are here to see to your hurts and to help you recover from the shock of your recent unfortunate experience. We must scan you to determine your hurts. Please hold still.*"

Ira held something that resembled a rounded cellphone over her head and then slowly brought it down before her, starting at the top of her head, pausing briefly at her heart and then proceeding to her feet. She expected to feel some tingling or some indication that something was happening, but there was no sensation at all. When the scan was completed, both the healers bent their head over the screen of the device, evidently mentally conferring.

"*We find no physical hurt other than shock, Jenny. You are in excellent health. We will give you a tea to take with your meal to* help your body deal with the shock and to allow you to rest. *I sense that you are overwhelmed and in conflict. This will pass.*"

Alla interjected, "*We are the Drimm, from the Ullah dimension. We recognize there has been a great burden placed upon you. In behalf of the Drimm and from our dimension, we extend both our sympathy and our support. Our Guardians will be assisting you in your training. You need not do this alone.*"

Jenny felt her eyes filling. She had managed to keep herself in tight control throughout the ordeal of the day, but this kindness brought it all crashing down. She buried her face in her hands and cried. Ira said, sending calm and comfort, "*We mourn with you, Jenny. Miriha was a friend to all. Weep as you must. It will help with the shock.*"

Alla turned to Tarafau and scanned him. After consulting, they said, that he would be sore for a few days due to hammering on the door to get to the Gatekeeper, but other than that, he would be receiving the same tea with instructions to rest.

When they left, Tarafau sat on the couch beside her. He extended a muscular arm to her and she threw herself into his arms, sobbing on his broad chest as he patted her gently on the back. "*I'm here, Jenny,*" was all he said, but it was enough.

Chapter 14: The Alliance

Jenny woke with a start. Looking around her, it took her a moment to remember where she was. The bedroom of the suite was lovely, as befitted someone of station. Muted tones of green, beige and white throughout the suite were calming.

She didn't remember much from the evening before. After she had cried until the tears wouldn't come, she had showered and changed from her dirty and sweat soaked clothing.

She and Tarafau had eaten the food that had been brought, barely registering what it was, mechanically bringing fork to mouth. They had dutifully drunk the tea they had been given and she vaguely remembered Tarafau removing the drooping cup from her hand and lifting her and bringing her in to the bedroom, laying her in the bed and gently covering her, after removing her shoes and socks.

It seemed impossible to her that only a couple months ago she had been ensconced in her comfortable life, writing blogs about things that, at the time, had seemed so important. She had hiked with her buddies and hung out with Sam. It now seemed somewhat dreamlike, unsubstantial, and yet, that had been her life and she had thought she was happy.

Now, here she was, on an alien planet in an alien dimension, interacting with the unknown, the unimaginable. Did she really see a dragon last night?

She got up and went through her morning routine pattern-breathing, showering and dressing. She could hear Tarafau in the living area of the suite, stirring around. She heard him open and close the door to the suite.

"*Breakfast is ready,*" he sent.

He had set up the little dining table with their typical training meal of cheese, rye cracker bread and fruit. "*I ordered for us,*" he said with a smile.

The meal reminded her of the weeks she had spent in Sanglarka, a happy time. She realized now that it was the calm before the storm and wondered how well she would measure up. She smiled at Tarafau in gratitude for the kind thought and ate slowly barely tasting the meal.

It occurred to her that this meal was probably not typical for the natives of this planet, nor for the other beings that populated it from the Dimensional Alliance. She was in awe that they could serve her this way.

"We will be meeting with the Chief Councilor and his officers when we finish eating," Tarafau said. *"They will want the full story of our encounter in the Gateway village. They will also give you instructions on your next steps and introduce you to your fellow Guardians from Earth. These have been called in to be briefed and to allow them to be a support network for you.*

You may ask any questions you wish at this time and they will answer you. After that, we will come back here and meet alone with the Earth Guardian delegation, so you can get to know them and assemble your resources. These individuals will be a great support to you in your work going forward."

Jenny only nodded. There was nothing to say, really. Her choices were limited. Moving forward she would need all the help she could get, and she was sure all of these Guardians had the experience she lacked.

Tarafau led the way to the elevator, saying, "Council" as they entered. After a moment, the quiet chime sounded, the voice echoed, "Council" and the doors opened.

They entered what appeared to be a reception area with chairs of various sizes ranged around the large waiting room. The being at the desk was covered in white fur, with a foxlike face and bright orange eyes. *"Tarafau and Jenny, you are expected. Please continue."* The voice in her head sounded female, but she had no idea for sure. She wasn't even sure if gender applied to any or all of the beings she met. One more thing she needed to learn to communicate with those she must work with.

She noticed that all of the doors and ceilings to this building were tall, no doubt to accommodate some of the huge beings she had seen in the assembly the day before. They entered the large double doors beyond the reception room into a circular room with a low dais at one end. There were a couple dozen seats arrayed in a single circular row. All the seats were filled with humanoid beings except two near the dais. Tarafau gestured Jenny to take one and sat next to her.

Looking around her, she was surprised to see the people in the room, until she remembered that her fellow Guardians were to be in attendance. In addition, there were other beings from different dimensions, one of whom she recognized as Drimm, who nodded towards her to acknowledge her recognition.

On the dais were the three Chief Councilors. The gnome stood and addressed the gathering. "*We are here to hear the report of Jenny Japhet and Tarafau Bane regarding the demise of The Gatekeeper, Miriha, and to decide what actions we can take to immediately secure the Gateway network. You have each been called here, at this time, because each of you have a key role in this process. When we are finished here, I will call the assembly and we will announce our decisions to the rest of the beings on the council.*"

He nodded toward Jenny. "*I trust you are well-rested and prepared to report?*" he asked, his fuzzy eyebrows raised and his eyes smiling. "*I know this has been difficult for you. You need not be afraid of judgement or censure. We are here to listen and to make decisions that will impact numberless beings across infinite dimensions. There is nothing personal in anything that will be said today. We must deal with the reality of the situation and do what we need to do, after we hear what you have to say. I ask you, therefore, to feel free to speak your heart and mind without fear.*"

Jenny gulped and nodded. She stood, assuming that was the proper way to report, and began.

She told them of the one word message from Miriha and the lack of gem eyes at the gateway. She told of the lamenting Linklings and the destruction in the village, the complete lack of either bodies or living beings. She told of the destruction that greeted them at the Gatekeeper building.

An then she told of climbing the rubble strewn stairway, and her eyes dimmed with tears. She paused to gather herself and went on to describe Tarafau's frantic efforts to get through the door to Miriha's office.

She described Miriha's injuries and her final words and by this time tears were streaming down her face. "*I'm sorry,*" she said, wiping at her tears. "*I'm so sorry.*"

Tarafau stood, reached out a hand and gently led her back to her seat. He turned to the dais. "*It happened as she said. We were too late to save the Gatekeeper. We sealed her body into the portal room. The gateway to earth sealed behind us as we returned. Only The Gatekeeper can now reinstate it, if ever. The people of the village have been abducted by the Groga. I do not know if they can be rescued and returned, for we found no evidence of how the Groga entered the dimension or how they escaped. We know nothing of the rest of her planet, or how far the Groga raid extended.*"

The Chief Councilor stood and Tarafau sat down.

"*This is what comes of allowing ourselves to get comfortable,*" he said, shaking his head grimly. "*We should have been more diligent in eliminating this threat.*

It is time to introduce you to the council and the Earth delegates in attendance. I am Ingot, elected Chief Councilor. My Second, is Liliath." He gestured toward the dragon to his right.

Liliath rose from her long chaise. Standing, her head nearly brushed the twelve foot high ceiling. "*Welcome, Jenny. I am of the planet Donali of the dimension, Totania. I see the legends of your Earth in your eyes.*" Her fanged jaws opened in what Jenny realized, with a start, was supposed to be a smile. "*My ancestors did indeed once fly and crawl on your planet. Our time on Earth was short, but for a time it was a favorite place to visit. There have been many of us who visited the Earth before the Earth Guardians were established formally.*"

Jenny suppressed a gape and nodded. "*It is good to meet you,*" she said simply, feeling like she should curtsy or bow or something. "*I have been raised with tales of dragons, some of my favorite stories. I remember wishing they were real.*"

Liliath, chortled aloud, startling Jenny. It was a deep, rumbling sound. "*Dragons...yes, I know we were called that anciently by your kind. We call ourselves, Alani.*"

Liliath sat, reclining on the specially made chaise set aside for her use. Ingot stood and said, gesturing to the tall birdlike creature to his right. "*This is Myla, my Third.*"

Myla stood from a seat that looked very like a nest. He had arms as well as wings. His colorful plumage, orange beak and bright eyes were very birdlike, but he gestured with his arms and hands in a very humanoid manner. His long slender legs were encased in feathers to his knees. "*Welcome, Jenny. I am of the planet Langtrey in the dimension, Alluvia. Our species, the Calyx, is one of several intelligent species in our universe. We have yet to visit your planet other than to pass through the gateway network. I doubt we will find our way there any time soon, but I have enjoyed a close association with Lizzie, your aunt. You can count on my support.*"

He sat, and Ingot stood again.

"*Now to introduce you to your fellow Guardians of Earth.*"

They each stood as he introduced them. "*Allow me to present, Juan of Puerto Rico.*"

A short, tanned man in a white shirt, white cotton pants and a hemp belt, his dark brown eyes twinkl in a big welcoming smile stood with a nod, his hands clasped in front of him.

"*You already know Lova, of Sweden.*"

Lova stood grinning at Jenny. It was evidence of Jenny's shocked state that she had not noticed her when she had come into the room.

"*Adelle of Switzerland.*"

A large blonde woman of square build stood and nodded to her soberly. Her pale blonde hair was put up into a braid that wrapped around her head like a crown. Her bright blue eyes reminded Jenny of the forget-me-nots that she had loved to make into garlands as a kid.

"*Mustapha, of Pakistan.*"

A wiry man with a short beard and dark tan complexion stood, his dark serious eyes looking into hers. He also nodded to her to acknowledge the meeting.

"Brendan of Australia."

Brendan's muscular frame topped Mustapha by a head or more. Brown hair and tan, his smile was welcoming, and he cocked his head slightly as if measuring her.

"Xao Ting, of China."

The short, serious, elderly Asian man bowed slightly in her direction, the streaks of silver in his black hair reflecting the light in the room.

"Leonora of Czechoslovakia."

She was large, but not fat. She looked to be in her middle years. Her short-cropped hair was dark as were her serious, piercing eyes. She nodded slowly to Jenny.

"Dhakirah of Ghana"

The woman who stood was very tall, easily as tall as Brendan. Her large dark eyes were slightly upturned, and she wore her black hair braided tightly around the cap of her head which streamed down her back in tight braids. Her African heritage was clear, the colorful tunic she wore contrasting beautifully with her dark skin. She smiled a beautiful smile of welcome.

"Aliki of Samoa"

The Polynesian man was perhaps in his 50's with a touch of grey in his dark curly hair. He smiled, gesturing welcome with open hands towards her. He had a kind of warmth about him, reminding her of a favorite uncle.

"Leland of Ireland."

The short, red-haired man stood grinning. He reminded Jenny of a gym teacher she had known in her high school years, always up to something mischievous.

"Guaray of India."

The dark-eyed man with wire-rimmed glasses stood and solemnly nodded towards Jenny, his hands clasped in front of him.

"*And, Megan of Canada.*"

A freckled older woman with auburn hair and green eyes, she reminded Jenny of photos she'd seen of farmer's wives. Her light brown hair was in a braid over her shoulder and she was dressed simply in a sweater and slacks. She also nodded to Jenny.

They all sat at that point and Ingot said. "*This is your Earth Guardian team. They are all experienced Guardians and have knowledge and resources you may rely upon in your duties. You will find your gate network now includes a portal directly to Sanglarka and all other Earth gates, so you can meet, plan and train together. Lova is the team leader for the Earth Gateway network. You will continue to train in your role as Guardian as you will train also for your role as Gatekeeper.*

Tarafau's role is The Guide. His centuries of experience will be invaluable to you. The role of The Guide is to mentor Guardians and Gatekeepers. You can trust his counsel and his wisdom to get you through this. Each Guardian has a Guide assigned to them. For the first few years, they constantly monitor and support the Guardian as they learn their duties."

Jenny gulped and stared at Tarafau, the awe in her face needing no words. Centuries? How old was this cat?

Ingot smiled at her reaction. "*It will take time for you to get to know your compatriots and to build the trust and teamwork that will become vital as we face the threat of the aggression of the Groga. At this time, Earth is not in danger, as far as we can tell. Based on what we know, our current theory is that they are accessing an ancient gateway that is not fully associated with the entire updated network. This still puts potentially millions of gateways at risk. All Guardians have been notified of this and the entire network is on alert.*

I will not lie to you. The options we have are few. We have become lax over the years. Evidently a remnant of the Groga has been nursing its wounds and growing their numbers and recovering old technologies. We thought we had taught them to keep to themselves. Obviously, the lesson did not sink in.

Our scouts tell us that the Groga no longer inhabit their former planet in their former dimension. It has become clear that our first task is to locate their base of operations. Then, we must determine the extent of their defenses and any new technology they have acquired.

Finally, we must prepare a plan to protect those who are most vulnerable and work to eliminate the threat permanently.

This is the task before us. And you, as Gatekeeper, are crucial to all of it. Do you have any questions?"

Jenny stared at him, her mind spinning. Questions? Questions?!

But she simply said, "*When do we start?*"

Chapter 15: Besties

Jenny stood in the middle of her cozy little living room. The week she had spent with the members of the council and her fellow Guardians had been exhausting. For one thing, the planet wasn't on a 24 hour day cycle. Days were approximately 37 hours long and they had taken advantage of every minute. When she first got home, she had slept for nearly 12 hours without stirring once.

Her fellow Guardians were wildly assorted in temperament and background. Each of them had been helpful and, since most of them had held their posts for long enough to know what they were doing, they were generous in their willingness to instruct and advise her. By the time they had concluded her initial training she had felt like her brain couldn't absorb a single additional fact or idea. They had said warm good-byes at the gateway door and as each had departed to their duties, Jenny had felt a pang of loss.

She had discovered that much about the gateway system was automated and, although that automation kept track of the comings and goings of all those passing through that network, she would not see most of the activity from her side. Those using the gateway system would enter a gate from their side and go directly to the door that would take them to their destination. Most of the time she wouldn't see any of them, unless they had business with her directly. Her previous fear of beings seen coming and going from her house had been assuaged. No one would have any idea that her house was a very extended version of Grand Central Station.

That sense of unreality returned as she looked around her. Tidbit lay in the sunny window seat contemplating the garden outside. Evidently his time as a cat was a restful interlude that he enjoyed immensely. He had already gone to terrorize Cinder this morning and chase butterflies out in the herb garden.

It all seemed so normal, and yet, Jenny now knew that what she thought of as normal was such a tiny, insignificant part of something so big, so alien and so amazing that her little house, with all its secrets, was just a speck on a bigger speck of the total picture.

She jumped when her cell phone beeped. A text message from Sam. "What's up, Jenn? Lunch today? My treat."

She texted back her agreement. Her instructions were clear. For the next few days she was to appear among her neighbors and friends to be doing all the usual things. It had been made clear that part of her responsibilities included interacting on Earth and keeping track of goings on in the world, as far as she could. It was not her responsibility to influence the events around her, but to observe and report, something she had already been doing for a long time.

She had been told, as part of her orientation, that this particular neighborhood had been built up around the house, and the neighbors were accustomed to the residents of 888 Infinity Loop being somewhat reclusive. And in that particular neighborhood, most of the residents were too absorbed in their own enterprises that they didn't have much time for interaction with their neighbors. This lack of curiosity on their part, insured that Jenny's extended absences would largely go unnoticed. And when Jenny was home, she should let herself be seen going about normal business, like going to the grocery store or picking up her mail. She routinely kept her little blue SUV locked in the garage so this would be harder to track her comings and goings.

It surprised her how much her experience as a writer had prepared her for her new roles. Not that anything could have completely prepared her for this. Her ability to think through scenarios and abstract potential outcomes would come in handy in creating strategies and tactics. And her inherent ability to communicate clearly would help as she was thrust into a leadership role.

Bob had dropped by earlier with a little pile of mail and had caught her up on the neighborhood. Cinder had gotten lost at one point earlier in the week and had been rescued from the local pound in the nick of time. Miss Longtree had won an award for her cross-stitch embroidery at the State Fair and two of the neighborhood teens were out doing a food drive for the local food bank. In other words, normal.

Sam arrived in her little red car. She took her to a local restaurant that served homestyle meals in a country kitchen atmosphere. The cozy little booth gave the feeling of privacy, even though the off-the-beaten path place was always full of customers.

"We missed you at the hike," Sam began. "I got some photos on Lake Arrowhead of the gang, though. I'll send them to your cell."

Jenny sighed. "Emergency meeting at work. You know how these executives can be. Everything's an emergency and then you find out they're just changing the branding or launching an ad campaign and they need, 'All hands on deck'."

"Yeah, I get it. We'd get so much more done without all of the staff meetings, most of which could be handled in a memo or email."

"So, tell me about your new gig," Sam said, after the waitress had taken their order, curiosity sparkling in her eyes.

"I'm still in training," Jenny replied carefully. "There is so much to learn. I met my team this week and we got to know one another. They're a really varied group, but they've been really supportive of the 'new girl'."

"Yeah, it's hard being the new kid on the block, for sure. I remember when I first came to the station. It was all pretty overwhelming. None of my training prepared me for the reality of working in a professional studio or the politics of working in a large group of creatives. Some of them are real prima donnas."

This was an old rant of Sam's. Sam was a technician, really good at production tech, but she had little patience for the eccentricities of the "talent" on the set.

"Have you gotten your first assignments yet?"

"Not yet. I have to do a tour of the company facilities. It will take me a few weeks of hard travel, but I have to familiarize myself with each area before I get my first assignment."

Part of what they had discussed during her training sessions had been the importance of learning to say just enough of the truth about what they did without giving anything away. There had been more than one story of near disaster when something slipped out that shouldn't have. Her team members had all agreed that the effort required to clean up these mistakes made it well worth the effort to get it right in the first place.

They had drilled her from different angles on how to reply to common questions and some not so common ones that could take you by surprise. Jenny had felt much better prepared by the time they had parted company.

"Hey! I could see you off at the airport!" Sam said suddenly. "I always hated having to park my car in those public garages. It will save you some cash, since you won't have to hire a cab."

Jenny paused. This had not been covered in her orientation. But the waitress arrived at that moment with their food and this gave her some time to think. There was nothing saying she couldn't fly to her first gate stop. Her passport was in order and it would give her another layer to her cover story. She would have to remember to be seen taking a cab from time to time, to give the impression that she usually got a ride to the airport when travelling.

"Sounds great, Sam. I haven't gotten my tickets yet. I'll let you know when I get them."

Jenny was starting her training in Puerto Rico. She would be spending a few days at each Guardian station. After having met all of her fellow Guardians, she was looking forward to spending time with each one, individually and learning what they had to teach her.

"So how are things at the station? I hear your 'weather woman' is quitting to pursue her acting career."

Sam laughed. "I think she just got a walk-on in a B movie from some director no one has ever heard of. I'm sure she'll go far. The studio is bringing on a meteorologist who just finished school. He's cute. Our female ratings are about to go up.

And, I hear I may be up for assistant director of the morning show. It's still in the works, but it's looking good."

"Oh, Sam, that's awesome! I'm sure you'll get it. One step closer to your dream."

"I won't be directing anything big for a long time, but it's one step higher on the ladder. Good experience and the director of the show has his act together. I'm sure I'll learn a lot. A nice change from being a floor director, working in the control room or mushrooming in the post-edit suite."

"So, have you dug into that shed out back yet? I know you've been busy with your new job and all."

"I've only just peeked in," Jenny admitted. "There's so much stuff in there. I think Aunt Lizzie was a serious pack rat."

Jenny really didn't want to get Sam involved in weeding out the storage shed. There was no telling what was in there.

Sam seemed to ignore the hint. "But that's half the fun! Maybe there is some pirate treasure or an ancient crystal with magical powers!"

Her enthusiasm made Jenny laugh.

"Or maybe it's just a lot of dusty old stuff I'll need to haul off to a thrift shop. At any rate, I won't be able to get around to it for awhile. This training tour is going to take up most of my time for the next several weeks, I'm afraid."

"Well, keep track of your adventures. I'll want to hear all about it. And take lots of pictures. I'm going to have to live vicariously, I'm afraid. The only travelling I'm going to be doing is to and from the studio in L.A. traffic."

Photos, what kinds of photos could she take that wouldn't give too much away? But as she thought of it, she realized she had gotten so used to the inter-dimensional nature of her life, that she had forgotten that people would never have any idea that this was why she was travelling, so as long as she was on Earth, she would be able to send photos of her travels without worrying about it too much. Just as if everything was…normal.

They spent the afternoon chatting and Jenny promised to make it to the next hike, as long as nothing came up in her "job".

When they pulled up in the driveway on Infinity Loop, Jenny was glad she got some time with Sam. It reminded her how important it was to get trained and why she had to do what she could to help prevent the Groga from raiding through the dimensions. She recalled with a shudder the utter devastation of the little Gateway village and tried not to picture what that would mean to her family and friends.

She invited Sam in, but Sam begged off, citing an early morning production meeting. So, hugs ensued, and Jenny waved her off. Bob was out in his yard and he too waved at Sam as she left.

"Hey, neighbor! Got a minute?"

"Sure, come on over."

Jenny let them into the house and Bob settled himself on the couch. Ensconced in her reading chair, Jenny noticed that Bob was somewhat soberer than usual.

"What's up, Bob?"

"It's the portal."

"The portal?" Jenny replied carefully. Was it possible Bob knew about the gateways?

"You know that Lizzie was very sick, and she was adamant that I not call any of her relatives during those last days. I stayed in the hospital with her. At the last, she was in and out of consciousness. Out, more often than in. She started to talk, as if to someone I couldn't see. Understand, she wasn't aware that I was there.

So, she started talking to Tidbit. I cottoned on that she was talking about something real, not a fantasy, but it sounded crazy. Lizzie wasn't the type. She was telling Tidbit to keep the secret, to not let anyone into the gateway. She talked about the Dimensional Alliance and someone called The Gatekeeper.

She said a lot of things I don't have any reference for, but she mentioned your name more than once. It's been keeping me awake nights. I have to know, if you can tell me. What has Lizzie gotten you into? And what does your friend Sam have to do with all of this?"

Jenny shook her head. How should she handle this? Nothing like this had come up in her training.

About that time, Tidbit wandered in.

"And I know about the cat. The cat who is not a cat." Bob said, pointedly looking directly into Tidbit's eyes. "I just thought you ought to know."

"*We have a problem*," Tidbit sent. "*No one is supposed to know.*"

"*I know*," Jenny sent back. "*What should I tell him?*"

Bob sat there, his blue eyes going from Tidbit to Jenny and back again.

Jenny sighed. If he knew, he knew.

"O.K., Bob. Tell me what's going on in your head right now." No need to panic, she thought, until she knew where he was heading with all of this.

He leaned forward, earnestly searching her face. "All my life I've worked in the sciences, watching technology go from basic engines and mechanics to rudimentary space travel, high end computers you can carry in a pocket and high speed communications that extend to nearly every quarter of the earth. I've seen research on dimensional physics, but nothing we have done so far even tells us that it is more than theory. And, yet, if I believe Lizzie's imaginary conversation with her cat," he paused and gave Tidbit a piercing look, "then there is something going on here that I want to be involved in.

I wanted to wait until I knew you better, before I approached you. But, unless I miss my guess, you're up to your neck in whatever Lizzie was doing and I want in."

Tidbit stared at Bob, his gaze intent as only a cat's can be. "*Tell him. I'll take responsibility for it.*"

Jenny made a mental note to hold him to that.

"Bob, if I tell you any of this," she hesitated, then took a deep breath and plunged forward, "well, it has far-reaching consequences. I'm not even sure I'm authorized to tell you anything. If you know anything about world politics, you know that some things cannot be made public, especially if it has the potential to increase conflict or cause panic. This is big, much bigger than I imagined, and I still don't know enough to tell anyone.

I do know that there is danger here, danger none of us are prepared for nor are we equipped to do anything about it. The fact that you know as much as you do already may actually put you into peril down the road and I would hate to be responsible for that."

Jenny knew Bob was probably old enough to be her father. He had a grown son of his own close to Jenny's age. It felt odd to be counselling him like this. But she hadn't even told her own father about any of this and she wouldn't. She somehow felt she could trust Bob to take her seriously and to not reveal any of this to anyone, however. Her friend, Sam, would call it "going with your gut".

Her friend, Sam. What had Bob said about Sam?

"Bob, what did you mean, how is Sam involved in this? She isn't involved at all."

"You couldn't prove it by me." Bob said, folding his arms across his chest. "She sure pokes around a lot when you aren't here, and she has been asking some pretty pointed questions about your new "job" and did I know where you were travelling to. I even saw her talking with Miss Longtree the other day. Of course, Miss Longtree doesn't really know anything about you, but it seems Sam spends quite a bit of time in the neighborhood.

I've even seen her letting herself into the backyard more than once."

"I think she likes the koi pond," was all Jenny could think to say. But, even to her, it sounded pretty lame. "I'm not sure what you're getting at."

"Isn't she a reporter or something for that little station in the valley?"

"She's a production assistant and may be getting a gig as an assistant director soon."

"Well, all I'm saying is to pay attention. You've got a pretty big secret and news folks seem to think that everything is their business. How fast they move up the ladder often is in proportion to the number of other people's secrets they can put on the chopping block."

Jenny really looked at Bob, as if for the first time. She never saw him in anything but his work clothes, not an imposing person at all.

Salt and pepper hair, his close trimmed moustache nearly all grey, dark eyes framed by bushy brows and laugh lines that indicated character more than age. On the surface, he looked like a middle aged man who no one would take a second look at. And yet, something about him was solid and strong, no doubt because of working with machinery of one kind or another all of his life. One of the most attractive things about him was his intelligent curiosity. And Jenny wagered, if she went into his workshop that it would be as orderly as an operating room.

Bob had already proven himself to be a staunch friend of Lizzie and had always treated Jenny with kindness and respect. His easy-going nature had charmed her from the beginning. Now she was seeing a side of him she did not expect.

She wondered what her aunt would have said about this development. The revelation of the gateways certainly wasn't anything Jenny had done, but somehow, she was the one who was going to have to deal with it.

Chapter 16: Dilemma

Tarafau shifted his stance, swinging his quarterstaff low at Jenny's ankles. Jenny jumped over and, swiveling, caught Tarafau mid-back with a stinging, "CRACK!", following the blow with and overhead swipe that caught him on the shoulder. Tarafau held his staff over his head in salute and surrender.

"Your practice is paying off," he said, only slightly out of breath. "That's the third time you've tagged me today."

Jenny was panting slightly as well. She grounded her staff and grinned. "Are you sure you aren't letting me win?"

"Not on your life. Your aunt accused me of that before. I would never let you win. Over-confidence can be as dangerous as incompetence."

Jenny tried to picture her aunt dodging and parrying and cracking Tarafau with a staff. She couldn't help but grin.

"Was she good? Did she ever beat you?"

"She was very good, but she never beat me. I saw her knock out a troll once, though. She could hold her own in a fight."

"And were there many of those? Fights, I mean," said Jenny, as she now tried to picture her aunt fighting a troll.

"From time to time our assignments take us to places that require us to be on our guard and use the skills you have been taught. It isn't like we expect to be in combat, like the Troopers or the Alliance Guards, but it happens. Which is why we teach you the staff and hand to hand fighting. It is best to be prepared."

"Speaking of being prepared. What about Bob? Did you know he knew about the gateways?"

Tarafau shook his head somberly. "And Lizzie never knew. She would have never revealed so much had she been in her right mind. Of course, they would have never let a cat into a hospital. I sat outside her window and mindspoke her whenever she was conscious.

But she seldom replied. At the last she sent one message…'Good cat.'" He smiled, but it was a sad smile.

"So, what do we do about this? I have racked my brain," Jenny continued, voicing again the conversation she had already had with Tarafau more than once, " I don't think Bob will tell anyone. He has a good mind and a good heart, I think. He seems genuinely concerned about whether Sam is up to no good, which I doubt."

Jenny paused, but what was Sam up to, she wondered. There was no reason she could think of why Sam would be driving all the way here when she knew Jenny was away. And going into her back yard to do…what?

"I wonder what Lizzie would have done?" she mused aloud. And then it hit her, Lizzie! She had the AI. She plopped down on the mat and pulled the tablet out of the MDP. Lizzie's smiling face appeared like the genie from the lamp.

"How can I help you?" she said, as she often did when invoked.

Jenny outlined the conversation with Bob and her dilemma. "First, what do I do about Bob? And second, what do I do about Sam? Bob has become a good friend and Sam has been my best friend since college. I don't know how much Sam knows, if anything, and as far as I know she might just be planning a prank on me or some kind of silly surprise. And Bob seems trustworthy, but this is a pretty big secret to have to keep, as you know."

LizzieAI looked grave. "I have some equipment in the shed that may be useful to help you figure this out. Bob can be trusted, but I want you to invite him over to lunch so I can speak with him. In the meantime, don't do anything out of the ordinary where Sam is concerned. No sense jumping to conclusions without proof."

Lizzie gave Jenny instructions about the equipment in the shed and how to use it. Tarafau had stood there behind her as Lizzie talked, quarterstaff in hand, his expression still somber and sad. Jenny realized that hearing Lizzie's voice and seeing her face, even though he knew she was a construct, must be difficult for him after all the years they had spent together.

Impulsively she jumped up, throwing her arms around him in a fierce hug. He was startled at first and then hugged her back. "I know you miss her," she said.

He released her, and she realized that the big man had tears in his eyes. "She was a great spirit with a fierce heart. All who knew her will miss her always. You are a worthy successor. She chose well."

Jenny ducked her head, a little embarrassed. She wasn't usually the hugging type. Oh, they had hugged a lot in her family, but other than that, she didn't generally give out hugs much, even to her friends. But Tarafau had become more than just "The Guide" to her. He was like an anchor in an increasingly stormy sea and she knew she could depend on him, no matter what happened.

They immediately left the workout room and went to the shed to retrieve the equipment Lizzie had described. She had given very specific instructions and the installation was simple. After completing it, Jenny showered and changed, considering once again the fix in which she found herself. Since she had been handed the keys to the house and walked through the door for the first time, it had been like a very precarious roller coaster ride and she was just getting started.

She remembered an old Chinese curse, "May you live in interesting times." And she sighed. Nothing for it, but to move forward. She was grateful for Tarafau and the LizzieAI. She was sure she would have made a mess of all of this without them, even with the training from the Council. She had never been one of those who struck out with total confidence in her own abilities to get her through. She knew she had some talents and strengths, but never considered herself to be out of the ordinary or special in any way.

Now, here she was with the fate of who knows what in her hands and she still felt clueless. She didn't feel like she could learn fast enough to keep up with the pace of events and be of any use whatsoever, but she was determined to do her part and that would have to do.

Tidbit followed her out the door and out the wrought iron gate. Bob wasn't out in his yard, as he often was. She went up to the front door and rang the doorbell. She waited for a minute and rang again. She saw his car in the driveway, but still no answer. He was probably in his workshop.

She walked down the driveway to the building that was about twice the size of Lizzie's storage shed, about the size of a large three car garage. She could hear Bob whistling as he worked at something. The door stood open.

"Hello?" she called. The whistling stopped, and Bob appeared from behind a large set of shelves with neatly ordered boxes and drawers, everything from bolts to tools sitting and hanging precisely in their places. On his shoulder perched on a leather padding was a beautiful Hyacinth Macaw. Ignatius, she remembered.

Bob grinned when he saw Jenny. "Hey there! Come on in!"

"Come on in!" repeated a somewhat scratchy, higher pitched voice. And Ignatius bobbed his head up and down excitedly.

She followed him around the shelving unit into the workshop proper. On tables were several projects, all of which looked somewhat mysterious to Jenny's eyes. "Contraptions" was what her dad would have called them.

One looked very much like a little robot about four feet tall, one arm detached and laying beside it on the table.

There were meters of some sort with needles vacillating, several computers all with active displays, and what looked like a radar display. Seeing all of this, for the first time, Jenny realized that Bob was much more than a self-described "tinkerer". She wondered who all of these projects were for.

He noticed her looking at the little robot. "Meet Fidget," he said, his eyes sparkling. "He's a little AI helper I've been working on for a long time and he's almost ready for final testing. He's no C3PO, but he'll do. He's going to be my shop assistant."

And to her surprise, Fidget turned his head and said, "Nice to meet you. I'm Fidget. What's your name?"

Jenny replied, bemused, and Fidget said, "Hi Jenny," then turning to Bob, "Is Jenny our friend?"

Bob laughed and said, "Yes, Fidget, Jenny is our friend. Please remember her."

Fidget nodded.

Jenny was impressed. The little robot stood. His face and body appeared to be some kind of shiny plastic, somewhat like a small astronaut. His "face" was generated with a graphical display and he seemed capable of expressing appropriate emotions through that display.

"And you made him in your workshop? That's amazing."

"That's amazing," agreed Ignatius.

"He's a prototype. There is a real market for AI robots in the making, and I can make him in pretty much any size, depending on what use someone would have for him. Even in his present state, he has the ability to extend his legs and arms to allow him to interact on any level. I'd appreciate it if you would keep him quiet for now. He's just in the development phase, at the moment and the industry is very competitive. There are some Japanese robotics firms that are very close to doing some similar things and I have to be set up to avoid unwanted attention."

"Speaking of that," Jenny put in awkwardly. "Can you come over for lunch today? We really need to talk about some things."

"Sure. Just let me tidy up a bit here and I'll be right over."

Jenny took another look around. "Good-bye, Fidget," she said.

"See you later, alligator," Fidget replied with a wink and Jenny couldn't help but giggle.

"Goodbye, Ignatius."

"Alligator." Ignatius replied with finality.

As she and Tidbit crossed the street, Tidbit remarked, *"He has come a long way on that project since Lizzie passed. Impressive. And he could be of assistance, in the future, assuming we can trust him."*

Jenny agreed. She went into the kitchen to prepare lunch and as she worked, she thought how nice it would be to have someone so close who knew her secret and in whom she could confide. It would make arrangements for her various absences a lot easier and somehow, she felt she could indeed trust Bob.

Bob showed up about the time she had some sandwiches and lemonade made. She got out some raw veggies she kept around for snacks and laid them out on the patio table.

Tidbit was laying out on the edge of the koi pond apparently watching the fish. As Bob and Jenny ate, Bob told Jenny about some of his adventures with creating Fidget, learning to create the plastic pieces with his 3D printer and designing the face and the facial expressions.

When they had finished, he helped her clear the dishes and they adjourned to the sunlit living room with Tidbit now ensconced in his favorite spot on the sunny window seat.

"I need to finish the conversation we started yesterday," Jenny began. "And I need to show you something that may be startling, and I need you to keep it in confidence, as I will keep Fidget in confidence for you."

Bob nodded. "Of course," he said.

Jenny sat next to him on the couch, holding out the tablet so they could both see the display. She invoked the LizzieAI and Lizzie's face beamed out at them, looking from one face to the other. "How can I help you, Jenny and Bob." LizzieAI said.

Bob let out a low whistle. "Facial recognition. Where did you get this?"

Jenny started to answer, but LizzieAI cut in. "I am an artificial construct created to allow Jenny to receive training as an interdimensional Guardian and Gatekeeper. I was programmed by Lizzie using advanced tech from another dimension. Lizzie counted you as a friend, Bob. Jenny has come to me with a concern that we need to discuss."

Bob's eyes widened and he looked at Jenny and back to the screen.

"The dimensional gates have existed on Earth, as far as we know, for as long as Earth has been a planet. No one knows the original purpose of the gates, or if they simply exist like black holes or quasars. The history of the first discovery of these gates goes past reckoning by intelligent species. But long before the Earth portals were discovered by Earthlings, an alliance of intelligent species was created to protect the various universes from those with ill intent.

The policy of the alliance is benign non-interference. Each universe is different and, as long as any universe does not infringe on the rights or territory of any other universe, we do not intrude.

Unfortunately, there have been those who, upon discovering the gateways, have decided on a course of invasion, exploitation, war and terrorism against other dimensions. This is what the alliance was intended to prevent. Peaceful interaction between dimensions has always been the policy, but only when a dimension was ready for first contact and they didn't infringe on the rights or properties of others.

At first, here on Earth, there have been random incursions into our universe, nearly all of which have been either unintentional or at the least, not aggressive. Out of these have sprung many of our myths and legends. Not all intelligent beings look like us and some of those incursions were purely by accident by non-intelligent species.

Thus, the time came when Guardians were chosen from among the various peoples of Earth, to guard the gateways and to keep them secret from the population that was not yet ready for interdimensional relations. I was such a Guardian, and now Jenny has taken my place.

In addition to the Guardians in the dimensions, one is always chosen to be The Gatekeeper. The job of The Gatekeeper is to monitor and coordinate all of the gateways in all dimensions and to lead the Guardians in the performance of their duty.

Due to circumstances we were not able to control, Jenny has also been chosen to be The Gatekeeper.

She is in the early stages of her training for both roles. The fact that my original self revealed the existence of the gateways to you adds an additional stress on her. My programming identifies you as a trustworthy, dependable companion of my original self. What we need to know, is, what are your intentions, knowing what you now know?"

Bob didn't answer at once. He gazed that the AI who had paused for his response. "This is amazing," he said in a soft voice that reflected awe. The thoughtful look on his face showed he was taking it all in as best he could, but, like Jenny, he was struggling to absorb it all.

"Of course, I will support Jenny in any way I can," he finally replied. "And I understand the need for secrecy. I agree the general population of our planet and the political machines in governments across the world are not ready for this. I will not divulge any of this to anyone. I would like, however," and his voice took on a tone of longing, "to be allowed to assist in some way, assuming you feel you can trust me to do so."

LizzieAI looked somberly at Jenny, "What do you think, Jenny? Ultimately this needs to be your decision. You have that right as Gatekeeper. You will, of course have to report all of this to The Council."

Jenny considered. "What are my options?"

"If you decide to trust Bob with these secrets, then you need only report it to the Council. Helpers and agents on gateway planets are allowed to Guardians and especially The Gatekeeper. The Council will decide whether he will be certified to go through gateways or not. If you decide to not involve Bob, then his memory of this knowledge will be wiped, and he won't remember either Lizzie's last words or these conversations. No harm will be done, and he will not need to be held responsible for this knowledge."

Jenny looked at Bob. "Which would you prefer? Knowing puts you under a grave responsibility to keep this secret. I can't guarantee you will ever be allowed to travel the gateways. It would be a help and a comfort to have one more person I can count on for assistance and counsel, but I wouldn't put this responsibility on you without your knowledge and consent. I'm not sure why, but I do trust you."

Bob stroked his salt and pepper moustache thoughtfully. "I treasure my friendship with your aunt," he said, looking directly into her eyes. "I am grateful you are willing to extend this trust to me. I would be honored to support you in this task. You only have to ask, whenever you need help." He extended his hand.

Jenny shook it in the spirit he offered it. It was a pledge and she understood it as such.

Tidbit sent, "*I think you have made a wise choice, Jenny.*"

Jenny sincerely hoped so.

Chapter 17: The Honey Trap

Jenny texted Sam with her departure date for the red-eye flight to Puerto Rico, where she would do her training with Juan. She was looking forward to the opportunity to spend time with Juan. He had been extremely supportive in their group training meetings and he had a gentle nature. He was a quiet man, but his face and voice were expressive, and he had been generous with his advice.

Sam picked her up in plenty of time to avoid the major traffic jams, which was good. The flight would be a long one. It would have been so much faster and easier to travel the gateways, but she still didn't know what to do about Sam and didn't want to foster any additional mistrust between her and her friend. She had deposited Tidbit in the Gateway office with food and water (and to his disgust) a litter box. She would fetch him out to the Puerto Rico gate at the other end.

Sam chatted animatedly about the last hike she had been on, the politics in her station and the pending approval of the assistant director's job. Jenny wished with all her heart that her enjoyment hadn't been tinged with the slightest suspicion of Sam's mysterious actions, as witnessed by Bob as she listened to her friend.

As usual, she asked Jenny about her job and Jenny gave her the canned responses she had practiced during her training.

They arrived at the airport in plenty of time. Sam had been surprised that all Jenny had was a carry on (her satchel) and her backpack. "You really know how to pack light," she commented. "I don't think I could have managed a four day trip with two small bags."

"It gets me through security faster and saves me a bag charge," was all Jenny replied in return. Of course, she had her MDP and the bags were only for appearance. It would have seemed very suspicious had she traveled without some kind of baggage such a long way, both for security and to her friend.

"Have a great trip and take lots of photos," Sam reminded her.

They hugged, and Jenny set off into the airport with a wave.

The flight was long, and Jenny took advantage of her first class seats to get some sleep. While she was awake, she read a book by her favorite mystery author that she still hadn't had a chance to read.

Juan was waiting at the baggage claim after she went through customs after landing. He was dressed in what the Hawaiians called an "aloha shirt" and jeans. The air was warm and humid, but a nice breeze was blowing. He grabbed her bags, stowed them in the back seat and off they went.

Jenny was grateful for the seat belts, as she quickly discovered that Juan liked to drive fast. They were quickly beyond the city and headed along the coast for awhile. The deep blue waters contrasted with white beaches, fringed by large palm trees and beach grasses. On the other side of the road rose a chain of verdant mountains.

"We are going to Los Piedras," Juan said conversationally, with his mild Spanish accent. "The view from my home is like no other. My wife has made accommodations for you." Jenny started at this. She hadn't even thought of the possibility of a married Guardian and she said so.

"Oh, yes. Many of us have spouses. We are, after all human beings. It is not forbidden. She knows what I do and why I do it and can be trusted not to discuss it with non-Guardians."

Jenny considered this. Her aunt had never married. She had spent all of her time with Tarafau. Jenny had assumed it was because Guardians were not permitted to marry. Perhaps Jenny would have a choice about that after all. She had dated some in college, but she had been so focused on her grades and her writing jobs, that left very little time for socializing. Fortunately, it wasn't a choice she would have to make any time soon.

He flew around the curves, keeping up a stream of information, like a tour guide, telling her about the lush rain forests of the area, the varied climates on the island and about the devastation of recent hurricanes.

"We were fortunate, as there is a spring on our property. Many on the island were struggling to get fresh clean water and food supplies were scarce. We have always kept a small emergency supply of food and fresh water due to hurricanes of the past. We had enough for ourselves and to share with our neighbors."

Jenny was in awe of the beautiful island and she was saddened by the destruction they had experienced. In Los Angeles it was more often fires, due to the drought, and earthquakes. Every place had their natural perils to deal with.

They wound up the mountain, surrounded by lush greenery and exotic flowers. Here and there bright colored parrot-like birds flew above the forest. With the windows open, some bird calls could be heard even above the engine of the car.

Finally, they turned into a long, narrow gravel road where two cars could almost barely pass one another, but they encountered no other vehicles. The forest closed in overhead and the sun was only seen in glimpses.

Then, suddenly, the road opened out into what appeared to be a large orchard with some of the largest fruit trees she had ever seen.

"Mangoes," said Juan, showing his white even teeth in a delighted smile at her reaction. "It's my wife's business. She sells them in the coastal towns. And she makes the world's best mango curry."

They entered a large iron gateway with a huge double gate that could easily be locked to keep out unwanted visitors. The fence around the property was easily ten feet tall, topped with barbed wire.

Juan noticed her glance to the top of the fence. "Keeps out wildlife, for the most part. We usually only close the gates at night. During the day they are unlikely to come into the compound."

The house they drove up to was not quite a mansion, but definitely was for a well-to-do family. Juan grabbed her baggage, despite her protests that she could carry them herself. He led the way to large carved double doors.

"Luz! We are home!" he called into the foyer. Jenny stepped through onto the tiled floor, as a middle aged lady in a white dress with a colorful belt and shawl rushed forward to greet her. Her long, unbound wavy brown hair fell past her waist and her dark eyes were crinkled in the corners with a bright smile that lit up her face.

"You're Jenny. Welcome, Gatekeeper, to our humble home." And she bobbed her head, not quite a bow. "Please come in and refresh yourself. You must be tired and hungry."

Jenny admitted that the eleven hour flight, not counting the two hours in the airport and the drive from her house, had worn her out.

Jenny didn't know much Spanish, but she knew that Luz meant "sunshine". Juan's wife definitely fit her name. She took Jenny up a long curved flight of stairs leading to a balcony-style hallway that overlooked the great room, including a large dining area that overlooked a beautiful view down the mountainside.

Her room was the second door. It opened into a suite that would rival any nice hotel, with a private bathroom and sliding doors leading out onto a balcony.

"Mi casa es tu casa. My home is yours. Please take time to refresh yourself. There is a snack and cold fruit punch on the balcony when you are ready and then, I think you should take a siesta before Juan puts you to work."

Jenny thanked her profusely as she backed out of the door, smiling. She slipped out of her shoes, grateful for the cool floor tiles in the heat. The open balcony windows let in a cooling breeze that barely stirred the curtains on either side of the balcony doors. A ceiling fan gently stirred the air and she walked out onto the balcony.

The view was breath-taking, overlooking the orchards and the slopes of the mountain stepping down to the sea. An occasional wispy cloud drifted across the deep blue sky. On a white wicker table with matching chairs under a colorful sunshade umbrella sat a salad, a bowl of rice with peas and other vegetables and what looked like pork. Next to the bowl, with condensation beading on the glass, sat a glass of what appeared to be the fruit punch Luz had mentioned.

She surprised herself by finishing every morsel of the rice dish which also contained olives, onions, peppers and capers. The tomato base was tangy, like nothing she had tried before. Before she knew it both bowls were empty, and she drained the last of the punch.

Yawning she took the time to take a shower before disappearing into sleep between white sheets on the very comfortable bed.

She awoke to the calling of birds from the forest below, the warm breeze still stirring the curtains from the balcony. She realized the light had faded slightly. It must be approaching evening. She jumped out of bed and dressed, concerned that she was being rude by sleeping so late.

When she got to the bottom of the stairs, she found Luz and Juan chatting amiably before the double doors that led out to the grounds. They looked up and smiled.

"I am going out to talk to the groundskeepers," Luz said to Jenny. "I'll be back in a bit. Please make yourself at home. Juan has been looking forward to showing you around."

She left, and Juan gestured for Jenny to follow him.

They went through the huge airy kitchen to a basement door. At the bottom of the stairs she felt the key on her neck begin to warm. "The gate recognizes you, Gatekeeper," Juan said. A door appeared, and they walked through it into a well-lighted office similar to her own, minus the cat bed.

"I need to go through and get Tidbit, er…Tarafau. It was necessary for my ruse." She had explained to Juan why she had to come the long way but had forgotten this little detail. Tidbit would have had to go through a quarantine after deboarding the plane, so this was the best solution. "He's been confined for nearly a day now and won't be in a very good state of mind."

He led the way to her gateway and she stepped in to her office. Tidbit started up from his cat bed. "Let's not do this often," he sent, disgruntlement clear on his cat face.

"Well, come on then," she said, trying not to grin. "Fresh air, sunshine and ocean breezes await."

She was surprised to see that he didn't transform on the other side of the gateway. "*Sanglarka is the only Earth gateway that is shielded so I can transform,*" he sent at her obvious confusion. "*So, every other place on Earth you visit, I am still Tidbit. Only in extreme emergency can I transform outside Sanglarka's shield,*"

"*Lizzie always loved coming to visit your beautiful hacienda,*" Tidbit sent to Juan. "*I know you two were also close. This was always a place of peace for her.*"

There was a short, sad silence as both the cat and the man bowed their heads, acknowledging their loss. Then Juan looked up at Jenny and said, "I will be taking you through several of my favorite dimensions over the next few days. While there I will introduce you to other Guardians and the necessary survival precautions for each one. This is per Ingot's instructions. You will need to pay attention to the details around you and when we are finished with each trip, you will report to me everything you noticed. We will continue to practice your martial arts and your mental exercises. You will need to especially work on the mental workout, as, once you have been trained by each of us, Lova will be introducing you to the key duties of The Gatekeeper and these will require that discipline. Any questions?"

As congenial as Juan had seemed, he definitely knew how to get down to business.

Jenny shook her head. "I am sure I will have many questions as we go along," she said.

"Then, take your rebreather from your MDP and we will begin. This will be a short trip before supper. After supper we will do another short trip and then your martial arts and mental workouts before bed. I recommend you eat well and sleep as much as you are able, as this will be very fast paced. Normally we would take longer to train you, but we are short on time, if your report to The Council is any indication of the danger we are in. The Groga are not patient. I am sure they are planning another raid and there is no way of knowing when or where they will strike again.

One of the reasons we will keep you moving is to avoid them putting a finger on how to find you."

Jenny wanted to gulp, but she just nodded and pulled the rebreather out. It was smaller than her hiking knapsack and weighed no more than her regular pack for a day hike. The line went to a small mask that was as clear as glass, but soft as kid leather. It adequately covered her mouth and nose and when she started the rebreather with an intake of breath, it sealed to her face. There was a button on the line that allowed the mask to release when needed. The rebreather simply recycled the air she breathed out through some very high tech filters, so a heavy oxygen tank was not required.

They stopped in front of the door they had gone through to her study. "Notice the markings on the door. You should realize that although the gateways appear as doors to us, they take on a different configuration that means the same thing to the other beings who use them. They really do not exist in a physical form. The format is sent as a signal to our brain and is transformed into something we recognize as an entrance or exit. Each door has specific markings, and some appear to be color coded. You can choose to color code a door for your own use by simply thinking it, but it may not translate the same for someone else, so the colors are strictly for your own reference, to easily sort out doors you use frequently or perhaps doors you may want to avoid or even doors that lead to environments where you have to adjust, such as wearing the rebreather and sometimes an environmental suit, such as an astronaut might wear. Is that clear?"

Jenny nodded, and he moved several doors down. "Note the markings. This is the Figard gate. The atmosphere on the host planet is not suitable for Earthlings. A surprising number of host planets are oxygen based, but not all. Figardians do not reproduce as we do. There is only a neutral gender. They bud, like trees and the buds then sprout into new Figardians. They are somewhat tree like, with a single eye and no mouths. They absorb their nutrients from soil and stream, but unlike trees, they are not immobile. They communicate mind to mind and will readily understand mind speech, but be aware, that on Figard what you say is said to all and any mind interested in listening can hear what you say.

Gravity is slightly less than Earth gravity, so you will feel light on your toes and when you return you will feel like you've gained several pounds. There are other creatures on the planet, but none appear to be intelligent enough to communicate with. That's about the best briefing I can give you. The rest will come with experience. Let's go meet the Figardians."

In retrospect, years later, Jenny would remember that it was this experience that finally brought home the fact that Earth was such a tiny speck in a wide universe. Over the next few days she met so many different forms of intelligent beings that she lost track. Only a very few were remotely humanoid. They even visited a water planet. The gate was an airlock and they wore environmental suits that were more like space suits than scuba gear, but the boots had a water option that turned them into flippers. On that planet, the intelligent beings were as large as whales and as gentle as bunny rabbits.

At the end of each trip, Juan had her recite everything she could think of that she noticed along the way. He was impressed with her ability to notice and recall important details and to sort out those things that were mostly insignificant. Her dreams at night were full of strange and wonderful things and her perspective of what intelligent life really meant was vastly altered.

He briefed her quickly at the beginning of each trip, but none of it had fully prepared her for any of it. A quick sketch of the details gave her only a small point of reference. By the time she was done with each visit, however, she realized that nothing anyone could have taught her in a classroom would have adequately prepared her for the incredible variety of lifeforms and planetary formats.

By the time her visit was finished, she had learned to love the hacienda with its towering mango trees, the sea breezes and such hospitable company. Luz was a delightful and warm person with a ready smile and a kindly, motherly air that made Jenny feel so at home.

"Please come and visit with us again soon," Luz said, as she left, giving Jenny a warm hug. "Next time, perhaps Juan will not work you so hard."

"Thank you so much for your kindness, Luz and Juan. I will be delighted to come and visit you any time you wish. But next time, I think I will come by gate," she said with a wink.

"*You're darned right*," Tidbit agreed and laughing Jenny stepped through the gateway to her home.

Then she stopped laughing. Whew! The smell of the litter box that had now been left in her office for several days was the first thing to greet her as they stepped across the threshold of the office. "*I told you, you'd regret this,*" he sent sourly.

She proceeded to take care of the litter box and was about to settle down in the living room when she realized that since she had come into the house a soft beeping had been coming from her office in the house.

There was a red light blinking on her computer. The trap had been sprung!

Jenny had left a key that didn't open anything on the ground outside the shed, as if she had dropped it. She had installed the advanced surveillance system that Lizzie had left in the shed and hooked it via Bluetooth to her computer which streamed the files to the Alliance cloud. The surveillance was set to only trigger on movement of something larger than a dog and didn't look anything like a camera. Whoever had designed it ironically made the cameras look like bugs.

When she called up the video, there on her computer screen appeared Sam, who circled the shed once, looking for an opening other than the door. Having found nothing, she discovered the key. She looked around and then tried the key in the lock. Of course, it didn't fit, but she pocketed it and went to the French doors and peered in. Then, it appeared that something occurred to her and she retrieved the key from her pocket and tried it in the French doors. No luck. She scowled and peered into the kitchen window, shook her head and then pulled something else from her pocket.

It wasn't her cell phone. It was a gadget of some sort. Nothing seemed to happen as she walked along the edge of the house, but when she walked past the door of the shed a blue light started to blink. She shook the door handle with frustration and left, her walk stiff as she stomped off, but at the corner she paused and returned to the door. She appeared to pause, facing the door and then, with a satisfied smirk turned and left.

So, what was this about? Should she confront her? That gadget in her hand had appeared to be some kind of scanner she was not familiar with. The look on her face was so much not like her friend that it was shocking in itself. She looked sly and hard and angry, nothing at all like the Sam she thought she knew.

"*Tidbit, come here. I need you,*" she sent to the cat.

She told him what she had found, and he just looked at her intently. "*Well, what do you think?*"

"*I think your friend cannot be trusted and that Bob is probably right. Save the footage. We may need it. You may need to postpone your next training. The Council will want to hear about this and about Bob, right away.*"

Chapter 18: Interesting Times

Jenny stood before the dais in the private Council room. She was mentally and physically exhausted. After two days of little or no sleep and retelling her story over and over again, the three Councilors finally seemed satisfied. They appeared to have forgotten about Jenny and she wondered if it was all right for her to at least sit down.

They had assured her after the first telling that they didn't lay any of this to her charge. Actually, they were impressed with the fact that she had used her resources so well. Although it was obvious that none of it was her doing, that didn't mean she still didn't feel like a total failure. All of the trust that had been put into her training was now seeming like a waste to her. How could they continue to trust her when the first breaches of the Earth gates had happened under her watch?

Tarafau stood next to her, his big hands clasped behind his back. They had questioned him as well and he had corroborated everything she had told them. It felt good to have him standing next to her. He faced The Council with an unblinking stare, his chin lifted, his shoulder's back and something about him evoked a feeling in Jenny of being protected and championed, like a queen with her knight of the sword beside her.

Thinking of that made her stand a little straighter, despite her tiredness.

As she straightened, Ingot stood. "*We have come to three conclusions. First, we repeat that there is nothing in any of this that indicates any fault on your part. Second, we will bow to your judgement concerning your neighbor, Bob. We will consider your request to certify him and make him a companion to The Gatekeeper. Third, we must arrange for your friend Sam to be questioned. She will not be harmed, but if necessary, we will erase any memories she has of you and anything she might have learned. This may sound harsh to you, but we may not have a choice, especially if she means you or the gate network any harm.*

Do you have any questions or objections?"

Jenny shook her head. If anything, their decision was better than she had expected.

"Tarafau, this will require extra vigilance on your part. If emergency measures are necessary, we give you permission to do whatever you must to protect the gates and The Gatekeeper."

"We also have news. The Groga have struck again. They raided a gate planet known as Lefia, strictly in and out without triggering any alarms. The gateway city was destroyed, and the Guardian and his people were abducted as before. They seem to want slaves as well as whatever wealth and tech they can take. So far, the gates they have raided have been low tech with the exception of the gate offices themselves. However, the office of this gateway has been completely stripped of any tech of any value at all.

We still have no idea where they are based or how they are getting through these gateways or why they started raiding again in the first place. Our best agents are on it and the Alliance forces are on standby.

In the meantime, we must deal with your situation. We will give you a pass, so you may escort Bob to meet with us. We will also be sending an envoy to deal with your friend Sam." He held his hand up, forestalling her comment. *"I promise, no harm will come to her, but this we must do."*

Jenny sighed and nodded. She knew that nothing she could say would change the decision and she understood why it must be, but Sam had been her friend for six years.

As the meeting ended, Myla stood from his nest chair and walked over to Jenny to put a hand kindly on her shoulder. His pupils pinned, and he spoke to her mind while making a crooning sound from his throat. *"Little sister, do not fear. We understand this is a severe burden to put on such young shoulders. All we can expect from you is your best effort. Our greatest fear is that you may be harmed before you can learn to survive and thrive in your calling. You need not fear us. We are not your judges. We are your fellows and your family. Be at peace."*

Jenny's eyes teared up and she sat, suddenly overcome with tiredness and grief. Grief for Lizzie and never having known her. Grief for

Miriha and her terrible sacrifice and now grief for the potential loss of a dear friend. Not to mention her horror at the terror and devastation to innocent beings she did not know. The kindness of Myla had totally undone her.

Myla continued to croon to her and to pat her gently on the shoulder.

Tarafau strode over to her. *"Come, we'll go to your suite where you can rest. Then we need to get the pass and the agent, before we can leave for home."*

Jenny followed him woodenly, her heart still hurting in her chest. He turned to her and extended his hand and she ducked under his arm. He put it around her shoulders and the two of them went to rest while preparations were made.

The healers were waiting in her rooms, the smell of the calming tea met them as they opened the door. They examined her carefully and sat her on a deep cushioned chair with an ottoman under her legs and a cup of tea in her hand. They laid a soft blanket across her lap and gave Tarafau instructions to allow her to rest quietly, after giving him a cup of the tea as well. They let themselves out without another word.

When she had drained her cup, Jenny set it aside and sat there, warm and comfortable everywhere but in her heart, but the tea had it's effect and before she realized it, Tarafau was patting her gently on the shoulder.

"Our escort is here," he sent quietly.

A young man stood there in jeans and a t-shirt. His thatch of brown hair was messy, and his blue eyes seemed full of mischief. In many ways he reminded her of Sam.

"I'm Burt," he said aloud, extending his hand. Jenny shook his hand, but before she could introduce herself, he added, "and you are Jenny, The Gatekeeper, with her Guide, Tarafau."

Jenny just nodded, still sleepy from her short nap. Tarafau clapped Burt on the back. Burt staggered a pace and grinned up at him. "Burt is an agent of The Alliance. He will be handling the issue with Sam as well as interviewing Bob before he is given the pass to come to meet with The Council. I know him and can vouch for his integrity and fairness."

This was quite a speech coming from Tarafau. He must have thought she needed the assurance and he was right. She wanted no harm to come to Sam.

When they arrived home, it was dark. Jenny made up the couch in the living room for Burt and went to bed herself, Tidbit curled up at her feet instead of on his usual nightly prowl.

The next morning, she dragged herself out of bed early, but Burt was already up and dressed, his blankets neatly folded on one end of the couch.

She offered him a bowl of cereal and some juice, which he accepted happily. They ate at the dining room table and were just finishing up when Tidbit presented himself at the French doors after his morning wander. Jenny let him in and fed him and filled his water bowl with fresh water.

She then offered to work out with Burt and Tarafau and they proceeded to the workout room. After doing her mental workout, which she now slipped into easily, Tarafau took advantage of having a third person to work on quarterstaff attacks from multiple sides. Jenny surprised herself by actually tagging each of them at least once while they came at her from either side.

At the end of the bout, they were all sweating. Jenny took dibs on the shower, but she showered quickly. When Burt finally emerged from the bathroom after her, somehow his wet hair was still standing up pretty wildly. He noticed her looking and shook his head. "I don't do gel and it won't behave any other way," he said, pulling a mournful face.

She laughed and shrugged. "I think you might look strange with your hair slicked down. The messy look suits you. Now, tell me what you're going to do about my friend Sam."

"Pretty simple, really. A pretty girl meets a charming young man," pointing to himself. "They engage in conversation (and he mimicked people talking with his hands) and the young man uses dastardly alien tech to check her motives and veracity. Assuming she passes with flying colors, the young man finds a good reason to be elsewhere and that is the end of it."

"In the case she doesn't pass, we arrange for her to have a romantic interlude, at which time we use our dastardly alien tech to find out what she knows, and we then use said tech to erase all pertinent memories and let her go on with her life.

Either way, I'm out of the picture. And she forgets me, and all is well in the multiverse."

Jenny knew she didn't really like it, but, if it went as he said, no real harm would come to Sam and she could be relieved of her worry and suspicion.

But before Burt took on Sam, he needed to sit down with Bob. Jenny dropped Bob a text and invited him over. Jenny was surprised at how quickly he was at her door. She introduced him to Burt and they all sat down out on the patio.

"Has Fidget gotten his arm back?" Jenny asked Bob, wanting to put him at ease.

"He sure has. He's nearly ready for some field tests."

Burt cocked his head, "Fidget?"

"My personal assistant, AI. He has a way to go yet, but he's coming along. He's kind of a secret project," he added with a sideways glance at Jenny.

"Oh, you can trust Burt," Jenny put in hurriedly, not wanting Bob to think that she was going around telling everyone about it. "He's here from The Alliance and wants to talk to you about what the Alliance is and how you can be involved. In the process he needs to know a lot about you, including your inventions. As a representative of The Alliance, he is authorized to give you a pass to go before The Dimensional Alliance Council to see to what extent you might be able to help us, as you offered to do."

Bob's eyebrows shot up. "Really? Wow, Jenny, I never expected this. Thank you." He turned to Burt. "Ask me anything," he said, earnestly, looking straight into Burt's eyes.

Burt nodded. "Do you mind if I use some dastardly alien tech to simplify the process?"

Bob's eyes widened at this and he shook his head. "Is it my birthday?" he asked, his eyes shining. "Are you an alien from another dimension?"

"Actually, I'm from Toledo," Burt admitted. "I kind of stumbled into this myself. I'm guessing you know Lizzie?"

Bob nodded. "Well, I was working as a personal assistant to an archeologist on a dig in Ghana. I met Lizzie and Tidbit who were searching for something. I offered to be their guide. Let's just say I accidentally ended up seeing more than was allowed without The Alliance taking a hand. I went through the same process you are experiencing now. And here I am. I couldn't be a Guardian, since all the known gateways were already guarded, so they made me an agent. It's been a wild ride, I'll tell you.

Now, are you ready?"

Bob nodded eagerly.

Burt reached into his pocket and Jenny felt her key warm, just slightly. Bob's eyes went unfocused for about a minute. Then the warmth faded from her key and Bob's eyes went back to normal.

"I'm ready," he said.

"We're done," Burt replied cheerily. "You pass. Hold out your hand."

Bob did so dazedly, and Burt pressed what looked like an ink stamp onto the back of Bob's hand. For a moment the emblem of The Alliance glowed there and then it faded away.

"That is your pass. It is valid for the next 2 weeks. You can only go through the gate escorted by a Guardian and this pass only allows you to go through the gate to Alliance headquarters. You and Jenny can arrange between the two of you when that will be. While there you will be supplied with accommodations. You need only bring a change of clothes and any personal items you may require, such as medications. Any questions?"

Bob appeared to be at a loss for words. Jenny knew how he felt.

He thought for a moment and said, "What does that gadget do, and can I see it?"

Burt laughed, and Jenny mentally rolled her eyes. This was so like Bob, who wanted to know how everything worked.

"Sorry, trade secret, although, after they interview you, you might get a peek at some pretty cool tech. The caveat is, that since you are 'a tinkerer', you especially need to remember you are not allowed to copy the tech you may receive from the Alliance in any way, for any reason. Us Earthlings aren't ready for this kind of power."

"I get it," Bob said. "It's the whole 'prime directive' all over again."

Burt grinned and nodded. "You got it in one. They don't call it that, but Gene Roddenberry had the right idea."

Jenny could see right away that these two were going to hit it off just fine. Kindred spirits, she could see that they could talk tech all day, if there was time for it. And, as if he had read her mind, Burt stood and, extending his hand to Bob, said, "I'd love to chat, but I have another assignment and they are anxious for me to complete and report. I'm sure we'll see each other again."

Bob shook his hand and replied with an almost childlike grin on his face, "I'll look forward to it."

As Burt made to go, Bob turned to Jenny. "I have to get back to my workshop. Thank you for this. Let's get together later today and plan when you can take me to meet with The Alliance Council. I'm not quite sure what I just let myself in for, but I have a feeling I'm going to be glad I did."

Jenny saw him out, then realized that her car was gone! About the time she was ready to dial 911, she got a text from Burt. "Mom, can I borrow the car? Sorry, I should have asked, but I really do need to get going on the Sam thing. I'll have it back in a couple hours."

Jenny shook her head and went back inside, where Tidbit appeared to be dozing in the window seat. She had no idea how Burt had taken the car without her keys or how he intended to find Sam, unless he was planning to find her at work, but she assumed he had ways of accomplishing things beyond anything she knew or understood.

She curled up in her reading chair and pulled out her tablet. The moment she invoked the LizzieAI, some of her tension eased. Though she had not known Lizzie in life, she now felt a connection with her aunt that fortified her resolve every time she connected with the AI. Whoever had programmed the AI had given her such personality and expression that it was easy sometimes to forget she wasn't just video chatting with the real thing.

"Good morning, Jenny. What can I help you with today?" LizzieAI's eyes were warm and caring and Jenny proceeded to pour out all of her worries, fears and frustrations with her new situation. LizzieAI listened intently, somehow managing to look into Jenny's eyes, as if she cared deeply for what she was saying. The sympathetic look on her face encouraged Jenny to get it all out. When at last she had poured everything out, tears were streaming down her face.

"You're having a rough time of it, I can see," LizzieAI said kindly. "But there is much hope in what I heard. First, you are not alone. You have companions who will support you and give you aid as you need it. Second, you are succeeding in moving forward in your training faster than anyone I know, even though it may feel woefully inadequate to you at the moment, with the burdens that have been placed upon you. Third, you have taken action exactly as you should have, as I would have done in the same circumstances.

In short, you have more resources than you may understand, and you have the spirit that is necessary for you to accomplish the tasks before you as well as any in your position might do. I am proud of you, Jenny. Always know that. I know I am an AI, a faint shadow of your aunt in life, but she programmed me to care for you as she did and to think of myself as her. As I have watched you grow, more than any of your cousins, I have been so impressed with your diligence and determination, as well as your kindness and imagination.

Don't shortchange yourself. It is easy to look back and criticize yourself with 'what-ifs' and 'should-have-dones'. Don't let that keep you from recognizing that no one expects you to do more than the best you are able to do, and, unless I am very much mistaken about you, you have what it takes to accomplish your tasks with honor. No one can ask more."

Jenny felt the tension go out of her. "But," she said plaintively, "It's all so big!" That had become the only word she could think of to describe the situation she had found herself in.

"Indeed, it is bigger than any mind can begin to comprehend. But there is an order to it and we are not helpless. You are not helpless. I know you are in conflict, with your friend under suspicion. The outcome may be that you don't see your friend again. If that happens, I won't lie to you. It is one of the most difficult aspects of the role of a Guardian or Gatekeeper. This is why it is important for you to focus on what you have, instead of what you wish you had."

Jenny nodded. She did have Tarafau, who had become like a big brother to her. And it looked like she would also be able to count on Bob's assistance, once he had been vetted by The Council. That was definitely a big plus. She yet had additional training to look forward to and so far, her training had been a very positive experience. She also had the other Guardians who had extended such a warm hand of fellowship to her.

But she couldn't write off Sam, not yet. They had shared so much over the years. She hoped fervently that Burt would come back with a report that her friend had just been in the wrong place at the wrong time and that would be that, but the footage from the security cameras still nagged at her mind and more particularly, her heart.

Chapter 19: Revelations

When Burt arrived that evening, he looked tired and disgruntled. "Your friend, Sam, didn't go to work today," he said, shaking his head. "I gathered from overheard conversations that she called in sick, but there was no one at her apartment. Nor was she at the coffee shop she frequents. Her car was not in her parking space, so I was pretty sure she wasn't on a walk."

Jenny turned this information over in her mind. It was unlike the Sam she thought she knew to call in sick without really being sick. Sam loved her job at the station and she willingly worked extra hours.

"Maybe she went to see a doctor or had some kind of appointment," she mused aloud.

"Perhaps. I hadn't considered that, but she has been gone all day and there are no lights on in her apartment this evening. Has she texted you or called you at all today?"

Jenny realized that she had not had any communication from Sam for over 24 hours, which was very unusual. Sam generally texted her with wry observations about her co-workers, ideas for pranks or funny memes they could both enjoy. And it was unusual for them not to speak at least once a day to catch up.

She shook her head. "I don't understand it. This isn't like her."

Burt looked grave. "Did you give her any indication you might suspect her at all?"

"No, I don't think so. I sent her photos of Puerto Rico while I was there, and we had messages going back and forth the whole time. I can't think of anything I might have said or done that would have made her think it was any different than any other time."

"Well, I'm not sure what is going on, but it doesn't look good. I get the feeling that she knows more than we even suspect. The last time you actually saw her was in the security footage, right?"

"Yes."

"So, let's retrace her steps from the footage and see if there are any clues as to what happened that afternoon."

When they went outside, Tidbit was stationed at his usual "happy place" at the edge of the koi pond. He looked up as they headed toward the storage shed.

"She walked all the way around the shed," Jenny said. "She appeared to be looking for a hidden opening."

As they slowly circled the building, Burt held his right hand out in front of him as if he had a flashlight, sweeping his hand up and down the building from the roof to the foundation and the grass surrounding it. He cocked his head, as if listening to something Jenny couldn't hear. She didn't voice the questions going through her head, as it was clear he was concentrating, and she didn't want to break that focus.

When they had circled all the way around the building, arriving at the locked door, he paused, looking at the door and especially the threshold of the door. He bent and slowly swept his hand back and forth, finally stopping above the center of the threshold.

"Stand back!" he commanded sharply. Jenny took several steps back. Burt touched his MDP and suddenly had what appeared to be a debit card in his hand which was flashing a red light. He pointed the card at the threshold of the door and there was a brilliant flash that appeared to be contained inside a transparent cube.

"It was trapped," Burt said in a flat voice. "Without the shield, had you tried to go through that door, the explosion would have killed you. Your Guardian key would have triggered it."

Jenny nodded, her heart in her throat. "Did Sam do this?"

Burt nodded. "I had noticed on the tape that she had returned briefly to the door before she left the second time. It only hit me today that she had a specific purpose to returning, not to just try the door a second time, that wouldn't have made any sense. The trap that was placed here was not apparent with the naked eye. Only my sensors would have detected it. It requires no installation, just drop it where you want it to be triggered. It was probably activated remotely as soon as she was out of sight of the cameras. I think she realized she was being watched.

There is little doubt in my mind that she is an agent of another dimension. Whether that is the Groga is impossible to tell without interviewing her. Your friend is not what she seems to be. I am so sorry."

Jenny let tears flow down her cheeks unnoticed. Sam had been her mainstay, her one constant, besides her family in her changing world. The counsel of the LizzieAI came back to her. Focus on what she had, not what she wished she had.

She wiped her face and realized Burt was awkwardly shifting from foot to foot, as if he wanted to leave until she got hold of herself.

"I'm ok," she said, "or I will be. What do we need to do?"

"Well, the first thing is that we need to get you out of here for awhile. Do you think Bob would be amenable to taking a field trip to see The Council right now? I will stay behind to see if I can catch up with Sam. And before I do, I will add a shield to this property. It will allow access to specific people, the gardener and the mailman, for example, but, if Sam shows up here again, it will set off an alarm and not allow her to leave. I am sure she is aware that her trap has been sprung and I am also sure she will show up here."

Jenny nodded and texted Bob, letting him know it was urgent and what she needed. Tidbit, who had been unusually silent now broke in with, "*Tell him to grab his bug-out bag. I know he keeps one by his front door.*"

Jenny looked at him curiously. "*Lizzie spent a lot of time with Bob when she was in the neighborhood. They were good friends and he always welcomed me right along with her,*" Tarafau sent.

That sounded like Bob, she thought.

After texting Bob, she went through her house quickly, putting things away and grabbing some changes of clothes. It occurred to her that she should keep a selection of clothing permanently in her MDP, so she wouldn't have to pack and unpack all of the time. By the time she had her stuff together, Bob was ringing the doorbell.

He was dressed as if going on safari, khaki shirt and pants, sturdy walking shoes and a knapsack slung across his shoulders. "I activated some special security precautions at my house and the workshop for while we're away," he announced. "Not sure if it will stand up to high tech, but it should at least notify the authorities if anyone tries to break in. I'm ready to go."

He put one hand on her shoulder, sympathy shining in his eyes. "Are you ok?"

"I will be. But we need to get out of here. Are you ready for an adventure?"

"Always," he said with a wide grin. "Are we bringing the cat?"

"Always," she returned, looking forward to his reaction when Tidbit revealed his secret.

"Then let's go."

He was puzzled when she led him to the closet door in the hallway. His eyes widened in amazement. After stepping through that impossible door, he stepped back outside the door, looked up and down the hallway, then stepped inside the gate office again.

"I'm pretty sure this isn't on the floor plan," he murmured, almost to himself. Tidbit had followed him in, nudging the door closed behind them. He looked from the cat to the cat bed. "So, now what?"

Jenny couldn't help but grin. "We're almost there. Follow me."

His eyes widened, but he followed her through the door into the gate room. He goggled, looking around himself down the long hallway that disappeared in the distance, and then he straightened his shoulders, nodded, as if to himself and followed her to the door. He whistled and cleared his throat.

"I always knew Lizzie was up to something interesting," he rasped. "All those years right across the street…" He trailed off, apparently at a lack for words to describe what was going on in his head.

"I get it. You can begin to see how hard it would be to keep all of this a secret, and we're not done yet. Are you ready?"

He straightened his shoulders, nodded and followed her through the door to The Alliance Council's dimension.

They stepped through the portal and she led him through the scanner. Suddenly there were three of them as Tarafau assumed his humanoid shape. Bob jumped. "Who are you?" he asked.

"Bob, meet Tarafau, otherwise known to you as Tidbit," Jenny said, barely suppressing a giggle at the wide-eyed look on his face. "It's a bit of a shock, I know, but there is so much more. You can begin to appreciate why we didn't sit you down and tell you everything. There is so much more than we could explain to you and doubtful that you would believe it, if we did. Are you okay?"

Bob shook his head and then said, as if contradicting himself, "Yeah, I'm fine. It's all just a little..." he trailed off again.

"Yeah, it is," agreed Jenny. So, let's go meet The Council, shall we?"

"Good to meet you," Bob said to Tarafau, looking up into his face and holding out his hand.

"And you," Tarafau said, shaking hands with Bob and showing his cat fangs in a welcoming smile.

They started down the path, to the city and, as they walked, Jenny told Bob about her first visit to The Alliance Council. Now, finally, here was someone who could relate to her feelings of overwhelm at all of these discoveries coming so quickly one upon another. Now finally she could share her awe of the responsibility that had been placed upon her, with someone who could truly understand how it felt to be exposed to so many alien concepts and experiences one after another.

The guards, this time, were different, albeit in the same uniforms as previously. They escorted them to a four passenger version of the automated taxi hover-cars, which Bob observed with wide eyes and twitching hands, as if he would have loved to take it apart and see how it worked. Off they hummed down the wide boulevard that let to the huge Council building.

It was gratifying to see Bob's head swiveling back and forth, trying to take it all in, the bustling foot traffic, the little hover cars weaving in and out without traffic lights and seemingly with no particular worries of an accident. Jenny realized this was like the proverbial "kid in the candy store" for Bob's inventive mind.

The vehicle came to a stop in front of the huge double doors, the guards beside them nodding to Jenny and Tarafau. *"We're here to see The Council."* Jenny told them. *"This is Bob. He has been invited to discuss matters with The Chief Councilor."*

"You were expected," One of the guards agreed in mindspeech, *"Go straight up to the private council room."*

Jenny saw the confused look on Bob's face and realized he didn't have the mindspeech ability, yet, and she didn't know how to give it to him. Miriha had done this for Jenny. One more thing she needed to learn how to do, apparently.

"To allow us to bypass the language problems, we use mindspeech," she explained. "I should be able to help you gain this ability once we have met with The Council. I haven't yet learned how to do that for other people. There is so much I have to learn, and I feel like there's no time."

She remembered that Miriha had simply touched her key, but Bob had no key. She had no idea how Miriha had done what she had done.

They went to the large elevator and Tarafau said, "Council Room". The elevator made its silent climb and opened onto the reception area. The receptionist greeted them with a smile. *"Gatekeeper, it's good to have you back. Please go in, they're waiting for you."*

Jenny realized that the guards who had put them into the hover-car had probably given The Council a heads up about their arrival. *"Thank you,"* she sent back and motioned for Bob to follow her into the council room.

As they entered, all three Chief Councilors were in their usual places on the dais at the front of the room.

"This is my neighbor Bob Reid," Jenny said, as they walked to the front of the room. *"He can't hear mindspeech, yet,"* she added hastily, lest they try to communicate unsuccessfully.

Ingot stood and stepped off of the dais, smiling, both hands extended in greeting. Bob took his hands. "*Welcome, Bob,*" he sent in mindspeech and once again Bob's eyebrows shot up. "Wow," he murmured aloud.

"*Simply think of who you wish to communicate with, and think your response,*" instructed Ingot.

"*Wow,*" sent Bob, "*This is amazing. Thank you.*"

Nodding, Ingot introduced Liliath and Myla. "*We have been briefed regarding the situation that brings you to us. We know that Lizzie would have never consciously revealed anything about the dimensional portals, and you are not at fault. What we do today is to determine the best course of action under the circumstances. Please be at ease, all of you.*" He gestured to the chairs that had been provided at the foot of the dais.

They seated themselves and Liliath spoke. "*Bob, we wish to know more about you and your thoughts about all of this.*" She gestured with a long clawed hand, as if the entire dimensional network were before them.

"*Begging pardon, ma'am,*" Bob replied, "*But I'm not really sure what 'all of this' is, if you take my meaning. I have a fairly good grasp of physics and science as they are a large part of my training, but I'm still getting my mind around the idea that there are truly other dimensions, other universes beyond anything we can see from Earth. It's a little mind-blowing.*"

All three councilors nodded their heads in understanding.

"*I observe, however, that you have a quick mind and a good basic understanding. Probably enough to be getting on with. Assuming we decide to, as I feel we must in this case, you will be fully trained in the mechanics of gate travel, or at least, as far as we understand it. You should know that much of it is still a mystery to us. We know it works, we use the tech necessary to access it all, but there is so much even our most advanced scientists do not yet understand,*" said Ingot.

"*I see,*" Bob said. Jenny could see he was now excited. Bob loved to know how things worked and now she could almost see the wheels turning in his head. "*So, to my understanding, within these portals, Jenny is now a Guardian and a Gatekeeper, both heavy responsibilities for a young adult, and she has accepted these responsibilities. She is very like her aunt in so many ways. She is very diligent and level-headed for her age, but she lacks experience.*

I notice you have provided a mentor for her," and he glanced meaningfully in Tarafau's direction.

Ingot nodded. "*Tarafau is her Guide. His function is to give her guidance in her responsibilities, to protect her from harm and to use his own vast experience to make up for that lack in her. All Guardians and Gatekeepers are given a Guide. We find it makes transitions easier and it allows the Guardian or Gatekeeper to focus on their mission.*

From time to time our Guardians and Gatekeepers also require additional aid. The reports we have received about your support and encouragement for Lizzie in the past and now for Jenny speak well for you. You have been vetted by Burt, our agent and I can see why."

He turned to Jenny. "*Jenny, what would you say to admitting Bob to the dimensional agent training, if he chooses to accept? He could be a great support to you, and he would accrue many benefits in the process.*"

Jenny bit her lip, thinking carefully. She had only known Bob a short while, and yet, she had a gut feeling that she could trust him implicitly. "*I agree. I believe he can be trusted to keep secrets. He does that already for the clients he creates for. He's smart, and he has been a good friend to me and to Lizzie before me. If he wants to do this, I say we give him a chance.*"

Bob looked at her, a mixture of gratitude and surprise in his eyes.

"*What would this entail?*" was all he asked.

"*You would be under the direction of the Council. Your assignments would vary, but for now your main responsibility would be to support Jenny during her training and in any needs she might have. You would be given a permanent token to give you access to the gateways. We would not ever ask you to do anything that violates your conscience or beliefs. You would be fully equipped with tech that you must promise not to attempt to duplicate or distribute on your planet, regardless of your good intentions. At some point you will be given access to technology that will allow you space travel to visit other species in your universe, but that is much later in your training.*

Do you agree to be faithful to this calling, to keep the secrets of the Dimensional Alliance and to serve faithfully to guard and protect the multiverse to the best of your ability? If you cannot, in conscience, swear to this, there is no harm done and the memories that have led you to this point will be erased. You will continue in your life with no feelings of loss or responsibility."

Bob considered this for only a moment, his face somber, then nodded. He held his hand up, his arm to the square, "*I so swear*," he said simply.

Chapter 20: Pick Up the Pace

They stayed there for three days, in which time both Bob and Jenny were training, counseling with the Council members and resting in their private suites in the building.

During that time, Jenny was glad to have the time to get to know both Bob and the Chief Councilors much better.

She was surprised to find that the draconic entity, Liliath was a gentle person with a mischievous sense of humor who was more than a little amused at the preconceived notions Jenny and Bob had about dragon-kind. She was exceptionally intelligent, often baffling even Bob with her lectures on the science of the dimensional portals. She admitted, again, that there was still much that even the most advanced cultures in the Dimensional Alliance did not completely understand.

Myla was also exceptionally intelligent, but of a more serious demeanor. He was a trained scientist, negotiator and scholar. He was fascinated about the variety of cultures on earth and had been a good friend with Lizzie, whose sense of adventure paired with a bright and inquiring mind was very attractive to the serious avian.

Ingot gave an appearance of gruffness, but when you got to know him, he turned out to be a sensitive soul, who listened carefully to everything that was said by all members of the group before making any pronouncements. He always continued discussions until every viewpoint had been heard and then reached a conclusion only after all had been taken under discussion.

It turned out that Bob knew way more than Jenny had suspected about the different theories about alternate timelines, contrasting dimensions and even theory about time travel. He had more than one PHD in physics, engineering and, of all things, social science. He was able to keep up his end of conversations that went way over Jenny's head, taking time to explain things to her in Earth terms when she got lost in the science that seemed to be beyond her. He was really good at breaking down complex concepts into terms that were easy to understand. His military service before college also gave him a fairly good grasp of tactics and strategy.

She commented to him that he would have been a great teacher. He was surprised, "Didn't you know? I thought I told you. I was an engineering professor at Cal Tech."

Jenny thought back on all the conversations they had had over the last few months. "Nope, but it fits."

Among other things, Bob received a necklace similar to Jenny's in function, but instead of a key, it was the infinity symbol. This designated him as an Agent of the Alliance. As an agent he had similar privileges as Jenny for the gateways, but he still needed to go through a Guardian or Gatekeeper to get access to the gate rooms. To his delight, he was also issued an MDP and a quarterstaff as well as having the Alliance apps installed on his cell phone. He was now included in Jenny and Tarafau's workouts. Jenny was surprised how quickly he picked it up.

"It's very similar to pugil stick fighting. It was part of basic training when I was in the military," he replied when Jenny asked him about it. "However, it hurts more when you make contact," he grimaced, rubbing his shin where Jenny had whacked him earlier. "You're pretty good at it yourself."

"I train every day with Tarafau," Jenny admitted. "I'm still learning."

"Well, Tarafau must be a great trainer," Bob said, wryly. "You sure surprised the heck out of me. I've got to learn not to 'go easy' on you." And he laughed.

Jenny giggled, despite herself. It had really helped her confidence to get in some good blows on both Tarafau and Bob that day.

The three days passed rapidly, with very little time to rest mentally or physically. Jenny's confidence was definitely shored up by all of the new information, training and the comradery she now felt with both the Chief Councilors and Bob.

She had been trained more thoroughly, alongside Bob on tactics using the MDP. She was taught how to transfer mindspeech to someone who did not have the ability, and she learned more about how her key worked as a universal pass to the entire dimensional network. She alone did not need another person to access every gateway in the network. It was politeness and protocol to access gates through the Guardian of that gate, but it was not necessary for her.

She also discovered that it was her responsibility to help Guardians choose their successors. Apparently, Miriha had been involved in her aunt's choice. And in the process of that training, she also learned that she had a method for observing potential future Guardians with tech that was painlessly inserted under the skin. This was why her aunt knew enough about her to choose her. As it turned out, she had not been the only one in her family that Lizzie had been observing, but evidently Lizzie had liked what she saw in Jenny.

One of the things she also began to realize was that the time would come for her to choose a successor. She would want to spend enough time with people outside the Earth Guardian council to allow herself access to potential candidates. Where she would find time for that, she had no idea.

Jenny wasn't sure what, in particular, her aunt had observed about her behavior that had helped her decide that Jenny would inherit the position, and she had mixed feelings about having been chosen. She was still filled with awe that her aunt had decided that she had the qualifications even for the Guardian position and she wondered, if Miriha had been able to choose her successor, if she would have decided to choose her, after all.

The time came for them to return to Earth. Ingot laid his hands on both of Bob's shoulders, looking directly up into his eyes. "*Your first assignment will be to protect The Gatekeeper and aid Burt in his search for Sam. She must be found and questioned. I have a really bad feeling about her. You now have the same tech as Burt, and he will instruct you more fully in their use. Keep a careful eye on Jenny and her house. It is doubtful that Sam will suspect you, as she could have no idea you have been received into The Alliance.*"

Bob nodded. "*I will see to it*," he said gravely. The determination in his dark eyes appeared rock hard. "*If it is within my power, no harm will come to Jenny. I owe that to her aunt. I am also glad to be able to call Jenny 'friend'.*"

He looked over at Jenny. "*I'll be your nosy neighbor. Maybe Burt and I can concoct some misinformation to send her way, if she doesn't suspect my involvement.*"

Ingot released Bob and stood before Tarafau. Unable to reach his shoulders, he looked seriously up into Tarafau's eyes. "*Take care, my friend. I know you to be a fierce warrior and a faithful companion. You are one of our most trustworthy and skilled Guides. I know you will continue to oversee the training of these with diligence and kindness. Know that our best wishes and hopes go with you.*"

He then turned to Jenny. "*Gatekeeper, you have come to your position unexpectedly and unprepared. You have shouldered a great burden with integrity and valor. I know we ask more of you than you ever expected to be responsible for. However, even in your youth, you have the qualities we value most in a Gatekeeper. Honesty, diligence, compassion and the willingness and humility to take on tasks greater than you think you are. If ever you need anything, you may text me.*"

Jenny goggled at him and he grinned. "*I have taken the liberty to add all three of us to your contacts on the dimensional aspect of your phone,*" he said with a smile. "*I hope you don't mind.*" And his shoulders shook with suppressed laughter.

Jenny threw her arms around him, surprising him only for a moment. He hugged her back with feeling then drew back and smiled up at her. "*Thank you, Jenny,*" he said gently.

Jenny then went to Myla and Liliath and hugged each in turn. Hugging a dragon…who knew they gave great, and gentle, hugs?

Her eyes now tearing up, she put one arm through Tarafau's and the other through Bob's and like Dorothy, she started down a road that she never expected to follow, with a faithful companion on either side.

Chapter 21: Cloak and Dagger

Jenny realized when she got up that morning that she felt safer and more like she was in a good place than she had felt in a long time. She had been encouraged by The Council to continue her training with the other Guardians, while Burt and Bob continued to search out the elusive Sam. She had no texts or phone calls waiting when she got home. It was clear that Sam knew that she knew. This made Jenny so sad, but she also felt more than a little angry that Sam had fooled her so very thoroughly.

All those years in college, hanging out, whining about being overburdened with homework, helping one another prepare for exams and pop quizzes professors were so fond of, and she had never had a single clue that Sam wasn't exactly what she thought she was.

"Don't let it make you cynical," Bob had advised her. "That's one thing about your aunt. She knew about the world and how not everything or everyone were like they seemed, but when it came down to it, she still found optimism, somehow, to treat every person she met as if they were as honorable, kind and caring as she was. We can all learn a lot from that."

She shrugged into her workout clothes and texted Bob that she was ready and to meet her in the workout room. She had made a point the night before to give him a quick walkthrough of the facilities. She had also given him her spare key to the house and shed. If she was going to need to trust him, she was going to trust him all the way.

To her surprise, he was already there, doing his warm ups. She remembered she had keyed the gate office to him and had given him permissions that included the workout room and the Alliance gateway. She and Tarafau joined him.

First mental workout, then quarterstaff. The graceful coordinated moves of the body and staff in the workout routine was much like a dance. It was a soothing way to get started on her day. As she moved through her paces, she allowed her mind to wander over the last few days. She realized that it was the best she had felt in a long time.

They took turns pairing off with the quarterstaff. They cheered one another on, occasionally making wry remarks about a particularly poorly executed move, without being critical. At the end, they were all sweating happily.

They took out time for showers and joined one another on the patio for a green drink. Tidbit dabbled happily at the koi as he lay at the edge of the pond. Jenny imagined he might have been too tired, after their workout, to chase butterflies.

They had only been chatting for a few moments when Burt showed up, coming through the garden gate.

"I've found her," he said without pausing for greetings. "She is holed up in a cabin near Arrowhead. There are a number of somewhat shifty types coming in and out. She does have wi-fi, however and she is using her cell phone. I put a tag on it and now we can track her when she decides to come out for any reason. She is having groceries and other things delivered. I may be able to find a way in by taking advantage of that little loophole."

Jenny gritted her teeth. She knew the little cabin well. She and the other girls in their hiking club had stayed there more than once, looking forward to a good hike and chatting and laughing together. Such good times…now tainted with Sam's betrayal.

"*So, what do we do next?*" Tidbit sent.

Bob started in surprised and then grinned and pointed at each of them. "*You two have been talking behind my back all this time, haven't you?*"

"*Indeed,*" Tidbit sent, with a mental feeling of a wicked grin. "*Such interesting conversations about all of your foibles.*"

"*Foibles?!*" Bob sent back. "*You're a cat. You chase butterflies and annoy the koi, not to mention terrorizing Cinder. You've got no room for comparison, Kitty. Foibles…huh!*"

Jenny couldn't help but laugh and Burt guffawed. "*Mindspeech can be a convenient thing,*" he added with a conspiratorial wink.

Tidbit repeated implacably, "*So, what do we do next?*"

Burt sobered up quickly. "*We stalk her carefully. Now that I have Bob to help, I think we can pull off a bit of subterfuge. I think the way in is through the delivery, like I said. I think between the two of us we can create a ruse that will work to get us into the cabin. Then I will show you how we extract information without damaging a person and without letting them know we were ever there. Let's leave these two to their breakfast and fish watching and you and I can work out the details.*"

They sauntered out through the back gate, evidently to have their conversation at Bob's place. Jenny picked up their empty glasses and headed into the kitchen, leaving Tidbit to his fascinating occupation.

She found it incredible that the big, strong, intelligent man could find such enjoyment in something so simple as fish or butterflies. Evidently neither existed in his home dimension. She often wondered about his long-lived species and what his life must have been like before he became a Guide for the Alliance. Up until now she hadn't had the courage to ask him about it. She made up her mind to have that conversation soon. By now she realized that there was nothing she couldn't discuss with Tarafau.

She cleaned up the glasses and put them away, then went into the living room with the idea she might take a break with that book she'd been trying to get to.

But as she sat down in her reading chair, book in hand, she heard a soft but emphatic mind-send from Tidbit. "***Jenny…***"

What he had been about to say, she never found out.

She dropped her book on the table and ran out to the garden. Tarafau lay at the edge of the pool as before, except he wasn't looking at the koi. He lay there as if taking a nap, the tip of his tail trailing in the water, a fish swimming up to it curiously. She ran up to him and looking down on him realized his eyes were indeed closed. She bent to rouse him and then saw stars, felt a sharp pain in the back of her neck at the same time. Then she saw nothing at all.

She awoke in darkness, not a speck of light. She tried to stand, but then realized she was tied to something, she thought it was a hard-backed wooden chair by the feel of it. Her wrists were painfully tied behind her and each ankle was tied to a chair leg. She felt dizzy, even sitting there, and her head hurt like blue blazes, as her dad would say. Her mouth was not bound, so she attempted to call out. "Hello? Hello!!! Is anybody there?"

Suddenly she realized that calling out might not be the best idea. Her captor or captors (she had a strong suspicion who that might be.) did not seem to be in evidence. Perhaps she could find a way to wriggle out of her bonds.

But a door opened before her, letting in a painfully bright ray of light. "Ah," purred Sam's voice, a note of satisfaction and smugness in it. "So, you're awake. Good. Looks like your bully boys fell for my ruse. I gave them what they were looking for, a mysterious hideout, suspicious types going in and out, groceries being delivered, my cell phone sending signals off and on. I was never there. It's an empty box, they're watching.

I may have injured your cat, I'm afraid. Perhaps fatally. I couldn't let him spoil my surprise."

She held her hands up in mock enthusiasm. "**SURPRISE**!"

Her shout sent spike-like pains through Jenny's sore head.

Jenny shook her head gently, not attempting to hide the disappointment and disdain from her face.

"Ah, I see you don't like my surprise. It's OK, I'll bear up under the grief."

She flipped the light switch and closed the door.

Jenny felt a shiver run down her back when she realized that Sam looked very different and not in a good way. Her auburn hair had been dyed black, or was that her natural color? She had a piercing on her lip and she was wearing something that looked like a black sorcerer's robe, belted with a chain of black metal. Sam's eyes were made up with black eyeliner and dark grey eyeshadow which made her eyes look sunken and dark. Even the irises of her eyes, which should have been green, were black. Her skin had a blue-grey tint to it.

"You're not from around here, are you?" Jenny asked, hoping her tone sounded flippant and didn't reflect the terror rising in her heart.

"Got it in one," Sam leered. "You always were pretty quick on the uptake. I'm sure you've figured out that we can't be besties anymore. My boss wouldn't like it much."

"You mean the executive producer at the station?" Jenny snapped back.

Sam shook her head. "Well, my real boss is more of an executer than an executive, but I don't think you really want to know about that, now, do you?"

Jenny clamped her mouth shut, refusing to be drawn into the taunt.

"Well, we shall see, what we shall see. I'm on a bit of a timetable and I don't have any time to waste with pleasantries." Abruptly she slapped Jenny's face so hard it made her already sore head ring like a gong. "That's for bringing in the troops," she said with a scowl. "I had this all worked out. I was going to worm my way into taking you to the airport on a regular basis and then just carry you off. But your new buddies put a kibosh to that.

So, I lured your A-team out to my cabin and here we are. You can be a really high-maintenance friend, you know?"

Jenny sat there in stony silence. She was sure, if anger expressed itself in lasers coming out of your eyes, Sam would have been fried where she stood. And then she realized, Sam was wrong. The A-Team wasn't at Sam's cabin. They were across the street at Bob's house.

"So, let's begin. You should know by now that I am not a very patient person. So, this is how this will go down. I ask questions. You answer questions. If I have to wait for an answer, I have an incentivizer." She pulled a small taser out of a pocket in her robe. "If you still refuse to answer, I have another incentivizer." She drew out a poniard from a sheath hanging from her chain belt.

"Are we clear?"

Jenny just sat there, praying she could be strong, knowing it was going to be a very long day, if she survived it.

"Hmmm, obviously not. Here's a taster." She applied the taser to Jenny's right leg, just inside her thigh.

Every nerve in her body hummed in pain. Her brain felt like it would explode. When Sam finally lifted the taser away from her skin, Jenny just sat there shaking and panting. A cold sweat had broken out on her skin and she felt like someone had grilled her eyeballs.

"OK, let's try it again. Are we clear?"

Jenny clamped her mouth shut. She knew this was a simple question that she could afford to answer, but she had heard that interrogators usually started with non-essential questions to get their captives used to answering. She was not going to fall into that trap.

"Well, who woulda thunk?" Sam said, her eyes wide in mock surprise. The whites around the black irises made her look like a cartoon villain. "Little Jenny has a backbone after all. But, tut, tut, we cannot allow this. Perhaps we should try something else."

She cradled the hilt of the poniard almost tenderly in her hand and pricked one finger, holding it out so Jenny could see it bleeding. She let the blood from the tiny prick drip onto Jenny's face. She grinned and licked the blood from her finger. "I've always wondered why you never got a tattoo when I went to get my sweet spider. I admit, I'm not much of an artist, but perhaps a butterfly?"

She bent over Jenny's exposed forearm. "I'd suggest you hold still. I'd hate to mess it up. It might hurt, just a little. Let's start with the antennae."

She held the poniard like a paint brush, cutting a fine line about an inch long on her arm.

Jenny didn't even care that tears were sliding down her face. She remembered her breathing exercises. In 2,3,4,5; Out 2,3,4,5,6; In 2,3,4,5,6,7…and as she breathed her patterns, she loosened each muscle in her body one at a time starting at her toes. She began to slide into that state outside of her conscious mind. The pain was still there, but it somehow felt far away.

"And another," said Sam, relishing the pain she was causing. Her voice was almost a caress. "Every butterfly needs two antennae."

Blood was now dripping from her arm onto the floor. Sam ignored it. "You have plenty of canvas for me to draw on. This is kinda fun. I almost hope you hold out for a long time."

She continued describing her bloody art. "Now the head, and the head needs two eyes. A nice long body to support some large wings." She paused as she drew and described each part of the butterfly until she finished that part and then continued through the wings, the design on the wings and each tiny leg. It seemed to go on for hours, but within the vortex of her breathing and focusing on each miniscule muscle, one at a time, she could almost ignore it.

By the time Sam finished and stepped back to admire her handywork, the blood was falling with an audible plop, plop, plop as it hit the floor.

Jenny started to hope that maybe she would bleed to death before Sam could get more artistic.

"So, are we feeling more cooperative?"

Flinching Jenny shook her head and then realized, to her chagrin, that this was an answer.

Sam smiled as if she had done something amazing.

"Very good. That wasn't so hard, was it?"

Jenny held her neck rigid, so her body wouldn't betray her. She only ground her teeth in an effort to keep her mouth closed and then returned to her breathing, now focusing on her jaw and cheek and neck muscles.

"Still haven't learned our lesson? What a shame. Let's see, what shall I draw next? Maybe a…" Sam began, but she never finished that sentence. Into the room burst Burt and Bob, quarterstaffs whirling.

Sam spun to face them and slipped in the puddle of blood at her feet. Burt hit her in the gut with the end of his staff and Bob followed it up with a sharp rap on the back of her head. Sam collapsed in a heap on the blood-slicked floor.

Burt quickly snapped handcuffs on Sam's wrists while Bob cut the bonds from Jenny's wrists and ankles with the same poniard that Sam had dropped when she collapsed.

Neither said a word. Burt threw Sam over his shoulder with a grunt and Bob slung Jenny on his shoulders like a backpack, her arms as straps. He held onto her, his hands gripping the bleeding cuts like a tourniquet. They rushed her outside to Bob's waiting car, throwing Sam into the trunk with a dull thud. Bob put Jenny gently into the backseat and sat next to her, while Burt drove. Bob pulled a first aid kit out of his MDP and proceeded to clean the wounds and put pressure on it with a large pad of gauze. "They're superficial cuts, even though they are bleeding freely. They may leave scars, though. Do you want us to take you to the emergency room?"

Jenny shook her head. "We need to get Sam to The Council, right now. The healers there can take a look at it."

Burt looked over his shoulder. "We found Tidbit and were able to rouse him. I think he'll be ok. The cell phone was a red herring. But what she didn't know is that I had placed a little beacon on her car. When we went back to the house to tell you our plan, you were gone, the cat was knocked out and the beacon was going off. We stopped to revive Tidbit and left him in your office in his comfy bed. We'll retrieve him on the way to the gate and take him to see the healer's as well."

"Can you try not to kill my car while you're at it?" Bob said querulously. "The paint job is new, and this is a classic."

Burt grinned. "Worry not, old guy. I've got this."

Bob moaned. "That's what I'm afraid of."

Suddenly Jenny realized they were putting on a show for her benefit, trying to keep her mind off of what had just happened, and she realized she loved them for it.

After zooming along back roads for what seemed like hours, they finally pulled into her driveway.

"I can walk," insisted Jenny, but as she tried to rise from her seat onto the driveway, she nearly passed out.

"I've got you," said Bob and Burt simultaneously. So, she looped her arms into each extended elbow and they walked her into the house, installed her on a dining room chair, closest to the door in the hall. They both rushed back out and came back in, carrying a still unconscious Sam between them.

"Let's do this," Burt said, grunting as Bob passed Sam to him.

Bob grabbed Jenny's arm and helped her up. "I've sent ahead," Burt said, huffing slightly with Sam's gangly weight. "They'll be waiting for us at the gate with re-enforcements. You won't have to walk."

As they passed through the office door, she saw Tidbit curled up in his comfy cat bed, his eyes shut. "Tidbit?" she sent, tentatively. He didn't stir. She saw he was breathing, his belly rising and falling, but he was obviously unconscious.

Bob hung the sleeping cat gently over his shoulders, his front paws hanging on one side of his neck and his back paws hanging on the other. The usually expressive tail hung limply.

"Heavens above," Bob exclaimed. "He's heavy! No more kitty treats for you, my boy."

Just as Burt had said, as they stepped through the gate, several guards were waiting with a larger version of the hover car. But when they started through the scanner a loud alarm went off.

"Oops," said Bob sheepishly and held out Sam's knife. "*I brought it as evidence.*"

The guard took it gingerly in a gloved hand. "*I'll process it, thanks.*" One of the other guards had pushed a button on his belt and the wailing of the alarm cut off.

Her ears still ringing, Jenny was escorted to a seat in the hover-car and slumped in the seat, feeling bad that she was getting blood on the pristine interior of the car.

They went down the hill to the city, but instead of parking in front of the huge double doors, they pulled past into what was apparently a parking garage, but instead of parking, they drove the vehicle into an even larger elevator than the one in the lobby.

"*We have instructions,*" said one of the guards briskly. "*We're not to make a public scene of this. Violence is rare in this city and we don't want to start a panic.*"

"*We're taking you into the guard station where we will incarcerate your friend here,*" he said pointing with a thumb over his shoulder, "*and where you will be transferred to the healer's center. After that, you will be taken to the Council room, where the Councilors will be waiting for you.*"

The elevator door slid open into a sterile looking space. A guard looked into the large room through a window that Jenny imagined, from watching cop shows as a kid, was bullet proof glass.

A wheelchair was waiting for her. She protested, but was installed into it anyway. "*You go,*" said Burt to Bob and the guards, "*we've got this.*" He placed Tidbit on her lap. Wait…Tidbit? What?

"*Why didn't he change?*" She had been too worried and dazed to realize that Tidbit had not transformed when they went through the gate.

"*I don't think he can do it when he's unconscious,*" Burt replied, concern etched on his face. "*I hope the old guy survives this. He owes me forty bucks.*" Jenny recognized it as a joke, if a weak one.

"*I'll take Jenny, to the healer's infirmary,*" Burt instructed Bob. "*Please stay here to answer questions. I'll be back as soon as I can.*"

Bob nodded, all business, and Burt pushed the chair out into the hallway.

The corridors seemed to fly by, Burt's long legs moving them along nearly at a run. Jenny clutched at Tidbit, feeling his steady breathing, but not even a slit of white peeked out from his eyelids. "*Please don't leave me,*" she pleaded mentally, focusing the sending directly to the cat and only him.

The bandage on her arm was soaked through, but she could no longer feel the pain. Her only thought, her only concern was the cat seemingly sleeping peacefully on her lap.

Onto and elevator and then within what seemed like something just short of eternity, the doors slid open. "Infirmary," said the disembodied voice.

There were healers waiting for them as they were wheeled off of the elevator.

Two of them whisked Tidbit out of her arms and two more wheeled her briskly into a curtained area. It appeared to Jenny to be a typical emergency room, a bed in the center of the curtained off space, some machinery that looked similar to machines she had seen in Earth hospital rooms and everything was white and sterile.

Jenny sighed.

"It's ok," said one of the healers. *"You're safe. We'll take care of you and Tarafau."*

Safe, thought Jenny, wistfully. It probably wasn't true, but it would do for now.

Chapter 22: Queen of the Groga

Jenny walked into the Council room, in clean clothes and a clean, white bandage on her arm. Her head barely hurt now, but she was assured that she didn't have a concussion and the pain would stop eventually. Tarafau was Tarafau again, but he did have a concussion and was ensconced in a very large bed with many pillows, a bandage around his head and an ice pack strapped to that. He was a little muzzy, but said he wasn't in any pain and wanted to get out of bed. The healer had put a guard in his room, as much to keep him company as to guard him.

Jenny felt relieved and saddened at the same time. Happy that he would recover, but it hurt to see him helpless and in pain, regardless of the brave front he put up.

Myla met her at the door, his arms outstretched to embrace her. *"We're so glad you and Tarafau are safe,"* he sent, cooing audibly as he was wont to do.

The other two were seated on the dais, looking into one another's eyes, obviously in the midst of a conversation. They turned, however, as Jenny walked to the front of the room.

"Welcome, Gatekeeper," said Liliath formally. *"Our commendations and commiserations on your ordeal and the way you handled it. Lizzie made a splendid choice."*

Ingot nodded; his brows furrowed in concern. *"What do the healers say?"*

"Tarafau will recover and my injuries are minor," Jenny replied.

"Not so minor," Ingot said. *"I heard you will bear scars for the rest of your life. The healer's say that something on that blade has insured it."*

"I hope I do carry them, as a reminder that I can do hard things. And Tidbit loves butterflies."

Ingot nodded, looking into her eyes. *"You carry also the gratitude of the entire Alliance. You have proven yourself worthy of your title."*

"All I did was keep my mouth shut. Burt and Bob were the ones who should be praised. They found me and rescued me and captured the spy. She is no Earthling, Ingot. I don't know where she comes from."

"You are right, Jenny. She is a Fleistian. They call her the Queen of the Groga, but she has no Groga blood, that we can tell. She is pure evil and has proven this over the course of many years. She institutes the raids and tortures and enslaves those they capture. She also has certain shape-changing abilities, which is why she was able to blend in so well on Earth.

You cannot be faulted for not recognizing her. We didn't and we have known of her for a very long time. It wasn't until she transformed into her regular appearance, we realized what she was. She has been well-trained and has scores more years of experience than you've been alive."

"That may be, but she is about to find out that Earthlings have a very important trait. We are survivors and we aren't very good at being pushed around. When all is said and done, we are more than we seem as well. I won't stand for her letting the Groga on my planet or anywhere in my universe, if I have anything to say about it."

Ingot grinned, but then sobered and shook his head.

"Contrary to what we previously thought, I am afraid they are already there. We must discover a way to locate them and purge Earth of their influence. We must discover if they have moved beyond the boundaries of Earth, into farther reaches of your universe. This isn't finished. It is only beginning. Until we have determined the extent of their influence, we may not rest or feel secure. I am sorry, but this is truth."

Jenny sighed, both grateful for his truthfulness and feeling unworthy of his praise. *"So, what are our next steps? I know she had some minions hanging about that cabin, so there are at least a few of them still there. And my first question is, how in the heck did they get there? I met Sam nearly 6 years ago at school. So, they may have been there at least that long. Miriha's first words to us, when we got to her was 'They're back,' which means they're not a new threat and at some point, they have gotten access to the network. This means the network is compromised. This means we're all in danger.*

My second question is, what can we do about it? How did you defeat them before?"

Ingot hung his head and Myla and Liliath shook their heads almost in unison.

"*We didn't,*" Liliath sent so softly in her mind that Jenny almost didn't catch it. "*We beat them back and nearly destroyed them, but we never defeated them. They stopped attacking us, because we outnumbered them and outclassed them in weaponry and tactics. When they stopped raiding, we stopped pursuing them. We had the best of intentions, but it was a mistake.*"

"*They are guerilla fighters, strictly hit and run,*" Myla put in. "*They are careful to sneak in, overwhelm their prey in a swift and unexpected attack and then they vanish with their captives before anyone can do anything about it, nor do they leave any trace to tell us where they might have gone.*"

"So, we're just gonna sit here and take it?" Jenny knew she was probably being unreasonable, and she hated the hurt she saw in their eyes. That didn't change the fact that she really needed some answers and for some reason she had thought she would find them all here.

"*No, Jenny, we are not only not going to sit here and take it, as you say, but we are mobilizing every agent we have in the dimensions that have been raided. This includes those on Earth. There will be a meeting at Sanglarka tomorrow, to organize your resources to begin to search for the Groga on Earth and to neutralize them. You will be in charge of the meeting and Tarafau will advise you as you go.*"

He saw the hope for Tarafau in Jenny's eyes and nodded. "*Our healers say he will be able to attend the meetings and will be able to help organize your effort. He must, however, not do anything physically strenuous for at least a couple weeks.*"

Jenny breathed out a sigh of relief. At least one thing was going right. She had been so afraid that Sam had killed her Guide. As Tidbit, he was very vulnerable, even though he was scary when he was in battle mode, as Cinder had discovered. As Tarafau he was formidable. Sam had attacked him when he was helpless, something, evidently that she was good at. "Sneaky Sam," she thought to herself.

As if it was a cue, suddenly an alarm blasted through the building. The klaxon was loud, and a bright light filled the room. It was a see-through read out that hovered in the air before them. Jenny got the feeling that each person saw the screen as if it centered on them and in their own language. "Subject escaped. Lockdown in progress." The message flashed in red letters on a light green background.

Ingot waved his hand and the image faded and the alarm ceased.

"Be seated, all. We can do nothing for the moment until security clears the building."

"Does this mean what I think it means?"

Ingot nodded morosely. *"Engoza has escaped."*

"Engoza?"

"You know her as Sam. Her real name, or the name she goes by, is Engoza. It translates as 'knife of death'. I doubt it is the name she was born with, but anything is possible, I suppose."

"I will never dignify her by calling her by that name. From now on, to me, she is 'Sneaky Sam'. She would hate that and that's just fine with me." She folded her arms in front of her chest, hugging that thought to her.

"So, she has escaped? Even with all of the security you have in this place? How is that possible?"

"We won't know for sure until the report from the security team," replied Ingot. *"I myself cannot imagine how this could have happened. In over a century, nothing like this has ever occurred."*

Liliath was visibly agitated. Up until now, Jenny had only ever seen the kind and stately side of her draconic nature. But now she could see how the legends of fierce and terrible dragons must have come about. The slitted pupils of her reptilian eyes had narrowed, her nostrils flared, and her teeth were bared in a snarl that made Jenny want to turn and run. She hissed audibly and turned to Ingot. *"We can no longer tolerate this. With Engoza free and the latest raids, it is like before. There is much more to this than it appears, and we must eliminate this threat once and for all."*

She then turned to Jenny and appeared to be forcing herself to calm. *"Jenny, there is no way for you to know how serious this is. On your world there have been horrific battles that have engaged your entire planet. Think of that same intensity of death and destruction across worlds, galaxies and universes. Think of the devastation that can occur when a malignant force such as the Groga have access to the network of gateways to unlimited dimensions. Even a relatively small force can wreak havoc and despair beyond our imagining, if their access is not revoked.*

Like your predecessor, you are in fearful danger. For whatever reason, you were targeted long before Lizzie made the final choice to put you in the position of Guardian. The fact that you attracted the attention of Engoza, as you did, is troubling. It means they have access to intelligence that we do not. It means this is much bigger than last time.

Originally, the Groga stumbled upon the network by chance at a gateway on their world that we had not yet established in the network. When we discovered this, through much sacrifice on the part of our agents and after much destruction on several worlds, we searched out the gates on that planet, in that dimension and closed them. It appears we missed a gateway and they have obviously searched it out. We know they are no longer on their original planet.

More than that, they have been careful this time to set up strategies and tactics that are very much unlike them. In the past they only took slaves and things of value, like jewels and precious metals. Now their target seems to be every bit of tech they can acquire and especially any tech related to the gate network.

I fear they have joined forces with a more devious race and therein lies our problem. Somehow, they may have access from a point that we do not know and that is not in our known network of gateways. Who knows what technology they may have access to that they did not have before? This is a new war, with new variables, and we cannot rest until we have destroyed their access permanently."

By the time she finished this explanation, Liliath seemed to have herself back under control, but a small wisp of dark smoke dribbled out of one nostril, which she waved away.

Myla nodded. "*We fear for you and the dimensions in the Alliance. At this time your Earth is in danger such as it has never experienced. If we are unable to locate and destroy the access of the Groga and whatever or whomever is aiding them, the entire network is compromised, and we may have no choice but to bring the governments of Earth into the Alliance, to protect themselves. As The Gatekeeper, it will become your responsibility to see to this, if it becomes necessary.*"

Jenny sat there in shock. It had all seemed an adventure until Sam and the Groga had been thrown into the mix. All of those dimensions to learn about and explore, everything she was learning and her kind reception into the Alliance as a Guardian. But since Miriha's death, it had escalated into a nightmare from which she couldn't awake. She couldn't go back to her comfortable little life. She couldn't view the world from her safe space online. The beautiful little garden with its herbs and butterflies and koi pond was no longer any kind of refuge.

There was nowhere to run or hide and these people and all of the people of the dimensions were counting on her, a twenty-something ghost-writer, to save them from ultimate evil. How insane was that?

But instead of voicing her fear, she said, "*What must I do?*"

Ingot's warm smile was as good as a hug. "*For now, you need to wait for the building to clear. Then we will prepare Tarafau to travel back to your gateway. We have already sent agents through to Earth to aid Burt and Bob. Bob has agreed to make his home headquarters for the agents there. The other Guardians have been notified and they will be in touch. It is vital that your training continue. It is also vital that you be protected. Therefore, we will continue as we have already decided.*"

At this point, another sound, less urgent, rang out. The transparent screen appeared again. "All Clear," it stated and then disappeared.

Almost immediately after that, two of the security squad marched into the Council room.

"*There is no trace of her, Councilors,*" the stern-faced guard reported. "We did a thorough search of the building by scan and room by room. She is no longer on the premises."

"*What happened? How did she escape?*" Jenny demanded, only realizing after she spoke that it wasn't her place to question him.

Ingot looked at her meaningfully and turned to the guard expectantly.

"*We don't know. We had visuals on her, both electronically and through the glass window to her cell. One moment she was there and the next she was not. We rushed inside and searched thoroughly then set the alarm and searched the building.*"

"*I think you will find, when you review the recording, that she was still in the cell when you searched it,*" inserted Myla dryly. "*We should have remembered that one of the abilities of the Fleistians is camouflage. Like the chameleons of Earth, they have an ability to blend into the background of their surroundings so well that they can seem to disappear. When you opened the door to search the cell, you allowed her to escape.*"

Both guards hung their heads, the shame apparent on their faces.

"*You could not have known,*" Ingot said. "*The fault lies with us. We should have remembered. Be at ease.*"

The guards nodded almost in unison.

Ingot said briskly, "*We cannot un-ring the bell. We can only move forward. Assemble the guards in the situation room and we will be down shortly. We must put some new security measures into place.*"

This was an obvious dismissal. The guards turned on their heels as one and marched back out of the room.

"*Now we will go see to Tarafau. Please come with us.*" Ingot led the way out of the Council room and onto the elevator. Crammed in there with the dragon, Jenny could now appreciate the size of the elevator, compared to the little boxes on earth. She could feel Liliath's breath on the back of her neck and had a flashback of reading The Hobbit as a kid. A phrase her mom had often said came to her mind, "Do not meddle in the affairs of dragons, because you are crunchy and taste good with ketchup."

She shook her head, this was no proper time for such thoughts, but it did make her smile.

They got off on the infirmary level. The stark whiteness was relieved somewhat by the dimmed lighting. A healer approached them and reached out a hand to Myla. She turned to the group.

"*Tarafau will be well. His concussion was milder than we first expected. It appears that his kind, partly due to their shape-changing abilities, have an automatic mechanism in their physiology that shuts them down when a certain amount of damage is done to the cranium and allows the body to begin repairs. He will still need to limit physical activity. No sparring or running or any activity that will jar his head. He does not like it but has agreed to cooperate.*"

Jenny's anxiety eased, just a little. She could no longer imagine her life without Tarafau. She knew she would never be able to complete her tasks and do her job without him to guide her and to be her friend.

"*Thank you, healer,*" Jenny said, grasping the healer's long fingered hands in her own. "*There is no way to express my gratitude.*"

"*We all have learned to love Tarafau over the years. This is not his first visit to my infirmary. Hard-headed old cat.*"

They entered Tarafau's room, where he was seated on the edge of the bed, a dressing wound around his head.

"*What happens to the dressings when we return to Earth?*" Jenny asked.

"*They will continue to do their job,*" replied the healer. "*We really don't understand the science completely. When he is bandaged in this form, the bandages continue to work, even though you can't see them on the cat. He will appear to be uninjured in that form. While you are in Sanglarka, have Arvid continue to treat him. I will forward him instructions.*"

"*Are you ready to go home?*" Jenny asked him tentatively.

"*Lead the way*," agreed Tarafau grimly, flexing his fists. "*We have work to do.*"

Chapter 23: A Shot in the Dark

The moment they stepped over the threshold of the gate into her study, Jenny knew something was wrong. She didn't know exactly why. Then she realized the skin surrounding her key was tingling. This had never happened before. She unconsciously picked up Tidbit, cradling him protectively.

Bob and Burt looked at her curiously, frozen in place, obviously concerned. "What's up?" said Bob, his voice sounding oddly in her ears as it always did after spending some time using mindspeech exclusively.

"I'm not sure," Jenny replied softly. "Something isn't right. My key is tingling."

Burt went around her, putting his hand on the door handle. "It's warm, but not hot. Don't follow me until I give the all clear."

Jenny nodded, and Burt turned the handle. The acrid smell of smoke and…was that gunpowder?...filled the room. Burt stepped through quietly and they all stood rock still where he had left them. In a moment he called out, "We're clear, but you aren't going to like it."

As Jenny stepped into the hallway the impact of just how real her danger was, hit her like a thrown brick. The area of the door to the gateways was blackened, as if someone had set off a small bomb. The floor was littered with ceiling tiles and the hall light was shattered. There was evidence of impacts, as if someone had tried to use a hammer to get through the wall.

As she moved into her living room, she vaguely noticed her books strewn across the floor, the stuffing of her reading chair pulled out down to the frame of the chair. Her china from her hutch was in pieces all over the dining room floor. The doors to her kitchen cupboards had been torn from the cabinet and a mixed odor of spices and decaying food wafted up from the floor.

She ran to the office and her computer was gone and all of her paper files were strewn as if someone had been looking for something.

In her bedroom it was the same. Her belongings had been trashed.

"The shed!" she cried and, with Tidbit still in her arms, she ran as quickly as she could through the shards of broken china out through the French doors that barely hung cockeyed on their wrenched hinges.

Like the gateroom door, there were obvious signs of an attempt to force entry, but the door remained locked and undamaged. Jenny heaved a sigh of relief. "I don't know what's in there that they could possibly want, but evidently Aunt Lizzie did a good job of protecting it."

She turned to her team. "I need some agents to come in and clean this up while we're at Sanglarka. We don't have time for it now. I wonder how they did all of this without someone calling the cops. It must have made a lot of noise."

Then she realized why they had taken the computer. They thought her security footage was stored there. She pulled out her phone. When they had altered the tech inside it, they had also installed an app that gave her unlimited cloud storage off world. Apparently, according to her training, they had hidden a tiny satellite among the space debris in Earth's orbit. Jenny had been sending the footage from Aunt Lizzie's security system into that cloud.

She brought up the security app. She watched in horror as two burly men smashed in the French doors with large hammers. Hadn't the neighbors heard?

"How could they have done this without attracting attention?" she asked the two silent men gathered around her.

"Silence shield. They must have extended a silence shield over the property. It's pretty common tech among the less honest of the dimensions. Most merchants on gate worlds know to use counter-tech against it, but I don't imagine Lizzie ever thought to need it."

Jenny continued to watch as these men went from room to room, ravaging her belongings. They didn't even appear to be looking for anything. However, they did search the walls carefully, probably looking for an opening into the gate room. Which was proved out after they had torn the bathroom apart, looking into the tank on the back of the toilet, throwing everything out of the medicine cabinet and the drawers and even unrolling the toilet paper roll.

As they moved toward the bedroom, they stopped in the hallway as if listening for something. One of them pulled out some kind of device and blasted exactly at the point where the invisible door existed that led to the gate room. There was a brilliant flash and when the picture returned, the wall was black, and they were attacking the spot with sledgehammers. Even as brawny as they were, they appeared to be making only the slightest dents in the wall.

They tried attacking on either side, supposedly to find a weak spot in the wall, to no avail. "The Alliance will be glad to know they get high marks for wall building," said Burt, almost gleefully.

When none of their efforts succeeded, they went on to trash her bedroom, but when they got to the computer room, one of the men, with a scruffy beard and a nose ring, reached toward the computer and ripped it out of the wall. This made absolutely no effect on the feed, as the security system was not tied into the computer. It only showed the footage on the monitor screen. "Bonus points," Burt breathed. "Magnificent."

They circled back to where the impervious door still hid behind the gate shield. One of them kicked the wall with a big booted foot, but only got pain for the effort. He hopped around on one foot, apparently swearing and shouting to the amusement of his companion until he hauled off and punched the fellow in the belly. The second man, clean shaven, even to his bald head, bent over in pain and then followed the bearded one out of the house.

Jenny regretted the lack of audio, as it might have given them a clue as to what their orders were and maybe where they were holed up or if there were more of them.

"But wait…there's more!" said Burt, who was practically dancing with excitement.

He pulled out his little multipurpose electronic device. It wasn't a cell phone; he had assured her the first time she had asked him about it. He called it his "swiss army knife". Apparently, it had many functions, one of which was to extract information from a person's mind and also to erase inconvenient memories. She shuddered to think what it would have done in someone else's hands.

He poked a few icons in rapid succession and his face lit up. "Gotcha!" And he actually did do a little jig on the spot.

"Gotcha?" Jenny inquired hopefully.

"It was a shot in the dark, but thanks to listening to my gut, we will now know exactly where they are from now on, thanks to my little bug friends. You see, when they went through the French doors, one of my little bug friends, actually tiny nanobots, dropped like a little spider on a web onto their backs and burrowed beneath the skin. They just feel like a little itch going in and, when the victim scratches at the itch, the bugs just burrow deeper.

It looks and feels like a mosquito bite. They can't be detected by any current tech and there is no additional sensation once they dig into the fatty tissue or muscle. These little hummers will tell us exactly where Curly and Moe are anywhere on the planet. Score a big one for dastardly alien tech! And the really cool thing is that they are dirt cheap and easy to manufacture. I keep a large supply of them in my MDP."

Jenny let out the breath she didn't realize she had been holding. "Do you think they will lead us to Engoza?"

"If not her, at least whoever is next in charge. I doubt she will risk being seen on Earth for awhile."

"Can I have a look at that?" Bob said, looking longingly at the little device in Burt's hand. "How do I get one of those?"

"Actually, they'll probably issue you one at the end of your Agent training," grinned Burt, but for now it stays in my pocket," and he suited words to action.

Jenny looked at Tidbit, who she had let down and had been sitting quietly at her ankles. "Are you OK?"

"*I'm fine*," he sent back. "*I think I want to check the koi pond. She may have left a clue.*"

Burt turned to Jenny. "I know this all looks pretty bleak from where you stand, but we'll get a lock on this. Was there anything valuable on your computer that wasn't backed up?"

Jenny considered. It had been her work computer, but other than email, she hadn't done much on her computer since all of this had started. Thankfully, she made a habit of trashing her read emails and dumping the trash folder nightly, so there was nothing there that might give them a clue as to what she might have been doing all of this time. Any emails she wanted to save, she saved to a highly encrypted cloud server, but she hadn't saved any of Aunt Lizzie's notes.

She shook her head. "I think I'm good there. And the laptop's no loss. It isn't like I can't afford to get a new one. I just hate having to reinstall all of that software."

Burt nodded sympathetically. "OK, well, I'd like to suggest we get on the road to Sanglarka, then. The house will be restored as much as possible while you're gone. Just think of it as an excuse to redecorate. A shame about the books, though," he said with a sigh.

Bob and Tidbit were examining the edge of the pond.

"Nothing here, but some cat blood," Bob said, as they walked up. "You might want to call Ted and find an excuse to give him a couple weeks off with pay until the clean-up crew is finished, though. Don't want him putting 2 and 2 together and coming up with 16."

Jenny nodded and texted Ted.

"So, let's go," said Burt.

"Wait a quick minute," Bob said. "I need to check on my house. Remember, they know I'm involved now."

Burt agreed, and they all trooped over to Bob's place, waving at Miss Longtree as they crossed the street. She waved back cheerfully and went on with pruning her prize-winning roses.

There was no sign of forced entry. Burt scanned for signs of Curly and Moe and they went in, after the scan revealed nothing. Bob and Burt did a quick tour of the house, then they headed out to the workshop. The lock was a fingerprint lock and an iris scan and once again Burt's scan found nothing. They went in and, to Bob's evident relief, nothing had been touched.

"I have Ignatius boarding with my son," Bob said. "And since it doesn't look like anything's been touched, while I'm here, I want to add a few things to my MDP. You never know when the right tool will come in handy."

After quickly gathering a number of tools and gadgets, many of which Jenny could only guess at their purpose, he paused. "Fidget goes too," he said, "and my main laptop and external drives."

After packing these into his MDP, he smiled and said, "Okies, kiddies, let's go."

Chapter 24: Seeking Sneaky Sam

As they emerged from the gateway in Sanglarka, Jenny was grateful to see Lova, Arvid and all of her fellow Guardians waiting to greet them warmly. These people were fast becoming as family to her. Lova pulled her in for a wordless hug. Beside her, Tarafau, with his head bandaged, gave a ragged sigh, as though he were very tired.

"*Come to the lodge*," Lova invited them, taking in all four of them with a sympathetic gaze. "*We'll get you fed up and then all of you will take to your rooms to rest. I have been given strict instructions, so there will be no arguments*." She looked pointedly at Tarafau.

He didn't argue, however. Jenny had never seen him look so weary.

The long dining room table had been extended and the lodge smelled of good food. There were many choices passed around, but Jenny took one of the large, fluffy home-baked rolls and a ladle of some kind of stew. It tasted like heaven to her weary soul.

There wasn't much chatter around the table as there otherwise might have been. Jenny was sure that her party must have looked like they'd been dragged through a rat hole. Most of them had circles under their eyes and Jenny realized that she hadn't slept in over 24 hours. The bandages on her and Tarafau were a mute testament to what they'd been through.

As they finished their meal, the others began clearing the table, shooing Jenny away when she rose to help.

"*Arvid will see to you and Tarafau. Go up to your usual suite and he'll be right up. The rest of you*," she said, looking sternly at Bob and Burt, "*will be shown to your rooms by Brendan*."

Brendan nodded to them. "G'day mates. Follow me."

Bob and Burt trailed behind Brendan, both looking at Jenny and Tarafau over their shoulders, reluctant to leave them.

"*Go on, we'll be fine*," Jenny said, waving them forward. "*We're right behind you*."

She and Tarafau mounted the stairs. She frowned. They hadn't seemed this steep the last time she was there.

It was both comforting and sad to enter her rooms she had spent so many happy days in. It seemed like forever ago.

They hadn't been inside but a few moments when Arvid came in, a basket in his arms, full of first aid supplies. "*Lova will be bringing up some nighty-night tea in a few, and you will both drink every drop. In the meantime, let's take a look under those bandages. You first, Jenny. Tarafau, go lay down on the chaise.*"

It was a mark of the strain of the last couple days and his injuries that Tarafau didn't argue or make a wise crack back to Arvid. He laid down with a sigh of relief and closed his eyes.

"*Don't go to sleep, you big lummox of a cat, you,*" Arvid grumbled. "*I'll need you awake to examine you.*"

Tarafau wearily opened his eyes. "*OK, but don't take too long, dwarf.*"

The comment made Jenny feel better. If Tarafau could make the effort to be playful, it was going to be all right.

Arvid gave a low whistle when he gently pulled away the gauze from her wound. "*A butterfly? Really?*"

Sam's artistry was already scabbing over. Jenny didn't know what had been in the healer's salve, but it was evidently doing its job.

Arvid cleaned the area gently, put more of what might have been the same medicine on the wound and rebandaged the area. "*It will scar, I'm afraid,*" he said echoing the regret of the healer who had treated her at the infirmary.

Jenny repeated her retort to Arvid, and he grinned. "*So be it. Few battle scars are this appropriate. She may have actually done you a favor. You'll never be able to look at this scar without remembering that you are strong.*"

Jenny thought she didn't feel strong at the moment, but she didn't say anything.

At this point, Lova came in with a tray with two mugs of tea.

"*It's just warm enough to drink,*" she said with a gentle smile, handing a mug to Jenny and sitting one on the table next to the chaise that seemed dwarfed by the big man lying on it as Arvid carefully unwound the bandage from his head.

"*It's a good thing you've got such a hard head, old cat,*" he murmured as he examined the wound on his head. "*And it's a good thing they missed your temple. That would have used up all nine of your lives.*"

Tarafau scowled, but Jenny could see his heart wasn't in it. And despite Arvid's gruff words, she noticed he was being especially gentle with his ministrations. Tarafau didn't wince once, but she could see the faraway look in his eyes and realized he was doing the breathing exercise that had meant so much to her when Sam was torturing her. "Sneaky Sam," she thought. "She's Sneaky Sam."

She was surprised how quickly the tea spread into her system. Lova, who had been standing there quietly beside her, took the empty cup gently from her.

"*Come, I'll tuck you in,*" Lova said.

Jenny didn't argue. There was a soft, flannel nightgown that Jenny guessed had belonged to her aunt, laying on the chair by the bed.

Lova helped her dress and true to her word, she tucked the downy comforter around her, pulled the drapes in front of the balcony window, turned off the lights and closed the door.

In her dream, Miriha walked before her in a flowing green gown, a linkling curled on her shoulder, its long tail laying alongside Miriha's long, thick braid.

She held out both hands as before. The linkling purred and crooned that soothing song. Jenny took her hands and suddenly, Miriha was Sam, the old Sam, smiling warmly at her and, just as suddenly, she was Sneaky Sam in her true form.

"Slippery little one, aren't you?" she hissed, her cheek beside Jenny's, her mouth by her ear. "Your dotty old aunt couldn't stop talking about you, that day on the train. How smart you were, how kind and creative. How you were going to be top of your class and hinting of adventures to come. I knew who she was, of course. She and I had a special relationship too.

And, yes, this is no ordinary dream. You can't get away from me that easily." She laughed, throwing her head back and grabbed Jenny's bandaged arm painfully turning it over to look at the wound. The bandage wasn't there, instead, the butterfly was bleeding again, drops falling audibly with a plop, plop, plop, as it had in that dark room that night.

Suddenly Miriha was there beside her, a quarterstaff of light in her hands. It whirled threateningly as she advanced on Sam. "You will depart hence and not return. Jenny's dreams are now guarded."

With a swift overhead stroke, she hit Sam on the top of her head and Sam exploded into dark tatters that hissed and disappeared.

"But you died, I saw you," Jenny spluttered.

"Indeed, you did. But when I transferred my key, I left a part of myself in your subconscious mind to protect you, when it becomes necessary. Remember there are dimensions as yet unexplored. I am here, dear Jenny. Sleep and wake refreshed. This evil one will bother you no more in your dreams."

Jenny woke much later, rested and refreshed. She remembered the dream clearly, but without fear. She would have to tell Lova, though, she realized. This could be important.

She rose and dressed. Tarafau was already up, rising early as was his habit. He sat at the little dinette, eating a thick porridge. Beside the bowl were an apple and an orange, several slices of cheese and some rye breakfast crackers.

He smiled when he saw her. "*Sleep well?*" he asked. He looked very much refreshed. The bandage on his head was a clear reminder that he still had healing to do.

"*I'm good,*" she replied, seating herself across from him. "*Er,*" she hesitated. "*Did you have any dreams last night?*"

Tarafau nodded gravely. "*I was visited by Engoza,*" he said simply. "*She won't bother either of us again.*"

Jenny nodded. "*I thought she might have visited you too. I think we should tell Lova.*"

"*Agreed.*"

They finished their breakfast in silence and walked down the stairs to the main lobby of the lodge. Waiting there were all of the Guardians, as well as Lova, Arvid, Bob and Burt. They had been standing in a loose group, talking quietly, but all cut off as they saw she and Tarafau descending the stairs.

"*No workout this morning for you two,*" Arvid said when he saw them. "*We'll meet in the dining room. It's one of the few rooms in the lodge large enough for all of us.*"

Once they were seated, Lova stood at her seat. "*Welcome all of you to Sanglarka,*" she said, spreading her arms in greeting. "*We are gathered here to deal with a serious breach of the gate network security system. The Groga are once again plaguing the dimensions with their raids and they seem stronger, more organized and better supplied than before. You have all been briefed on the main points, but Jenny and her team have more to tell us. As Gatekeeper, Jenny presides over this meeting of the Earth Dimensional Alliance Guardians.*"

She nodded to Jenny, as if to turn the meeting over to her.

She stood, but her knees felt like overdone noodles.

"*Um, welcome all of you. As you know I am new to this position and these responsibilities. I frankly don't have the slightest idea how to proceed, so I will be relying on your collective experience to get us through this. One thing I do know is that we can't drag our feet or take too long to get our act together. Earth is in danger. Let's start with Burt's report and then I will want all of your input.*"

She sat down with relief that all eyes now went to Burt. She hoped she hadn't sounded too much like a kid asking for permission to play with the bigger kids on the playground.

Burt stood and recounted their story from the time he arrived at Jenny's house for the first time up to the present. As young and flippant as he could often be, his report was concise without leaving out any important details. From time to time he had Tarafau, Bob or Jenny fill in parts where he had not been present.

When he was finished, he looked around the long table into each face. *"We are not without resources, but our adversaries are several steps ahead of us. If we don't get our act together quickly and catch up this could be very bad, not only for Earth, but for every universe attached to the gateway network. I'd recommend that we shut the network down and trap them in their own dimension if it wasn't for two things: One, they aren't in their own dimension. Reports tell us they have raided several worlds over the past few weeks and that they have agents still on many of the gate worlds. Secondly, there is actually no way known we could shut down the network even if we wanted to. The Gatekeeper can shut down a single gate, but only temporarily."*

Hands shot up from several of the Guardians and Burt patiently answered their questions, clarifying what wasn't clear. When he was finished, he said, *"Tarafau tells me he has something new to report."*

He sat and Tarafau stood. He easily dwarfed even Brendan. He told them simply about the dream he had experienced the night before. The only difference between his dream and Jenny's was that in Tarafau's dream Sam came into his dream as her own self and no disguises. Miriha had appeared with her quarterstaff of light and defeated her in the same way.

Then Jenny stood and related her dream as well. When she was finished, she remained standing.

Like Burt, she looked into each face before she continued. Each gave her an acknowledging nod.

"As you can see, we have a difficult task ahead of us, but Burt knows where Sam's henchmen are holed up and that's a start. What I'd like to do is hear from each of you about your strengths and weaknesses, so we can break up into groups to tackle specific problems with the best possible team for each. Does that sound reasonable?"

They all nodded their assent.

Evidently, they had been prepared for this eventuality. A transparent screen appeared, floating above the table. Bob inhaled; his eyes gleaming. Jenny could almost hear his mind whirring, studying, considering possibilities. Jenny was relieved that she had not shown her ignorance by asking for a whiteboard and markers.

Lova stood. "*I am Lova Norstrom, of Sweden. My strengths are organization, training, the ability to see patterns. I have been the Guardian of the Sanglarka gate for over 40 years. Friend of Lizzie and Miriha. My faults are that I tend to be overly tender-hearted, I am impatient with slothfulness or dishonesty and I tend to make snap judgements that I regret later.*"

As she spoke, her words were listed in two columns on the transparent screen next to her name, labeled "strengths" and "weaknesses".

Lova sat and Arvid stood. "*I am Arvid Longhammer, not of this dimension. I am an Alliance Agent, keeper of the grounds and master trainer here at Sanglarka. My strengths are armed and unarmed combat, tracking, training, first aid, woodcraft and I'm a pretty good cook.*"

The group laughed appreciatively at this comment, as they had all enjoyed the benefits of Arvid's cooking.

"*My weaknesses are technology that requires anything but simple verbal commands. I have no diplomacy and I say what I think. I work best on my own as I am headstrong and have my own way of doing things, though I get it done in the end. I don't like being pushed.*"

Evidently, many of them had been on the receiving end of Arvid's sharp tongue as furtive smiles went around the table.

"*I am Bob Reid,*" Bob said as he stood. "*I'm from Los Angeles, California. I am a scientist and an engineer, Army veteran and tinkerer. I'm good with tech, can hold my own in a fight. I'm familiar with many types of weapons and I'm a pretty good shot. However, I tend to be over-curious, which sometimes gets me into trouble. I got into this by accident, but I'm committed to it. I am new to this, so I need training and to familiarize myself with the tools we have available to us. I hope that won't hold us back.*"

Burt grinned around the table as he stood. His wild hair matched his grin and his intense blue eyes twinkled mischievously. Evidently, he was acquainted with a number of the Guardians, as many of them returned that grin. *"I am Burt Scout of Toledo, Ohio. I am an expert in Gateway tech, and I like to blow up things. I have been an Agent for about a dozen years. My weaknesses are a flip tongue and a casual disregard for rules I see as unnecessary or foolish. I do my best work with deadlines. Some people would call that procrastination. I call it efficient use of time. I've got little tact and I'm OK with that."*

Lova shook her head with a twist to her mouth. Others nodded.

Mustapha stood next. His dark eyes scanned the group. *"I am Mustapha Kashani, Guardian of the Pakistani gate. My strengths are logistics, strategy and tactics. I am also expert in communications and international political intelligence and hand to hand combat. My weaknesses,"* at this he raised his chin arrogantly, *"are firearms and explosives. I am not a good shot and I detest loud explosions."* He looked pointedly at Burt who grinned and shrugged.

Adelle's warm smile when she stood was such a contrast to Mustapha's serious air that the room seemed to lighten perceptively. She looked over her oval wire rim spectacles as she spoke. *"Good day to you all. I am Adelle Becker, Guardian of the Swiss gate. My strengths are research, particle physics, and astrophysics. My weaknesses are anything having to do with violence, and I tend to get easily distracted, according to my husband."*

Juan nearly jumped up from his seat. *"I am Juan Roman, Guardian of the Puerto Rico gate. I am also a pilot,"* a nod to Brendan, *"a hunter and tracker. I have a good head for deciphering codes and riddles. My wife says I have no head for balancing the books and that I sometimes do not take things as seriously as I should. I tend to leap before I look, which has sometimes gotten me into trouble. That being said, I take my duties very, very seriously and I have little patience for those who don't pull their weight."*

Jenny found herself impressed with the variety of disciplines and personalities of this team. She had gotten to know each of them somewhat during her training at the Alliance, but from the perspective of what they needed to do, she was yet at a loss on how to create an effective effort to stop the Groga. She had no time to ponder this, however. Xao Ting had stood.

The diminutive Asian man bowed slightly to the group before speaking.

"*I am Xao Ting. I have the honor of being Guardian of the China gate. I will tell you that I am strong in herbs and ancient medicines. I am a philosopher and a fair poet. And this humble one also is a Bei Shaolin Grandmaster. I submit that I fail miserably at outdoor living as I have a very poor sense of direction,*" he glanced at Brendan, "*and I am allergic to wool.*"

As he sat, he hung his head, as if these failings were beyond bearing.

Brendan stood, looking straight at Xao. "*He failed to mention that no one here, including Arvid, has ever defeated him at quarterstaff, even when there were three of us to his one. I am Brendan Lisle, the Aussie Guardian. I am a sharpshooter and hunter. I also am a pilot. There's pretty much nothing I can't fly. I can't cook, and I am lousy at tech that doesn't involve things that fly.*"

The tall Ghanaian stood gracefully. "*I am Dhakirah Jelani, Guardian of the gate in Ghana. My strengths include art and dancing as well as computer science. I am afraid my weakness is that I have no combat skills. I can master the forms for the quarterstaff, but I cannot bring myself to use it to strike someone. Under most circumstances, I feel this is a good thing, but I admit that my pacific nature could be a drawback in our current circumstances.*"

Jenny couldn't help but return her beautiful smile as she sat down.

Then Leonora stood, her hands clasped behind her back, as if at parade rest. Her mental voice was low for a woman and she looked directly at Jenny, ignoring the others. "*I am Leonora Svodboda, I guard the gate in Czechoslovakia. My strengths are good discipline and I can run very fast. I was a gymnast in my youth, and I am still supple and balanced. I climb mountains for relaxation, and I raise cattle, so I am strong. I have no sense of humor and I don't like being idle. I hate waiting.*" And she sat and returned her gaze to the center of the table in front of her.

Aliki nearly bounded up. "*I am Aliki Malala, the Guardian of the Samoa gate. I have a photographic memory. I remember everything I ever see. I am a sailor and can sail every type of vessel from ancient to modern. I can't dance. I don't play the ukulele and I have a horrible singing voice. Besides that, I am a stickler and I have a tendency to point out other people's errors before I think about it.*"

His smile had never wavered during his report. Jenny imagined that even when he was pointing out other's failures, he would do it with a smile on his face.

When Guaray stood, he seemed as grave as Aliki was cheerful. He looked straight into Jenny's eyes after nodding to Lova and Tarafau, who were seated on either side of her. "*I am Guaray Varma. I guard the gate in India. I am a scholar and have something in common with you, Jenny. I was not chosen. I found a woman perishing in an alley. She transferred her key to me and her MDP. The beacon had been activated and those who located me introduced me to my duties. I have been the Guardian only for seven years. I have no skills but teaching and writing. I don't know in what way I can be of assistance, but I will serve.*"

Jenny had a feeling if she hugged him, he wouldn't appreciate it, but she still felt some kinship with the man. He had not shared this during the training they had done together at Alliance headquarters, but she was glad to know it now and sure that they could find a way to use his skills. She had a suspicion that he was naturally humble and not used to telling others of his talents.

Megan of Canada stood nervously, her hands clasped in front of her, as if to keep them from shaking. "*I don't do well speaking in front of crowds,*" she began. "*I am Megan Smythe. I guard the Canada gate. I am what you in America would call a park ranger. I know woodcraft and the care of living creatures, as I have a degree in zoology. I know how to track, and I can handle firearms and I am a certified drone pilot. I'm physically strong. I don't like crowds or large cities. I don't do technology much in my job and I have poor people skills.*"

She sat down abruptly and put her head in her hands, as if to shut out the faces before her. Jenny got the feeling that Megan would be much more at home with the animals in the woodland than she was dealing with so many people all in one place.

Leland hopped up. *"I'm imaginin' you saved the best for last,"* he said with a wink at Jenny. *"I'm Leland O'Flaherty. I'm the Guardian of the gate o' the Emerald Isle. I'm quick on the uptake, fast off the starting line and I can lick me weight in tigers. I've the strength of ten and I never quit. I know how to take orders as I am a proud veteran of the Defence Forces of Ireland. I admit to a quick temper and a long memory for folks who intend to do harm."*

He saluted Jenny and bowed to the rest and sat, looking pleased with himself.

Lova stood, turning to Jenny. *"These will serve as your resources and team-mates on Earth, Jenny. You should also remember that you have the backing of the Alliance to pull from as well, but they are also organizing the defenses for the entire network. Our job for now is to find the agents of the Groga here on earth and 'interview' them in an attempt to discover their plans and how they are getting into dimensions without using the portals, or if they are using them, how they are by-passing the scanners. The weapons they carry should have set off alarms and instigated other defense mechanisms.*

Earth is the only gateway planet where we know for certain there are Groga agents in place. Finding them may be the key to defeating the Groga once and for all."

She paused, as if waiting for Jenny to say something.

"I want to tell you how much it means to me to have all of you on my team," Jenny began, mentally running through everything she had heard and observed, as she scanned the screen in front of her, which was now full of the information revealed by the other Guardians. *"I'm new to all of this and I don't pretend to be a great leader or an expert in much of anything that pertains to the task ahead of us. Therefore, I'll need everyone's help and input to get this done. I would like Burt, Tarafau and Lova to be my counselors in this. Let's adjourn for a couple hours so we can take all of this,"* she waved at the screen hanging in the air above the table, *"into account and then we'll divide us up into teams and create a plan to go on with. Fair enough?"*

There were nods of agreement around the table and a scraping of chairs as they rose to leave.

"*One more thing*," she added, and they all paused before turning away. "*I know I'm just a kid where most of you are concerned and I could never truly replace Lizzie or Miriha, but I promise you I will do my best to listen, learn and I won't quit on you.*"

There were murmurs of agreement and looks of appreciation, and, on some faces, grim determination, as they contemplated what her words meant.

She turned to Lova and Burt, who had remained seated. "*OK. Let's get this done. It's time to find Sneaky Sam and her minions and get the Groga out of the gateways*"

Chapter 25: Shedding Light

Jenny watched Tidbit sunning himself on the window seat. Like Leonora, Jenny hated waiting. It wasn't that she didn't have anything to do, but Burt had headed out with Brendan, Bob, Xao Ting and Leland on the hunt for the Groga, based on Burt's locators. Even though she knew there was no way they could have gotten to them in the Louisiana swamp where they had located them. There was no way they could have even found them by now, much less hatched a strategy.

The house had been swept and the ruined furniture had been removed. Her old camping cooler was the only thing to sit on in the house, at this point. Burt had assured her that all repairs would be made, and furnishings would be provided by the time she had time to return. She was glad she had put clothing and hygiene supplies into the MDP on her last trip.

She had taken some of the time to set up her camping cot in the bedroom for a temporary place to sleep and had gone out and bought some paper plates and cups as well as some freezer dinners, sandwich supplies and some fruit. Burt had told her to resupply her food stocks when the clean-up crew was finished with the place, as anything that did get left behind would be suspect.

She had put Lova, Mustapha and Aliki on the team for organizing and logistics, interacting with Burt's team for keeping track of strategy. She had explained that she would be keeping the rest of them in reserve to have access to their skills as stage one of the operation to find Sam's minions moved forward. She sent the Guardians who could be spared back to their gates with instructions to report anything out of place or unusual as they went about their duties.

Tarafau would have been a real resource for Burt's team, except that for now he was Tidbit. In a few minutes she would retire to the gate study, as Alliance Agents would be coming through her gate with the express purpose of protecting her and Tidbit. This made her feel like less of an asset and more of a burden to the team, but Lova had pointed out that she was a vital key to the success of their mission and every general she had ever read about had bodyguards and aides de camp. Though she understood their reasoning, it had done little to assuage her thought that they would have been much better prepared if someone else had been in charge, even with the guidance and direction of Tarafau, Lova and Burt.

She had been surprised how business-like Burt had been as they had conferred about what to do next. She was very used to thinking of him as a smart aleck kid near to her own age, but he had been working with the Alliance since he was a teen, having stumbled into things that did not concern him. Lova said he had taken to the Alliance training like a bird to the wing, and he knew things about this kind of warfare that surprised her.

Jenny couldn't help but grin when she thought of him, however. She was learning that even with his seemingly casual attitude, he was a sensitive and kind person and there was something about his smile that warmed her heart.

Lova had revealed that she also had a military background and had been an officer over troops. Jenny could imagine this easily, considering the matter of fact way she directed everything at the Sanglarka training center.

Tarafau had been around when the original Groga raids had come up before, so he had valuable information as to what Burt's team should expect. Having fought them before, he knew strategies that had worked in the past.

The team had worked from the chart that had assembled itself during their conference with the other Guardians. It was obvious there was a wide range of skills to choose from and none of the weaknesses any of them had admitted to needed to be a barrier, depending on how they did assignments.

Once they had given the assignments and the others had departed, Lova had seen Jenny, Tarafau, Burt, Bob and Xao Ting off through the L.A. gate with hugs and assurances that her team would stay in close touch.

Burt's team had run off in Bob's car to depart for the airport to Louisiana, where Burt's bugs currently resided, and Jenny had been left with Tidbit to await her Guard detail.

"*You coming?*" she asked Tidbit, as she began to head for the gate office. Tidbit looked up with his lamp-like eyes. "*I should be there to greet them,*" he agreed.

The green light above the gateroom door lit up after they had been there only a few minutes. It was nice to know that her Guards were punctual, she thought wryly.

To her surprise, the three who stepped out of the portal were humanoid and female.

"*Lyra, Nona and Mynn,*" said the first one who had stepped through the gate, pointing to each of them in turn. "*You are Jenny and Tidbit and we are your Guard.*"

Jenny noticed they were dressed in what her dad had called "civvies", no uniforms.

"*We're your cousins from Arizona,*" Lyra said with a smile. "*We'll be your guests for awhile. Our rental car will be arriving in the night, while your neighbors are sleeping, and, in the morning, your neighbors will be none the wiser. Just say we caught the red-eye. We know your cover is blown for Engoza's henchmen, but we still want your neighbors to think that everything is normal here.*"

The three women couldn't have been any more different than one another. Lyra was a short curly-haired blonde with pale skin and big blue eyes. The top of her head just came up to Jenny's shoulder. Nona was a few inches taller than Jenny and her skin was only slightly lighter than Tarafau's with black hair pulled back into a knot at her neck. Her eyes, surprisingly, were also blue, almost aquamarine. Her height made Lyra look even shorter, if possible. Mynn's short brown hair was straight and spiky and her eyes were brown as hot fudge. She was about Jenny's height and had a mischievous glint in her eyes.

"*Hey, Tidbit!*" Mynn said, reaching down to scratch behind his ears. "*I hear you've been in a cat fight that you didn't win, lately. I didn't think that was possible.*"

"*It is, when your opponent sneaks up from behind and knocks you on the back of the head,*" he sent grumpily.

"Tish posh, you silly old cat. What happened to those reflexes like lightning?"

Tidbit laid his ears back and stalked out of the open door into the house, his tail waving behind him in indignation, not deigning to reply.

"I'm not sure where to put you three," Jenny said, uncomfortably. *"I guess you could camp out in my home office. There's nothing in there now. Not even any furniture."*

"Not to worry," Nona said, *"We are equipped."* And she tapped the MDP on her wrist.

"OK, I'll leave you to it then. Make yourselves comfortable. I'll make us some lunch. If you'd like we can eat it in the garden."

The three nodded their assent and went into the office.

While Jenny put together some sandwiches and a tall pitcher of cold water with orange slices in it, she mulled over what it would be like to have so many people in her little house for an extended period of time. The last time she had had a roommate had been Sam, in their tiny little apartment off campus.

She flinched at that thought and touched the still tender butterfly cut into her flesh. She was sure she could trust these women. They were, after all, Alliance Agents. But the hurt had been so much more than the physical torture Sam had put her through. She felt violated and used, feelings she had heard others talk about, but something she had never fully understood.

It was true, what her mother had always told her, that oftentimes the pains of the heart were much more hurtful than any physical injury.

Her guards finished setting up their bedroom quickly and joined her out on the patio, bringing out a couple of dining room chairs, so they all had a place to sit around the little wrought iron table. They oohed and aahed over the little herb garden and the koi pond, setting Jenny at ease, instead of the other way around.

"So, while we're here, is there anything we can do to assist you?" Lyra asked.

Jenny thought about it. There was still the issue of the storage shed. She had put it off for way too long. Sam had been really focused on it, as if she knew there was something important in there. Perhaps she had only thought it was the gateway, but Jenny didn't think so.

She told them about the shed and Sam's strange behavior in front of the door, including the exploding trap she had laid for her there. They listened attentively.

"I'm glad you waited for us to do this," Lyra said. *"We have some tools that may make this safer. Just because you disabled one trap, doesn't mean you caught them all. Your 'Sneaky Sam' sounds like a conniver to me. I'm betting she had more than one trick up her sleeve. Stay here."*

Mynn stayed with Jenny while Lyra and Nona started a slow circuit around the shed in opposite directions, holding their hands up, palms extended toward the building, as Burt had done. When they met again where they had started, in front of the shed door, they nodded at one another and returned to sit down at the table.

"There's a net around the shed," Nona said. *"Its purpose isn't clear. It may have been put there by your aunt or by Sam. There is no way for us to know. However, if it was put there by your aunt, you may be able to question LizzieAI about it."* She noted the shock on Jenny's face as she realized she hadn't told them about LizzieAI. *"We were briefed before we came about your training and resources,"* she said simply.

Jenny pulled her tablet out of the MDP. "What can I do for you today, Jenny?" came LizzieAI's cheerful voice. Jenny quickly outlined their dilemma, pointing the tablet camera at her three guards. "Ah, I see. Stand in front of the door and say, "The Cat's Pajamas" and the net will come down. It is mostly there for surveillance purposes anyway, but there are things it won't allow you to remove from the unit unless it is disabled. I suggest you don't disable it unless you intend to take something out of it."

Jenny decided they may need to take some things out of the shed, especially if it might help them in their quest to eliminate the Groga. She said clearly, "Cat's Pajamas". She noticed nothing, but took out her key to the shed door and opened it. She couldn't help remembering the flash of Sam's trap when Burt had sprung it. Nevertheless, nothing happened.

As they entered the shed, the lights sprang up and the seeming chaos inside was exactly as Jenny had remembered it the one time she had taken a moment to go inside. At the time it had been overwhelming to even consider going through all of this, and it seemed that hadn't changed. Jenny's insides were in a knot thinking of how much stuff there was to go through and there seemed to be no particular order to any of it, which seemed a little out of character for Lizzie.

As she recalled, there were two rooms. The front part of the shed appeared to be the furnishings and decorative items from the house that the executor of the will had moved out to make room for Jenny's things. When she got to the door that went through to the other part of the shed, however, it was locked. Jenny tried the outside door key, but it didn't fit. She took out her tablet again. "Um, Lizzie, how do I get through the second door?"

"Oh, sorry, Jenny. The key is taped under the desk drawer. You should find the desk somewhere in the first section."

Sure enough, after a quick search they found the desk and on the underside of the main drawer was taped a key which fit perfectly.

The door opened into a warehouse type space, very similar to the one inside the MDP, except not so large. This was not an interdimensional space, such as Jenny has suspected it might be. It was only as big on the inside as it appeared to be on the outside.

This felt more like a space her aunt would create. Orderly and clean. The tall metal utility shelves were labeled. and each thing, most of which Jenny did not recognize, appeared to have its own space. Lyra, Mynn and Nona looked around with delight.

"There's enough tech here to equip a whole platoon," Nona said in tones of wonder. *"How many missions had she completed in her 60 some earth years in the Alliance? It seems like she was involved in way more than just tending her gate."*

Jenny thought of the photo she thought of as "the safari" of Lizzie and Tarafau smiling exultantly at the camera. She had since visited that spot. It was the outside of the building that had housed Miriha's gate. She was now certain that Lizzie hadn't spent as much time at her gate as she had initially assumed.

"Is there anything we can use once we have found the Groga here on earth?" Jenny asked.

"Oh yes," enthused Mynn. She cocked her head, considering. *"Of course, it depends on the terrain and our need to not attract the attention of the locals. But there are definitely some things we can use that will even the odds, depending on what the odds are, naturally."*

"Naturally," Jenny agreed with a twist to her mouth. It seemed that everyone knew so much more than she did.

"You three know what all of these things are. Do you see anything that doesn't seem to belong or that might be key to something the Groga may be planning?"

Lyra looked around for a moment. *"You know, this may take awhile. Nona is our specialist in weaponry tech. I think Mynn and I will sit out in the garden for a bit."* And suiting actions to words, she and Mynn headed out the door.

Jenny's look at Nona was a question.

"They want to be sure no one comes at us while we're occupied," she said. *"Come on, let's take a look."*

"Take out your tablet and get a photo of each shelf and their contents so we can look at it in more detail later," she advised. *"The LizzieAI will be able to give us a commentary on each one in the comfort of the gate office, to be sure we are secure. In the meantime, I will look at the shelves behind you and see if anything stands out."*

This sounded like a good plan and a lot faster than going over every single thing on every single shelf. Jenny proceeded to follow her instructions as Nona went from shelf to shelf behind her, seemingly murmuring to herself, keeping up a running commentary.

"Wow, that's an old model. I didn't know they still made them," she said at one point, picking up what looked like an oddly shaped rifle with a solid barrel. She saw Jenny looking at her. *"Energy weapon,"*

she said, answering Jenny's unspoken question. *"About 20 years behind current tech, but a nice piece of work nevertheless."*

They continued to scan the shelves. Jenny was amazed at the variety of things on the shelves. There were even some regular books on one set of shelves. She came to a tray of what looked at first like watchbands until she recognized them. *"Nona, look! Are these what I think they are?"*

"MDPs!" Nona's intense blue eyes lit up like a Christmas tree. *"I wonder if they have anything in them?"*

Jenny picked one up and thought, "peek" and suddenly she saw before her endless shelves of tech, supplies and even a couple of the hovercars like she had ridden in to the Alliance headquarter building.

"Jackpot!" she said, scooping them all up. *"Let's just get these shelves photographed and retire to the gate office."*

Nona nodded, saying not another word. They finished photographing the shelves and left, locking the door and putting the keys into her MDP.

Lyra and Mynn were lounging, apparently completely relaxed, sipping from their glasses of what was probably now just warm, orange-flavored water. They stood immediately and followed Jenny and Nona quickly into the house.

"You coming, cat?" Mynn called out to Tidbit. *"You might want to see this. Jenny and Nona have found something."*

As they shut the door to the gate office behind them and Tidbit curled up in his bed, Jenny laid the MDPs, 5 of them, on the desk before her.

Lyra and Mynn gasped. *"Are they full?"* Mynn asked eagerly.

"One of them is. I haven't checked the rest. Could this be what Sneaky Sam was looking for?"

"I wouldn't be surprised," said Nona. *"If all of these are full, anyone could supply an entire army, depending on what's in them."*

Jenny agreed. *"I think Lizzie must have keyed them to me, since I was able to peek into the one I looked at. Can I transfer that key or* add you three to be able to access these? If they are full, this is five warehouses of stuff. It'd take me years to catalog it all."

"*Unless of course, the catalog is in LizzieAI,*" Lyra said, rolling her eyes, as if it was so obvious anyone should have thought of it. And she may have been right, Jenny thought, with a shrug.

Sure enough, when she queried LizzieAI, she affirmed that all of the MDP's were full. Jenny was so glad that the tablet would only open at her command.

"*Asking permission to transmit this to The Council,*" said Nona, a salute implied in her crisp tone.

"Of course. They should know. What can we do to secure them? Should you take them back to headquarters?"

"I don't know, Jenny. That might be an obvious move and we don't know how far the Groga have infiltrated the network. They may actually be safer right here. This gate office has proven to be impervious to attack, so far, at least with the weapons the Groga brought to bear last time. Either way, I will let The Council know and you should send a message to Lova."

After she had done so, Jenny asked LizzieAI where she would recommend keeping the MDPs in the office.

"There is a floor vault under the desk, with the keyword, '88badWolf88'," LizzieAI told her.

Jenny never ceased to be amazed at the forethought and precautions Lizzie had taken in all she had done. Jenny hoped that this would eventually come with experience.

She stooped to peer below the desk. Sure enough, there was a tile on the floor that looked different from the others. Rather than a combination lock such as you would expect, there was a button. Jenny pressed it and a keyboard slid out with a plain grey and black display. She typed the password in and the tile slid away, revealing a small safe with a number of small items in it. She didn't take time to examine them, however. She felt an urgency to put the MDPs in a secure place. She definitely wasn't going to carry them around with her.

No sooner had the tile slid back into place, she rose to find all three of her guards standing, facing the door to her house, with their quarterstaffs in their hands, Lyra with a finger over her lips.

"There was a noise," she sent in mindspeech and pointed to the door that led into the house.

"I'm sure it's just the boys back to report," Jenny sent back.

"And if it isn't?" Lyra arched an eyebrow. Jenny shrugged.

"Stay behind us." Nona sent as they headed for the door.

They opened the door silently, and as they entered the living room it was as if time slowed. Several things happened all at once.

Three workmen stood as if frozen in a moment of time. The shock on their faces was evidence that they didn't expect to see anyone in the house. Their grey coveralls and the toolboxes in their hands told Jenny there was probably a work van parked out in her driveway. But if these had been the workmen Burt had contracted, he would have warned her they were coming, and they wouldn't be scowling at the four women as if they meant murder.

Before the moment of shock was dispelled, Tidbit was in the air, leaping with an enraged howl, claws extended, directly at the face of the workman in the front. Jenny had no idea he could leap so high. He dug his claws into the man's face and shredded his eyes, leaving bloody streams running down his face and continued to attack. The man screeched in pain and rage and tried to pull the cat off of him, but Tidbit had dug his front claws into his shirt and was now clawing his belly with his hind feet.

In the meantime, Lyra, Mynn and Nona had surrounded the two other men, their quarterstaffs whirling. From the toolbox one man had grabbed a long handled wrench and was swinging it in an attempt to ward off Nona's attack and the other had a large maul in his hand. But neither of them had the reach allowed by the quarterstaffs and their weapons were unwieldy.

Whack! Whack! Crack! Lyra and Mynn alternated rapid blows from either side of the man with the beard. The dark-bearded man with the maul had no chance to connect because he couldn't strike at one without exposing himself to the other.

Jenny saw that the first man was laying on the floor, moaning, clutching his bloody face in his hands, Tidbit standing over him and making that curious half howl, half growl she had first heard when he had attacked Cinder what now seemed like years ago. The front of the man's shirt was oozing blood. He wouldn't be a problem any time soon.

She decided she could do the best by aiding Nona. She and the grizzled fellow with the wrench were circling one another cautiously. Jenny's mind flashed back to all of those practice sessions when Arvid had insisted she retrieve her staff over and over again out of her MDP until it seemed to appear in her hands like a magic trick and how useless it had seemed at the time.

But now it flashed into her hands and the man who was circling with Nona had his back to her. Evidently, since she appeared to have no weapon, he hadn't thought of her as a threat. Her staff came down on his head with an audible "CRACK!" and the man fell like his bones had melted.

Now the last man, his maul in his hands and his face in an enraged scowl was surrounded by four angry, armed women who circled him, whacking at him from every angle. With a growl of disgust, he threw the maul down on the floor so forcefully that it cracked a tile. "I GIVE! I GIVE!" he shouted, throwing both hands into the air.

Lyra gave him a final whack in the gut, and he fell to his knees.

Nona went straight to work, handcuffing each of them roughly while Mynn pulled out her first aid kit. *"We want you to be healthy when we interrogate you,"* she purred sweetly.

The man groaned as she cleaned his wounds. *"He won't be able to see again,"* she said cheerily. *"but we can't afford to have him die of an infection now, can we?"*

The fellow Jenny had cracked on the head lay very still. *"Is he dead? Did I kill him?"* she asked, and she realized she was trembling.

"No," said Nona briskly. *"But he's gonna have one heck of a headache when he wakes up. He's probably got a concussion, but*

that's for the healers to determine. Help will be coming through the gateway; you'll want to greet them."

Jenny almost collapsed with relief. In all of this time, it hadn't yet occurred to her that she might actually kill someone. The sandwiches they had eaten earlier roiled in her stomach.

Sure enough, when Jenny entered the gate office, healers and guards were streaming through the gateroom door. Jenny thanked them and led them into the living room which now seemed excessively crowded. But not for long. The healers took in the scene quickly and started giving orders to guards who manifested stretchers from their MDPs and began to put the two injured men on them and take them directly back to the gateway without pause. The remaining man they roughly stood on his feet and frog-marched him out of the room. Two guards gathered the toolboxes, the wrench and the maul and, as they turned to leave, one said, *"Well done. I assume we'll see you back at headquarters to report what just happened here?"*

Lyra nodded, the man saluted and out he went.

Jenny looked around herself in shock. It had all happened so fast that, if it wasn't for the over-turned cooler, a cracked floor tile, and the small puddle of blood on the floor, she wouldn't have believed it had actually occurred.

"So much for no physical activity," she murmured to Tidbit. "You never cease to surprise me. Are you OK?"

"Groga don't taste very good," was all he said, licking the blood off of his paws.

"Let's see what our friends left us," Nova said, heading for the front door. It was too late to worry about the ruse of the rental car. The need for information trumped the need for secrecy. Jenny was relieved, however, that the street seemed to be empty at the moment.

Out in the driveway was a white panel van with "Jerry's Plumbing, since 1996" painted on the side. The intruders hadn't bothered to lock it, assuming a quick and easy getaway. They had obviously assumed Jenny was alone, with only Tidbit for protection, not counting on his ferocity. They opened the back doors. It was empty.

Not a gum wrapper or a pop bottle or even any other tools or equipment. It was spotless.

Mynn sighed. *"They weren't taking any chances. Maybe the forensics guys will have more luck with their toolboxes."*

Before they closed the doors, they checked to see if the keys had been left in the ignition, but they hadn't, and they went back into the house, Jenny's Guards leading the way. This business of bodyguards going everywhere she went was going to take some getting used to, Jenny thought, but she didn't object. After all, they had just saved her life moments ago and this was only going to get worse. "Girl power," she said to no one in particular and all three of her guards grinned.

"OK, let's get to headquarters," Jenny said. *"It's time we got some questions answered."*

Chapter 26: Q&A

They arrived at headquarters minutes later and were escorted directly up to the council room. The Councilors were not on the dais. A circle of chairs, one perch and a chaise on the main floor were mostly filled with Earth Guardians, a large Alliance Guard and another uniformed being she did not recognize. There were only two free chairs, one for Jenny and one for Tarafau, so her Guards stood at rest behind her.

As she sat, she noticed that Ingot seemed more agitated than she had ever seen him. He always had seemed to keep his cool, even when alarm bells went off. Seeing him this way, worried her.

The other two Councilors were not quite as easy to read, although a small rivulet of smoke occasionally escaped Liliath's nostrils.

"*Welcome, Jenny.*" Ingot said from his seat. "*Congratulations on the capture of Groga agents. They will be interrogated by some of our best, and I doubt they can hold out for long. Please recount how this came to pass.*"

Jenny looked around the circle. As Ingot had not stood when he had spoken to the assembly, she remained seated and told the gathering about the circumstances of their capture of the three Groga agents and about the MDPs they had found in the shed. If anything, by the time she finished her report, Ingot was even more agitated.

"*This is grave news indeed,*" he said with a sigh, shaking his head. "*But there may be some hope in the MDPs you found. The enemy is moving much faster than we had hoped and it is obvious that the Groga now know where the new Gatekeeper portal is located. We will have to take some additional precautions. I am sorry to tell you that you won't be spending a lot of time in your home for awhile.*"

Enemy agents must not see you coming and going. Let them think that you have fled the gate. They will see workmen going in and out, presumably to repair the damage they did to your home. They will make a great show of installing heavy security precautions. We want them to think we are afraid they will try again."

We ARE afraid they will try again, Jenny thought to herself.

"*For the next little while, you will need to come and go only from the gateways, never out your front door. I would have you work from your gate office, when you are on Earth, or at any of the other gateways. When you were in Puerto Rico, you sent photos to Sam, did you not?*"

Jenny gasped. She had sent photos of her on the mango plantation and in the forests. "*I did, but I don't think there was anything in them that would have identified the hacienda or where it was located.*" She paused, thinking. "*There was one photo I took from the balcony. Could your techs look at it and determine if she might be able to locate the hacienda by looking at that photo? It's the only one that had any details that might possibly help her. All she really knew is that I went to Puerto Rico.*"

Ingot smiled at her wearily. "*I will have them download the photos from your phone, with your permission. Did you take any photos of you and Juan or Luz? We really don't know how much they already know about the other gates on Earth. I would hate to think they might have been exposed to her agents.*"

"*I would have liked to have had photos of the two of them, but I didn't take any. I thought that would have been a security risk.*" Arvid nodded and Jenny looked at Juan. His usually cheerful face was somber. "*Have you seen anything suspicious around your home?*" she asked Juan worriedly.

"*There have been no breaches of security at this point, and you know I have taken precautions. I can see anyone coming from a long way off, due to security cameras along the jungle road and the path leading to the hacienda. My wife's assistants in the mango grove serve a second purpose. They are all ex-military and they go armed. Partially, this is because of the jungle predators who roam in the jungle beyond, but they also serve as security and they know their jobs well. And I must reveal that, as many of you know,*" glancing at the three councilors, "*Luz is not without her own defenses.*"

"*I am hopeful that there are not enough clues in any of the photos that might help her pinpoint the gateway. But, since we can't know for sure, we will need to add extra security; shields, net sensors and the like,*" replied Ingot thoughtfully. "*We would do the same for the house on Infinity Loop, but there are too many people too close who might cross the boundaries. We will have to get creative. In the meantime, we also need to determine what to do about the MDPs you found, and we need to discover, what, if anything, we can get from the three men you so handily defeated. Is there anything else?"

He looked around the circle, encouraging anyone who had anything to add to speak up.

The uniformed being that Jenny had not recognized sent to the group. Now that she looked at him properly, she realized he was like a much enlarged version of Ingot, stocky in build, with a square face and a dark beard...that wiggled? He wasn't quite as tall as Tarafau or Brendan, but Jenny could imagine that face when angry and shivered. *"Jenny, I am Gariel. I am the chief of the Alliance Troopers. What do you know of the Queen of the Groga?"*

"Nothing more than that we think she's Sneaky Sam's boss."

He looked puzzled; his beard squirmed more animatedly. *"She means Engoza,"* put in Tarafau.

He nodded. *"The Queen of the Groga is not a Groga. No one knows much about her dimension of origin, but the thinking, for now, is that the Groga may have been taken to her home dimension. We have no clues as to where that may actually be in the gate network or whether that dimension is even in the network at all. Among the infinite number of potential connections, we have a nearly impossible task. We currently have no way of tracing their path unless we get information from those you have captured or from those Burt is tracking. One of the key pieces of information we must obtain is where they are coming from and how they have been able to infiltrate the network to have access to the planets they have raided.*

We believe that Engoza is the commander of all of Groga forces and a skilled agent, as you have discovered." He glanced at her forearm. *"We are hoping she will slip up, but so far our hope is in vain. Right now, the only strategy we have, is to find and capture any agents who may still be on Earth. The agents on your team are even now homing in on the location of what we believe to be their headquarters on Earth and when they find them, we will be ready to* assist in capturing them. If at all possible, we need them alive, to interrogate."

"*Lova has instructions to pass anything pertinent directly to the Council and to me.*" Jenny said, nodding to Lova.

"*We still await news from Burt's team,*" Lova said. "*Last we heard; they were preparing to enter a swampy area in Louisiana. Normally there would be no cell signal there, but the team is equipped with Alliance signal enhancers. We could communicate with them even if they were in a cave deep in the earth or under water. All of their communications devices are shielded, so they shouldn't be able to be detected by the Groga.*"

The Councilors nodded to Lova. "*It sounds as if, everything that can be done is being done by our Earth team,*" said Ingot, approvingly.

Suddenly Ingot went still, his eyes unfocused. Jenny realized he must be receiving a private mindspeech message.

He stood. "*They have begun to interrogate the one prisoner who is conscious. He is resistant, but they will report when they have anything noteworthy. The one is still unconscious and the one who has so many wounds from Tidbit's claws is in pretty bad shape, but they say he will survive for questioning. I would like to suggest that when they do that, Tarafau be in attendance as Tidbit. The chief guard seems to think this will be an effective way to 'encourage' him to be forthcoming.*" He grinned at Tarafau wickedly.

"*Wait,*" said Jenny, "*Tarafau can become Tidbit away from Earth?*"

"*And Tidbit can become Tarafau on Earth, but only in special circumstances. There are many reasons, including his ears and fangs why it would not be politic for him to run around Earth as Tarafau. This is why he is currently only allowed to become Tarafau in the shielded space at Sanglarka and in your dimensional gym. In an extreme emergency in the past, he has changed while he was on Earth, but those transformations were not seen by anyone living,*" he concluded grimly.

It seemed there was no end to surprises where Tarafau was concerned, she mused. She tried to imagine Tarafau shopping at her local mall and suppressed a giggle. Controlling her expression, she said, looking at her fellow Earth Guardians. "*I think I will stay at Sanglarka for awhile, at least until we have a clear path to follow. I will check in at the gate on Infinity Loop from time to time.*"

Something occurred to her. "*I thought you could just extract information with your ' dastardly alien tech', as Burt puts it. How can the Groga henchman be resisting?*"

Liliath answered. "*You have been taught the mind training exercises, yes?*"

Jenny nodded.

"*So, have our enemies. Their approach is different, but it has the same effect. The next step in your training will be to learn to close your mind to anyone you don't wish to have access to your thoughts, regardless of the methods they use. This is just one of the mental techniques you will need to learn.*

You have already seen the benefits of this training in your ordeal with Engoza, even though you are still learning. It is key to your position to learn every type of mental power you are able to learn. This varies from person to person. Lova is very skilled in this. Being able to use your mind, as well as your body, to protect yourself is one of the things that all Guardians and the Gatekeeper must continually practice.

In order for us to break down a skilled mental block, it may take days we do not really have, but there is nothing we can do to change this. This is one reason we feel Tidbit may be an incentive to breaking the resistance of the man he attacked. There is already fear there. If he knows the cat is in the room with him, he may break more easily than the others. We shall see."

Jenny thought that maybe having Liliath in the room with the others might be a great incentive as well, but she wasn't sure she felt brave enough to say so. Liliath's eyes were slits, which usually meant she was upset or angry about something. Her mom's old saying kept repeating in her head. Liliath had never been anything but kind to Jenny, but she didn't want to ever give her reason to feel otherwise.

Ingot stood, looking somberly from face to face. "*You all have your assignments. We will be asking much from all of you until this situation is resolved. I fear, whether it takes weeks or months or...longer, we will all be strained to the maximum of our capacity. We will communicate to your headquarters immediately, if there are any changes or news regarding our prisoners. Gariel will be travelling to meet you at your headquarters as soon as he has something to report concerning the progress in the interrogations.*

His second in command will take over his general duties, but he will be running our efforts from Sanglarka for now. We want him on the ground and ready to move quickly when the Groga agents are found and a plan is devised to capture them. We will transfer the MDPs you found to Sanglarka, so we may inventory them and discover how they can aid us in our fight and to potentially puzzle out why Engoza was so intent on retrieving them.

Be well, all of you. Much rests on your well-being. You are not alone. We will not fail you."

It was a dismissal. The company rose. All of them looked determined and grim.

Jenny turned to the Councilors. "*How long do you think until the man Tidbit shredded will be able to be interrogated?*"

Myla replied, "*The healers say a few days. We will notify you when we are ready for Tidbit.*"

Tarafau nodded. Jenny hugged each of the councilors in farewell and left behind her fellow Guardians. Most of them would be going home to secure their gates and then would be returning to Sanglarka as needed. Jenny had already secured her house, as much as it could be until the techs from Alliance headquarters were able to set up some new shields for both the house and the shed.

She thought about the little safe under the floor tiles. What were in those MDPs and why hadn't LizzieAI told her about them? So many questions and little time for answers.

Chapter 27: The Lair

Since she had returned, Sanglarka had become a buzzing hive of activity. Everyone had their assignments, and not all the Guardians were there at any given time, due to the necessity of continuing to step up security at every gate. Lova had increased Jenny's mental training sessions and Arvid was putting her through unarmed combat techniques, which meant more bruises both to her body and her ego.

Between that and the endless meetings and exploring the MDPs, the three days they had been back on Earth had seemed like weeks. Every night, after doing her breathing exercises, she had collapsed onto her bed like every bone in her body had dissolved. She didn't remember her dreams, but there had been no reoccurrence of Sam invading them. She was sure she would have remembered that.

Since Juan had been notified about the potential danger that Sam may be able to pinpoint his gateway, he had immediately been sent home to see to the protection of the estate. He assured Jenny when she had tried to apologize that this was a part of his job and he had prepared for it. "*I have a few tricks up my sleeve,*" he had said with a wink and a grin. "*I would never leave Luz unprotected, and she is by no means helpless.*" He got that dreamy look on his face that he had whenever he talked about his beautiful wife.

Aliki, Adelle and Guaray had undertaken to inventory the MDPs. The three of them had communicated with their Guides with instructions to assist the Alliance in securing their gates so they could stay in Sanglarka for this task. Between Aliki's photographic memory and Adelle and Guaray's background in research, they were well equipped to do a thorough job. That being said, they had only gotten through the first two, and the lists of equipment and supplies was more than a little surprising. The MDPs, when filled, were more like one of the "big box" stores than anything, large warehouses that expanded at need.

They had gotten very excited about a lot of tech that Jenny didn't begin to understand, but Aliki had said, "*This changes everything.*" He assured Jenny that both Burt and Bob would be extremely excited to see what Lizzie had accumulated over her 60 plus years of working as a Guardian.

He also told her that there was some of the tech in the first MDP they had explored that was unknown to him. He was hopeful, however, that Burt and the Alliance scientists would know more about it.

Lova and Tarafau had gone over the lists of equipment and supplies that had been found so far with blooming hope in their eyes.

Lova explained, "*We will need to be able to shore up security at every Earth gateway. This means using tech that is not scannable by any of the current technology available to Earthlings or the Groga. It also means employing more mundane methods that have been used for centuries on Earth by various cultures. We want to keep the Groga off their guard.*

In addition, much of the equipment on this list are surveillance related, which, when installed throughout the network, should give us advanced warning of imminent attack and will allow us to watch our enemy, hopefully unnoticed."

As Jenny continued her training, she concluded that, although she was constantly learning new things, her tasks were not impossible, as long as she took it one day at a time and was willing to rely on the experience of her team members. Trying to comprehend the entirety of it was just too overwhelming. Her dad had always said, "Do the work that's in front of you and do it well." It often surprised her how often the sayings she had rolled her eyes at as a teen turned out to be useful, after all.

At the end of the fifth day, Lova assembled them at the gate. In the waning light, Burt, Bob, Leland and Xao Ting stepped through, all looking tired and rumpled. "*We found them*," said Burt wearily, shaking his head. "*Let's get to work.*"

They followed the four into the lodge. Lova insisted they eat and rest before reporting, but Bob shook his head. "*We'll eat and rest, but first we need to bring you all up to speed.*"

They retired to the dining room. Arvid bustled off to the kitchen. When all were seated, Burt began.

"*If they had hidden out in pretty much anywhere but a Louisiana swamp we would have been back sooner. The beacons I planted in Moe and Curly are still active and sending a clear signal. But there are few roads where they have set up headquarters and there is no way to go in clandestinely except to hike in. There are no straight lines in a swamp and the swamps in that area are home to some of the most dangerous wildlife pretty much anywhere else on earth.*

Most everyone knows that there are alligators in the Louisiana swamps, but there are also bears, and more varieties of poisonous snakes as anywhere I've ever been, not to mention constrictors. Add to that bobcats and mosquitos big enough to carry off a Smart Car and you can begin to see what we're up against.

That being said, they haven't done much in the way of other security. I'm guessing they figure to let the native reptile population keep out unwanted visitors. There is definitely some kind of tech being used inside their compound and I do mean compound. They've got a force there, probably a few hundred Groga, which doesn't count for much against the forces just the Louisiana National Guard could bring to bear, but no one knows they're there and I think there's way more to this than it appears.

It isn't just a few brutal henchmen. This many Groga in one place could only mean one thing. They're planning something bigger than any of the raids they have done up to this point. I don't know if they are just using the swamp as a staging ground for raids to other dimensions or if they mean to do something here on our planet, but either way, it isn't good.

We got footage of their operation for the team to analyze, and we installed some recording equipment up in some of the cypress trees that surround their lair. We'll know if they appear to be getting ready to make a move. I don't think we were noticed, but I have to tell you, if they see us coming it won't be pretty. I'm voting we get the Troopers involved in this. If we're going to take this camp without letting any of them escape and without attracting attention, we're going to have to have a solid attack strategy. I would be surprised if this was an in and out mission. There's likely gonna be some fighting and there's gonna be some big risks.

One of those risks is alerting the governments of Earth that there is a combat mission right under their noses. We have to make sure that the satellites that survey that region are looking the other way, somehow, and we're going to have to keep it as quiet as a raging battle can possibly be. There isn't any human habitation for miles, but some sounds carry for a long way, if we don't figure out how to curtail that.

I want Gariel to head this operation up. He's a tactical genius and he may have some resources we don't have."

Aliki piped up. "*And we may have more resources than you think,*" he said with a big grin.

"*You found something?*" Bob asked excitedly.

"*Yep, five MDPs from the storage shed behind Jenny's house, and we're only mostly through the second one. That Lizzie was the ultimate pack rat."*

Lova nodded. "*And we'll brief you about it over your meal,*" as Arvid came into the dining room laden with trays of food which he sat before Burt's team.

None of them argued the offering of food even for a moment.

Lova brought them up to speed on everything that had happened in their absence. Bob sent a worried glance at Jenny when they recounted the attack by the Groga in Jenny's living room. She tried to smile back encouragingly, but Bob just shook his head in disbelief and the look of horror on Burt's face would have been funny, if it wasn't so unexpected and sincere.

"*Have you heard anything back about the interrogations, yet?*" Burt asked clearing his expression.

"*We expect to hear soon. It appears the one who was still conscious after the conflict is very mentally resistant to our extractors, so they are attempting,*" she paused, pursing her lips, "*other means.*"

Xao Ting had been sitting quietly between Burt and Bob, but now he spoke up. "*I may be of some assistance in that area. There are some herbs…*" he left the words hanging in the air.

"*I'll let them know,*" Lova replied.

She turned to Jenny. "*What are your thoughts, Gatekeeper?*" she asked respectfully.

Jenny hesitated, looking into the faces of the Guardians, Guards and Agents assembled before her. When did a twenty-something blogger become the leader of an interdimensional force? She saw hope and confidence and worry all at once on those faces. She felt very small and inadequate at the moment.

"I am not a general or a statesman. I am a girl from Earth who has gotten herself way in over her head, but I have the best possible team and councilors anyone could ask for. I'll try my best to do my part, but I must depend on the collective experience and skills of each of you. Between us and the resources we can call on from the Alliance, I believe we can do this. We must do this.

The people of our planet are unaware, with all of their petty squabbles and big plans, that an inimical force has become entrenched here. We must try to keep it that way, if we can, because I don't think than anyone on Earth is any more ready for this than I am.

Lova, please acquaint The Council with our current situation and consult with Burt as to what we need. Burt, I think you should add Brendan to your team. Aliki, in the morning, I want you to do a walkthrough with Burt's team of what your team has found in the MDPs, so far. There has to be something in one of them that Sneaky Sam was aware of and that she wanted bad enough to blow her cover at this stage.

You also need to speak with Megan. She knows a lot about wildlife, and I think there may be some ways we can use that to our advantage.

As for the rest of us, it will be important to increase our vigilance in the gateways and their surroundings. I would like Adelle to put her brilliant mind to work on how these Groga are circumventing the gateways. With her grasp of science, she should be able to get together with the Alliance physicists to figure this out. If the Groga can do this, then they might not be the only ones. We need to know how they are managing to slip onto Earth without using any of the known gates.

That's all I can think of right now. I need everyone to reassemble here right after breakfast tomorrow morning, so we can work out the details and make any additional assignments any of you can think of that I've missed."

Lova nodded. "*Jenny has the right of it. This is bigger than any one of us could handle on our own, but together we have the resources and the talents necessary to get this done. Right now, everyone needs to get some rest, so we can get an early start.*"

Next morning, the entire group did their run and workouts together. It reminded Jenny of the many wonderful hours she had spent with her hiking group and that memory brought pain to her heart again. All those happy times completely ruined by the blatant and unfeeling betrayal by her best friend. She pushed it aside. "Think of what you have, not what you don't have," came back to her mind.

This group of Guardians, Guards and Agents were fast becoming something more than a team dedicated to a mission. Jenny knew that when it came down to it, she could trust any of those gathered at Sanglarka with her life and the fate of her planet. She had to keep reminding herself that the fate of the Dimensional Alliance also hung in the balance. But for now, it helped decrease the immensity of it all to focus on saving Earth.

All of her life Jenny had been fascinated by space and had dreamed of space travel. The universe had been bigger than she could imagine and now she found out that she lived in one universe among billions, each as vast as her own, and that somehow the actions she and her little team would take in the near future would impact more than she could possibly count or even envision for eons to come.

After a good night's sleep, workouts, showers and the usual Sanglarka breakfast, the diners helped clear the table and returned to meet about last night's revelations.

Jenny stood, and they got quiet. "*I hope everyone is rested and your minds are clear,*" she began. Unlike the day before, she had spent time before sleep considering carefully everything Lova, Tarafau and Burt had revealed to her and what she needed to do to organize her resources. She felt much more prepared. "*I don't want to spend a lot of time just batting things around. I'll be coming around to get a report from each team once we separate into groups, so we can put together a plan as quickly as possible. I'll give everyone until the end of the day to come up with the best tentative plans you can. We are expecting Gariel and Brendan sometime later today who will be joining Burt's team. We have sent them each a brief, so you won't have to start them from scratch.*

Arvid is setting up a buffet so that people can go ahead and eat as they are ready to take a break without having to worry about a mealtime schedule and I want you to feel free to continue to work while you eat."

At this there was a chuckle that went around the room. Like they would even consider slowing work for something so mundane as eating, unless, of course, it was Arvid's masterful cooking!

"In the meantime, if you have any questions for Lova, Tarafau or me, just let us know. Is that clear?"

A concurrent nodding of heads and chairs scooting back told her that they were ready to get started.

Bob sidled over to Jenny who hadn't yet risen from her chair. *"Wow, kiddo. I'm impressed. I had commanders in the military that didn't take charge this well. Obviously, all that training with Lova, Tarafau and the LizzieAI is paying off. We'll get this done. Mark my word."* Jenny realized that maybe Lizzie's slip would make all of this much easier. Bob was going to be a true asset, both for the team and for her.

Some of the groups headed out to the balcony that stretched the length of the lodge overlooking a valley filled with wildflowers, a magnificent view of the snow-capped mountains framed in a crystal blue sky frosted with wispy streaks of nearly transparent clouds. Others convened in one or more of the private offices or the library. Tarafau gathered Jenny's guards and headed toward the workout room. When they all had dispersed, Nova steered Jenny out the front door toward the gate. The Sanglarka gate actually looked like a white picket garden gate, arched by a white trellis draped in wild roses.

"Brendan and Gariel will be coming through soon," Lova said, as they stood before the gate. *"I thought it would be nice to meet them, so we can get them into their groups as quickly as possible. Both of*

them will be meeting with Burt's group first and then Gariel will be meeting with you, me, Arvid and Tarafau."

"*Lova, I'm glad I got to spend a few moments privately with you. I think you probably know that I am 'scared spitless' about all of this, as my dad used to say. I am not afraid of the conflict, although I've never been in any kind of a fight in my life, but I'm mostly afraid I'm going to mess this up. I know next to nothing about fighting or strategy or subterfuge, except what I've read about in books. I'm not afraid of technology. My generation was raised with it, but I don't know enough about what the tech we have can do. Isn't there someone else who can take over for me?*"

Lova arched her eyebrows, puzzlement clear on her face. "*Are you saying you want to quit? I don't believe that of you for one moment.*"

Jenny shook her head vehemently. "*No, I'd just like someone else to be in charge.*"

Lova put an arm around her shoulders. She smelled of herbs and fresh air. She put a finger under Jenny's chin, tilting her head up to look into her eyes. "*You, my dear, are more than you know. I can see why Lizzie was so excited about you. Few more experienced people could do what you've already done for this group. You have organized them into teams that make sense, based on the tasks at hand and the skills represented. You are willing to take counsel and you aren't afraid of hard work. You have acted even through your fear and you have done more than any of us originally expected of you.*

It's true you weren't given much of a choice when The Gatekeeper passed her key to you, but you didn't flinch from the responsibility." She stepped back, her hands on Jenny's shoulders. "*You will do well, as well as anyone could do under the circumstances and better than most.*"

Jenny embraced Lova in a grateful hug. "Thank you," she whispered. "Thank you."

They pulled apart and stood there for a moment, looking into one another's eyes. Then her key warmed and they turned in unison toward the gate.

At that moment, Brendan emerged from the gate, followed by Gariel. The tall muscular Aussie greeted them with, "G'day" and Gariel nodded at them.

"*We got the briefing,*" Gariel said. "*That should make this move a lot faster. We have gotten a bit of intelligence from the one conscious prisoner and the healers expect the man Tidbit shredded to be well enough to interrogate by tomorrow. There have been no additional raids, as far as we know, since the last one reported. I get the feeling the Groga are planning something on a larger scale and that we're not going to like it. The sooner we can get a working strategy and assemble the troopers, the better.*"

"*It looks like the one who is still unconscious may have a bit worse concussion than originally thought. He will live, but they're not sure how functional he'll be. Amnesia isn't uncommon in that kind of skull damage. I hear, our Jenny took that one out,*" Brendan said, clucking his tongue. "*Give a woman a stick...*" He shook his head and grinned at her like a little kid.

Jenny didn't know what to say to that, so she nodded her head.

"*They've already separated into groups,*" Lova said as they entered the foyer of the lodge. "*I believe Burt's group is out on the balcony.*"

Brendan and Gariel headed towards the windowed doors leading out to the balcony and Lova led Jenny to the workout room. There, Tarafau the bandage still wrapped around his head, and Arvid were back to back, sparring with Lyra, Nona and Mynn, three on two. The Guards were holding their own, circling and getting in a tap here and there, but the two men's staffs whirled in a nearly impenetrable barrier.

"Time out!" hollered Lova in what her dad would have called her "drill sergeant" voice.

The staffs immediately stopped, except Lyra's who exacted one last "crack!" on Tarafau's backside. Tarafau growled at her, but she just laughed and ducked quickly behind her fellow Guards.

"*I seem to recall the healers said, no physical activity for you, old cat.*" Lova said, her hands on her hips.

Tarafau and Arvid had the grace to look embarrassed and Lyra jumped in with. "*We were going easy on him,*" and then clamped her mouth shut at the quelling look Lova sent her way.

"Tarafau and Arvid, we need to visit Burt's group. Brendan and Gariel are about to brief them on the interrogation and I don't want to miss it."

Arvid and Tarafau nodded. Lyra, Nona and Mynn fell into step right behind them. By the time they got out there, Gariel had just stood, preparing to speak. Arvid grabbed some chairs and pulled them over as Gariel began.

"*As I told Lova,*" he began, "*we haven't gotten as much information as we would like, but it appears the Groga have teamed up with a group of rogue agents who were kicked out of the Alliance for one reason or another. They don't come from any one dimension. They're a rag tag lot and we could probably have mopped this whole thing up if it wasn't for the fact that they seem to have a sponsor from an unknown dimension besides the Groga and the Fleistians. It is this unknown element that has us worried.*

The good news is that they don't seem to be using the Alliance network.

The fact that they attacked and killed a Gatekeeper and have raided in several dimensions already is bad enough, but knowing they have access to a way to sidestep the gate network is beyond terrifying. These preliminary raids were just to assess their strategy, I believe, and since they have been successful, the evidence suggests they are planning something much bigger.

This means your mission to capture the Groga in their lair here on Earth is vital, if we are going to stop this threat before it gets any bigger. The damage they could do to the multiverse could be irreparable if whatever they are planning succeeds, since there is no way to keep them from encroaching on many unsuspecting worlds when we have no idea how they're doing it. So much of the multiverse actually lives in relative peace and is therefore not prepared to defend themselves from this kind of threat.

This is why the Dimensional Alliance has sent me here. Your operation here is first priority and a large part of our forces are on standby. That being said, we have to be in readiness to move as we are needed. After we assess what you will need, we will deploy whatever resources you require."

Every face in the group was grim. It was Bob who broke the silence. "*Well, us Earthlings won't lay down and let them run over the less prepared. First, let's get them off of our planet and figure out how to seal those gateways. Then, let's kick them out of the multiverse once and for all.*"

Chapter 28: Out of Small Things…

As they sat down that evening at the long dining room table, every jaw was set and every eye was determined. Each team had conferred, and, using their own specialties and skills, they had come up with a plan that surprised Jenny. It used an ingenious combination of high tech and no tech in a way Jenny would have never considered.

Megan, the quiet, shy woman, who had interned at the Henry Doorly Zoo in Omaha, Nebraska, home of the largest indoor swamp in the world, had come up with an idea to use the local wildlife against the interlopers. Brendan, who had hunted crocs in Australia, had teamed up with Megan and between them and Bob, they had concocted a somewhat bizarre plan that would more than just distract the Groga and soften them up for the Troopers, who would be there to keep the enemy from escaping and mop up when it was done.

Their plan for stage one would require a platoon of small drones, which, as it turns out, a number of the Guardians flew as a hobby. They had discovered a couple score of drones in the MDPs. So, it was totally doable, and this part of the plan wouldn't expose any of the Alliance troops to danger or expose the use of "dastardly alien tech".

Jenny noticed that Megan seemed a lot more at ease with the other Guardians than she had at their first meeting.

Bob reported his part of the plan next. He couldn't resist employing some alien tech that had been discovered in the first MDP. It was amazing how quickly he fell back into his military training. He stood, his hands in his pockets, rocking excitedly on the balls of his feet, "*Sometimes if you want to do big things, you have to think small. We found some flying nanobots that have some unique programming. It will make the overall plan work more effectively and it will minimize casualties, at least on our side.*"

As he continued to reveal the unique way he would be employing these little flying bots, Jenny realized that Bob had a mean streak she had never noticed before now. She made a mental note to never make him angry.

By the time they had each laid out their individual facets of the plan, Jenny and Lova had to remind them that they needed at least some of the Groga to survive the attack. "*We won't be able to get any intelligence out of them if they're all dead.*" Lova commented wryly.

Tarafau stood up behind Jenny, his hand on her shoulder. "*Gariel tells me that it's time for Tidbit to put in an appearance at headquarters to encourage a blind Groga to tell us his darkest secrets. Jenny, her Guards and I will go to Alliance Headquarters to interview the man that Tidbit attacked. I expect the results will be interesting.*" The satisfied look on his face said much more than his words.

"*The Troopers assigned to the first stage of the operation will be here in the morning and Burt's team is going to the staging site to get set up for the attack. We've hired a number of different transports to get us there, hopefully without attracting any notice. There will be no uniforms. And the non-humanoid forces will be transported in closed vehicles. The idea is to filter in as quietly as possible,*" Gariel said. "*Burt and his team have put together a solid plan that's tactically sound. Assuming the plan is successful, no one outside of that swamp will be any the wiser.*"

"*Does anyone have any questions?*" Jenny asked. "*While they are setting up the operation, the rest of us will set up a situation room. I'm assuming that the surveillance recordings can be made available here?*" she asked, turning to Lova. Lova nodded.

"*Good. The other teams will continue to work on their tasks. We especially need to finish the inventory of the MDPs. Tarafau and I will return as soon as we finish with the interrogation, hopefully with more information about where we stand,*" she paused, remembering the other point she needed to emphasize. "*Please remember, that some of those Groga need to survive your attack. We need as much information as we can gather, if we're going to stop this.*"

They adjourned, each of the members of Burt's team bustling off to prepare. Jenny stood and Tarafau and her guards followed her and Lova into the dining room. Arvid had prepared a nice buffet complete with salad bar and desserts. They each grabbed a plate and, at Jenny's request, retired to the office Jenny had used before. "*This should work just fine for a situation room,*" Jenny said to Lova.

"*Is there a floating screen here?*" referring to the screen that had hung above the dining room table earlier.

"*This office is fully equipped,*" said Lova. "*I'll make arrangements to move some of the furniture and install an appropriate table and chairs. We'll have it all ready when you and Tarafau return.*"

Lova saw them off to the gate. Xao Ting had given them some special herbal tinctures that he claimed would produce agitation without reducing mental clarity. Jenny pocketed the vial.

When they stepped through, there was a contingent of Guards waiting for them. This was unusual. Generally, the gate was protected by the scanner and the Guards waited at the bottom of the pleasant walk down the hill.

When Jenny questioned them about it, they simply replied that security was being stepped up at all gateways and she would be getting instructions when she got to the Council room.

When Jenny and Tarafau walked into the Council room, all three Councilors were there, in addition to a couple of Guards.

"*These two will be escorting you to the interrogation section. It is a highly secure area and this is standard procedure. Before you leave, do you have any questions?*" Ingot said, getting right to the point.

"*The Guards that escorted us from the Gate, said there would be instructions on the new security procedures?*" Jenny countered.

"*When you and Tarafau are finished with the interrogation. We thought it would be good for you to be in attendance as well as Tidbit. You may have some insights we may miss. We'll be viewing the interview from here.*"

As he said this, a new transparent screen popped into view directly in front of the dais.

Jenny and Tarafau followed the Guards down the elevator to the Guard Station without speaking. The two Guards looked so somber and official, Jenny admitted to herself that she felt somewhat intimidated, even though she knew they would not harm her.

When they filed through the security scanner, another official greeted them respectfully. "*The subject will be shielded, but he will be able to hear you and to*", looking at Tarafau, "*smell you.*"

Jenny thought she detected a slight smile on his lips that came and vanished before she was sure. "*I've brought an herbal tincture, created by Xao Ting, one of the Earth Guardians. He seemed to think it would help increase the effectiveness of the interrogation. He said to put a drop on each wrist of the prisoner and wait about 2 minutes for the effects to set in. That is when Tidbit should make himself known.*"

The guard nodded and accepted the little vial from Jenny. They followed him into a room that wasn't much different from the small rooms in the infirmary, except that, instead of a bed, there was a large, heavy metal chair with a big burly man, restrained by what appeared to be leather straps on his arms, feet and his neck and fastened to the chair.

He scowled at the sound of footsteps but said nothing.

Jenny was shocked at the all too apparent damage to his face, neck and arms. Tarafau hadn't exaggerated when he had said he had "shredded" him. His eyelids were tatters and the eyeballs that showed between strips of skin were no longer white, but dark red, as if filled with blood. His entire nose was scabbed over and his lips were as ragged as a torn cloth. Jenny wondered how he would be able to speak until she realized that this interrogation would probably be conducted entirely with mindspeech.

The guard turned his hands over to add the drops of tincture on his wrists. Jenny was not surprised to see the amount of damage to his hands and wrists, most likely inflicted as he had tried to pry Tidbit from his face.

The guard sent to the group, "*We have a few questions.*"

The man spat in his direction through ragged lips.

The satisfied smile on that ravaged face changed to pure terror when Tidbit, now transformed, let out that eerie "mrrrreeeeowww!" The man looked fearfully around, although unable to see, and struggled in his bonds. "*Get that THING away from me!*" The thought was a piercing shout that hurt Jenny's mental ears.

"*We have some questions,*" the Guard began again. The man shook his head frantically, his body arched in the chair. The Guard simply stood there, saying nothing while the man struggled.

Tidbit growled deep in this throat and then stropped the man's ankles. As the cat touched him, Jenny thought the man was going to strangle himself trying to get away. Tidbit hissed and spit.

The guard continued to stand there quietly, and Jenny suddenly remembered something from her mom's favorite cop show. "Good cop, bad cop," she thought with a grin.

"*Please, Mr. Guard, can't you take the cat away? The man is terrified!*" she sent with a note of sympathy thrown in for good measure. "*Please! I can't stand to watch this.*"

The guard replied sternly, "*I can do nothing if the man chooses not to talk. The cat has a right to be here to witness the interrogation as much as you do.*" He nodded with understanding at Jenny, encouraging her to continue.

"*But if he talks can you take the cat away?*" she pled with the guard. "*If he answers your questions?*"

"*This sort don't answer questions, Miss,*" he replied gruffly. "*I guess I'll just have to turn him over to the cat. Come with me. You won't want to watch this…*"

"*NO!!!*" the man wailed in their minds. "*Please, don't leave me alone with him!*"

"*I can do nothing if you won't cooperate.*"

The man was becoming more and more agitated as Tarafau "mrrrrreeeowed" once more, his cat voice starting low and rising to the screech of an animal about to attack.

"*I'll talk! Please! I'll talk!*"

The guard nodded, and Tidbit walked back to Jenny, purring loudly. He waved Jenny and Tidbit out the door with a finger to his lips and turned to the man.

The Guard who had been standing outside the door smiled broadly as she and Tarafau followed him back to the Council room. When they got there, the Councilors were engrossed in the screen before them. They motioned for Jenny and Tarafau to take seats on the dais next to them.

"So far, he has only confirmed what we already know, but he is getting more and more willing to answer questions as he goes. The other man chewed his tongue off between sessions and bled to death. The unconscious one has revived, but as we feared, remembers nothing. So you see how important this one has become." Myla told them once they were seated.

As they sat there, Jenny was surprised to find that instead of speakers, the audio feed was direct mind contact. She heard both the Guard's questions and the answers of the scarred and frightened prisoner, very clearly.

Most of the questions sounded almost routine. How was he recruited? What was his commander's name? What was his mission? All of these he answered freely.

He was recruited from a merchant's guard on his planet. His commander's name was Morgent. His mission was to find The Gatekeeper's gate and to pillage the storage shed of any items that might be useful. But when the Guard finally asked him what dimension he came from and how they had come to Earth, he suddenly stiffened, his bloody eyes wide, his ragged mouth in an "o" of surprise. He coughed once, blood spewing from his mouth and went limp.

The Guard turned away from the lifeless, shattered thing still suspended in his bonds. He looked up at what was probably the camera and shook his head morosely. *"I was afraid of that,"* was all he said.

"*Trapped!*" Ingot fumed as he terminated the screen, "*trapped to implode when a certain question was asked.*"

"*I don't know how to get around a mind trap like that,*" said Liliath. "*We're going to need as many prisoners from the Earth raid as we can get. It may take some time to figure this out. In the meantime, we aren't much ahead of where we were before.*"

Jenny put her head in her hands. As grisly as it had been, she felt no compassion for the man who had died, only disappointment that they still didn't have the information they needed. The life and survival of her planet depended on it.

"*What do we do now?*" she asked, hoping she had kept the plaintive note out of her mental voice. This was no time to appear to be weak. People were depending on her.

For a moment, no one spoke. Finally, Liliath raised her head. At this moment she reminded Jenny of every scary dragon painting she had ever seen. She seemed to grow as she sat before them, tendrils of smoke leaking from her nose and mouth, her eyes narrowed and the end of her tail twitching like Tidbit when he was agitated or angry. Then Jenny realized that her colors were shifting from blue and green to red and purple.

For one startling moment she thought that Liliath was responding to her whine, then she realized that Liliath wasn't looking at her.

"*We have been too soft.*" The murmur in her head accompanied the low auditory rumble that was emanating from Liliath. "*Words burn in me. I can no longer suppress them. We cannot afford compassion or benign non-interference in this case. While it is true that we do not advocate force, we cannot sacrifice the peace and growth of worlds without end for the avarice and violent natures of a small minority. I can no longer tolerate it!*" And she brought a clawed fist down on the dais so hard that it nearly threw Jenny out of her chair.

Myla stood and placed one hand on Liliath's heaving shoulder. "*I'm with you,*" he sent quietly. "*We need to finish this once and for all.*"

Ingot nodded solemnly, reaching up and placing his hand on her chest. "*I agree. This is an infestation that cannot be allowed to continue. Our patience is at an end.*"

The three turned as one to Jenny. "*Earth has become the lynchpin.*" Ingot said, "*If we are to be successful in routing the Groga, it all begins there. Set your plans into motion now. While you are accumulating the intelligence we require, we will assemble the other Guardians and put enhanced security on every known gate. Most of the worlds where there are gateways are as vulnerable as Earth.*

Planets and universes that are fully aware of the gates are few for reasons you have probably guessed by now.

The Guards who will be returning with you will brief all of the Guardians on Earth of the new security procedures which will be implemented immediately. This includes increased, on the ground, personal Guards for every Guardian and their Gates, as well as automated weaponized security measures that are being installed on every gate even as we speak, starting with the Earth gates. We do not think these incursions are happening through known gates, but we are taking no chances.

There is a reason why they are attacking gateways, but it is puzzling if they have their own ways of getting into other dimensions. There also seems to be a deadline they need to meet, at this point. We need to focus on getting this information, as well as their points of egress and their overall plan. So much depends on this.

The cultures are rare that are fully ready to embrace the gateways and their best uses. For the most part our function is to prevent incursions such as the Groga from happening. I do not know the purpose of The Creator in making the network of gateways, but I do know that this isn't the first time the cause of evil has been facilitated by them. Those of us who stand for good cannot allow unsuspecting populations to be ravaged in this way, if it is within our ability to stop it."

"*I cannot promise success,*" Jenny replied, looking each in the eye in turn. "*I can promise that my team is dedicated to doing our best. With your help and the guidance and training that is being generously provided, I hope to grow into my calling. For now, however, I will continue to depend on the experience and wisdom and skills of those who support me. Thank you for the trust you have put in me.*"

Tarafau laid his hand on her shoulder. "*We must return. The operation is ready to set into motion and we need to be there. I assume the Troopers who are supporting us have already arrived at Sanglarka?*"

Ingot nodded.

"*Then we will be off.*"

"*May the Creator of All Things grant you the strength and courage you require.*" Ingot said.

As they turned to leave, Jenny, straightened her shoulders. There was work to do.

Chapter 29: Into the Swamp

Sanglarka was quiet. With the exception of Jenny's Guards, Lova, and Tarafau, the others were all at their tasks, either on the operation in the Louisiana swamp or setting up the increased security at their gates. At this point, they were waiting, something that Jenny despised. It gave her way too much time to think and to worry. A million what-ifs went through her mind.

All of her troops had begun their journey, but they had to rely on standard air and ground transportation, for the most part, departing from various gateways in small groups, careful not to trigger security measures in the various countries they were filtering through. It would be a few more days before all would be in place. In the meantime, time dragged on her like lead weights.

Reports were coming in from the situation room as each unit fell into place. At the point when the operation would be set in motion, it was likely they would not budge from that room. In the meantime, Lova continued Jenny's lessons in mind control and she worked out daily with Lova, Arvid and Tarafau. She did all of her running on a treadmill to stay close to the action and to be able to handle anything new that came up.

She had come to a point in her training where Lova would test her strength in many ways, with distractions, loud noises, even pain. Jenny got to the point where she could hold the pain and distractions away from her conscious mind without even having to think about it. When Lova or Tarafau or her Guards would attack her randomly, her mental shields automatically bloomed in her head and they were getting stronger by the day.

Her ability to use her hands and feet to defend herself was also increasing. It was amazing to her, as short as she was, that she could throw Lova and that she could even give Tarafau a good fight, even though she had yet to throw him. When she had initially started training with Arvid, she had been intimidated about fighting without her quarterstaff, which by now felt very natural to her hand. Now, although she was still mostly a novice, she could break most holds and had learned to use the other person's strength and weight against them.

She fervently hoped the time would never come where she would need to use it, she continued to work very hard to learn as fast as she could.

She spent a lot of time with LizzieAI, learning more about different dimensions and her dual roles as both Guardian and Gatekeeper since, at this point, the training by the other Guardians had been put on hold until they could get past this vital mission.

Finally, after all the waiting, it was almost startling to realize that it was finally time. Everything was in place and the team was about to launch the attack. There was a seven hour time difference between Sweden and the swamp. Burt had opened up the surveillance feed and kept a running commentary on the action taking place in front of them.

"Today we are using a combination of ' dastardly alien tech ' and good old mother nature to set up the Groga for a rout. They're mostly big brutes, none quite as hefty as our sweet kitty cat, but big enough to be going on with.

Bob is his own team. He has rigged several hundred of the tiny flying nanobots to imitate the nasty, hungry mosquitos who live here. Their job is three fold. First, they make this horrendous buzzing noise, aiming mostly for the ears. This will help distract and keep them from noticing the drones which are in the second wave of the attack. Second, they actually bite, even if they don't suck blood. But it will feel like a bug bite, itching and all. Third, they have a feed to the memory extractor device.

We think that if we can distract them enough, their defenses will be down, and we can get information they wouldn't give us consciously. Several nanobots will attack each Groga they can get to.

The second wave will be using the extremely cool drones we found in MDP number 2. Adelle and Megan have programmed a blue tooth controller with a special 'dastardly alien tech' booster that will allow us to fly the drones in formation. There are sixteen of them, each with a hook on the belly of the drone. Suspended by four corners, one hanging from each of four drones, is a bag of cow blood that is set up to drip blood down on the heads of the Groga, as well as on their equipment and the ground around them.

Were you aware that alligators stalk and kill prey starting at dusk and through the night? Just after supper time, as the light is starting to fade, we will launch the first wave. While they are busy swatting at our 'mosquitos", we will start the drones over the camp, dribbling blood over everything as they pass."

Jenny couldn't help but wonder at this part of the plan. She remembered something about an old horror movie with blood being dumped on someone, but how could this possibly hurt the Groga?

"Along with dribbling blood, the drones will be broadcasting the roar of the bull alligator in every direction. The camp is mostly surrounded by water, infested with alligators, which we have been privately feeding around the area for awhile. We haven't fed them in 24 hours, so I imagine they are ready for a snack.

The smell of blood and the roar of the gator will attract them. They will go tearing through the camp and there is only one road out, which we have blocked and surrounded on both sides with hidden armed troopers.

If the plan works, the Groga won't even take the time to grab anything as they leave the camp. If there are any documents or other clues, we will be able to scoop them up while we are loading Groga into moving vans. Once in the vans, we will pipe sleepy time gas, courtesy of Xao Ting, into the storage compartments and remove them to a nifty little storage unit we have prepared specifically for their 'special needs'.

So, what do you think?"

"I'm speechless," admitted Jenny, looking at Tarafau who was beaming with a wicked, cat-like smile, baring his fangs. Lova simply nodded her approval, since she had been very much a part of the planning of the operation.

Burt looked at his watch. "Operation Gator Bait, commencing in, 5...4...3...2...1...Liftoff!"

He grinned, and the camera view switched to above the trees, apparently one of the drone's point of view.

The sun had nearly disappeared to the west, but under the canopy of trees, it was already dark. Finally, it passed over a dirt and gravel road. As it traveled up the dirt road, Jenny could barely see the moving vans, covered in jungle netting and she assumed that the troopers were camouflaged to the point that no one would see them in this half-light.

The camera switched to night vision mode as the sun finally sank below the horizon. Jenny realized she was holding her breath only after she let it out with a huge sigh. Lova grabbed her hand and held it. "*Breathe*," she sent. "*Remember your breathing.*"

As the road opened into the camp, Jenny was surprised to realize the Groga had somehow obtained U.S. Army tents and equipment, probably from a surplus store. There were six large barracks-sized tents, one with the sides rolled up that looked like they were using it as a mess tent.

Men were seated, or standing, some working on equipment, some with cups of some kind of beverage in their hands, talking about whatever Groga soldiers talked about. They looked like larger and heavier-than-usual human beings. No one would have suspected they were aliens.

Suddenly a few of them scowled and swatted, as if at mosquitos or gnats. The assault had begun. If the situation hadn't been so important, it almost would have been humorous. Those who hadn't yet been attacked by the little bots, stood looking at their fellows dancing around and some of them did point and laugh, that is, until they too found themselves trying to fend off the little pests. In less than a minute, nearly every one of them were dancing wildly, slapping at themselves.

"Did I mention? Xao Ting helped us add a little extra itch to their bite. They won't be comfortable for quite awhile. And, according to Xao, they should be feeling the effects for about a week," he chortled.

In the meantime, phase two was beginning. The small drone army flew over, emitting the roar and challenge of a bull alligator while sprinkling the dancing Groga with cow blood. From the edge of the water beyond the camp came answering bellows. At first the Groga didn't seem to notice, because they were entirely engrossed in combatting the bite'ems and squirming to scratch the intense itch generated by their bites. By the time they noticed the first alligator charging from the bank, it was almost too late for them to run. In the confusion, they dropped everything, pushing for speed.

"According to Megan, an adult alligator can run up to 11 miles per hour and they can jump up to 6 feet. They can even climb trees and fences to get to their prey," Burt cut in conversationally. *"Especially when they're hungry, poor things."*

The Groga were running full out toward the road. They had no idea their vehicles had been disabled by simply cutting the battery cables. Once they realized their safe transportation was non-functional, they scattered down the road. The gators had stopped chasing them, of course. Gators by their nature are somewhat lazy hunters. But the Groga didn't realize it, since the drones were following behind them, still broadcasting those horrifying roars.

By the time they passed the part of the road that hid the troopers, they were nearly spent in the panic of running flat out for nearly a mile, so that when they found themselves surrounded by armed troopers, most of them simply collapsed to the road in a panting heap. The few that thought to continue running, were stopped in their tracks, by the menacing weapons of the troopers.

The troopers loaded them onto the waiting moving trucks and slammed the doors shut.

Amazingly, not one of the team was hurt and, as far as they knew, they had captured every single Groga in the camp alive, although some of them had been injured in their frantic flight from the charging gators.

"We'll lure the gators away to another part of the swamp, now, and wait for the other denizens of the swamp to settle down, then we'll go in and clean up the camp. It'll all be packaged up and sent to The Alliance for examination. Most of the team will be headed back to Sanglarka tonight. It will take a day or two to collect everything the Groga have left behind, once the gators have been redirected. A platoon of Troopers will help us with clean up. We'll stay in touch. Burt, signing off."

The feed went black and then suddenly lit up again. Data was pouring into a file labeled, "Groga mind feed".

"We're already getting some results in from the mind extraction program in the bots," Lova said, relief etched plainly on her face. "We'll let it fill up and then we'll sort through it after we eat."

After supper, each of them took a different set of files to review. Most of it was very similar to the information they already had. The majority of it was stream of consciousness of minds that seemed to have just one focus. Follow orders, eat, sleep, follow orders. Many of the coarse thought processes made Jenny sick to her stomach. The ones she went through in the beginning were violent, crude and greedy, with no thought for anything but their mind-numbing routine. (Not that, she was sure, they had much of a mind to numb in the first place, after having read several of the files.)

Suddenly Tarafau grunted and held up a hand for them to stop.

"I've found one of the officers. They don't seem to be all that much more intelligent than their soldiers, but evidently, they were entrusted with a little more information. As it turns out, they are definitely using an alternate portal that was not officially linked to the Alliance network. From what he was told, there are many such spread across the dimensions that work on a slightly different frequency.

This fellow doesn't have the capacity to understand the science of it and he doesn't seem to have the frequency or any access information in his head. There is, however, something there that concerns us greatly. We have a spy among us. One of the Guardians is not on our side. And he names the traitor. It's time we take steps and cut off their source.

We will wait until our teams return and then we will assemble at Alliance Headquarters for a," he paused, considering his next word, *"debriefing."*

Chapter 30: The Dissembler

With the agreement of The Council, the only thing the Earth Guardians were told about the meeting In The Alliance Council room was that it would reveal the results of the interrogations and the information that had been found by the ground crew at the end of Operation Gator Bait.

Every Guardian was in attendance, as well as Tarafau, Burt, Bob, Lyra, Nona, Mynn. Gariel and a couple of stone-faced, uniformed Guards. Jenny could feel that there were mental conversations passing between the attendees as they waited in audible silence for the Councilors to mount the dais.

The Guardians were seated in a large semi-circle, in no particular order, with the Agents and Guards mixed into the group, a seemingly casual meeting about the events of the previous week.

Jenny found herself doing her mental exercises to calm her racing heart. The rest seemed their normal selves. Megan wasn't fidgeting as much as she usually did. She was beginning to feel more at ease, after having worked closely with several of them during the raid on the Groga camp. It was clear that she and Adelle were having a mental chat. Aliki was his usually cheerful self. Dhakirah sat calmly, her dark almost liquid eyes unfocused, probably also in conversation with Adelle and Megan. Guaray sat silently, his arms folded across his chest, seated, somewhat uncomfortably between Tarafau and Brendan. The rest sat more or less patiently for the meeting to begin.

Ingot got to his feet and stood before the group, scanning each face until sure he had their attention.

"We have much to discuss today. Let me begin by congratulating you, one and all, for a brilliantly planned and executed operation. 274 prisoners, most of them uninjured, now are detained in an ultra-secure site in the mountains of Colorado. All continue to be sedated and guarded 24 hours a day.

The strategy to distract them so skillfully that we were able to get past their mental guards was mostly successful. We did indeed get some key information from them, which we will discuss in a moment.

We also were able to extract some additional intelligence from a few documents they left behind. Once again, this will be explained later in this session.

Our first order of business, however, is high priority. It appears we have a traitor among us."

Gasps and shocked faces showed throughout the room, with the exception of those who were in on the secret.

"And we know who it is…" but before he could finish, Guaray jumped up from his seat, turning to flee, only to be intercepted by Tarafau and Brendan. He turned away from them, only to find Jenny's three Guards before him, quarter-staffs held menacingly in guard position. The two grim guards who stood in the back of the room moved forward.

It was as if he was one of those blow-up punching clowns that had been punctured. He deflated as if he were going to faint. Tarafau and Brendan each grabbed him by an arm.

"What *do you have to say for yourself?*" Myla demanded, standing between Ingot and Liliath, his feathers fluffed and his eyes pinning.

Guaray didn't even make a pretense of denying any of it.

"The reason I found that Guardian in that alleyway that day was because I killed her. She didn't know I was her killer. I got her with a poison dart that is fairly quick acting. She thought I was trying to help her, but she knew she was dying. She willingly surrendered her key to me. I have been passing what little I know to the Groga leaders for 7 years.

You should know they threatened my family. Said they would kill them in an apparent suicide bombing and let one of the terrorist factions take the blame. I felt I had no choice. I knew I would be caught eventually. I admit I am a great coward, and this has been eating my heart from the beginning.

I know the consequence of my actions. I surrender to my fate. But please, can you protect my family before they discover I have been found out? I know I am undeserving of any kindness from you, but my family is innocent of any wrong-doing. It is all I ask."

Ingot's expression did not soften. "*This has seldom happened in the eons since The Alliance was founded. But your gate will be locked, and your key will be suspended. We will painlessly terminate your life, but before we do, I promise we will see to the safety of your family.*"

Guaray sagged between the two large men holding his arms. He nodded resignedly. "*I am almost relieved,*" he said with a deep sigh. He turned his head to Jenny. "*You must be sure to pay attention,*" he said urgently. "*They are watching all gates, but more particularly, they seem to want you personally, and not just for your Gatekeeper access. I do not bear you or the Alliance any ill will. I did what I had to do.*"

He nodded again, as if to himself. "*I will tell you anything I know before you kill me. I'm ready. Let's go.*"

Tarafau and Brendan handed him over to the waiting Guards who escorted him from the room.

As if it had been practiced, the rest sat themselves almost in unison. Only Ingot remained standing.

"*It is a sad thing. I hate the necessity to do it, but we cannot afford to be lenient, regardless of the circumstances. Guaray will be given time to put his affairs in order, under strict guard and the highest security. As soon as we have assured him that his family is safe, he will go to sleep and not wake.*

But for the rest of us, we have no time to mourn or to dwell on this. For now, we will simply disable the India gate. When we are certain we have the leisure for it, we will choose a new Guardian.

Now let us move to the most important reason for this gathering. You need to know the outcome of your labors.

Firstly, we didn't get as much as we would have liked from our mental extractions. The majority of those we have detained are simple soldiers, with no knowledge of any strategies or plans. They simply react to their orders, which never actually reveal the intent of their masters. We did, however, extract some interesting facts from the commanders of this small force.

We were happy to discover that our gate network does not appear to have been compromised at this time. However, it's seems obvious that they haven't given up on attempting to do so. This may mean only a limited number of dimensions have been exposed. I have no illusions, however, that they will be satisfied with that.

We also discovered that they are coming out of a dimension that is not connected to the network, which means we have two reasons to discover their gate network and figure out how to either close it down or negate it in some way.

According to our current intelligence they have a much larger force secreted somewhere on Earth. Although this force numbers in the thousands, based on the intelligence we acquired in the raid, it doesn't appear to be even a small fraction of the forces they have at their command.

Evidently not two, but three dimensions have allied themselves to eventually conquer The Alliance. The Groga are actually subservient to the other two entities, which at this point we know little to nothing about. The Queen of the Groga, who gives Sam, a.k.a. Engoza, her orders is from the unknown dimension who instigated this plan. They conquered the Groga not long after we thought we had subdued them. At that point the Groga were in a weakened state.

Over the last couple of centuries, they have been nurtured by the other two dimensions as a source for soldiers, like so much cattle, breeding for traits specific to a warrior class, but not specifically for intelligence.

This is as much as we could ferret out from the disjointed mental state of the commanders of this small force, and the documents we have been able to decipher, but it is a good start.

As I see it we have a number of issues we need to pursue:

> *First, we need to discover the whereabouts of the alternate portal or portals on Earth, since it is our best starting point.*

> *Second, we need to somehow get the frequency or frequencies of that gateway, so we can figure out how to enter their portals and discover the extent of their gateway*

network. This should give us a key to potentially either disabling it or eliminating it permanently.

Third, we need to discover and eliminate the large Groga base they have established on Earth, but before we do that, we need to know specifically why they are there and keep them from accomplishing their objectives.

This is going to require the dedication and diligence of every person on your team as well as all of the resources we can bring to bear in your behalf. For now, of all of the dimensions in The Alliance, Earth is in the most immediate danger, so we will focus on getting them off of Earth while we continue to research the other issues. This is only the first phase towards ultimately eliminating this threat, but we can move no further until it is accomplished. Any questions?"

It was obvious from the looks of concentration on nearly every face that each member of the Earth delegation was still absorbing what Ingot had said.

Bob's face reflected the gears turning like mad inside his head. Burt's face had transformed from the triumph of the success of his mission to a grim determination, his blue eyes narrowed and his mouth a thin line. Even Juan and Aliki, normally cheery and optimistic looked seriously contemplative.

Jenny realized they might be waiting for her to speak first. "*Where do you suggest that we start? And what resources will my team have access to?*"

Liliath answered, "*I think the obvious choice is to start with the large Groga force. We need to determine where they are and their mission. My suspicion is that they are established on a portal site and, if we can observe them, we may be able to discover the necessary information to shut down their access once and for all.*

If we are able to do this, it may allow us to avoid a cross dimensional conflict. The consequences of war across the network would be unimaginable. Last time we had to fight them; billions suffered. Some of the gate planets were completely eradicated. At the time we thought they had infiltrated our gate system. Now we know otherwise and may be able to prevent this from ever happening again."

"But what about the dimensions they may have access to that are not attached to our network. Won't they still be endangered, even if we shut down their access to the Alliance network?" asked Dhakirah.

"*You are correct in that assumption*," interjected Myla. "*Naturally, our first responsibility is to the universes in the Alliance. If, however, we can eliminate the threat entirely, we will.*

Your science and technical team and ours will have to be very involved in this. Adelle's laboratory and observatory in Switzerland is probably the best environment for them to pursue their labors. The tactical team will continue in Sanglarka. For security's sake, and in the absence of any Guardians from their gateways, we will station Guards and Troopers at every gate. For most of you, this will not be a problem.

The Gatekeeper's gate will now include a barracks gate for the Troopers and Guards to stay in, as her house is too small to accommodate them. They will be staying out of sight of the neighbors, never appearing outside of the gateway office, unless absolutely necessary. New levels of technical security are being installed at every established gateway system across the network, starting with the Earth gates.

In the case of Jenny's gate, since there are already workmen coming and going for the 'remodeling' that is going on, her neighbors will not notice anything amiss.

Jenny must be seen from time to time coming and going. This can be accomplished by simply entering the gate office, going outside for a few minutes, collecting mail, that sort of thing. Jenny will not be staying in the house, however. Lights have been programmed to turn off and on at appropriate times, as well as sounds and shadows that will make it look normal. Tidbit will be also seen in the neighborhood here and there.

In the meantime, we will continue to examine the evidence brought to us from the swamp. We think there may still be clues.

Have you gone through all of the files created by the mental extractor, yet?" he asked turning to Lova.

"*We are about halfway through the files at this point. If we put a couple more sets of eyes on them, we could be finished in the next 24 hours,*" Lova replied.

"*What will we be doing with the Groga prisoners?*" asked Jenny. She realized that she might not like the answer, but she needed to ask.

"*We are still considering this in the main Council,*" answered Liliath. "*There are several options available to us. Of course, the easiest, but the most distasteful would be to simply kill them, but that would only be as a last resort. At the moment, the majority in the council are leaning toward wiping their memories and settling them someplace where they would have no access to a gateway of any kind. We would provide teachers and initial supplies to allow them to survive and fend for themselves. We would do this for all of the Groga, if it were possible. It is a lot more effort and resources on our part, but the hope is to take away not only their option to harm others, but their intention as well.*"

Jenny nodded. It helped to remind herself about the difference between The Alliance and their enemies. "Live and let live," seemed to be the Alliance philosophy when dealing with other cultures in the dimensions.

"*If there are no further questions, we will adjourn, for now,*" said Ingot. "*As soon as we have everything we can possibly get, out of the information available from the documents and mental extraction files, we will hopefully be able to create a strategy for our next steps. We can only hope they don't choose to raid again in the meantime. We don't know how often the swamp base communicated with their home base, considering there was no gate there that we could observe. However, because of the traitor among us, they may already know we have defeated them.*"

They all stood to leave. Myla stopped Jenny before she could turn for the door. "*We want you to know that we understand you have been placed in a very difficult position. I know there will be times you will be uncertain, times when you will doubt your ability to cope, but it is important to remember that you are not alone and that we believe you have abilities you have not even begun to explore. We are confident you will fill your positions with the same honor and strength as Lizzie and Miriha."*

"Thank you, Myla. That means a lot to me. It is all so much more than anything I ever imagined, even without the Groga crisis. I've decided to take it one step at a time and hope that my best effort will be enough. My dad always says: 'All you can do is all you can do.' And I'm finally beginning to understand what he meant."

Chapter 31: The Devil in the Details

Shopping at the local mall was somehow jarring. Jenny, Nona, Lyra and Mynn, wandered through the weekend crowds commenting on this and that, having lunch in the food court and trying on clothes in the shops as if all was well with the world and she didn't have the fate of innumerable dimensions directly on her shoulders.

Jenny had decided that, since her house had been trashed, and all but the few changes of clothes she had stored in her MDP, had been torn to shreds, she needed to resupply her wardrobe. It seemed so odd to be doing something so normal, but they laughed and chatted like old friends. It was comforting to know that, although it may have appeared that her little entourage was totally absorbed in spending money and doing the silly things girls did while shopping, her Guards were on hyper alert.

Lova had agreed with Jenny that the Groga were unlikely to attack her in such a public place, but that she needed to get used to taking her Guards with her everywhere she went.

So, she picked up all her wardrobe essentials, some of her favorite accessories and played her role. While they were out, Jenny treated each of her Guards with a couple of new outfits and they were no different than any woman would be when choosing something new to wear.

They arrived back at Sanglarka and went to their rooms to unpack their various shopping bags. When Jenny came down into the great room of the lodge, she went straight to the situation room where Tarafau and Lova, along with Adelle and Dhakirah, were going through the extraction files.

"*Anything new?*" she asked as they looked up from their research.

"*Not really,*" Dhakirah replied. "*These fellows almost seem like they were made with a cookie cutter. Not an original thought in the bunch. The breeding plan for the Groga seems to have been custom-made for their conquerors.*"

Tarafau nodded. "*It seems obvious they had some genes modified in the process. On the one hand, they are ferocious warriors with no conscience whatsoever, and yet they obey their leaders almost docilely. No grumbling and never questioning any of their orders. I wonder if there is a way we can use that.*"

"*How was the shopping trip?*" asked Lova.

"*Weird. I felt like I was just play-acting, doing normal things when I know nothing is really as normal as it appears. I looked at all of those people, going about their very normal lives, with no clue what's hanging over them. That used to be me.*" And she sighed, taking a seat beside Lova. "*The house is looking better, though. They're bringing in some of the new furniture tomorrow.*"

Adelle nodded. "*I often feel very estranged from my friends and family, doing what we do. The compensation comes when we realize that it is because of us that they can continue to live their normal lives. All of the drama and politics that go on from day to day and yet, the total impact of all of it is confined to the small borders of our tiny, nearly insignificant planet. And now, here we are, the center of a conflict that is beyond any of our abilities to contemplate fully.*" She looked at Jenny, compassion plain in her bright blue eyes. "*The one thing we can each hold onto is one another and the realization that we are not limited to our own puny resources.*"

Jenny stood and went over to Adelle, surprising the scholarly woman with a grateful hug. "*I am so glad to have you on our team, Adelle. You nailed it. We have one another and that will have to be enough.*"

The older woman smiled up at Jenny from her seat in front of the readout. "*I think you will do well, Jenny. Now shall we get back to it?*"

A couple hours later, Arvid called them to supper. It always amused Jenny that Arvid happily did most of the cooking for the group. He was a great cook and he seemed to take great pleasure in the happy sounds of people eating what he had prepared. The teams assembled at the table carried on mindspeech conversations as they ate, evident by the looks that passed between them, non-sequitur chuckles and occasional gestures with fork or knife in hand.

Finally, when stomachs were happily full and even the silent conversations seemed to have slowed down to nearly nothing, Lova called for their attention. "*We are making progress through the files and should be done before bedtime. I know the team at Alliance headquarters have been working through the detritus from the camp. Have you heard anything from them yet, Burt?*"

"*They did find a document that seems to be encoded. Bob and I have been working on an algorithm to crack it and I think we're close. I'll let you know the moment we have anything. Other than that, most of it is just trash. This group didn't go in for tech or anything remotely resembling luxuries. They were strictly a grunt unit, which makes me seriously wonder why they were there in the first place.*"

Jenny considered that. Why were they there, after all? In Louisiana, of all places. Of course, the swamp made a pretty good hideout, but why so far away from any of the Earth gateways? And why a force of brutes with no useful leadership? It didn't seem right to Jenny, now that she thought of it.

"*Perhaps we will yet find a clue in the files or the encrypted document,*" Tarafau added. "*I don't think we've harvested everything that's there yet.*"

"*In the meantime,*" Burt said, "*I've been watching Homeland Security memos fly around and there's pretty much next to nothing going on out there. At least nothing that applies to our situation.*"

Jenny's jaw dropped. Homeland Security? He said it so casually, as if it wasn't a big deal. It was easy, with Burt's age and his sloppy appearance to still think of him as just a geeky kid her own age. But his time in training with The Alliance had honed him and there was so much going on under that mop of wild hair, that he never ceased to surprise her.

Bob added, "*I've been checking with Interpol. Other than the usual, there's nothing to indicate they've discovered anything worrying.*" Jenny's head swiveled from one to the other and back again. Interpol? Talk about underestimating her resources!

Bob saw her surprise. "*It's a little device Burt put me onto. ' dastardly alien tech' scores another one for the home team,*" he laughed.

"*Then let's get to work,*" Tarafau said dryly. Then to Jenny he said, "*You haven't worked out today. Grab your Guards and go to the workout room. I'll meet you there when you've done your mental exercises and your warmup.*"

Jenny started to protest, as she felt like she had been goofing off today, even though it was part of the plan to make everything look totally normal at 888 Infinity Loop. It was a little disconcerting to see Troopers on guard in the gate office, for sure, and she had been apprised of the fact that, since they had been able to extract a DNA sample before Sam had escaped and also from the captured Groga, they were able to attune the shields to her and any Groga that came within 100 feet of the house.

She changed into her Gi and sat with her Guards, who were fast becoming her good friends, on the mat doing her mental exercises. These days she had three workouts, one with the staff, one in hand to hand and the last was the attacks from four or more different minds testing her shielding ability along with physical attacks of pain to test her mental distancing abilities. Most of the time, now, she could withstand a great deal of pain as if it were less than the tiniest pinprick, but this had yet to be tested under fire, with the exception of her interlude with Sneaky Sam.

Her quarterstaff workouts and hand to hand were usually divided into one on one sparring matches and six way free-for-alls, sometimes two teams against one another and sometimes her against all of them. Tarafau and Arvid pushed them hard.

"*Weapons are all well and good,*" Arvid told them, "*and we'll start working with some distance weapons soon, but better yet is the surprise element of being able to defend yourself in close quarters with nothing but your hands and feet to defend yourself. Most of your enemies won't expect this of you and many of them never bother to learn hand to hand beyond simple punching and brawling. As you have seen, force directed against you, when properly re-directed can be a powerful asset in your favor.*"

When they finished and had cleaned up, Jenny headed into the situation room only to find everyone else gathered there and nearly all talking at once. They quietened as Jenny entered.

"*Listen to this,*" Lova said, and began to read from the file in front of her, "*Message received from headquarters: 'Operation to begin in three Earth weeks. Have (unintelligible word) in readiness...' Alligators? What are you talking about? Attack? What do you mean? Run! Run!*"

Lova couldn't suppress a chuckle, but immediately got serious. "*He didn't end up reading the rest of the message. We're assuming the word we couldn't understand was a technical term for a weapon or strategy. We also believe that this is the document he was reading when so rudely interrupted by mosquitos and gators and is the encrypted document that forensics is working with. This small snippet from this extraction could be the key to that message. This also means we are working on an extreme deadline.*

I forwarded the transcript of this extraction to Alliance headquarters. By the time they finish decoding the document, we will have to move quickly, as we are now 4 days into that three week period. This means everyone needs to be on extreme alert and ready to move within minutes as soon as the translation is received. We will have next to no time to come up with a strategy and we can only hope that there will be a clue as to the whereabouts of their secret base somewhere in the document."

Jenny looked around her. She was so proud of her team. On every face was stony determination. If it could be done, this team would do it.

"*OK, then,*" Jenny said, "*I want each of us to assemble every tool we think we might be able to use as well as clothing and rations.*

I want everyone on the team to host one of Burt's little bug friends. It may be important at some point to be able to track you as things heat up.

Bob, I need you and Aliki to continue to inventory Lizzie's MDPs, so we know exactly what our local resources are. Knowing what is there and extracting the things we need ahead of time is going to be important.

Even with all the preparations we need to make, everyone needs to get as much rest as possible, so when we move, we'll be prepared for what will likely be a grueling time with not much opportunity for sleep. Also, one thing I learned as a hiker was to 'carb up' before a long and difficult hike to give our bodies the resources for energy and stamina in a long haul.

Burt, notify all the Guardians who are not here. Not all of us are going to be 'on-the-ground' in this effort, but everyone needs to know the plan. Lova, notify the Council that we are making preparations and to have Troopers standing by. Let's do this thing."

They all separated to their various tasks. Tarafau approached Jenny, concern in his eyes. *"I've seen that look on Lizzie's face before, Jenny. You intend to be 'on-the-ground', right in the middle of it, don't you?"*

Jenny straightened to her full 5 feet 4 inches and looked him in the eye. *"Isn't this what I have been preparing for? Gariel will be directing troop movements and strategy. I don't think I can handle sitting here watching, while my team is out there risking their necks. I know I'm not a warrior maiden out of some fantasy tale, but I'm invested in this and I won't sit on my hands."*

Tarafau cocked his head. She could almost see cat ears pointed forward and a twitching tail in his expression. Then he shrugged and sighed. *"I could never keep Lizzie out of it either. I will be with you and your Guards, regardless of what part you play. You won't go haring off on your own?"*

"I'll stick with my A-team," Jenny agreed. *"I've got business with a certain sneaky person and I won't hand that off to anyone else. And I'll get one of Burt's tracking thingies, so you can't lose me."*

"The Gatekeeper usually doesn't go into combat situations. We can't afford to lose you. But I know better than to argue with someone who is so much like your aunt. I would like to suggest that you take on the role of a field commander. You'll be close to the action, but not in the middle of it. Will that do?"

"For now," Jenny agreed.

Lova looked up from the file she was reading. *"We need to go to the gate,"* she told Jenny. *"Troopers will be coming through and we need to get them set up in our field barracks."*

"*You have barracks?*" Jenny asked in surprise. "*Why would you have barracks?*"

"*Technically, we don't have barracks, but we will in a few minutes.*" Lova answered mysteriously. "*Come on, I'll show you.*"

They got to the gate just as Troopers came spilling out. As the uniformed troops emerged, they ordered themselves into ranks, standing at ease. There were a couple hundred of them, by Jenny's estimation. Gariel came out of the gate last.

"*You have your orders*," he called out in a commanding voice. "*Proceed.*"

"*Over here*," said Lova, moving to a level, cleared field, a few hundred feet away. A man Jenny assumed must be a platoon leader, walked to about the center of the area and from his MDP he drew a cube about a foot on every side and placed it on the ground. He then went another 50 feet and repeated the process until there were four cubes laying at angles with one another.

He pressed a button on what looked like a utility belt and the cubes simultaneously began to expand. In less than a couple minutes, four buildings stood there, complete with windows, doors and tent-like roofs. Jenny gaped. She could see where a non-tech person would consider this sort of thing magical. The only thing lacking was a wand or a staff and some magic words.'

"*Would you like to see inside?*" Lova asked Jenny, her mouth twisting in amusement.

"*Sure,*" said Jenny, following Lova through the door of the closest building.

Inside there were cots similar to the standard army cot, a small break space with tables and chairs and what might have been a privy. All of it was lined up very meticulously with spaces between beds, enough for 50 people.

"*Wow,*" Jenny said. "*Just when I think I'm used to all of this…*"

As they exited the barracks, Jenny noticed there was a fifth building being erected, somewhat larger than the barracks. "*The assembly building, so they can brief all the soldiers at once without *distractions. All of these buildings are shielded, and communications are in the admin building,"* said Gariel.

The empty field was beginning to look like the barracks had always been there. But, unlike standard Earth Army barracks areas, there were no vehicles or weapons in evidence. The gates were all the transport they required here, and their weapons were stored in their MDPs. None of the soldiers wore backpacks. Any transport they might require on the battlefield or when they did not have gates available would also be stored in their MDPs.

Jenny imagined this made for a very mobile force which could march farther and respond faster than any earthly force she was aware of.

Then, Jenny realized that this **was** a very small force, if the numbers reported regarding the hidden Groga force were even close.

"Where are the rest of the troops?" she asked Gariel.

"This is just the advance party," he replied. *"The rest will be deployed once we know where we need to be. "The Troopers in this unit are the elite and their main purpose is to scout and gather intelligence for the rest of our forces. Remember, that one of the requirements of this operation is to leave as small a footprint as possible to the watchful eyes of satellites and other intelligence devices on Earth.*

We don't want to cause concern to the governments of your planet. This battle must be waged as quietly as possible. We hope to develop a stratagem that will lure their troops off world. That would be the ideal situation, but if not, we will use every resource at our disposal to make this conflict as brief and as quiet as possible."

"That would be preferable on so many levels," Jenny agreed. There was something about Gariel, even with his squirming beard and his commanding air that was very comforting. He exuded a vibration of cool competence. She never had seen him at rest. Every minute he seemed to be on point. This, of course, was a trait to be desired in a military commander, but Jenny wondered what he was like when he had the opportunity to relax. She suspected that it was a rare thing, considering the scope of his responsibilities.

Burt strode up, his wild hair fluffing in the breeze and his blue eyes intent. "*Hey there! Looks like that snippet from that extract has done its job. They have finished decoding the document. Meeting in the situation room in five minutes.*" He turned on his heel and headed back to the lodge.

No one hesitated. Gariel, Lova and Jenny followed on his heels. The situation room was crowded. Most were standing, but they had saved Jenny a seat. Arvid stood, what appeared to be a dispatch in his hands.

"*The message contained in this document is long, so I will summarize. The Groga have assembled themselves in the Vale do Javari, a part of the Amazon jungle about the size of Australia. This massive jungle is inhabited by just over a dozen small indigenous tribes of just over 2,000 people, which leaves a vast hole in the center of the jungle that is not populated. Furthermore, the canopy is so dense that nothing, but very expensive high-tech equipment can penetrate it.*

The closest gate to the Vale do Javari is in Puerto Rico. There are about twenty five hundred troops located deep in the heart of the jungle. They chose their spot well. Getting a large enough force in there to attack them without anyone's notice will be quite a feat, especially in the time allotted.

Based on our current intelligence, they must be guarding one of their portals there and in about sixteen days they will be transporting those troops to another dimension to raid. From what we can deduce from the document, they have been staging their latest raids from earth all along.

So, our priorities will change for the moment. Instead of trying to annihilate this force, as pleasant a thought as that may be, we need to use their position and this potential raid as an opportunity to find the gate, get some readings and more intelligence. Once we discover their destination, we will attempt to put troops in their way to hopefully protect their target.

Once the bulk of their troops are through the portal, the troops here in Sanglarka should be enough to get into their camp with very little resistance. And we'll leave them a little surprise before we vacate the premises. Nothing, of course, that will damage or harm the indigenous people.

There were no references to the portal, other than as transportation, so we must assume that the commanders of this force are already trained in its use, or they have documents existing somewhere in the camp with that information. Either that, or they use a device such as a Gatekeeper or Guardian key to access the portal. If that is the case, we will need to capture one, preferably with the person attached to it." At this he gave one of his evilest grins. "Bonus points," he growled.

The rest of the team gave an approving chuckle.

"Looks like we have our work cut out for us," Burt said ruffling his wild hair. *"Tactical team, meeting. Now."*

The room half emptied. "Aliki, since Bob will be in the Tactical team meeting, can you head up a group to inventory the remaining three MDPs? We'll need anything we can use in the Jungle environment. I can only hope that may include some kind of watercraft, considering that the Amazon jungle is crisscrossed with rivers that have some nasty surprises for those who are unprepared." Lova, said.

Aliki recruited Adelle, Dhakirah and Megan and they left for the other library which had been co-opted for MDP research.

That left Lova and Jenny. *"Let's take a cup of cocoa out on the balcony and catch our breath,"* Lova said. *"I have a feeling things are about to get really intense before the day is out. I sent a message for Juan to join us, now that he has the Puerto Rico gate secured. He has a really great companion in Luz. She is so much more than just a wife and hostess. Did you know she is an awarded sharpshooter? She has more medals than anyone on the team, except maybe Brendan."*

They sat on the balcony looking out onto the peaceful valley and up to the snow-capped mountains sparkling in the sunlight.

"The days are getting shorter," Lova sighed. *"In another month it will be dark more than it will be light. It has a different kind of beauty, the dark. From our lovely little valley surrounded by*

mountains and far from city lights, some nights the stars are so bright, it's like you can reach out and touch eternity. Where we live, we have the opportunity to truly appreciate both. But when it comes to the darkness of the soul…" she trailed off.

Jenny nodded. "*I think I am only beginning to understand what that means. You'd think someone who writes for a living would be more based in reality, but even knowing what I know, I tend to focus on the good things in the world. I think I get that from my mom. And I've been fortunate, as I don't write about world events. Most of the time what I write is more about technology, science and industry than anything else.*

I know there is evil on the earth, but it seems so far away from my comfortable little world. And now I come up against it on a scale I have not imagined in my worst dreams or nightmares. The idea of multiple dimensions was so much science fiction to me. None of the research I have read about has come to any firm conclusions about their existence and more often than not it is pooh-poohed as pseudo-science or the overactive imaginations of a small group of physicists."

Lova agreed. "*Reading some of the 'scholarly' works of those who disbelieve in other dimensions makes me smile. We have so far to go before we are ready for what's 'out there'*," and she gestured toward the startlingly blue sky, as if to encompass all of time and space.

Suddenly they heard raised voices from inside the lodge. As they burst through the glassed French doors, they realized it was coming from the library where they were doing MDP research.

She quickly realized it was not panic or fear. Someone was celebrating.

Chapter 32: Out of the Frying Pan

There might as well have been confetti in the air. Aliki and his team were doing what could only be described as a "happy dance". Whooping with hands in the air and jumping up and down and hugging in congratulations.

"*We found the motherlode!*" Bob exclaimed as he saw Lova and Jenny walk through the door, followed rapidly by Jenny's guards and the rest of their comrades. "*That Lizzie is a pip! I don't know how she acquired all of this, but I doubt she ever threw anything away that was of any use. The fourth MDP was a goldmine of tech and equipment. Also, enough rations to field a small army as well as more of those cubes that make barracks buildings. But, on top of that, it turns out that Fidget has cousins!*

We have about 50 little robots along with manuals. And let me tell you, these little guys can do some pretty amazing things. For one thing, they can fly. They are armed, and they can lift as much as a forklift, but they are so small they look inoffensive. They can color shift to blend into their environment, and they can communicate through the Alliance broadband network. In addition, they can be tracked, even through a gateway. Whoever designed them evidently put a version of Burt's bugs in them. These would work as a nice little advance force.

I don't know if this was what Engoza was looking for, but, if not, we haven't finished exploring these MDPs. One of them even has the equipment for a field hospital.

But when I said we hit the motherlode; I was being literal. There's gold in them thar MDPs." This last was said with a drawl, his fingers in imaginary suspenders. "*She has a stash of gold coins like I've never seen before as well as a goodly hoard of gemstones. What was she preparing for? Did she have some kind of premonition? Or was she under orders we don't know about?*"

Jenny wondered herself. How had her aunt obtained such a wealth of resources, even over 60 years as a Guardian? She itched to get out her tablet and talk to LizzieAI, but she decided it would be best to do that in private until she knew more.

"*Congratulations, MDP team,*" she said effusively. "*This should give us an edge. Aliki, please take this list to the tactical team, so they can decide how best to use this in their plans. Some of this will want to be distributed among various MDPs for our unit and this may alter their tactics and will hopefully save some lives.*"

As she said this, it suddenly loomed in her mind that this wasn't just an adventure, with happily-ever-afters at the end. There would inevitably be injuries and deaths. So far they had managed with few casualties, but that would not continue. The force they were up against was formidable and they had no compunction about harming others, in fact, they gloried in it. She steeled herself, realizing just how unprepared she was, on a personal level, for what was to come.

She wasn't sure how Lizzie had acquired such wealth, but the interesting thing was that the gold had to be the least important of their finds. With the resources of the Alliance to draw on, money didn't seem to mean much.

They went back to work, knowing that every moment had to count. Once again, Arvid set up a buffet table that people could dip into and take their plates back to where they were working. They took breaks only to work out and they did that in shifts.

Lova had been teaching Jenny how to discern the strength of another person's mind control and Jenny was struggling with it. Lova had told her that this was important, because if you didn't know this, you could mistakenly attack someone who could easily break you. It was difficult to shield yourself when attacking. But for purposes of shielding, knowing what you were up against was a helpful skill.

At first Jenny had been appalled that these mental techniques could be used in this way. Lova had explained that, first of all, not every mind was able to do more than a weak shield, much less use their minds to attack another mind. Secondly, those who did have this ability, at least within the Alliance, would not consider using mental control to harm another person, unless they were under attack themselves.

Liliath, for example had a very high level of mental control including the ability to coerce someone to do something against their will (It was one of the inherent traits of her species.), although this kind of control could only be maintained for a short period of time, as it was very draining and could even damage the person doing the controlling. Another thing Liliath could do was something called "the shout". This was a very mentally loud sending that could momentarily disarm another person. The problem with "the shout" was that it could not be made specific. It affected everyone in a certain radius from the person performing it. Secondly it also sapped the person doing it, so it had to be used sparingly and with some kind of immediate plan in mind.

But Jenny wasn't close to that kind of power, yet. She was getting very good at shielding but lacked the mental strength and will to use her mind to attack someone. Lova continued to help her hone her shielding and explained that when Jenny was away from Lova that Tarafau would continue her training.

By this time, Jenny found that the bonds of friendship continued to grow for each of her team members in a way she had never quite experienced before. The people on her team, each with unique qualities, were more than even family to her. She felt she could entrust each one, not only with her life, but with her heart.

This did much to soothe her disappointment and hurt about Sam. Even as angry as she still was with Sam's treachery, after years of believing she was her friend, the sense of loss was keen. Only the support and friendship of the people on her team made a difference in that. She couldn't very well talk to her parents or anyone in her family about it or any of her other friends from before.

Jenny finally decided it was time to confront the LizzieAI with the mystery of the MDPs. She needed to know more about how they had been acquired and get counsel on how best to use them. In all of the hullaballoo of the past couple of weeks, she hadn't consulted her since that day in the gate office.

She settled into one of the cushioned chairs in the lobby. She didn't feel that she needed to keep it completely private. After all, she would have to share everything she learned with her team at any rate.

LizzieAI's cheerful face greeted her with the usual, "How can I help you?"

"I need to know where the equipment and supplies in the MDPs came from and whether you have any advice on the best way to deploy the resources in them. I know you must have an inventory of what's in there. I intended to ask you earlier and there has been too much going on."

"You know that I was a Guardian for over 60 years, but what you may not know is that I also was sent on agent missions with Tarafau during my training. Had your training been of the usual sort, you would have done the same thing. I was given permission to hold onto any resources we used in those missions for the use of the Guardians on Earth, if we ever had the need for them. The Council of that time felt that it was important that it not be held in the main headquarters, Sanglarka, so that our enemies wouldn't have access to them, if Sanglarka was ever attacked.

The Los Angeles gate was one of the lowest profiled gates on Earth. As a result, it was unlikely anyone would expect that we would store them in my little backyard shed.

I am up to date with your situation, as my algorithm is connected to the communications network of the Earth Guardian. You can use anything in the inventory to implement your strategies in combating the Groga. There is, however, a compartment in MDP number 5 that you should leave alone. It is a last resort and I won't even tell you about it at this time. You can't even access it without a key that I will give you, if it ever is necessary.

The gold will be of little use in this project, but it is good to have resources when you need to travel outside the gates. I used to cash in a little every month into my bank account to give the appearance of a regular income and avoid suspicion. I never minded paying the taxes on it, as it gave me a nice addition to my cover. It is the reason the property taxes and other bills are able to be paid automatically. Consider it wages for your duties, as that is exactly what it is.

Funny enough, it comes from a dimension where gold is as common as sand is here. They thought I was crazy when I loaded up with those 'yellow rocks' every time I went there. I acquired the rights to an old played out mine in Alaska and bought a derelict smelting facility. As far as they know, the coins they were smelting came out of the mine. I paid them well enough, in gold, that they were happy to keep my little secret.

By the way, you own the mine and the smelting facility as well as the house and some other properties we haven't yet discussed. Ask me about it after things settle down.

My advice is to trust your team. Each of them has been chosen, including yourself, for certain qualities that, when combined, make the Earth Guardian team a force to be reckoned with.

We must gather the necessary data, if we are to succeed at any cost. You, in particular, have skills you haven't discovered yet, that may be the key to this conflict. Trust your instincts. They are very good."

"So, we pretty much know all we can know at this time, then?" Jenny queried.

"Until you get the intelligence we need, we can do nothing more," agreed LizzieAI. "Focus on that."

Jenny signed out of her tablet and sat pondering the fact that she really didn't know much more than she did when she logged in. She sighed and went to check on the tactical team.

They were all pouring over a large map, projected on what Jenny had decided to call an "air screen".

"The native population of this area have had little to no contact with the modern world. There are a little over a dozen small tribes in this huge area and their approximate locations are marked on the map. I can only guess at this part, because the camp will have been shielded from thermal scanning, but it looks like the most likely area is this part here," Burt said and he stabbed a finger at a space between the icons that represented the various tribes. *"It's still thousands of square miles, but it would allow them to operate without impacting the little tribes, which are monitored very carefully by the Brazilian government, due to laws protecting the indigenous people, much like our endangered species laws.*

This means, getting in and out of there without attracting attention is going to be our first hurdle. It is doable, but it will require a great deal of coordination and considerable subterfuge on our part.

Bob, can you have the robot force programmed and ready by tomorrow? And did you test to see if they will come up on normal tracking, such as radar if we fly them in?"

"Yes, and we also found a replicating device that creates those little flying nanobots. We can have a huge supply within the next day or so. I already started producing them and storing them in my MDP."

"Awesome. And, Gariel, do you have any suggestions about how to get your troops in under the radar as well? It's the solid humanoids we will have the most trouble with."

"Yes, Burt, we have determined to launch from the Puerto Rico gate. No uniforms. Just camouflage gear, which is very common clothing in the rain forest. We'll be landing our transport plane on a private airstrip not far from the jungle. From there we will be using the transport hover cars found in the MDPs to get into the jungle in small groups. The hover cars have a chameleon circuit that will shield them from casual observation, and they make no noise. They will also leave no trails for others to follow.

Communication will be handled through the Alliance network, which is not trackable by any Earth technology that we are aware of. We will provide the same transport for all of the participating Guardians and any of their teams who need to come along."

"Great. That takes care of the first priority. I am sending a report to Lova about our needs, so we can get all of our MDPs loaded tonight. She will be in charge of issuing equipment based on everyone's assignments.

We will coordinate each stage via the Alliance network. For now, it's all about getting all of our teams in place as quickly as possible and gathering as much intel as we can get our hands on. As soon as we have answered as many of our questions as we can, we will hone the strategy." He turned to Jenny. *"I will brief you a little later this evening, as soon as we have gone through our checklist. I understand you will be coming along. You, your Guards and Tarafau will be with the tactical team.*

Lova Arvid and Adelle will be coordinating communications between our forces in the field and the Alliance. We will be immediately updated if they receive any new intelligence. Their research departments are standing by to process anything we discover as we go. We only have about a week and a half to find the Groga forces, infiltrate their operation and get the portal coordinates, as well as do what we can to protect the dimension where they plan their next raid."

"*I just talked with the LizzieAI about the resources in the MDPs,*" Jenny put in. "*All of it is authorized for our use. There is a compartment in MDP number 5 that you need to leave alone. You can't get into it and it isn't authorized for this operation. That's all I can tell you about it. What time do we want to leave in the morning?*"

"Sweden is five hours ahead of Puerto Rico, so we can start our troops through the gate at about 8 a.m. here. That will mean that by the time we have everyone through the gate, it will be about 5 a.m. there. Juan has arranged for a private charter plane to take us to an obscure private air strip, once used by smugglers, and since purchased by the Alliance, to offload. From there we have a very long overland trip in the hovercars to a certain place in the jungle from which we will have to proceed on foot, so be sure to bring your hiking shoes," he added with a grin.

"*If there are no additional questions, everybody can scatter to prepare.*"

No one spoke, so he clapped his hands with a "Crack!". "*See you in the morning. Get your stuff together and get some rest.*"

Bob sidled up to Jenny. "*I want to show you something*," he said, beckoning for her to follow.

She followed him to the library where they had been inventorying the MDPs. In one corner of the now deserted room, there was what looked like a statue covered with a sheet.

He pulled the sheet off with a flourish. "TADA!" said the AI voice of Fidget, a happy grin and a wink on his digital face. "Hello, Jenny. So good to see you again. Do you like my new look?"

Fidget's gleaming white body had been painted with camouflage. "You look like you're ready for combat." Jenny said.

"I have been promoted." Fidget said enthusiastically. "I'm now the robot force battle commander."

"I see Bob has been working on your emotion circuits again. You appear to be excited."

"It is a grave responsibility," Fidget said, his face changing to a serious demeanor.

Bob couldn't conceal his grin of delight when Jenny responded by nodding back soberly.

"I think I've taken him as far as I can, but he definitely has come a long way, even since you first saw him. I've backed up all of his programming and his data, as well as all of my notes on his construction. Burt knows someone here on earth who might be able to help me put him into limited production."

"I'm going to have siblings?" Fidget asked, his digital eyebrows shooting up in surprise.

"You are," Bob agreed. "You will be the big brother to many siblings."

"Awesome!" replied Fidget and Jenny giggled.

"You've added some real personality to him. When will you make one for me?"

"Oh! Now you've gone and spoiled my surprise. I actually was going to give her to you tomorrow before we left, but now…" He turned to a cabinet behind them and opened the door. There, an exact duplicate of Fidget appeared and opened what were obviously female eyes in a female face.

"Meet Lizziebot," he said with a flourish. "I got permission to download LizzieAI into her. Now you have her experience and a very useful companion for the coming days."

"Hello, Jenny," Lizzie said, her eyes crinkling. "It is good to see you."

Jenny couldn't stop the tears of joy and overwhelm that streamed down her face. "Oh, Bob!" she exclaimed, throwing her arms around his neck and hugging him with all her might. "You are amazing!"

Bob hugged her back and then, pulling back looked into her eyes. "I always wanted a daughter. My son was an only child. May I adopt you? I mean, I know your parents are still alive and all, but could you use a bonus dad?" His kind eyes were serious, but full of warmth.

"Oh, Bob! You have been such a good friend. Yes, by all means. Someone like me can use all of the love and support she can get. I could never tell my real dad about any of this, if for no other reason than that I wouldn't want to put him in danger. It will be good to have a guiding hand in addition to all of the support I have from our team. Is Lizziebot completely operational?"

"I am," Lizziebot replied. "May I suggest I ride in your MDP until you're ready to use my many talents?"

"Great idea," agreed Jenny. "In you go." She installed Lizziebot into her MDP.

"You too," said Bob to Fidget and suiting action to words installed Fidget into his own MDP. "These things are amazing," he said, tapping his wristband with true awe on his face. "I have half of my laboratory in here now. Burt and I made a second trip through the gate the other day to pick up a few things."

"This is an amazing gift," she told Bob. "I know you and my aunt were very close. Perhaps this is also a comfort to you? I had no chance to get to know my aunt, but now I can carry her everywhere I go and have the benefit of her experience as well as the innumerable skills I am sure you have programmed into her."

"I have added a few surprises for you," he held up both hands, "Nothing alarming, I promise you. But I think you will find Lizziebot entertaining as well as useful."

They headed out into the lobby. A line of troopers waited outside the library. Lova strode up. "*Time to load the MDPs of our Troopers,*" she said to Jenny. "*Aliki, Burt and Gariel will be aiding me. As soon as that is complete, I will help the rest of the team get loaded up. I'll let you know when it's your turn.*" She smiled at Jenny and beckoned to the first Trooper in line.

She and Bob passed Aliki and Burt hustling past the Troopers into the library.

The Lobby was filled with the Trooper's on line, so they went to the dining room where the buffet had been laid out.

"We're going to miss all of this excellent food for the next little bit," Bob said to Jenny, *"so, dig in and enjoy it while you can. An old soldier's advice."*

As they seated themselves, Jenny mused. *"I really don't know a lot about you. My dad was in the military. When did you serve?"*

"It was just before Desert Storm," he said. *"I only served a 4 year term, but it gave me the money to go to college and get my degrees. I was part of the team that manned the Patriot surface-to-air missiles during Desert Storm. Hotter than the devil's underpants and nerve-jarring to boot. I was glad to take off the uniform and use my skills for more peaceful endeavors."*

"And now I've dragged you into another war." Jenny said sadly.

"It's what needs doing and I'm very glad you 'dragged' me into this. Other than Fidget, I haven't had a project that caught my imagination like this in a long time. At middle age, I'm just hitting my stride. Besides, what's a few grey hairs between friends?"

Jenny laughed despite herself. *"My dad started going grey in his thirties, to his great dismay. Mom kept telling him it looked 'distinguished'. I told him it made him look 'extinguished'. Now that's what he tells everyone if anyone notices how grey he is."*

Bob laughed. They finished their supper just about the time Tarafau and her Guards approached. *"I hope you didn't fill yourself up too full. We're going to have a skirmish in the workout room to get everyone good and tired before we go to bed. Lova says she'll be ready for our loading when we're done...after we've showered, of course,"* he added with one of his catlike grins.

Bob and Jenny took care of their dishes, changed into their Gis and arrived to find most of the team, with the exception of Lova and Adelle who were finishing up the last of the Trooper's load-up. They started with the basic breathing exercise, went through the forms in unison, led by Arvid and then Arvid split them up into 2 groups.

"*Tap strength only. We need you all fit to leave in the morning. If you're tapped, you're out. Other than that, any move you wish to practice is acceptable. Remember, our enemies have no scruples or conscience. They won't hesitate to 'cheat' or harm you in any way they can think of.*" He rubbed his hands together. "*This should be fun!*" he exclaimed with his wickedest grin. "*Begin!*"

Jenny's Guards had ended up in her group, with Tarafau, Aliki and Bob. The other group comprised Arvid, Burt, Gariel and Brendan. Jenny figured even though the numbers were uneven, counting strength and experience, the mix was about right.

The air was soon filled with the noise of quarterstaffs colliding and the grunts of the participants. Lyra, Mynn and Nona took on Brendan. Tarafau and Aliki faced Gariel. Bob engaged Arvid and Jenny found herself up against Burt.

He grinned at her, circling. Jenny didn't attack but watched his eyes. His blue penetrating eyes. He swung almost casually at her, his staff meeting her block with a gentle tap. He pivoted, countering with the other end of his staff and soon they were exchanging blows, calculated only to leave small bruises instead of serious injuries, as they had been instructed.

Jenny couldn't even watch the others out of the corner of her eye, but she heard Mynn exclaim, "I'm out!" indicating she had been touched. She kept her eyes locked on Burt's, intent on not being one of the first ones out. She held no illusions that she could defeat most of the more experienced fighters, but she wanted to reflect well on her mentors.

She and Burt continued to circle, their quarterstaffs falling into a rhythm of clacks and taps. Around them they could feel the pace increase, taps coming closer and closer together. Suddenly Jenny saw Burt's gaze shift just the smallest degree to his right. She prepared to block his blow in that direction, but instead, he reversed, ducking below her block and sweeping his staff along the floor from the other direction. Jenny over-balanced and slapped the floor, Burt's staff poised over her bottom. "Tap!" he said triumphantly, tapping her bottom lightly.

Jenny was relieved to see she wasn't the only one sent to sit on the bench at the side of the mat. Mynn, Nona and Brendan were all sitting there watching the melee intently. "*You need to watch Lyra,*" Brendan said morosely. "*She's so cute with that blonde curly hair and those dimples, but she gives no quarter, and she has some pretty slick moves.*"

Lyra had moved to help Bob against Arvid. Arvid was smiling wickedly, but between Bob and Lyra, they were keeping him on his toes. Gariel was lightning fast, but both Aliki and Tarafau were experienced with the staff and they worked well together, doing their best to keep him off balance.

Burt joined Gariel and on it went. By the time the contest was over they had recombined several times, but in the end, it came down to Tarafau and Arvid. Jenny knew the competition between Arvid and Tarafau was a long-standing one. She was rooting for Tarafau. Now the quarterstaffs whirled at blinding speed, nothing to indicate they were even there except when they made contact with rapid clacks back and forth. Both of them were focused entirely on one another, not even seeming to blink.

When Arvid finally tapped Tarafau, not all that lightly on his calf, with a similar sweeping motion to what Burt had made to topple Jenny, Tarafau just shook his head. "*Someday,*" he said wryly. They shook hands and the group applauded.

"*OK,*" Arvid said, clapping his hands together, "*shower and get yourselves a snack. Lova will call each of you as she is ready for you.*"

When Lova called Jenny, she handed her a number of packages. "*This first aid kit is specialized to deal with medical issues you may encounter in the Amazon jungle. It includes insect repellent, a couple of epi pens, in case you react to something that bites you, a snake venom removal and antivenom serum kit, sunscreen, pain medications, salt tablets to prevent dehydration, an antimalarial drug, an antibiotic, and the usual things you would expect in a first aid kit, including a CPR mask. The MDPs make it possible for us to carry a much more extensive kit than if you had to pack in.*

There are several paracords, carabiners, a survival knife, a machete, rations for a week, fire-starters, flint and steel and a standard compass. I have included three changes of military grade camouflaged clothing with hats, extra pairs of socks and weather gear in your size. You can use your usual hiking boots, as I remember they are very sturdy, and you've already broken them in. I also included some non-reflective sunglasses and some night goggles.

Since you are first aid and survival certified, you are familiar with the uses of all of these. Instructions for any medications are included on their containers. Standard issue MDP contains many other survival supplies, such as a tent, wet weather poncho, rations, etc.

Can you think of anything else you may need that you don't have?"

"*Do you have anything to make my gut stop churning? I'll be honest. I'm scared.*"

Lova smiled. "*Jenny, you are one of the bravest souls I've met. In the past few months, you have already dealt with more than most people ever deal with in their lives. You have taken on responsibilities that would be overwhelming for any mortal. I can't see the future, nor do I claim any prophetic gift, but based on what I have learned in the short time we have spent together, I believe that you will not only conquer every obstacle that lays before you, but you will lead us to ultimate victory.*"

She stretched out both hands to Jenny and pulled her into a hug. "*Just keep being you,*" she whispered into her ear. "*That will be more than enough.*"

Jenny let out the breath she had been holding. "*Thank you, Lova. I'll do my best.*"

"*No one would expect more than that,*" Lova returned. "*Now tell Bob to get in here. I'm almost done and it's time for everyone to settle down and get some sleep before tomorrow.*"

Jenny relayed the message. The dining room and the lobby had nearly cleared out and the lodge was quiet, compared to the bustle of the past few days. Jenny headed up to her suite. Tarafau was waiting there.

"*All set?*" he asked, handing her a cup of chamomile tea. "*I thought you could use something to relax you. You've got a lot on your mind and that's normal the night before an operation like this. When you get into bed, do your breathing and combined with the chamomile, it should allow you to get a good night's sleep. An old soldier's wisdom says that you sleep every safe opportunity that presents itself. The next several days will be grueling and will tax you in ways you can't imagine, even with your experience in hiking outdoors.*"

"*Thanks, Tarafau,*" Jenny said, taking the tea and sipping. "*The tea was a great idea. I'm pretty well set. Lova made sure I had everything I need, and I've got the entire team to back me up. I know this won't be easy and I know what we're about to do is very dangerous. But, if this must be done, I think we have the best possible team to make it happen.*"

Tarafau nodded.

"*Oh, and did you know about this?*" Jenny called Lizziebot from her MDP.

"*Hello, Tarafau,*" Lizziebot said, as she scanned the room.

"*What is this?*" Tarafau was obviously startled.

"*Lizziebot, meet Tarafau...Tarafau, Lizziebot.*"

The expression on Tarafau's face was both confused and somewhat sad.

"*I am not Lizzie, Tarafau. I am the AI that was in Jenny's tablet.*"

"*Is this a Bob project?*" he said, finally. "*I had no idea he had gotten this far. Does this mean Fidget is also functional?*"

"*Bob got permission to download me into this latest robot form. I will be able to be a companion to Jenny and aid her more actively in her task. I hope this is not upsetting to you. I know you and Lizzie were very close. And yes, Fidget is also functional and ready to go.*"

Tarafau looked at Jenny. "*I won't pretend this isn't a little disconcerting, but I can see how this could be very useful. I look forward to learning more about this. But, for now, we need to get to bed. See you in the morning.*"

"*G'nite, old cat,*" Jenny said tenderly. "*Rest well.*"

The next morning all were in their places at the breakfast table. Cheerful greetings met her as she seated herself. She had dressed in the camos Lova had provided for the whole expedition. Looking up and down the table as she ate, she was happy to see the interaction between all of her team. From the time they had begun this task, she had seen them coming closer and closer. Not to say there weren't occasional disagreements, but all-in-all, they not only got along well, but the range of skills and temperaments were so complimentary that the diversity worked in their favor.

After breakfast, they assembled at the gate. Gariel and the Troopers had already gone through. The field where their barracks had been was once again just a field. You wouldn't have known that just the night before it had contained 200 soldiers and their gear, except for the rectangular patches where the grasses had been compressed and yellowed slightly. In a day or so there would be no sign they had ever been there.

Lova and Adelle were on hand to bid farewell to the Guardians and Lyra, Nona and Mynn were waiting patiently for the go ahead. "Protocol," Lyra said, "says we go through, two in front of you and one behind. Mynn will be the behind." And her eyes crinkled at the double entendre.

Mynn rolled her eyes but didn't say anything. This kind of banter that went back and forth between her Guards was common. However, she had learned that when it was time to be serious, they had no problem being the professionals they had trained to be.

As she came through the gateway, Juan nodded to her and waved her forward, out of the gate office. Inside the hacienda Luz was waiting dressed in her usual white with a colorful shawl knotted around her waist. She offered Jenny a warm hug and a smile. "It is so good to see you again, Jenny. Your Troopers are assembled in front of the hacienda. We have worker trucks out front to transport them to the charter plane. You will go in the van with Juan. While you're waiting, may I offer you and your team some fruit punch?"

She looked at Tarafau. "Well this is a treat! We seldom get to see you in your natural form."

"Special dispensation, considering we are taking more than a few extra-dimensional beings in our entourage and there is almost no possibility that anyone besides the enemy will see me," Tarafau said, grinning. Luz gave him a big hug and turned back to her hostessing duties.

Jenny accepted the cold fruit punch gratefully. For some reason her mouth was decidedly dry. The rest of the team was through the gate just as Jenny finished her punch. "Let's move out," Juan said to the group. "We've still got a long way to go and the timing on this is very particular due to government patrols."

Luz walked Jenny to the van and before she climbed in, Luz grabbed her for a quick hug. "When this is all done," she said, her dark eyes looking deep into her blue ones, "You must come and just relax here with Juan and me for awhile. I have a feeling you and I will be good friends."

Jenny enjoyed the ride down the mountain, listening to the birds calling here and there and taking in the colorful blooms that abounded along the narrow road from the hacienda to the main road. As usual, Juan sped around the curves in a way that made Jenny glad for her seat belt. They soon turned off of the road that wound around the coastline onto a road heading to the sea.

A large, old passenger airplane with no logo or markings sat on the tarmac of the tiny private airstrip surrounded with jungle foliage. Evidently the Troopers had already loaded.

"The Alliance has purchased a number of properties over the years. This airstrip actually belongs to us as does the strip where we will be landing," said Juan. "Get on board. Brendan will be our pilot today and I will be his co-pilot. Aliki has consented to be our flight attendant, which should be interesting. It's about a five hour flight and the weather is favorable."

On board the aircraft, Jenny took her seat toward the front of the cabin in what would have been first class. Behind her, she could see the Troopers row on row, faces bland, all dressed in camo. They didn't appear to be nervous, their faces indicating that there were a number of silent mindspeech conversations going on, sometimes resulting in soft chuckles.

The interior of the plane was not as shabby as she had expected, and she noticed that it was cleaner than most commercial planes might have been. This plane was reserved for Alliance business and was not frequently used, but evidently Juan had taken as good care of it as he did his magnificent hacienda and grounds.

Takeoff was routine. Bob was seated next to her and Tarafau across the aisle. She had expected conversations to be about the upcoming mission, but Bob chatted with her about the neighborhood. Evidently, he had been putting in regular appearances, chatting with neighbors, so it would appear that all was going normally.

Tarafau asked about Cinder. It amused Jenny that his time as a cat was so entertaining for him. According to Bob, Cinder had been in the doggy hospital, having run in front of a car, but was recuperating and would be terrorizing the neighborhood again in no time. Miss Longtree was on the east coast, lecturing at several major universities on ethics. All in all, everything was quiet. There had been no sign of Sam or her minions. Ted was back working the garden, since the shields had been programmed to allow him into the backyard and all traces of the damage to the house and altercations in the back yard had been removed.

Tarafau said he was glad they would have this respite, so Cinder could heal in time for his next attack. Jenny laughed at that.

Bob went into much more detail about the additions he had made to Fidget and Lizzie.

"They can both defend themselves, if necessary and they are constantly backed up in the Alliance cloud. Obviously, if I make a commercial version, those features will be left out. Their emotional response circuits are much improved. They can sense from body posture and facial expression the mood of those with whom they interact and respond accordingly. They have communications circuits that allow them to act like a cellphone. They can also document actions around them, similar to that surveillance equipment on your property.

By the way, I didn't steal that from the Alliance. I have a similar system on my own property that has been in place for years."

They went on like that throughout the flight. At one point, Aliki came around with lunch, serving them with a huge smile, acting like the maître d in a fancy restaurant, a towel draped over one arm. It was nothing special, however, sandwiches, fresh veggies, an apple and water, but it was filling and broke up the time.

Brendan's voice came on the loudspeaker. "This is your captain speaking. We have just sighted the Brazilian coastline. We should arrive at our destination in about 20 minutes. There is no control tower and no air traffic, so we will be able to land quickly. Troopers will exit the aircraft first. Please go immediately to the tree line at the end of the runway and set up your transport craft and load in. Gariel has his orders and the units of the hovercraft caravan will begin into the jungle within 15 minutes of landing. Please fasten your seatbelts and put your tray tables and seatbacks in their original condition. Thank you for flying Alliance Air. Hope your flight was out of this world. G'day."

Jenny grinned. Obviously, Brendan was enjoying his role as pilot for this venture.

Aliki cleared up all the leftover trash from lunch and belted himself in for landing. Jenny could feel her heart speed up. This was it. Up until now it could have been any of a number of flights she had experienced, but now they were headed into the unknown. Few human beings beside the native population had ever penetrated as far into this jungle as they would be. And, if it had been a sight-seeing journey, that would have been concerning enough, but their destination and what they must do when they arrived loomed in her thoughts.

Every single person in this venture was in serious danger from here on out and they looked to Jenny for leadership. Not really, she amended quickly. Gariel, Tarafau and Burt were in charge of the main force and the Troopers would follow their lead.

The landing was smooth, the sea rushing by on one side and the jungle on the other of the long runway. Deplaning from the air conditioned aircraft, the heat and humidity hit her in the face like a blow. She noticed her face felt moist. Squinting against the sun, she saw the others moving quickly to just inside the edge of the jungle.

The crystal blue sky and the deep greens of the jungle vegetation were a stark contrast to the bright white clouds scudding across the sky. All of this beauty, she thought and yet it hides one of the largest threats humankind had yet to face. And even as that occurred to her, another thought raced across her mind like one of the big white clouds. What if it wasn't? How many times in the past might her planet have been on the verge of annihilation without anyone on earth any the wiser?

As she entered the jungle canopy the heat dropped only a few degrees. The insistent moisture that surrounded her was much like entering the steam room in Sanglarka. Not quite dense enough to blur her vision, but enough that she suddenly felt damp from head to foot. She was glad she had taken Brendan's advice and brought plenty of clean cotton socks as well as using the foot powder each of them had been provided. Foot rot was a common issue with rain forest expeditions. Fortunately, they wouldn't be trekking by foot for hours, yet.

The hover transports had already been extracted from their MDPs and the Troopers were mostly all loaded into them. Gariel was in the leading craft with Burt in the next to last, along with Jenny, her Guards, Aliki, Tarafau, Brendan and Bob. A rear guard transport full of armed Troopers followed directly behind them.

"The cars are programmed to follow the lead car, which Gariel is guiding via GPS," Burt explained to their group. "We'll mostly be able to sit back and enjoy the ride. I recommend you get some rest. When we leave the vehicles, we have a good 4 hours to trek in the half light of the jungle canopy. We'll have to set up a camp when we get to our first camp site. We will be pushing very hard for the two days following on foot, at which time we will send out robot scouts to see what they can find. If we're lucky the final leg of the hiking part of the trip will take only another day, if we really push and there are no incidents to slow us down. At some point we may also find ourselves on the water. Your seats do recline a bit, if that will help."

Despite her nervous energy and the heady experience of being in a real jungle for the first time in her life, Jenny obediently went into her breathing exercises and relaxed. If everyone survived and they succeeded, there would be time for sight-seeing later.

She felt the slowing of the hover car through the haze of the nap she had not expected to be able to take. The snake of hover cars was coming to a stop.

The Troopers immediately exited their cars and assembled themselves in a formation in the small clearing they had paused in. As soon as all had left the cars, they disappeared into the MDPs of those who were responsible for them. Jenny remembered that each of them had a small hover car in their MDP, if it became necessary for them to flee, but she doubted, considering the density of the trees ahead of them that they would be much use in the deeper parts of the jungle.

Gariel had plotted their trek to avoid contact with any of the native inhabitants, so it wouldn't be "as the crow flies". This jungle extended for thousands of miles in every direction and Jenny knew she would not be straying from the group, if she could help it. If it wasn't for the compass included in her emergency kit, she would have had not the slightest idea how to point in any particular direction due to the heavy jungle canopy which would block any attempt to find direction by the sky or landmarks. Each of them was equipped with a map, of course, but how much good that would do if one of them got truly lost and were on their own, she had no idea.

She had gone through the required survival training course when she started with the hiking group a few years ago, but she'd never had to use more than the most basic parts of the training. She was hopeful she would be able to recall it, if the need arose.

Fortunately, Burt, Brendan, Gariel and Tarafau all had significant experience and she guessed that it was also part of the training and experience of the Troopers. She breathed a mental sigh of relief that this wouldn't all be on her and moved over to the huddle of her team by the assembled Troops.

Gariel turned from the huddle to the Troopers, his beard twitching animatedly as he spoke. *"I want the platoons to split into an advance and a rearward formation. The rest of the party will advance between the two platoons. Your first priority is to protect the Guardians. Be aware that we may find ourselves threatened by more than enemy forces. This jungle is crawling with creatures that are dangerous in many ways. Most predators will stay away from such a large force, but some of the deadliest creatures in this jungle are small enough and silent enough to be easily missed.*

Vigilance is easily worn down over long marches, especially in this heat and humidity. Stay alert and, if you feel yourself wearing down, remember what awaits us at the end of this long march. We go from the frying pan," and he wiped the sweat from his brow, *"into the fire."*

Chapter 33: Out-sneaking The Sneak

Jenny walked beside the hovering stretcher, her hand on the chest of the Trooper laying on it, to calm him. As they walked, she whispered what she hoped were comforting words. *"We caught it in time. You're gonna recover. I'm right here."* The Trooper still trembled, but his breathing was not as ragged.

They had stopped for a short lunch break, only taking time to get their food out and take care of other needs before intending to eat on the march. By this time, Jenny was beginning to understand the enormity of their task. It was Gariel's intention to get in 25 miles before making camp for the night. This meant pushing at a steady pace with very few breaks.

One of the Troopers had sat on a mossy log to change his socks. Suddenly he yelled, swatting at something on his ankle. "Wandering Spider," said Brendan worriedly, "otherwise known as the Banana Spider. Bad luck, mate. They usually only come out at night." In an instant, the venom treatment kit was in his hand. First, he used a suction cup to pull as much venom out of the wounds as possible. *"These buggers are very aggressive and often bite multiple times by the time you notice the first bite,"* he went on calmly as he selected a vial from the kit, inserting it into a type of hypo-pen. "Fortunately, they do make an anti-venom for it." He stabbed the hypo into the man's calf above the wounds. "Now we'll bandage this, put you on a stretcher and elevate the leg to slow the spread of the poison. We can only hope you don't have an allergic reaction in addition to the other symptoms."

The man had been strapped onto the stretcher. They pulled out a bedroll to put under his leg. He had trembled and twitched with muscle spasms for nearly an hour, but Brendan had told her, that if he made it past a half hour, there was nothing more to do but keep him hydrated and let him rest, until the poison worked its way out of his system.

Before they had set out again, Gariel reminded his Troops of the consequences of inattention and once more emphasized the importance of vigilance.

It was nearly 4 p.m. when they paused again. Jenny had been on some long and difficult hikes, but nothing had prepared her for this. First of all, unlike the calming redwoods of her native California and beautiful Sanglarka, the jungle was never silent. Things seemed to be constantly stirring from the various insects who buzzed and clicked and reptiles that slithered, swishing through the underbrush, to the various wildlife, such as birds, monkeys and large predators. It felt like there were eyes constantly bearing down on them. And she never felt the urge to pee, as she was sweating out every drop she drank.

The man had finally sunk into a restless sleep and she turned the watch over to Nona. She drank another half bottle of water, grabbed some rations and ate standing. She knew if she were to sit down, she would probably fall asleep.

"We'll be at our projected campsite in about an hour," Burt told her as he was about to walk by and noticed her standing there. "Can you manage it?"

Jenny nodded tiredly. It felt like even that was too much effort. "Setting up the campsite will be a little more complicated than you may have experienced even with all of the hikes you've been on," he said. "In addition to setting up tents, and all of that, we also need to see to a defense perimeter and coordinate multiple night watches. We're going to rise soon after dawn, before the real heat sets in to give ourselves a bit of head start tomorrow, since we will also have the morning rain to contend with. At the end of that day we will set up our first semi-permanent camp while we send the bots out to reconnoiter. Once we have more intel, we will make some decisions. This part of the Amazon basin is crosshatched with rivers and streams. We may decide to do part of the trip on the water to speed things up and take it a little easier on our forces."

She later wouldn't be able to remember exactly how she got through it, except that she called on her breathing exercises to distance herself from the pain, heat and exertion.

When they finally arrived, they set up camp in a little clearing. According to the information they already had, they were far away from any of the native tribes, so they wouldn't risk any cultural or biological contamination. Jenny hoped that none of this conflict would affect any humans in the area. The Groga already had so much to answer for.

Bob was busily assembling his bot army. Burt and Gariel were setting up the command tent and the Troopers went about setting up the rest of the camp. Jenny, her Guards and Tarafau would all be bivouacking together in a small cabin-sized building, complete with cots, chairs, a curtained space with a porta potty and a small table.

Once Jenny had settled in to her small space in the cabin, she decided that she should go to the command tent, but, if she was honest with herself, she was exhausted, she didn't have any clue how much use she would be. She had no battle experience and she had competent advisors, but she couldn't just sit and wait for all of the decisions to be made even though she knew, in this case especially, she was leader in name only.

Burt and Gariel were studying a large map of the Amazon basin on an air screen when she arrived. She and her Guards pulled up chairs and waited for the others of the tactical team to arrive. It felt good to sit in the relative cool of the tent. Gariel had explained to her that they deliberately had no air conditioning in the tents, although they had the tech to do so, since they needed to acclimatize themselves to the heat, if they were to survive this trek.

Tarafau, followed by Bob, Juan, Aliki and Brendan strode into the tent. Soon after, the squad commanders entered, reporting that the camp was set up and secured and the watches had been put into place. The men were currently eating and would be on stand-by for instructions.

"*OK. Let's start with Bob,*" said Gariel.

"*The bots have been deployed in pairs into the most probable areas. They are in complete camouflage mode and are employing heat and sound sensors. Their programming is set up to eliminate beast and critter sounds as well as anything that isn't man-shaped. They are* streaming constant reports and we'll know the moment any of them encounters troop sized numbers."

"*Great*," said Gariel, his beard twitching mildly. "*Aliki, have you checked out the local waterways to see how many of them might be a path to our potential destinations? And have you checked out the watercraft?*"

"*Yes, boss,*" Aliki replied amiably. "*We have a lot of options, depending on what the bots tell us. The boats are shipshape and watertight. How many of your men know how to handle watercraft on a river?*"

"*Easily half of them,*" said Gariel confidently. "*We had a mission not long ago that required them to navigate similar boats. And Brendan, have you set up our little 'surprise'?*"

"*Easy as pie.*" Brendan's eyes sparkled with mirth. "*Thanks to Lizzie, they won't know what hit 'em. At least, not until it does.*"

"*Those MDPs sure made all of this simpler. But I don't want any of you thinking this is going to be a walk in the park, like our last encounter. Even if these Groga are as mindless as the last bunch, there are way more of them and they may have tech we haven't anticipated,*" Gariel intoned seriously, looking from face to face.

"*Bob, when should we start receiving reports from the bots?*"

Bob scratched his head. "*Hard to say. It all depends on how far out our friends have camped. At the widest point, the jungle stretches across 1,200 miles and covers over 3 million square miles in dense rainforest with few clearings. It's also crisscrossed with multiple waterways from small creeks to wide rivers. At this point we're only about 200 miles in and most of that was because of the hovercraft. It's a lot of area to cover, even flying over the canopy. If our luck holds, we could hear by morning. If not, we'll just have to keep our fingers crossed that we can pull this off before they head out of that portal.*"

"*Then, there is nothing to do but wait, for now. All our resources are organized, and we can be on the move with 20 minutes notice. Get some rest while you can and stay hydrated. I know I'm being repetitive, but you'll be glad you took my advice."* And Gariel looked pointedly at Jenny.

Jenny shrugged. She knew that her concern probably showed on her face. She wouldn't neglect herself. As an experienced hiker, she knew the importance of both rest and hydration and in this heat where you sweated water out nearly as fast as you could take it in, it would be doubly important.

She looked at the map stretched out in front of her. They had specifically blown up the area that featured the rainforest. It was vaster than she had realized. Stretching across 9 countries in South America, it appeared to be about half the size of the entire United States. The proverbial needle within the haystack didn't even start to describe the near impossibility of their task.

She hoped that clever use of technology would give them the edge they needed to find the Groga and implement their plans to find the portal, prevent the defeat of yet another culture and allow them to infiltrate, find and defeat the Groga and their allies once and for all. Piece of cake, right?

The mess crew had brought food into the command tent and the team ate quietly, each lost in their own thoughts and plans. When Jenny rose to head to their tent to get some rest, Lyra, Nona and Mynn got to their feet and followed her out to her tent.

It felt like she had no sooner laid her head on her pillow than Tarafau was shaking her awake. *"There's news,"* he said. *"We're gathering in the command tent."*

Her Guards were already on their feet. They strode back across the encampment. Inside the tent the air seemed electrified. All heads turned to Jenny and her escort.

"I don't know what the odds are, but the bots have found them. About 135 miles as the crow flies, or the robot, in this case, and they don't even appear to be covering their tracks that well. They're well away from any native villages and appear to be going about their business without a lot of urgency. The portal appears to be in the center of their camp. If we travel upriver, instead of whacking our way through the jungle, we could be there in a few days. That

doesn't leave us a lot of time for planning." Bob said as they seated themselves around the map.

We have less than a week before their deadline, if our intel is accurate," said Gariel gravely. He turned to one of his commanders. "Disassemble the camp and assemble the troops outside in an hour. We should have our travel plan completed by then."

The commander nodded curtly, turned on his heel and left.

"We'll be travelling by boat during the day as long as the light lasts, and we'll camp long enough to get some sleep at night. I want this council in one boat, so we can plan as we go. In the meantime, Aliki, which of these waterways will get us there the fastest all in one piece?"

Aliki grinned. *"Well, boss, with the boats Lizzie so generously provided us, we can use this waterway here."* He pointed to a not-so-wiggly blue line that extended from where they were to the big red dot someone had put over the area where the Groga were camped.

"It's a fairly straight shot, as these rivers go, and we should be able to make the trip with only a couple of stops each day. Be sure to remind everyone to use their sunscreen. The reflection of the sun off of the water can cause some really nasty sunburns and there will be little shade during the trip. In a few places the trees shelter the water from the sun, but those are few and far between.

The watercraft are an adaptable design. We tweaked them and now they're like river tour boats you may have seen. They will hold about 24 people each, not counting the pilot. This means eight troop craft and one command craft to hold all of us. They should be fast enough to get us where we're going in two days with rest in between.

I'd like to recommend that every trooper is armed for a potential fire fight, although, if that happens, we are going to be hard pressed to defend ourselves, or so anyone watching would think. However, as an added precaution, we'll be deploying Bob's handy little bots along the river route, following us as we travel. Anyone lurking in the undergrowth on the banks will have a nasty little surprise waiting above them.

Jenny, in addition to your Guards and Tarafau, I want you to keep your bot next to you in the boat. We want to keep you safe."

Jenny found herself more than a little annoyed at this "keep Jenny safe" thing that had been going on since her fight with the three workmen in her house that day. It seemed like, since she had experienced two encounters with the enemy and come off not much the worse for wear, they would trust her to take care of herself. On the other hand, she guessed it was more about the importance of her position as Gatekeeper. She earnestly wanted to tell them she could take care of herself, but she knew their intentions and their reasoning were sound.

Gariel thanked Aliki and looked at Burt. "*Have you transmitted our findings to Lova?*"

Burt nodded. "*I have all of the bots set up to transmit all of their intel to Sanglarka, in case they see something we may have missed. I would like everyone to use mindspeech as we travel. I want to be as quiet as possible. Sound carries farther on water. The engines of our craft are quieter than most, but I don't want us yelling back and forth to communicate.*"

Gariel turned to Bob. "*Do we still have access to those handy little flying nanobots? It worked so well as a distraction last time and if the trackers were activated on them, we would be able to track any strays, not to mention as they go through the portal and we end up fighting them.*"

"*Yes, although we don't have enough to handle the numbers we'll be facing. I replicated as many as I could while we were in Sanglarka. But any distraction is better than none. If we are strategic on how we use them, we should be able to take advantage of their special talents.*

Also, if we can get one on someone going through their portal, it might give us a clue as to the frequencies or coordinates they are using. I'm hoping they're using some sort of transmitter to key up the gate. If that's the case, we should be able to quietly liberate one so we can send one or more of them to the Alliance to examine."

"*Agreed,*" said Gariel, his heavy brows furrowed. "*And we should have more information available as we travel. OK. Get your gear. I'll meet with the Troopers and we'll head out.*"

It only took a moment to gather the few things she left on her bunk. She considered the MDP one of the big compensations for the choice she had made. No heavy backpacks or luggage when she traveled. She knew Bob would love to get his hands on the scientific principles that made them work, even if he would never be allowed to reproduce them for Earth consumption, at least until Earth technology caught up.

The Troopers were already formed up in the now empty clearing. By the time she had walked over to stand beside Gariel, her cabin had disappeared into someone's MDP and you could barely tell they had ever been there.

When the last were assembled, Gariel sent to his Troopers, "*Who are we?*"

In one mighty mental voice they replied. "*We are The Troopers of the Dimensional Alliance, dedicated to protecting the weak. We defend the right and the liberty of all beings by the grace of The Creator of All.*"

"*What is our creed?*"

"*Peace is our first priority. True to the cause of freedom and faithful to our companions and our mission.*"

As they stood at attention, mental voices reciting with conviction and power, Jenny really looked at them for the first time. They all appeared to be no different than any soldier she had ever seen. She remembered as a kid, her dad in his uniform. He always looked like a superhero to her. He too, had that light in his eyes that told her that his convictions were deep, and he did what he did to protect their family and the families of all of her friends.

These men and women were diverse in so many ways. All humanoid, skin colors ranging from the slightest tinge of green to every racial skin tone on earth. She did not doubt that they varied also in other ways that couldn't be seen by her, but the one thing they all had in common was that fervor. They believed intensely in those words.

"We go once again into the unknown as we have so many times before. We cannot allow the incursions of the Groga to continue. Our force is smaller, but each of you have been hand-picked for your ability to work as a team and make intelligent individual decisions as they are required. As we travel on the river, you will receive your orders and instructions. We are the shield of the dimensional gateways. There will be no welcoming victory parades for us. We serve those who do not know us and who may never realize the sacrifice each of us have chosen to make for their protection.

I would trust every single one of you with my life and the lives of those I hold dear. You are my brothers and sisters. We would not harm the Groga or their allies, if they would attend to their own business, but we cannot allow them to continue to harm innocents for whatever reason. We go to victory, regardless of the outcome, either to conquer the Groga or to find ourselves in the arms of The Creator of All Things."

At that point he held up both hands and they began to sing. It reminded Jenny of the Gregorian chants her mother had been fond of. The deeper voices harmonized with the higher voices in such perfection that the air vibrated. Jenny couldn't understand the words, but it made her feel peaceful and there was an ascending warmth and joy emanating from the chorus.

"It is a prayer," Tarafau sent to her. *"They are petitioning The Creator of All Things for victory over evil in the multiverse and in their hearts. They are giving thanks for the abundance of life and beauty. They are asking for strength and courage. They are also praying for the Groga, that they will have a change of heart, that they might not have to destroy them."*

As the music stopped the vibration hung shimmering in the air for a moment. As one, all of them, including Tarafau and her Guards, extended a fist in front of them and placed them on their heart. Jenny and the rest solemnly copied the gesture. After a moment of complete silence, one of the commanders sent. *"To the boats by ranks."*

The ranks peeled off one at a time and they walked to the water's edge where the boats had been tied. At no time had the Troopers marched in unison while in the rainforest. They made less noise when walking at a staggered pace as they would have if just hiking with a group.

Once Tarafau had handed Jenny into their boat and she had seated herself, she got Lizziebot out of her MDP per instructions. She didn't have to brief Lizzie, as she had access to the same stream of information that the other bots had, plus her own connection to Sanglarka and Jenny's phone. Lizziebot also was linked to the "bug" Burt had installed in her hand. Part of her programming was that if Jenny was in a situation that the bot couldn't get her out of, the bot was to immediately report to Sanglarka for further instructions.

They started down the river. At one point Jenny had trailed her fingers in the water beside her, but Tarafau had reached out and grabbed her hand firmly, pulling it out of the river. *"You don't want to do that. The water seems peaceful, but my research..."* and he trailed off, nodding out to the river. Jenny's eyes widened as she saw coils of something very large undulating alongside the boats. It appeared to be as long as the boat and thicker than Tarafau's thighs.

It was no trouble after that to keep her hands well inside the protection of the boat.

The river curved to the right or left as they went, sometimes drifting them under canopies of trees that blocked out most of the light, but mostly they were exposed to the baking sun and the dense humidity that permeated the rainforests of the Amazon basin. It would have been completely quiet, if it weren't for the various calls, hoots, whistles and sometimes roars and shrieks that emanated from the vegetation that surrounded the river. The boat's engines made almost no sound, and no one spoke aloud, as instructed.

They didn't stop to eat, relying on prepared rations stored in their MDPs when they were hungry.

Jenny watched the bank slip by. It would have been hypnotic, if it wasn't for the fact that each stretch of bank held new and interesting things to see, or that they were on their way to a battle where many might possibly be seriously injured or lose their lives. Jenny would have found the trip almost pleasant, with the exception of the buzzing insects, some of which were not deterred by the insect repellent and the overpowering heat.

All heads were covered with brimmed hats, but that only shaded their faces from the sun. It did nothing to stop them from sweating until every hat was ringed with sweat around the headband, even soaking out towards the brim.

The boats had been equipped with a kind of porta-potty cubicle. Unlike other public toilets of this type, there was no terrible smell. Waste was simply evaporated with no telltale odor or dumping it into the river. One blessing at least. This meant that they didn't have to stop the boats at all on their journey until night fell, since each had been provided with rations in their MDP.

They wouldn't travel in the dark. Night was when most of the big predators came out, especially on and along the river, and lights on the boats would give them away to anyone who might be watching.

The first day passed with no incidents of any importance. They had seen wildlife as they floated past the banks faster than Jenny had expected. These weren't speed boats, but they were way faster than they could have walked. The fastest pace they could sustain on the march was about 3-4 miles per hour. The boats covered 25 miles in that same amount of time. Since they weren't going "as the crow flies", they had a lot more than the 150 or so miles to travel, but they would still reach their destination in a couple of days, since they didn't have to make any stops except to sleep.

Jenny found herself wondering how they could go so far without refueling. Burt explained, *"We aren't using standard fuel, such as you understand it. These boats could go a year or more without having to pay attention to fuel. If we have issues at all, it won't be because we need to look for a service station."*

Jenny had to let herself be content with that. Her mind was far too focused on the impending mission to wrap her head around dimensional science. It was hard enough to mentally prepare herself for a new experience she had never coveted. Of all of the adventures she had imagined herself pursuing, going into battle against alien beings in a jungle had not been on the list.

The morning of the second day, Jenny assiduously applied her sunscreen, jammed her hat on her head and left with Lyra, Nona, Mynn and Tarafau in tow. Lizziebot hovered beside her as well. She was on print speech mode to comply with the no verbal speech orders. When she would speak to Jenny, her digital face would disappear, and a text readout would replace her smiling face and those intense blue eyes.

During the previous day, once she was finally able to relax, Jenny had amused herself by asking Lizzie questions about the things they saw. Lizzie was a fount of information. She had noticed, after awhile, Lyra, Nona and Mynn were peering over her shoulder as well to see what Lizzie had to say. The tiny pop-out touch keyboard that extended from Lizzie's chest made it easy to have a silent conversation.

The forest around them was noisy. The birds and creatures of the forest greeted the day with loud contact calls, bird-song, shrieks and what almost sounded like laughter. And, of course, the insects contributed buzzing and something that sounded a lot like the little drones Brendan was so fond of. Jenny really didn't want to see the insect that made that noise.

The Trooper who had been bitten by the Wandering Spider had since recovered, but Jenny still was very careful to not sit or stand too close to the vegetation where they were known to hide. Burt claimed that snakes wouldn't attack people unless you frightened them, but Jenny still couldn't repress a shudder when she heard the dry, rasping sound of a snake or lizard slithering through the underbrush.

Back in the boats, they began their journey again. This time, however, instead of sitting in silence most of the way, Gariel began to relay the reports of the bots, broadcasting via mindspeech to everyone in each boat. They were nearly there. They would pause in their trip about halfway through the day in a clearing about a half day's march from the nearest Groga sentry. The bots had plotted a map of the occupied area, including marking out the location of the portal.

While in the clearing, all would put on their battle armor and ready their arms. Jenny was relieved to discover that the battle armor was actually air-conditioned and treated in such a way that casual surveillance methods such as radar would not detect them on their approach.

They had issued Jenny something that looked like a blaster out of a space opera. After demonstrating its use, they had been impressed with her accuracy. She was no sharp-shooter, to be sure, but her dad had taken the kids out to the weapons range fairly often to teach them gun-safety and to be sure they could defend themselves that way. Jenny had never chosen to own a gun, but she knew one end from the other. She could hit a target, but she wasn't sure how accurate she would be when she was running or when the target was moving too fast.

Gariel told them that the bots had also determined that the portals did work via a device. These devices had been issued to each of the platoon commanders. The first part of their mission was to acquire one or more of those devices, preferably without alerting the Groga of their presence. The second priority would be to discover what dimension the portal was pointed at. Once they were able to provide Alliance scientists with a device to study, they would attempt to discover how far the enemy portal network extended, and what, if anything they could potentially do to disable it once and for all.

The final push would not be limited to the Troopers in their party. Assuming the dimension being attacked was in the Alliance interdimensional network, a suitably large army of Troopers would be waiting for the Groga when they emerged through the portal on the other side.

It all sounded so simple and logical to Jenny, like they just couldn't lose. Maybe it wouldn't be as bad as she had imagined? But Tarafau squashed that thought like a bug.

"It's as good a plan as we can have, but we all know that there will be contingencies we didn't plan for. What are our fallback instructions?"

"We will establish a command post a hundred yards or so from the Groga camp. The hovercars will be stationed there. If things go bad, get back to the command post and fill those hovercars or use one from your MDP. They are programmed to take you to a safe place where you can reconnoiter. Each of us have accepted Burt's

bugs. *If you get lost, find a quiet spot and stay put, if possible. We will not leave anyone behind, if we can help it.*

All of our decoys and distractions are in place and everyone has received their orders. We will start infiltrating the enemy camp as soon as we are in range. The bots have marked all of the sentries they could find and have left us the schedule of the guard changes. Each sentry point has two guards and they are armed with blasters as well as com devices to alert their command post of anything untoward.

Stage 1 will be to wait until a change of guards, put the new guards to sleep with a bite from our nanobots and take over their posts. We will steal their uniforms and go looking for the portal devices. Preferably we would like more than one device. It will be high priority to preserve one for examination by our techs at Alliance headquarters."

Bob twitched and added wistfully, "*Any chance I can be in on that?*" The look of suppressed eagerness almost made Jenny laugh.

"*We'll have to see,*" Gariel said with an amused twist to his mouth. "*Your clearance for tech may take a bit. They're pretty careful with that. Tech pollution in the early days of the Alliance was the cause of more than one failed culture. That kind of infection can cause so many more problems than it solves and in some cases it has proven disastrous.*" He held up his hand to forestall Bob's objection.

"*We know you are trustworthy, and we know that your intentions are good, but despite that, there are protocols we must follow. As a veteran of Earth military, I know you understand.*"

Bob nodded; a bit chagrined.

"*Jenny, do you have anything you would like to add?*"

Jenny's head jerked up. She had been so wrapped up in the instructions and her jumbled feelings about the impending conflict that the question blind-sided her. She thought a moment then nodded her head.

"*I have learned something important today about myself and about our cause,*" she began, tentatively, weighing each word carefully before she said it. "*I don't know for sure why my aunt Lizzie chose* me to do this, but I do know that I am on the right side of this conflict. I know we are doing what is right and I know that we stand for something important. It is comforting to me to know that my associates in this cause feel as I do. I too would rather never harm another living thing in my lifetime, but I cannot sit still when I know that others are being wrongfully attacked, killed and enslaved, for whatever reason. I admit I am afraid, but I am consoled by the fact that I can count on every person on this team and I want you to know that I will not hang back when the time comes to fight."

All faces turned to her in what appeared to be alarm. "*You are with us as our leader. We will not have you engage the enemy. If I had my way, you would be at the command center in Sanglarka,*" Gariel said bluntly, but without heat. "*You are precious to the Alliance. Your task will be to oversee the command tent and coordinate information as it comes through the communications network. Tarafau, Nona, Lyra and Mynn will also be with you to assist you and protect you. I thought you understood this.*"

Jenny gaped. She didn't know how to reply to this. Not fight? Be protected? There it was again. She did not want to appear sullen, but Gariel had just sucked something important right out of her. She had to sit in the command tent while everyone else was risking everything?

Tarafau put one hand on her shoulder. "*Each person on the team has their part to play. Will you not choose to do your task?*"

When he put it that way, it made her sound selfish and petulant. Slowly she nodded at Gariel. "*I will do my part. I promised it and I will not go back on my promise, but I don't have to like it.*"

Gariel nodded and went on, detailing the various posts and tasks of the platoons of troopers and the techs who would be running the various decoys and distractions. Jenny realized there would be a lot more going on in the command tent than she thought and that Burt, Bob and Gariel would also be with her in the command tent, so perhaps it wasn't as much of a big deal as her mind had made it at first.

When they arrived at the clearing, they disembarked, and the watercraft were installed back into the MDPs. They set up camp and made their preparations. Each of them went about their various tasks without fuss or comment, having been thoroughly briefed during their time on the water.

Even knowing she would not be in the middle of the action; Jenny's stomach was churning. By tomorrow morning, they would be fully engaged with the enemy. By tomorrow morning Jenny realized that her life would have changed even more than it already had, for good or ill.

They took their march once again, through the dense canopy and undergrowth of the forest. Jenny thought, as she hiked with Tarafau in front of her and her Guards surrounding her on either side and to her rear, that somehow time had sped up as they approached closer and closer to the Groga camp.

All at once they were halted and Jenny realized they must be at their command post. The Troopers were already assembling the barracks and the command tent. One group of them were parking hover cars on one side of the area, the cars' camouflage shielding in place, so that they were difficult to see visually or with any kind of detection equipment unless you knew where they were. Everyone was in armor and had weapons at their belts and strapped to their backs. All in all, the scene was somewhat like the science fiction movies she had always been fascinated with.

She noticed the command tent was ready and she decided she might as well get to work. There were no more inspiring speeches or even quiet discussion as all was put in readiness. Everyone knew their duty and, if they needed to communicate, mindspeech was the order of the day.

As she entered the tent, she noticed that the map above the conference area had changed. Now it was a real time aerial view of the Groga encampment. The camp lay about 1,500 yards away from their command tent. It was laid out like the spokes of a wheel, tent-like structures, similar to their own radiated out in neat lines from the center. In the center was a large clear space that looked like it was probably used to assemble their army. On the side of the wheel closest to their own camp was a large tent that had soldiers coming and going, clearly the command center of the Groga forces.

At the top of the inner cleared space of the wheel was an area labeled on the map as "portal". It might as well have been an empty patch of ground, as there was nothing to even indicate it was there. It didn't appear to be guarded, probably to avoid drawing attention to it, but Gariel had explained to them during the briefing that it had been identified by the bots in their fly-over, after having observed troops coming and going through it. The portal seemed to go to more than one place at once. They had to assume devices controlled the destination.

"We will be neutralizing the sentries in about an hour from now," Gariel began, as the last of the command team arrived. *"We have about 8 hours from that time to try and get as many of the portal devices as we can without being detected. The guards change again in 8 hours and we need to get Troopers in place before the Groga plan to launch their attack. The big distraction to allow our guys to sneak through the gate ahead of the Groga soldiers has already been prepared and we will trigger it after we have obtained the portal devices.*

Once the last of the Groga attacking force is through the portal, our Troopers here will move to attack the few remaining forces and secure the Groga encampment. If all goes well, we will have neutralized the Groga forces deployed here and will be able to fortify this portal against any further incursions. They will no longer be able to use it to get to Earth.

Lova and her team will be streaming our reports directly to Alliance headquarters. They have twice the number of Troopers than the Groga assembled, and they are in readiness to immediately deploy to the dimension being attacked.

Bob, have you activated the first round of distractions?"

"Ready."

"Burt, are you ready with round two?"

Burt grinned evilly, *"Ready and willing."*

"So now we wait until we get the signal."

The view of the screen changed to a grid view of eight sentry posts. The Groga guards didn't seem all that attentive. They stood back to back, their weapons slung on their backs, looking almost disinterestedly at their surroundings.

"*They have very good hearing,*" Gariel continued. "*But their eyesight is questionable. I think they may have trouble with low contrast, especially in the shadows, based on past intel. This could work very much in our favor. As a matter of fact, one of our distractions is very much based on that assumption. Burt and Bob have passed their decoy and distraction strategies on to the Alliance troops back at headquarters, for which they were very grateful. You Earthlings have very devious minds. I'm glad you're on our side,*" he said grinning at Bob and Burt.

The two of them sported twin grins and fist-bumped to celebrate that praise.

Jenny smiled. Burt and Bob had made a real connection. You nearly never saw one without the other. Mynn had taken to calling them "BnB" and it had caught on with most of the team.

Gariel's face went serious again. "*Jenny, I want you to monitor communications between Sanglarka and the Alliance. We need to coordinate these attacks very closely to be completely effective and to give us the least chance of casualties.*

Tarafau I need you, Lyra, Nona and Mynn to watch the perimeter of our camp. Do not engage any enemy you see unless it is necessary. You three have access to the sleepy-time bots, as Bob calls them, and can deploy them at will. If they don't see you first, that will be our best strategy."

They immediately stood up and left the tent without looking back.

Bob interrupted. "*What are we planning on doing with all the sleeping beauties we're creating? That sleeping potion will keep them out for at least ten hours, based on what your scientists know about their physiology and Xao Ting's suggested dosage. We can't leave them here and I think your current holding facility is full up.*"

"*The council is still debating the final disposition of prisoners. Half of them are all for trying to rehabilitate them and put them on a non-gated planet that would be under their surveillance. The other half want to euthanize them and be done with it. Ingot is still unsure how the vote will go, but it has to be unanimous for euthanization. By the way, a bit of good news: You should also know that Guaray may not end up being executed. He has been very useful to the Council and they are considering also taking into account that his family had been threatened."*

Jenny's heart swelled at this. The impending execution of Guaray had never been completely pushed to the back of her mind. She couldn't help but wonder how she would have reacted under similar circumstances and she knew that most of her fellow Guardians felt the same.

A small chime sounded from the split screen above them showing each sentry and all eyes were riveted. Two of the guards collapsed like puppets with cut strings, followed by another and another. Jenny wanted to hold her breath until the final pair of sentries collapsed.

A soft cheer went up from Burt and Bob and there were smiles all around as the Troopers came into view and dragged the sentries off into the underbrush. They returned, dressed as Groga and gave the thumbs up sign, one at a time until all were accounted for.

The viewpoint of the bots suddenly changed to a different set of bots atop the perimeter of the camp. Gazing down, it all seemed business as usual. Soldiers milled about, either set at different tasks or drilling or moving from one area to another in small groups or as individuals. Nowhere did anyone seem to be hurrying or excited.

"And now it begins," said Gariel.

Chapter 34: When All Else Fails

Jenny peered through the darkness. Once again, she found herself tied to a chair, helpless and furious.

It had all started out so well. The assigned Troopers had infiltrated the edges of the Groga camp and found and liberated three of the portal devices and had brought back three sleeping Groga, adding them to the sentries they had captured, restrained and put under guard in one of the hovercars. Two of the devices had been stored in a bot and were sent flying back to the mainland where a pilot waited to fly it to Puerto Rico and from there it would be sent back through the gate to Alliance headquarters. The other device had been examined by Burt and Bob.

The extractor had been used on the Groga captains and they were able to decipher the use of the various knobs and buttons. The location of the intended assault had also been extracted and sent to Lova. They were exultant to have this first part of the plan go so well.

When they had gotten word that the Alliance did indeed have a gate on that world and that the Troopers were deploying, it seemed they couldn't help but win.

As soon as the Groga force was seen deploying through the gate and the last one stepped through, Gariel had sent their 200 Troopers to the camp. There only seemed to be about 150 left behind to guard the camp.

It had been a wonder to Jenny that all was working so well, especially after Gariel's grim statement that even the best plans had their unseen flaws.

Bob's nanobots went to work, buzzing and biting and making the Groga nearly dance with frustration and irritation.

Then Burt's drones invaded the sky with an angry buzz. They could be as silent as a gentle breeze when programmed to do so, but in this case, they sounded like gigantic angry wasps as they flew at the Groga, dropping something that looked a lot like maple syrup on their heads.

The Groga fired at the buzzing nuisances, occasionally hitting one, but the drones were so quick and nimble that the hits were few and far between.

As soon as the enemy was fully sticky, the syrup coating heads, hands and even their weapons, the Troopers poured in, their weapons trained point blank at the Groga who had been herded by the buzzing drones into a bunch, facing out.

Almost in unison most of them put their weapons on the ground in front of them in obvious surrender, but a few fired at the Troopers who corrected that mistake with quick shots that put those who had fired down. The first casualties were on the Groga.

Jenny quietly sent up a thank you to "The Creator of All Things" and was turning to comment to Bob and Burt, who were conferring on next steps, when she realized they were standing there with their hands raised in surrender. That was when the lights went out.

Now, as she tried to peer through the darkness around her, she noticed the sound of breathing around her. From her earlier experience, she knew better than to call out vocally. "*Burt? Bob? Tarafau?*" she sent cautiously. Someone exhaled loudly behind her and Tarafau responded, "*We're here, Jenny. I'm sorry. We have failed you.*"

Bob's mind chimed in. "*Tarafau, there was nothing you could do. Everything pointed to a win and we never saw anything in the surveillance cams until they were right on top of you. Blow darts, really? Of all the primitive, low-down, sneaky…*"

If Jenny hadn't been so frightened, she would have laughed. It was definitely ironic that their enemies had used a variation of their own tactics on them.

"*They weren't even Groga,*" Burt added suddenly just beyond Bob. "*Evidently, the Groga aren't as concerned about polluting the culture of the natives as we are. The glimpse I got of our attackers tells me they were probably Amazonians. We were just lucky that they didn't coat those darts with curare. Obviously the Groga want us alive, at least for now.*"

Jenny was pretty sure she knew who their orders had come from.

Lyra piped up, "*Does anyone have any idea where we are?*"

"*We could be pretty much anywhere. We may still be on earth or they may have taken us to one of their conquered worlds or even one of the home dimensions.*" Burt replied. "*Were any of us awake when they transferred us?*"

The lack of a reply said all it needed to say.

Jenny suddenly realized that it wouldn't be like last time, with Burt and Bob busting down the door to rescue her. She had never felt more helpless and alone. And then she remembered the counsel her father had once given her, before she had joined the hiking club.

"It's easy to panic when you find yourself in a difficult situation. You need to remember, OODA," he told her as he drove her to her first hiking club meeting. She had been in junior high school at the time and she rolled her eyes at the funny word, assuming her dad was poking fun at her.

"OODA is a term," he went on, ignoring her teen age reaction, "used by the military to make decisions when things aren't going well. Every commander knows that strategy and battle plans tend to go out the window after the first shot is fired. And people in combat often find themselves in unexpected situations.

But this happens a lot in life. Panic usually brings the very worst consequences, because it is based on fight or flight reactions that completely by-pass your brain.

OODA stands for: Observe. Orient. Decide. Act. Let's say somehow you got separated from your hiking group in unknown territory. Instead of running around in circles or plunging off onto the first path that looks inviting, you follow the steps.

First, observe. Take a deep breath and take inventory of your surroundings and your resources. If you know you have enough rations and supplies to last for awhile and you observe that there appears to be nothing dangerous in your vicinity, the best plan might be to stay where you are.

Then orient yourself. After taking stock of what you have, you may realize that you have the ability to make some kind of signal, preferably one that won't attract the beasties around you who might be looking for a snack.

That puts you in a position to decide. After taking stock, line up your choices and choose one that makes sense.

Finally, act. Once you have decided, get moving. Thoughtfully act on your decision immediately and with confidence. By going through these steps, you know you have made the best decision you can. Don't second guess yourself. Got it?"

Jenny nodded to herself as she had on that day. Her dad's advice had come in handy many times in her life.

"*OK, everyone, let's take stock. Do all of you still have your MDPs?*" Jenny wiggled her wrist as much as she could. Amazingly enough, the MDP was still there.

Burt said, "*MDPs can only be willingly removed, kinda like the ruby slippers. If someone tries to remove them, for instance by cutting off your hand or killing you, they will explode into bits of confetti. Which is why I can guarantee all of us still have them.*"

All of a sudden something occurred to Jenny.

"*Mynn, Nona, are you here?*" No reply. "*OK, either they are still unconscious or somehow they escaped, or...*" she trailed off realizing she didn't want to think about the "or".

"*They can take care of themselves,*" Lyra said, cutting her off from going any further into that thought. "*If they escaped, they have already fallen back to the contingency plan and are heading out to the rendezvous place. We won't know until we can count heads, if that is a possibility. We must assume the worst and work from there.*"

Jenny knew that Gariel had led his Troopers to the Groga camp following Burt and Bob's distractions and wouldn't find them missing until they had secured that area.

"*So, we have our MDPs, probably none of the weapons we were carrying outside of them, we're all tied up and there is a possibility no one knows where we are. We do, however have* our little *bug friends and we have one another. Everyone keep your eyes open and your mouths shut. We don't want them to have anything more to go on than they were able to see in the command tent, which was way more than I ever wanted to give them."*

Bob spoke up. His mental touch was so much him that Jenny could almost hear his matter of fact baritone. *"Well, one more bit of good news. All of the bots are waiting the next command signal, and no one can give it without the 64 bit hexadecimal password code. If they try even once to access any of it without that code, the whole thing will blow up in their face."*

Burt said, *"I just remembered something. As soon as we saw that the Groga were nearly drowned in syrup and our people had cornered them, I automatically triggered phase 2 of my distractions. And the drones are on search and destroy for a 2 mile radius from the Groga encampment to track down any strays. The first little distractions were humorous, but those drones mean business now. I'm guessing whoever grabbed us, if they went through the portal had to do it under fire. They won't stop searching for Groga until I give the code to Stage 3, so maybe..."*

He never finished his sentence. The place they were in was suddenly flooded with brilliant light as, what looked like a heavy curtain was drawn across a small door, spilling in sunlight. The bright light was somewhat painful.

She knew before a word was uttered who stood silhouetted against the bright light.

"Looks like we have all the ingredients for a party. And you know how much I love parties, don't you?"

Sam gestured, and two short native women came in to light torches that stood in all four corners of the little house. The walls of the hut, for that was what Jenny assumed it was, looked like it had been woven from palm fronds or some such. The little native women hurried quickly out of the hut, their heads bowed, looking at the ground. Their posture bespoke fear and subservience. At least now Jenny knew they were still on earth.

The curtain fell as the women hurried out. Sam/Engoza, stood with her arms outstretched as if greeting hoped-for guests. "So good to see you all. Even the kitty cat. Only, what brought you out of your disguise, big man? What? No purrs for your good friend Sam?"

Sam was fully in her Engoza persona. Her long robe hung open, a short tunic and sheer leggings peeking out, all of it in black and silver. Her long black hair was plaited into dread locks and her claw-like nails were painted (unless it was her natural color in this guise) the color of blood.

She grinned, walking a full circle around Jenny. "Look at you! Playing soldier, I see. Unfortunately, you lost your blaster somewhere along the way. And last I checked, R2D2 is in a galaxy far, far away. Your cavalry is in the room, so I doubt a rescue is on the way. A pity about your girlfriends..." and she trailed off, wrinkling her nose.

Jenny refused to engage her. She just sat there, glaring back at her, willing herself to be brave.

"Do we have to go through THAT again?" she demanded, hands on her hips. "Really, Jenny, this is just so very tiresome. You already have one beautiful art treasure ala moi. Certainly, that's enough for anyone. You should know the time will come when I will drink your blood. I got a little taste and I like it. But for now, I have orders to the contrary." She licked her lips as if in ecstasy.

Jenny thought of the butterfly on her arm and took courage from it. She noticed the others weren't saying a word and she was grateful for the solidarity. She knew what was coming next and winced at the thought, but she knew her companions would not thank her for giving in, if they were tortured. Even knowing this was true, she also knew that Sam didn't think of Jenny as brave. She knew she would try torturing at least one of her team, even potentially killing one of them, if she thought that might get her what she wanted.

Suddenly, there was an outcry from outside the little hut. Sam growled, an almost bestial sound. "You'll keep until I return. I think we understand each other." She whirled around and sped out the curtained door.

There was a clamor of voices and shouts not far from the hut and the smell of smoke. It seemed that one or more of the buildings were on fire. Sam's voice could be heard above the rest shouting orders.

Once again, the curtain drew back and a very old little native man peeked in. Looking from side to side he entered and drew a knife from his sash above his loin cloth. Jenny tensed. "*Oh well,*" she sent to the group. "*We did our best...*"

The little man bobbed his head and grinned. "*You speak the mind,*" he sent. He pointed to his chest. "*I too.*" With his knife he hurriedly cut Jenny's bonds, mind-speaking as he worked. "*I shaman. You shaman too?*" Jenny shook her head.

"*Ah well,*" he sent as he freed her ankles. "*You good. You kind. Your mind says so.*"

He moved from one of them to the other, each of them standing in turn, rubbing their wrists and ankles. "*You come. You follow.*"

He moved what appeared to be a set of shelves to reveal an opening smaller than the door, but simple enough for all of them to get through. Tarafau had to struggle, but he made it. The little shaman pulled the shelves back in front of the hole and beckoned to them grinning. The hut backed up against the rainforest. He slipped between two banana trees and they followed him.

The forest canopy in this area was so dense that it felt almost like nighttime with the exception of the tiny pinholes of light that glimmered here and there on the jungle floor. It was as if the constellations had been plucked from the sky and placed beneath their feet.

"*I light fire,*" the little shaman continued. "*Old building. We make it again. Water is not close by. They must stamp it out with blankets and things until they get water. Keep them busy. We hurry, yes?*"

Jenny nodded at him, wondering where they were and where they could possibly hide quickly enough to avoid being found. She didn't know if Sam had Groga soldiers with her or if she was relying entirely on her native "friends".

The sounds of the panicked cries fell quickly behind them as they walked so fast as to nearly be at a run, barely avoiding tripping on vines, stones and the detritus of the jungle floor. Finally, the little man, who had managed to stay well ahead of them, despite their level of fitness, stopped in front of what looked like a large rock.

"You stay here. I go back. I be mad at the strange woman. I tell her to not make fires my village. I yell very loud. She not know to check on you for a time. You disappear. Poof! I go now." And he sped off back along the way they had come.

Without saying a word, Tarafau moved beyond the rock and disappeared. He sent, *"Come around the rock. It's a cave."*

They all moved quickly around the rock where the path rose a few feet and then, sure enough, there was a path downward behind the rock into a fairly spacious, dry cave.

Tarafau had already removed a camp lantern from his MDP. It was considerably cooler in here and Jenny could see that, since there was that little rise on the path before it moved down into the cave that, even when it rained, the little cave would stay dry.

"Is everyone ok?" Burt asked. *"Besides some sore wrists and ankles, that is,"* he said, rubbing at his wrists reflexively.

Jenny looked around at the weary little group standing there. Her team. *"What about tracks? Can they find us? I don't think we are out of the woods yet,"* she sent, pursing her lips at the weak play on words. *"And I think, based on what I know about caves and echoes, we should probably continue to use mindspeech."* They all nodded, waiting to hear what she had to say, which flummoxed her. Why weren't the more experienced ones taking control of this situation?

Burt spoke up. *"I did what I could to cover our trail. Thank heaven for boy scouts, right?"*

"OK, what are our resources? How do we find out where we are? How do we contact the cavalry, if they're still in the vicinity? How much time has elapsed? And what are our next steps?"

Bob scratched his head. *"Well it all depends what each of us have in our MDPs, I guess. But I can tell you where we are. We are about four and a half miles from our command center, based on intel from our still operational bots. Evidently no one has given them any new commands, which may come in pretty useful. As far as the cavalry is concerned, we're currently on radio silence, since the attack on the Groga. I assume our troops found our abandoned hover cars near our command tent and have scattered, per instructions. It may be some time before they break that silence, if at all. I'm guessing we've been out for about 24 hours, which means it will be dark in about two hours. As far as next steps are concerned, that isn't my call."*

"*Well said,*" agreed Burt. "*Most of the plan worked. Our sticky little wicket isn't quite so bad as it could have been. I say let's think this through while we have that luxury. Step one is eat food and hydrate, as we haven't done that in over 24 hours. Then we need to set a watch schedule and get some sleep. Let's get out the gear we'll need to stay comfortable tonight and go from there.*"

"*That sounds like a good plan, Burt. Even though we slept for about 24 hours, drugged sleep isn't the same as natural sleep. Once all systems are go again, we should be able to come up with a plan to get ourselves out of here, find out where the others are and how to proceed from there,*" said Tarafau.

The entrance to this cave is pretty defendable with weapons from our MDPs and the Lizziebot and Fidget, who were not captured, based on the fact they are now in two way communication with us, which should help. They will wait for orders. We also need to put something across the cave opening to insure we aren't leaking light. That would be like setting up a big sign that says, 'Idiots in a cave. Come and get us.'"

They all set to their tasks and in a short time they were all wolfing down rations, not caring that they weren't heated. After cleaning up any stray crumbs so as not to entice the crawlies in the area, they set up cots, Lyra took first watch at the cave mouth along with the two bots outside the cave and Tarafau turned off the light. Lyra would do her watch in the dark so as not to compromise her night vision. It would be lonely, but short. They decided to split the watch into five two hour shifts. Which meant everyone would get a good amount of natural sleep. Jenny volunteered for the last watch and, even though she didn't expect to sleep a wink, the next thing she knew Tarafau was gently shaking her awake.

"*Your turn,*" he sent to her. She rubbed her eyes. The interior of the cave was no longer pitch black as the sun had already risen. Only the sleeping bag they had used to block the entrance kept the cave as dark as it was. Tarafau laid back down on his bed and Jenny sat on the boulder by the entrance, pondering what could possibly be done for their situation.

Breakfast was rations again, but Jenny didn't even consider complaining. She found herself incredibly grateful for the preparations they had made for this trip. She could easily survive a few weeks on the amount that was stored in her MDP. And, if she needed to survive for longer than that, she could fall back on the survival training her hiking club had sponsored every year, and she would stretch the rations much farther than that by supplementing with the fruits so abundantly available in the jungle.

She knew that she couldn't be complacent, but she felt a lot more optimistic, being out of Sam's clutches once again. When would she ever be rid of her? It was becoming clearer every day that there was only one way to do that. She must defeat Sam once and for all.

When they had cleared up and packed everything but the lamp and the sleeping bag over the door into their MDPs, they sat cross-legged in a circle on the floor of the cave.

"*Have you heard anything new from Gariel or anyone from Sanglarka?*" Jenny asked Bob.

"*Not yet, but the bots are still gathering data and my drones await our command once they have located us. Based on the last images they sent us, the Groga are not showing up on any of my tech. Their camp is a ghost town. Our command center is also deserted, and I only see one of the hover cars, which hopefully bodes well. I believe radio silence will probably be lifted in the next 24 hours, as long as the drones and bots don't detect any further movement.*

And before you ask," he said, holding up a forestalling hand, "*No. Neither our drones nor the bots have found us yet. There is some interference that is keeping them from being able to find our bugs. I think it has something to do with the frequency of the Groga portal. They will have to come closer before they locate us. The GPS seems to be working, however. They appear to be running a search pattern at the moment.*"

"*OK,*" said Jenny. "*That at least gives us something to work with and information to plan from. Burt, what do you recommend, based on this intel?*"

"We stay put for the next 24 hours. I don't recommend we even put our heads out, at this point. The door of the cave is defendable. One person could hold off an army from here. The only concern would be if they tried just blowing us up. But, if they don't know we're here, that's unlikely. So, we wait.

Once we get in touch with the drones and bots, we can also get in touch with Sanglarka, so they know where we are. They will know that Jenny is still alive, since the Gatekeeper key is still active and hasn't passed to another."

Jenny took it all in and sighed. She really did hate waiting, but she didn't see an alternative based on the facts in their possession.

"*OK*," said Bob, "*who's up for a game of Spades?*"

They all laughed and, in good humor actually took him up on it.

She quickly discovered that Lyra was highly competitive and evidently, she had picked up the game while they had been in Sanglarka from Burt and Bob. Tarafau confessed to have played with Lizzie during downtime in their suites at Alliance headquarters. Jenny hadn't played in a long time, but it was a game they often played as a family when she was growing up.

After a bit, the game and the socializing had calmed Jenny down considerably and it gave time for her mind to wander. What now? She hoped the Troopers had been successful in defeating the Groga on the other side of the portal. Obviously, the portal would have to be put under guard, to prevent access to earth and hopefully the portal control device had made it successfully to the Alliance.

They had two options, as Jenny saw it, to create a permanent base by the portal, although it was unlikely that it would go unspotted, or they would have to disable the portal. That, of course, assumed the scientists at the Alliance could figure out a way to do that.

In the meantime, Sam was presumably still out there.

She threw the question that occurred to her out to the group.

"*Do you think the Groga portal is a natural portal, like the gateways, or do you think they have a technology to create portals?*"

She could see the wheels in Bob's brain turning at light speed and the rest looked both thoughtful and somewhat startled at the question.

"I suppose, it is theoretically possible to create a gateway like those that occur naturally. There has been a lot of study by physicists into wormholes, for instance, by introducing exotic matter into a wormhole in an attempt to stabilize it. Wormholes are still a mystery, but some have theorized that wormholes may give entrance to other universes or dimensions. We just don't know enough about how all of it works. And from what I understand from my discussions with Alliance techs, they don't really completely understand how it works either," Bob said.

"It is still very much of a mystery," Tarafau agreed. *"All of the scientists of the dimensions who are aware of their gateways study the phenomenon of gate travel constantly. They concur that it has to do with certain vibrational and magnetic forces, but although, at some point eons ago the gateway network was developed by beings far advanced from us, those origins are lost in the mists of time as we know it. The network only connects known gateways. It doesn't create them.*

We operate a machine that we do not completely understand. The gates have their own laws, which the gateways follow, but we don't know enough. We follow the protocols for their use carefully, mostly by tradition. We know, if somehow we violated one of those laws, the entire system might collapse and the access to the gateways would become random again and allow forces, such as the Groga, to reign in blood and terror across the multiverse."

The card game had come to a screeching halt with this discussion. All looked thoughtful. There was a long silence.

"We should eat and rest," Lyra said, breaking the moment. *"I, for one, want to be ready to get out of here."* All of a sudden Jenny realized that Lyra had not been her usually buoyant self, as she had always been, even when things had been difficult. It occurred to her that Lyra didn't know the fate of her companions.

Jenny covered Lyra's hand with her own. *"I'm sure they're all right. They probably left with the rest of the team. I'll bet they're in the library with Lova right this minute trying to figure out how to rescue us."*

"*They'd better be*," Lyra growled with a very non-Lyra-like scowl. "*I don't want to have to break in a new team.*"

Jenny reached across and hugged her. Lyra looked up in surprise. Her face softened. "*Thank you, Jenny.*" Jenny surprised herself. She realized that she had become a hugger, something she had never really been before. So much about her was changing so rapidly, but she supposed that if changes were happening, the hugging thing was a pretty good one.

Jenny laid down on her cot after another meal of cold rations. She hadn't intended to sleep, but she drifted off almost immediately in the quiet.

She was walking along a long path among towering sequoias. The usual peace she was always able to find among the ancient trees seeped into her bones. The path beyond her was dimly lighted except at the end, which seemed to lead to a meadow and glowed brightly ahead.

As she strolled, her mind tried to remember why she had felt so tense, but the thought drifted away into the green serenity that surrounded her. When she finally stepped into the meadow, she saw she was not alone. Dressed in a flowing white gown, with wildflowers in her hair, was Miriha. As was her wont, she held out both hands to Jenny with a warm smile.

Jenny reached for her and Miriha pulled her into a fierce hug. Drawing back, she looked intensely into Jenny's eyes. "Once again you are up to your ears in alligators, it seems," she said with a smile. "I wish I could bring you comfort and tell you that you are over the worst, but I come to you with a message: When you awake, you and Tarafau must leave the cave without your companions. This will send you into deeper danger than you have yet experienced, but, if you do not choose to do this, all of you will perish and the consequences will reach into every dimension across the multiverse."

"A message? From who?"

"This comes to me as part of my calling. I am what some would call your guardian angel. The Higher Power would have you know this. One of my responsibilities is to communicate these things to you."

"What? And what are Tarafau and I supposed to do when we leave the cave? Sam is out there and whatever minions she may have recruited. What can just the two of us do?"

"You are to return to the Groga camp and to the portal."

"But I don't have a device to access it and, even if I did, I don't know how to use one."

"A way will be provided. I cannot tell you more. This mission must proceed due to choice and not by direction. This is no dream. When you awake, Tarafau will also be awake. The exigency that allowed him to be Tarafau on earth is past. He will now be Tidbit, as before and may not return to his true form until your mission is complete. Your key will be warm and will continue so until you leave the cave. By this you will know that this message is a true one. Your companions have all drifted into sleep and will not wake until you leave, unless you make the choice to stay."

Jenny peered up into Miriha's sparkling green eyes. "So, it is my choice? And this will help us eliminate the threat to earth and save the gateway network?"

"It will. Your road is yet long and neither you nor Tarafau will emerge unscathed. Will you do this?"

Jenny straightened her shoulders. It was her choice. And somehow, she knew that Miriha spoke the simple truth.

"I will."

Miriha nodded and placed one hand on Jenny's head. "May the blessings of the Creator of All Things go with you. You will find a new item in your MDP. You will not need it just yet, but when you find yourself on the brink of destruction, it will be a shield to you. You can only use it once, so choose wisely." At that, there was a flash of brilliant light and Miriha was gone.

Jenny started awake, sitting bolt upright on her cot. All was completely still around her, with the exception of Bob's gentle snore and the purr of the black cat sitting on the floor of the cave next to her.

"*Are you ready?*" Tidbit sent to her.

"*I am.*" She rose quietly, donned her boots and walked past her sleeping companions, including Burt, who was asleep at his guard post by the door. Jenny knew he would feel guilty about that.

"*Should we leave them a note?*" she sent to Tidbit.

"*Miriha will have taken care of it. She has quite a different mission for these three.*"

Chapter 35: The Road Less Travelled

Jenny and Tidbit stood quietly on the edge of the deserted camp. Most of the enemy tents had collapsed and those that remained, often as not, had gaping holes in the canvas or were askew on their poles. In the center of the circle of ground that had been used as a gathering place for the enemy soldiers, lay a pile of cloth, evidently a banner of some sort. Abandoned weapons lay here and there, but there were no signs of bodies or anything living.

The lively sounds of the jungle surrounding it mocked the silence of this place where once two thousand or more bustled about their chores and other activities.

She stepped as noiselessly as possible onto the grounds, not entirely sure what she was supposed to do next. She almost felt foolish, acting on what may have been only a dream, but her key had warmed, as Miriha had said it would and Tarafau was once again Tidbit. Trust was becoming more and more difficult with the betrayals she had experienced lately, but if she could trust anyone, she felt she should be able to trust Miriha.

As she neared the place where she knew the portal lay, she couldn't see any trace of it. Another thing she must take on trust. The bots had shown soldiers coming and going through it, so she guessed she would just need to be patient and alert and wait to see what came next.

She halted a few feet from where the footprints of heavy boots simply cut off in the dirt ahead of her. It appeared that the portal was large enough to allow several soldiers to go through shoulder to shoulder. She knew from her training that the width of the gateways was not really the size of a doorway which was just a convenience for visualizing the gate.

"*Tidbit, how far can a gateway expand so that larger groups to go through at once?*"

"*Remember your instruction, Jenny. The doors are simply a visual representation. A draconic Guardian, for instance, would probably see an entrance 20 feet tall and a dozen paces wide. A guardian from Ingot's race would see an entrance considerably smaller, but either one of them could go through the other's gate without any problem."*

She heard a sound ahead of her. The last person she ever wanted to see again was striding from behind one of the tents that had not collapsed. She steeled herself not to flee, squaring her shoulders and looking defiantly into Sam's alien eyes. She continued, even within the confines of her mind, not to give her the courtesy of her real name. One small victory, but for now it would have to do.

"So, did you lose your little pals? The jungle can do that. And what have we here? Here, kitty, kitty!" she added in a mock little girl's voice. *"I have cat treats."*

Jenny continued to gaze at her scornfully and, without looking, she knew that Tidbit had leveled his golden eyes at her, unblinking, waiting.

From behind Sam, a dozen large Groga soldiers marched from their hiding place inside the tent.

"Are you ready for a sight-seeing tour? I'm going to take you home to meet my parents. That's what besties do, after all, right?"

To her amazement, Jenny's key warmed again. Was that a prompt? Was this how Miriha could communicate with her?

Jenny kept her policy of silence, for now. When she said nothing, Sam spat on the ground. *"Take them,"* she commanded the Groga.

Tidbit surprised Jenny. He allowed himself to be picked up by one of the soldiers, looking at Jenny the entire time. His message was clear, so when she was grabbed firmly by her arms on either side by a stocky soldier, she did not resist or speak.

They followed Sam through the portal, the other soldiers plodding behind them.

They emerged into darkness. As her eyes adjusted, she realized that it was not fully dark. The sky was dark grey. Tatters of darker grey clouds skittered along, highlighted by twin moons.

"*Home sweet home*," Sam sighed, stretching her arms out as if to encompass the entire scene before her. Ahead of them on a rise loomed a large black stone building. It was a big cube, probably about 20 stories tall, with few windows. There was no decorative stonework or embellishments of any kind. The stone appeared to be rough cut out of a single piece, window slits hewn out and almost randomly placed.

From this distance she could see only one entrance, at least on the two sides facing them. There were no trees in sight, but they weren't walking on sand or grass, either. As far as she could see the barren land stretched far and away with no identifying features. The surface they walked on was spongy, like some kind of moss, and grey like everything else that wasn't black. She could see no constellations or any other lights in the sky other than the two moons. Either, it was too early in the evening or morning (which time it was wasn't clear) or they were on the farthest edge of some galaxy where starlight didn't reach.

They marched along in silence. It seemed to take forever before they got any closer to the building. The distance was apparently distorted by the lack of landmarks. When they finally began to make their approach, she realized she had vastly underestimated the size of the building which now seemed more of a small mountain than a building.

The entrance, which had appeared to be of average height now seemed to be three stories high. On either side, just inside where they could not be seen from a distance stood two beings the size of what she imagined a troll would be. But instead of the clubs usually associated with such creatures, these carried alarmingly large versions of the blaster rifles of the Groga and their eyes bespoke cruel cunning.

They snapped to attention as Sam approached at the head of her little party. The ebony doors before her slid open without a whisper of sound. As they followed inside, Jenny nearly gasped. The gigantic room they had entered seemed to have no ceiling, although the sky could not be seen. It appeared to be an endless tunnel of blackness. The walls, black as the outside of the building were lit dimly by flaming torches spaced far enough apart that the light from one did not fully extend to the light of the next one.

The floor beneath their feet glistened like black slime, but their boots rang hollowly as they moved forward. There didn't appear to be anyone there in all that empty space. They walked and walked, the torches fading behind them as they went and new ones appearing before them.

At some point, two lights appeared ahead, as if they had just come into being. Between the two lights were two black thrones that appeared to be cut from obsidian, all ragged, sharp edges and points. The personages seated on the thrones were also dressed in black, so that their faces, seemed to float in mid-air.

The woman was so like Sam as to be recognizable immediately as a close relation, either a sister or a mother. The man had a vibrant streak of white on his right temple and his brows were thin and arched.

The guard who still held Jenny in a firm grip, threw her sprawling onto the floor. One of them placed his boot on her back, preventing her from rising

The thought of the man on the throne pierced Jenny's mind like a spike of fire. "*Is this the Gatekeeper you bring us, daughter?*"

Sam had dropped to one knee. "*It is, father. And the sly one, Tarafau in his cat-like guise. I do not know why he has not transformed, but he is now in your power.*"

Jenny started. That's right, she thought. Miriha had told him he would not transform. Was this an effect of the alien portal? Jenny knew in his cat form he was vulnerable. He had already been injured as Tidbit. What would they do to him?

Even with everything that had already happened, up until this moment, Jenny had not felt afraid, confident that Miriha would not lead her astray. Had she once again put her trust in the wrong place?

The woman inclined her head toward the man and sent, "*This bears some consideration, Your Majesty. We should put them somewhere so that we and they can consider their fate.*"

The king nodded. "*It is the decree of King Namal and Queen Ohaz of Fleist, that Jenny and her cat,*" and he arched one brow in Tidbit's direction, "*be placed in the 'thinking room' until we determine what fate will serve us best.*"

Once again, the two Guards grasped Jenny by the arms and hauled her up to her feet. Without a word, they marched her through a door to the right of the throne room and into a nearly pitch black hallway. The guards seemed to have no problem with the lack of light, stomping along beside her, her arms tightly in their grip. But Jenny had no thoughts of escape. She had absolutely no clue where she was or how she could even consider getting home, much less to any place of safety.

Besides, she still didn't know why she was there or what she was supposed to do. Miriha had said she would know when she needed to know. So now she would wait.

The guards came to an abrupt halt before what appeared to be a stretch of wall, no different than any other. A part of the wall slid open at no command or gesture that she could discern. The guards shoved her forward into the darkness. She landed on her hands and knees, and she heard a small thud and a yowl just ahead of her. The door, such as it was, slid silently closed behind her.

"*Tidbit?*" she queried silently. There was absolutely no glimmer of light.

"*I'm all right. A cat always lands on its feet, you know.*" She felt his head butt up against her shoulder.

"*Can you see anything?*" she asked, "*I understand cats can see in the dark.*"

"*While it's true cats are nocturnal creatures, they can't see any more in a complete absence of light than you can,*" he replied, and she thought she detected a wry twist to his sending.

"*OK, so OODA still applies. I'm going to stay on hands and knees and feel my way to the edges of the room to start with. Then I want your thoughts on our situation.*"

"*Very slow, very careful,*" he agreed.

"*Very careful,*" Jenny echoed, her mind considering how many things might potentially be waiting in the pitch black. "*I'd get a light out of the MDP, but I'm afraid that would give us away. The night goggles won't work unless there are critters in here with us who would give off body heat, especially since there doesn't appear to be a source of light in here.*" Her skin crawled with the idea there might be some kind of alien rat-things in here with them. She scooted carefully back, putting her back against the doorway they had just come through.

"*I smell nothing but the two of us,*" Tidbit replied, almost conversationally.

She crawled warily forward, sliding her hands and knees and counting her crawling steps as she tried to determine the edges of their captivity. Just as she was beginning to wonder if there were no edges, a silly thought under other circumstances, her hand hit air. She almost pitched forward but pulled back onto her heels.

"*I've found an edge but be careful. It appears to go out into nothing, and I don't know how far down the nothing goes or how far it is across.*" She had a picture in her head of Alice falling down the rabbit hole.

She took a coin out of the wallet in her MDP, hung her hand over the hole and let it drop. There was a long moment and then a soft faraway ping as the coin hit something hard. Jenny shivered. Sliding her hand carefully to the left until she found the wall she started from, she then edged around in an undulating circle that eventually came around to the same wall.

When she got to the wall, she took out her quarterstaff and held it at arm's length past the gap, trying to determine how far the pit extended before it hit another wall, with no success. Her staff was 5 feet long and the gap was definitely farther than that. Whether that was an inch or a mile farther really made no difference at this point. She moved away from the pit and sat with her back to the wall.

"*Tap lightly on the floor in front of you,*" sent Tidbit, "*so I can find you.*"

Jenny did as instructed, and Tidbit curled up beside her. "*Now let's think. It is, after all, 'the thinking room'.*"

Jenny wondered what her team was doing, as she and Tidbit sat here, mentally twiddling their thumbs. She thought of her family and friends back on Earth, blithely going about their lives, unaware of the threat that hung over them. She wondered if the portal device had made it to the Alliance and, if even now, they were shutting down the portal, not realizing that Jenny was stuck on a planet, in a dimension, neither she nor they knew anything about.

Then she brought herself up sharply. No pity parties for her. She needed to stay focused.

"*Tidbit, what do you know about this place? Have you ever heard of Fleist before?*"

"*Although I have heard of Fleist, I don't know what dimension they are from. I don't think they have an Alliance gateway here, however.*"

A gong sounded above their heads, making Jenny jump. Its sonorous vibrations filled the dark space. The echoes went on and on for what seemed like several minutes. From the sound of it, the ceiling to this room was very high and the pit below them also threw the echoes upward, bouncing them and multiplying them until they finally faded away.

"*Any chance that was the dinner bell?*" Tidbit sent hopefully.

Jenny couldn't help herself. She laughed. She pulled some rations from her MDP and the two ate in silence. When they were finished, Jenny felt around where they were sitting for any crumbs or wrappers. She wanted to leave no clue of what their resources were to inform their captors. She had a strong suspicion they were being monitored somehow. When she and her family had played rummy when she was a kid, her dad was always admonishing her, "Don't show anyone your cards." It was good advice. Especially now.

Within minutes a bright light flared and filled the room only for a moment. In that moment, Jenny was grateful she hadn't attempted to walk around in this room. The after image on her retinas showed that the pit that surrounded them was a good 20 feet across. There was absolutely nothing else in the room except her and Tarafau.

Soon after the brilliant light the gong sounded again. It dawned on her that they were trying to assure that she and Tarafau didn't just curl up and go to sleep while they waited to hear from their captors. She had heard of political prisoners being mentally assaulted, deprived of sleep and randomly stimulated with a variety of frightening images, sounds and even electric shock to soften them up for interrogation.

She decided. She told Tidbit, "*I am going into hibernation*," a term Lova used for distancing the mind from outside stimuli. During her practice sessions with Lova, she had become nearly as proficient in this aspect of mind control as her instructor. Now was the time to use what she had learned.

After drifting for a time, she set herself to working through her dilemma about what to do next. She knew the simple act of surrendering herself to Sam was only the first step and she almost understood why she was only given that part of the puzzle to start with. In her hibernation state, she could concentrate. She vaguely felt the continual racket and odd lights inflicted on them in the thinking room, but it was something she could placidly ignore. She knew Tidbit was doing the same.

She had set her mental alarm to sound when the door finally opened. At that time, she would instantly be awake and alert and ready to confront whatever came next.

She tried to work through it all logically. She found herself in Dorothy's situation, which might work to her benefit. Just as the ruby slippers would not work for the wicked witch if she murdered Dorothy, the key and the MDP would not work unless they were given willingly by the one they were connected to.

In this case, at the moment, she was probably not in danger of her life, but potentially her sanity and maybe being damaged in such a way that she lived but would be unable to function physically for the rest of her life. So, in the words of the witch, "These things must be done delicately."

Her best strategy might be to be patient until she knew more about the actual situation and her location and surroundings. When they opened the door to their prison, they would expect them to be broken and pliable and ready to spill their guts. She would find a way to use that. What concerned her most was what they might do to Tidbit. She would have to cross that bridge when they came to it.

Tidbit's mental voice came drifting into her mind. He was the one person who could do this with her under her mental protection. Lova had taught her how to give him a key that would allow him to pass her mental barriers.

"*I must tell you something important,*" he said. "*It was never time to say this before, but it is vital that you understand it now. There are things about me that I determined not to reveal until I was sure the time was right. I had hoped it would be a long time from now, but here we are.*

I was probably as surprised as you were when Lizzie revealed you would be her choice for replacement when she passed. At that time, the crisis was far away, or so we thought. You were still in college and she and I had just come off of a series of missions for the Alliance, exploring potential dimensions to determine whether they were ready for the general population to know about the gate network. There are relatively few that are admitted to the Alliance at that level. Most of them are similar to Earth. They have Guardians, but the beings of that world and that universe are not ready to know that the gateways exist.

When Lizzie told me she had chosen an heir, I was skeptical. I knew you were very young and although you had a lot of the qualities we require, I couldn't see how you could take on this responsibility, even though your aunt was about the same age when she became a Guardian.

I have since learned that you have all of the qualities your aunt did and some I did not expect. I'm telling you this, so you may understand that it has only been the last couple months that I have finally been at peace with Lizzie's decision. You are worthy of your position, although you still need to grow into it. I want to give you the chance to do that.

Therefore, I need you to know that besides long life and the ability to change my form, my people have an additional natural talent. We can pass dimensional barriers without a gate. There is no gate to my world. We have been travelling the dimension since before the organization of the Alliance. If things look grim, and if it is necessary, I may leave you, if only to bring aid to you. But our captors will not realize I am gone. I will appear to exist in a shadow form that will feel tangible to them and will respond naturally to whatever they do to me, but it will be a mere shell, so that nothing that happens to it will actually harm me. Do you understand why this is important?"

In Jenny's calm mental state, technically she knew what he was telling her. She understood his words. She also knew that it meant that at some point she might be very alone here. "*I understand,*" she said, but she somehow knew she really didn't.

"*I'm going to do something cruel to you, Jenny. When you come out of your meditation, you won't remember I told you about my additional talent, because the enemy must not know, but when you truly need to know, it will return to you. Your reactions to what will surely follow in this place must be genuine. I want you to know that I think of you as a daughter. I would rather give you temporary pain than to lose you entirely. On a subconscious level, you will know this. It will give you strength to overcome the darkness.*"

Tidbit faded from her consciousness. She didn't know how long she had floated in the void she had created for herself, with the distant lights and sounds only a slight disturbance, when she actually drifted off to sleep.

She awoke to someone shaking her shoulder. It surprised her that she had not woken when the door had admitted this person. Evidently, she had been more tired than she realized. She looked up muzzily to see a little man, about as tall as she was seated. She had slept in a sitting position, her back against the rough black wall. His short white hair was meticulously coiffed with deep waves and he wore a crisp white shirt, deep red velvet vest and a cravat, underscored with dark pants and shiny black shoes.

"You must have been very tired, young miss," he said repeating her own thought with something like concern in his large dark eyes.

Jenny nodded. She unconsciously put her hand out to touch Tidbit, who was curled up by her side.

"*I am to take you to bathe and eat and then we will get started.*"

Get started with what, Jenny wondered. He gestured for her to rise. When she stood, his head was slightly higher than her waist. "*Follow me, young miss.*" He gestured without a backward glance. Back they went through the dark hallway. As they walked the end came into sight. It was a stairwell, once more torchlit, of black stone.

They ascended what seemed like forever. Jenny was bemused by the lack of guards, but once again she realized that escape was not an option, at least not until she knew more about this place and what she was supposed to do here. So she followed the little man up several flights of stairs. You'd think, she thought grumpily, that a culture smart enough to use portals would have invented an elevator.

They came out of the stairwell into a well lit corridor of black stone. This was utterly different than any place she had seen in this fortress. There were tapestries along the walls, although not of pleasant scenes as she had seen when she visited a castle in the Bavarian alps long ago when her father had been stationed in Germany. These were of battle and slaughter and what appeared to be ritual sacrifices, all very meticulously worked and in what had probably been brilliant colors when they were created. Now they gave off a look of worn antiquity.

All in all, she could see where anyone living in such a place wouldn't have much of an optimistic attitude towards life, if they had to look at those every day for any length of time.

They stopped in front of a large grey door and the little man pulled out a large ring of keys, selected one and let them in.

Jenny was shocked. This room did not correlate with her picture of this dreary place. The room was decorated with shades of beige and white with damask-like wall covering, somewhat in the style of French Provincial. The flowing and soft lines of the furniture and the delicately embroidered framed tapestries on the walls were soothing and lovely.

He turned to her. "*My name is Mynah and I will be your tutor and servant, while you are here. You need not consider yourself a prisoner, but you may not leave the castle without express permission of the Queen. My job is to teach you the niceties of noble life and about the culture of our realm. I will also see to your needs, including appropriate clothing,"* and he eyed her up and down, not looking at all impressed.

"Seamstresses and some lady's maids have been assigned to you and they will attend you shortly. Once you have been attended to, bathed and properly dressed I will return. There is a necessary for you and your, ahem, cat, on the other side of that doorway, as well as bathing facilities. Please make yourself comfortable. Your attendants will arrive shortly."

Before Jenny could acknowledge anything, he had said or ask a question, he turned on his heel and left. She heard the lock click from the other side and sighed.

She turned to Tidbit. *"What do you think of this? I admit to being more than a little confused."*

"You can rely on it being a very carefully thought out stratagem, 'young miss'," he sent back, parroting Mynah's term for her. *"Keep your eyes and ears open and your guard up."*

"You sound like Arvid," Jenny retorted.

"Where do you think I got it?" and his tail went up with that peculiar curve that always looked like a question mark to her.

"So, which of you is older, you or Arvid?" but before he could reply, there was a soft knock followed by the entrance of three women, one with a tray in her hands, with the same skin tones and facial characteristics as Sam. Instead of being dressed in black robes, however, they were attired in what seemed to be typical servant's attire no matter what dimension you came from; grey skirts, white blouses and small aprons with no lace or adornments.

The shortest one also looked to be the oldest of the three. *"Mistress Jenny,"* she sent with a little bow. "My name is Wellis, and these are my assistants, Gras and Cheb." And both girls bobbed their heads as well. *"We will be your attendants while you are here. The seamstress will be here shortly to take your measurements for suitable attire."*

The girl named Gras held out the tray she was carrying. "*Before all of that, we must feed you.*"

She set the tray on a small table, just large enough to accommodate two chairs, and laid the place setting with what looked like chopsticks as well as something she recognized as a finger bowl. Last she placed a tall goblet which probably held water. This was the most inviting as her throat was horribly parched.

"*Thank you*," she said, inclining her head. The three faces before her looked as if she had used a vile curse word.

"*Kind miss,*" Wellis sent, "*we are not of a station to deserve any thanks. We do as we are told. There is no honor in this.*"

Jenny nodded, though she felt she should shake her head instead.

She sat at the table and for a moment she wanted to weep. She was so tired and confused and scared. However, she would not want to show any weakness to these or any of the inhabitants of this place.

So, she sat and ate what appeared to be some vegetables that had been steamed atop some kind of noodles. The glass did indeed hold water and when she downed it in nearly a single gulp, one of the girls immediately refilled it. The napkin in her lap felt like fine linen and the chair she was sitting on was upholstered with something similar to the damask-like curtains that hung over the windows of the room.

She almost felt like there should be a minuet being played on a harpsicord in the background.

Another knock about the time she had completed her meal admitted the seamstress and her minions. She had Jenny stand up and turn before her, clucking her tongue and shaking her head as if she faced an impossible task to make Jenny fit for polite society. Jenny rolled her eyes and suppressed a sigh.

She felt swarmed. The seamstress was taking measurements and calling them out loud in a language that might have been some variation on German, guttural and harsh. The consonants almost sounded as if she were spitting them.

Finally she stopped, harrumphed without saying a word to Jenny mental or otherwise and stomped out of the room, her minions stomping behind her.

"*She didn't even ask what colors I like,*" Jenny sent sullenly to Tidbit.

Wellis made a shooing motion towards the bathing facilities. "*Clean clothing will be brought to you when you are finished. All necessary things are prepared for you. Please leave your garments in the basket next to the bath. There is a robe hanging behind the door.*"

The "bathing facilities" took Jenny's breath away. The tub was more like a small pool, not actually long enough to swim in, but Tarafau could have stretched out in it and had room to spare. There appeared to be steam rising off of the surface of the water, so Jenny tested it and breathed deeply. It was perfect for the long soak that she so desperately wanted.

She undressed and slipped into the tub, immersing herself completely before floating for awhile, doing her mental exercises, relaxing every muscle one at a time. Once she began to relax to the point that she felt she might fall asleep, she set about washing herself and found soap, and shampoo. The towels that had been laid out on the edge of the tub were deep and soft. There was one for her body and one for her hair, which she had lathered three times instead of the usual one, having not had any kind of real bath or shower for days. The soap they had used on their trek had not had a pleasant smell, because anything even lightly resembling perfume would attract insects. And then it had only been washcloth baths.

As she wrung out her hair with the towel, she realized it was getting quite a bit longer than she usually wore it. There had been no time to even consider other than basic hygiene for what seemed like a long time. She brushed it out and wound it into a knot on top of her head and donned the soft, plush, resort-style robe.

When she went out into the salon of the suite, her maids were standing there as if they had been at attention the entire time she was in the bath. Tidbit sat on a cushion with a disgruntled look skewing his cat face. "*They brushed me,*" he sent. "*I'm 'such a good kitty', or so they tell me.*"

Wellis waved toward the door opposite the bathroom. "*I have set out some clothing for you to sleep in. Get some rest and we will see you in the morning. If you need anything just ring.*" And she pointed to a button on the wall next to the bed. The clothing they had laid out was a grey granny-style nightgown, similar to what she had worn as a kid, but with no trace of the flowers, lace or ruffles a little girl might wear.

Jenny simply nodded and closed the door behind her, after letting Tidbit in. Interestingly enough, they had laid a blanket on the floor next to her bed, apparently to accommodate Tidbit.

"*Lay it on the floor next to the door,*" he sent. "*Don't block it, but make it so I could catch an ankle, if I needed to.*"

Jenny did as he asked, got dressed for sleep and climbed into the queen-sized bed between clean sheets and under a soft thick blanket and fell into a deep sleep before she could have another thought.

Chapter 36: Where's the White Rabbit?

For the first four days she followed the exact same routine. Her maids would knock on her bedroom door and when she responded, they would bustle about pushing back curtains that let in only the dimmest grey light, lighting lamps and preparing her bath.

By the time she emerged from the bath, her clothing for the day had been laid out on her bed and once she was dressed, there was a breakfast of the same vegetables over something like rice, noodles or quinoa. In the meanwhile, her maids would make over the "nice kitty", brushing him while he endured it with wise-crack remarks only Jenny could hear.

The clothing the seamstress had created for her was all in various shades of grey and black. No wonder she didn't ask Jenny for her color preference. The only spots of any color in her rooms beside the beige and tan were the tapestries which held colored mandala-type designs. Instead of the robes worn by Sam and her parents, these clothes reminded her of paintings she had seen of the Quaker settlers of the United States. Plain dresses with loose fitting bodices, high necks, gathered skirts and simple satin slippers, with optional bonnets. None of it was trimmed with anything like lace or ruffles. A good thing, in Jenny's opinion. The cloth was soft, however, which was a relief as she had been dreading the idea of some scratchy penance-inducing material.

As soon as her breakfast was finished, Mynah would come to "instruct" her. These teaching sessions were more than a little strange, but actually somewhat useful. She still had no idea what Sam and her family were planning for her, but she did know somewhat more about the dimension and planet on which she found herself.

It turned out that this planet was on the very edges of the solar system it belonged to. The sun was so far away that the only light was grey and even the two moons that orbited the planet were wan and almost misty, more like a nightlight than anything else. The galaxy that claimed its orbit was far away from any other and their solar system was on the far edge of that. They were so tenuously connected to any of it that their planet could very possibly go rogue at some point, breaking away to float between galaxies and solar systems, at which point all life which existed here would be snuffed like a candle that had burned out.

This would happen eventually. Mynah had been certain about that, but it wasn't an urgent concern, as things went. This was thousands of years in the future.

The only thing that prevented the planet from being a ball of ice, with no atmosphere or liquid water was a very hot core and strong gravity. Jenny felt as if she weighed an extra twenty pounds, which took some getting used to, but she was adjusting.

The food they ate wasn't vegetables at all, as it turned out, but several types of fungi that was the only thing that would grow in the low light of this world. Jenny began to understand the lack of color in her surroundings. Color was seen by the human eye only when light was present. She wondered where the colors had come from in the tapestries she had seen, so she asked Mynah.

He replied that the planet had not always been so dark. Their planet had been drifting farther and farther to the edges of their solar system for thousands of years. Over time they had developed many types of artificial light, but their eyes were not used to it, so they only used the brighter lights for things such as surgery or research. Because of this, the irises of their eyes were covered in a black film to protect them from bright lights. This was kind of like having permanent sunglasses, which also inhibited their ability to see and appreciate color.

Day in and day out, Jenny learned that the history and culture of the Fleistians was long and, as Jenny had suspected based on the tapestries in the hall, bloody. There were two very different, very separate cultures on the planet, and although King Namal claimed to be the "true" king of the planet, there was another king as well who he labeled "the usurper".

His name was Nivi and he reigned in the kingdom his people called the Kingdom of Cindu. Cindu translated to "continued light" and they believed that the people of Namal had strayed from the original teachings of their forefathers. Nevertheless, they would have let King Namal rule as he would, over those who wished to be reigned by him, as long as Namal would leave them to pursue their own beliefs.

There were two portals, one in each kingdom and many wars had been fought over them. King Namal had wanted to control both of them, but the people of Nivi had defended their portal to prevent Namal's armies from dominating the ability to travel. Recently there had been a period of relative peace mostly because of Namal's involvement in the Groga raids. His tactic was to eventually gain full access to the Alliance gate system, which would mean that the Nivian's access to the gate would be a moot point.

"*So why are they giving me all of this information?*" asked Jenny one day. "*I don't understand.*"

"*I would think it would be obvious,*" replied Mynah, a genuinely puzzled look on his face. "*They know if you know the truth, you will be amenable to aiding our cause. Engoza says you have a logical mind and will fall in with our plans as soon as you realize how important it is.*"

Jenny had mulled this over carefully.

"*And if I don't 'fall in'?*"

"*We will have to extract information from you unwillingly. I do not suggest it.*" He scratched at his immaculate head as if he was completely mystified by this thought. He didn't look at all threatening, just stating a logical fact.

By the fifth day, Jenny was having trouble sitting still. She knew her team was still out there fighting and although she now knew a lot more about Sam and her people, she hadn't been out of the room once in that five days, not that there was much to see, if she did get outside. She realized that this was nearly as effective as the sleep deprivation would have been in the thinking room. She blessed Lova for the hours she had spent strengthening her mental skills.

The absolute boredom was a bizarre form of torture. No one spoke an unkind word to her. She wasn't deprived of food or sleep. Her surroundings were as nice as any grand hotel. She was completely comfortable, and she just wanted to run.

She asked Wellis about a gym or workout room, but the concept was foreign to her. Mynah said she should not strain herself.

So, to the horror and protestations of her maids, she cleared a space by moving some furniture and started running in place. It was a bit awkward in skirts, but she managed it. "*I can listen while I run, Mynah*," she told him when he looked alarmed. Her maids were beside themselves, burbling in their strange language and wringing their hands. But Jenny persisted, and Tidbit sent a feeling of great amusement. If he had been in his human form, he would have been holding his sides laughing. As it was, his rumbling purr spoke of his enjoyment of the spectacle.

As she continued to jog in place, Mynah shrugged, gestured to the maids to settle themselves and continued his instruction. At no time had he asked for any information from Jenny. She would tell all as soon as she had a full understanding of their plans, Mynah assured her, and if she did not, well, she was made very aware of the consequences.

Today's lesson was to be about King Namal's allies. Although they tried to make it appear that the Fleistians were in charge, Jenny had a growing suspicion that King Namal wasn't pulling the strings.

 It turned out that their allies were a powerful entity in a separate dimension who had conquered most of their own universe. Their appetite for power was not quenched and they wished to spread their influence. When they had discovered the portal that led to King Namal's domain, they swarmed in so fast that they were in the fortress before there was any chance of response.

King Namal had immediately welcomed them as if they had been invited and made a pact of friendship on the spot. The Insenium, as they called themselves, seduced Namal to see their side of things very easily as it expanded his horizons from global domination to see the bigger picture of what they could do with full access to other dimensions. Not to mention an opportunity to use the Groga, whom Namal's people had conquered a couple hundred years past.

Thus, Namal had instituted the Groga breeding program to raise himself a huge army of soldiers who didn't have the wit to even know they were slaves. He had established a large city not far from his fortress where Groga were trained from striplings to be a cog in Namal's war machine.

The majority of the Groga population, however, lived on a planet in another dimension entirely, accessible by Namal's gate.

So far, the Insenians had not stirred themselves beyond giving instructions to Namal which he promptly executed. The early raids did not start with Miriha's gate village, but with dimensions not yet established with the Alliance. The plan was to use the smaller raids to train their soldiers. Ultimately, when they were up to strength, they would tackle the Alliance more directly.

"*How many soldiers will it take to be 'up to strength'?*" Jenny asked, dreading the answer.

"*We are nearly there. Right now, there are nearly a billion in training and many times that on the Groga world. There are two classes of Groga, the soldiers and those who serve the soldiers by providing food, clothing and weapons. For now, they wait in readiness to serve the great cause of King Namal.*"

"*And what exactly is his 'great cause'? I don't recall you saying.*"

"*Why, to put all universes on an equal footing, to eliminate all crime and war, and to take away the necessity for beings to make decisions for which they are not qualified. When King Namal conquers all, he will be given the power to control everything. There will be no poverty or conflict. All will live in harmony and the multiverse will be in order.*"

Jenny barely controlled a gasp, turning it into a cough. She stopped jogging and simply stared.

"*And what decisions are we not qualified for, again?*"

"*Why, pretty much everything: What career to pursue, where to live, who to turn to for help, what to believe in. All would be generously given to each being in the multiverse by those much wiser than they. They need not worry about making wrong decisions for they will be taught everything they need to know and no more. In this way, the* stress of choosing wrongly will be eliminated and they can live peacefully, confident that their lives are ordered."

"*And you think this is a good thing, do you?*"

"*Do you not? By putting your trust in those put above you, you will never have to be worried about anything again.*"

"*Except dying of boredom and being forced to be something someone else wants me to be,*" thought Jenny to Tidbit.

"*This is the worst evil,*" agreed Tidbit. "*The ability to choose and to make mistakes is part of what allows us to grow and learn. Beings who are not allowed to struggle and learn from their choices eventually stagnate and are reduced to simply supplying basic needs. There is always a hidden motive for those who espouse this line of thinking. They never do it from the kindness of their hearts.*"

"*My dad used to say, 'the reason so many mice die in mousetraps is that they don't realize why the cheese is free'. You know I can't stand for this, Tidbit. I think I'm done playing around. What do you think?*"

"*I think you should follow your instincts, Jenny. They are usually very good.*"

"*Mynah, I'm afraid I can't agree with your agenda. The whole, 'under the control of the evil empire' thing, doesn't work for me. It's a total deal breaker.*"

"Pardon? I don't think I understand," he said, clearly confused. "*All would be peaceful, and everyone would have what they need. We would keep them from making horrible mistakes…*"

"*Or any progress. You would stifle that which makes life worth living. Peace is not worth the price you are charging for it.*"

Mynah shook his head and wrung his hands. "*I have failed then. Failure is not pleasant, no it isn't. And you refuse to reconsider? Engoza said you would be reasonable.*"

Jenny looked into Tidbit's golden eyes. The cat gave the slightest nod.

"Indeed, Mynah. Bring on the torture. It can't be much worse than this."

Her maids began to wail and Mynah, mumbling aloud and shaking his head, slammed the door on his way out.

"Now what?" she sent to Tidbit.

"Change your clothes. You can't do much in that outfit," he sent dryly.

Ignoring the howls of her attendants, she marched into the bedroom, slipping out of her slippers. Her old clothes, remarkably, were in the clothes press and her boots where she had stowed them under the bed. She knew she would be unlikely to escape, but she couldn't just sit around.

As she left the bedroom, one of the maids, grabbed her arm. *"Young miss, you mustn't. They will punish us all,"* gesturing to the other maids who were cowering together in a corner.

"I have no choice. I cannot agree to this foul plan to destroy the multiverse. People will not just lay down like trained animals. They will fight and fight and fight. The multiverse will be plunged into unending war or destroy itself in the effort. Not all cultures are like the Groga, and many of them are so much more advanced than Earth, where I come from, or your planet. I must do what I must, and I'm sorry if it harms you. How about you help me escape and we can all get out of here?"

The two maids in the corner began to moan and wring their hands, but the one who had addressed her paused thoughtfully. *"Come with me,"* she sent. And her fellow maids wailed even louder than before.

They went out the door, Tidbit at Jenny's side. The maid led her the opposite way from how she had entered the suite, down the corridor to another staircase, narrower and steeper than the one she had come up nearly a week ago.

Several floors down, the maid put her finger to her lips in that universal gesture of quiet. They entered another hallway that could have been an exact copy of the one from which they had come. Jenny couldn't even tell if any of the gruesome hangings were different. A few doors down the hallway, the maid tapped quietly on a door. As it opened, a liveried maid peered out. She and Jenny's maid conversed quietly in their own language. "*Come,*" her maid said as soon as the other nodded.

She walked into a suite very similar to hers, but all in dark greys and black. From an over-sized armchair with it's back to the door a figure rose.

Sam! She had been betrayed, again! Sam grinned. "*This one will be rewarded for her faithfulness. The others will lose their lives for their cowardice.*"

Sam was no longer dressed in her voluminous robes. She wore what her mom would have called a "cat suit". Black, spandex-like material hugged her every curve. Her blood red nails betrayed the only color. Around her neck, a necklace of ebony stones, like black diamonds, hung past her scooped neckline.

Sam paced a circle around Jenny. "*Well, well, well. You have decided to decline our hospitality then?*"

Jenny decided in that moment to continue her policy of silence with Sam. She just stood there impassively, her head up and shoulders back, waiting to see what would happen next.

Sam put her hands on her hips, her mouth twisting in derision. "*Still giving me the silent treatment, then? You'll find that won't sit well with my friends in the discussion room.*

OK, look. I tried to give you a chance, because of our friendship, but your chances have run out. I refuse to be responsible for what happens next." She pressed a button on the wall similar to the one on Jenny's former bedroom and a soft knock came on the door moments later.

"*My guards live in the room next door,*" she explained as her maid rushed to open the door.

Jenny fleetingly wondered if the guards were there to protect her or to keep her out of trouble.

The two guards went to one knee, awaiting instructions.

"This one seems to think she prefers the discussion room to her quarters, and I intend to oblige her. Please send for the Chief Conversationalist. I will attend him there."

"Come on, Jenny. I'll escort you to your next adventure." She said this with as much flippancy as if she were talking about lunch at the mall.

They walked back down the corridor to continue down the narrow stone stairs for what seemed like 20 stories. *"Elevators encourage slothfulness,"* Sam commented. *"Strength is paramount in our kingdom. We'll soon discover how you measure up."*

As they exited the stairwell, Jenny realized they had entered a large indoor stadium of some sort. It looked as if it would hold forty or fifty thousand attendees. Once again, the ubiquitous torches lined the walls and hung from the ceiling. *"Lights,"* Sam commanded and very bright, white lights sprung into being above them, reflecting off of the black polished marble in a way that made it appear to be nearly white.

On the stage below the tiers of benches that ran around the amphitheater, were two black stone tables a few feet apart from one another with two guards standing on each side of each table and one standing at the head of both in a white lab coat, his hands clasped behind his back. *"We've been preparing for this. I had hoped you would see reason, but I know how stubborn you are."*

As they arrived at the bottom and walked onto the stage, Sam said, *"Do you wish to climb up onto the table, or shall I have my friends help you?"*

Tidbit hopped up onto one of the tables and Jenny followed his lead. She determined that she would put herself into her protected mental state as soon as possible, setting up her trance to collect all information like a tape recorder without having to invest any attention into any of it.

"I have a plan," Tidbit sent to her. *"Nothing that occurs here is what it seems. I have taken precautions. Guard your mind and all will be well."*

"*I'd like to say I agree,*" she sent back, "*but this looks pretty grim. Are you sure?*"

"*I am. Guard yourself now. This will not be pleasant, but we will triumph.*"

The guards grabbed her roughly and tied her hands and feet to leather-like straps attached to the table. The restraints gave her no room to move except her head. Tidbit passively allowed them to do something similar to him, growling that weird cat warning, part growl, part howl. The guards laughed.

Sam stood silently while they made their preparations, oddly enough the whole scene reminded Jenny of an operating room. Trays of implements were laid out, rough looking towels lay in stacks, and the big man in the lab coat observed it all without expression. The brilliant lights, focused entirely on the stage, were eerie in contrast with the darkness that seemed to hover beyond its influence.

"*Allow me to introduce you to the Chief Conversationalist. He will assist me today.*" The man in the white lab coat nodded curtly at Jenny.

Sam stood there, her hands clasped in front of her, a smile of satisfaction on her face. For a moment she transformed, her features melting like warm wax into the Sam she remembered. All of those happy days, giggling together, doing one another's nails, researching in the library or binge-watching their favorite old television shows rushed through her mind like an arctic wind. And then there was a rush of grief for her loss of what she had thought was such a great friendship.

She knew there were times she felt she wouldn't have made it without Sam's encouragement. And now it came to this. She knew what Sam was doing. She knew this transformation was a move calculated to tenderize her. She knew there was no kindness or nostalgia in this act. It was one last, cold, conniving measure designed to make Jenny more receptive to their torture.

But she knew Sam now. An evil princess out of one of the fantasies she loved to read, Sam was nothing now, but her nemesis, and she would treat her as such. Sam would not get the satisfaction of any answers from her, if it meant her death. She set her determination and began to go through her exercises, distancing herself from the ordeal to come.

"*You know I'm not going to make this easy.*" Sam's voice was almost a purr of pleasure. "*This is definitely going to hurt you more than it will me. I've been looking forward to it, actually. Little Jenny perfect. Always top of her class. Always upright and honest. Never in for a little cheating or an unkind prank.*

Now I will break you. When I am finished, you will love me for what I am, and you will be my perfect sycophant. We will be besties again. Doesn't that sound wonderful? But, as they say, 'No pain, no gain.' And I promise you, there will be pain."

Jenny listened, almost bored as she floated inside her protective mental bubble. She knew Sam meant every word, but she also knew that there were people counting on her. She must hold on. Tidbit had a plan. Then her key warmed on her neck. She almost felt Sam would be able to see it glowing, but Sam paid no mind. Was this an assurance from Miriha that she was doing the right thing?

Jenny was surprised, then, when Sam turned, instead of to her, to Tidbit.

"*You, sly old cat, will be my tasty little sample. We want to give Jenny a preview of coming attractions, don't we? I've wanted to get my delicate, genteel hands on you for years. Do you remember Lizzie's friend Marie? That was little old me.*"

Her features melted again and now she was a petite dark haired middle-aged woman with a bob hair-do wearing a checkered shirt and jeans, a pair of gardening gloves in her hand.

"*Remember all of those garden club meetings and shopping at the farmer's market? Oh, of course you don't. After all, Lizzie couldn't take a cat with her to a public place like that. It would have seemed way too weird. I worked on her for nearly ten years, hoping she might consider me as the guardian of her gate. Evidently, I didn't measure up for some reason.*

It was always Jenny she went on about. I soon determined that it would be best for me to connect with Jenny instead. So, I ended up moving away to be closer to my grown children (who of course didn't exist) and just kept in touch with newsy little letters about my garden and news about impending weddings and grandchildren. That correspondence went on the entire time I was wooing Jenny."

Jenny turned this over in her head. How old was Sam, really? She knew that lifespans of beings within the Alliance varied wildly, from hours to eons. Earthlings had a fairly good lifespan, but many of the beings she had interacted with were hundreds of years old. She still didn't know how old Tidbit/Tarafau was, but she knew he was old when he met Lizzie, over 60 years ago. And where was Sam going with all of this reminiscing?

Sam reached out and chucked Tidbit under his chin. *"Why is it that you haven't transformed, my little changeling? Why aren't you the great beast you are when you aren't on Earth? I had hoped to have more to work with, but then, we can get creative, can't we? Let's start with all of this fuzz and see what powerful muscles lurk beneath? I think you need a shave."*

She gestured at one of the guards who handed her a straight razor.

"Now hold still, I'm not sure how sharp this little guy is, and I'd hate to cut you...before it's time." The nasty smile on her lips that Jenny could only see from the side before Sam leaned over Tidbit gave her chills even deep in her mental protection.

Sam lifted his face and started at his throat. For a heartbeat, Jenny thought she was going to slit his throat, but she didn't. Carefully she shaved the fur from his neck and then from his belly. She didn't speak as she worked, concentrating on removing every bit of fur from Tidbit's body and finally his face, without cutting him once. He lay their very still, the golden orbs of his cat eyes fastened on Sam's face the entire time he was facing her. When she had thoroughly stripped his underside, she had her guards turn him over on his belly, at which point he gazed into Jenny's eyes, nearly unblinking.

"She hopes to un-nerve you, by harming me. Remember, I have a plan. Remember, I have never failed you. Remember, you are the key to everything. You are loved. You are respected, and you are valuable to the entire multiverse. This doesn't end here."

Once Sam had stripped him of every vestige of fur she turned to Jenny. *"What a handsome cat, yes? Now that we can see what we have to work with, where should we start? Not so intimidating without your armor, are you, kitty cat? Now that we have removed your armor, let's remove your weapons."*

Without his fur, Jenny could see even more clearly the muscles rippling under his black skin. He looked smaller without his fur, but something about his attitude still made him look larger than life to her.

Sam reached for something similar to pliers and grabbed a toenail on his forefoot. *"Let's see if we get a reaction from this, oh stoic one."*

She started to pull, not quickly, as one would if they were trying to minimize the pain, but very slowly, extending the claw until you could see the base of the nail starting to ooze blood. The somber Chief Conversationalist nodded approvingly, as if he and Sam were having a mental conversation, not directed to Jenny. Tidbit's entire body shivered with the pain of it, but he did not cry out. One by one Sam pulled each of his claws until all four feet were bleeding. By the fourth foot, Tidbit was yowling in pain as Sam pulled the last five claws.

"Now that we've got the claws, the only thing deadly about you are your fangs. I'll need a stronger implement for that, but first I need to clean up this mess we've made."

She grabbed the top towel off of the stack and wiped up the blood that was strewn across the surface of the rock slab. Now, she had the Chief Conversationalist hold Tidbit's head. The end of his now snake-like tail lashed in frenzy and Jenny could see the effort with which he clamped his jaw closed.

She wanted to cry out. She wanted to tell Sam to stop and she would tell her anything she wanted to know, but she knew that Tidbit would not thank her for it. He had a plan. He had told her so twice, and she believed him, but could the damage Sam would inflict on him in the meantime be repaired?

A long screech came from his mouth as Sam levered it open, stuffing a rubber dental dam between his back teeth, which held his tongue down and made his yowls sound even more odd than before.

At that point Jenny saw what must have been a combination of the excruciatingly bright lights and her distress. Tidbit glowed briefly with a green tinged light. He was still yowling, but his eyes appeared unfocused and there was a slight change in the tone. More than likely the change in the sound was due to Sam slowly yanking at his fang. Tidbit's back arched and he squirmed frantically now. Jenny realized that tears were streaming down the sides of her face onto her ears as she looked away toward the ceiling.

When the first one came loose, shooting blood onto Sam's cat suit, she cursed and used a towel to dab at it. The second one broke soon after she grabbed it with the pliers, evidently because she was angry at getting his blood on her, as if it was his fault. She then proceeded as she had done with his claws, grasping each of his fangs and pulling slowly and firmly, all the while Tidbit was making that gurgling howl.

Jenny closed her eyes. She could no longer watch. Evidently Sam noticed this, so she kept up a stream of conversation about what she was doing, the look on the cat's face, the fact that his screams were fading and that he wasn't so tough as she thought, all in almost a drawl, as if she wasn't even interested in what she was saying, just talking out of boredom.

Finally, there was silence. Jenny had no idea if it had been hours or days since they were strapped to their stone slabs. As Jenny opened her eyes, she knew what she would see. Tidbit lay there like so much meat, slices in his skin, his mouth still open with broken teeth and missing fangs. His flesh on his belly lay in tatters and there was blood everywhere. There were even spots of blood on Sam's face, or rather the face of Marie. Her assistant was also spattered with blood, once again standing at the head of the two tables, his hands clasped behind his back, staring straight ahead with no expression.

For the first time, Jenny struggled against her bonds, wanting nothing more than to pound Sam's face into hamburger, to wipe that satisfied grin out of memory and change that smile into the look of terror frozen on Tidbit's face. She found Tidbit's growling yowl coming from her own throat. But she didn't speak a word. She would not give Sam the satisfaction of even one word coming from her mouth.

"There, there, sweetie. He was just a cat. No big deal from a cosmic point of view. He must have used up all of those nine lives, though, I think. Either that, or he didn't want to come back for more of this." And she waved her hand negligently at the bloody corpse.

"But what about our sweet Jenny? Will anyone miss you when you're gone? Besides that ragtag bunch of crusaders holed up on Earth. I imagine they have disabled my portal there by now. Not important, for, when you and I are finished with our little exercise, you will gladly hand me the Gatekeeper's key, and all will be well. My father will turn the multiverse over to the Insenium and will be exalted as the first power, just under the Insenium overlord himself.

I will be given your dimension as a gift for my service and will live happily in your little house on Infinity Loop, with all of the resources of your universe at my fingertips. Not bad for a hometown girl like moi."

And she morphed into her Sam guise. She grabbed one of the rough towels from the stack which was now shorter by about a fourth. She gently wiped at Jenny's tears, a look of mock concern on her face.

"*I don't want to miss a moment of our fun together and I am tired. I will go catch a cat nap and leave you to do the same.*"

Jenny heard her footsteps fade away, followed by her guards. Obviously, Jenny was in no position to escape and she was fairly sure there were guards stationed outside the exits. As the door slammed behind them every light went out abruptly. Once again, she was in total darkness.

She floated in that darkness, her mind turning in her protective bubble. She had no desire to face the full impact of the last several hours. Even distancing herself from the pain and sorrow of her ordeal and the fear of the coming torture she was sure to receive at Sam's hands, she still felt unable to cope with what it would be like outside of her mental shield.

She tried to relax, as Sam had recommended, realizing, if she was going to get through this with her resolve intact, she would need to be as rested and energized as possible.

Then, suddenly, Tidbit's voice was in her mind. "*I now release the memory of what I said to you in the 'thinking room'. Remember.*"

And she did. It bloomed in her mind like a candle in the dark. There really was a plan! Tarafau had known all along that his torture and "death" would be used to soften her up. He also knew her response would need to be genuine. So he allowed her to suffer, knowing in the end she would be glad for his subterfuge.

"*Tarafau?*" she queried into the darkness.

"*We're coming,*" he sent, to her delight. "*Hold tight for a minute more. When we cut you loose, be prepared to access your staff. You may not need it, but ready yourself mentally and physically for a fight.*"

Jenny nearly cried again in sheer joy. Fight or no fight, he was coming, and he was bringing others with him. She could face anything knowing that Tarafau was alive and on her side.

She felt the air stir in the darkened space. She nearly jerked away when a hand gently touched hers. "*Hold tight, I have to cut this,*" sent Arvid. "*Stay very still.*"

She didn't move, realizing he would be doing this by feel. As he cut the final bond holding her foot, she sat up carefully.

"*We'll get some light on the subject in a moment,*" sent Tarafau. Jenny wasn't really sure how she always knew the difference between Tarafau's sendings and Tidbit's, but she knew this was Tarafau and she knew somehow, he was standing right next to the slab upon which she now sat.

"*But before we do, you need to know there are quite a few of us and we're getting you out of here. The Fleistians just discovered we have breached their dimension. Right now, their guards are assembling. We have only moments. Stay close to Arvid and listen to his directions.*"

"*Thank you, Tarafau, I will.*"

In the utter silence, she heard the doors at the top of the amphitheater open. Jenny suddenly remembered something her dad had said about the advantage of the heights in a battle and felt very exposed as she slipped off of the stone table. Her staff appeared in her hand. She grasped it firmly in the fighting stance, grateful for the feel of the sleek wood in her hands. Her key warmed and she realized she was still being guided.

"*Look down*," came Arvid's command in her mind, "*And keep your eyes to slits. Look up when I tell you.*"

Jenny obeyed, realizing that this was to prevent the blinding effect of coming from pure darkness into light.

The lights came on and even with her eyes averted to the floor and closed to slits, it was still almost painful.

She heard a collective gasp and then Arvid said, "*Look.*"

At first, she looked to the top of the amphitheater, noting Sam at the forefront of a group of Groga soldiers. Sam and her minions looked shocked and looking around, Jenny realized why.

On every row starting at the top, the stair-stepped benches were filled with…Tarafau! Well, not really Tarafau, but an army of beings enough like him as to be nearly indistinguishable. Every one of them had a blaster rifle trained on the pitifully small force surrounding Sam.

"*You will not prevail!*" she sent, her face twisted in shock and fury. "You'll never get out of here alive!"

Tarafau did not reply. He thought to Jenny, "*I think we have a bit of a surprise for her. I'd have you out of here already, but I thought you'd like to see this.*"

She followed his glance up at the wall extending above Sam's head behind her. Perched on an extinguished torch bracket, directly above her was something that looked very much like a spider the size of Sam's old Smart Car. It spat something from underneath its pincers onto Sam's head which instantly covered her in a web that was attached to a filament which began to draw Sam upward.

Sam yelled something urgent to her Grogan soldiers, but they didn't budge, looking down the bores of the thousands of blasters pointed at them. Some of them edged towards the exit door but froze when a full platoon of Tarafau's cousins swiveled to aim directly at them.

Another couple of platoons strode forward, encircling the Groga soldiers menacingly. Tarafau's troops each put a hand on the shoulder of a Groga and flashed out of existence. Jenny blinked and returned her gaze to the now shrieking Sam who continued to be drawn higher and higher towards the waiting spider.

"Don't worry," sent Tarafau. *"Your Sam is not going to be eaten by our little arachnid friend."* He smirked and put one hand on Jenny's shoulder and one on Arvid's. *"Let's go."*

Immediately they were somewhere else, surrounded by Tarafau's people in a meadow. Not far from where they stood, were Lova, Burt, Bob and the rest of the Guardians as well as Jenny's Guards who looked at once shamefaced and relieved to see her. She would talk to them later and could hopefully make it clear that they were in no way at fault for her recent adventure.

Sanglarka had never looked so good.

Chapter 37: Debriefings

Tarafau's people attended to setting up camp in the meadow, which now looked like a small city between their encampment and that of the Troopers. Only a portion of the force Tarafau had brought to free Jenny and capture Sam had come with them to Sanglarka. From her recent experiences, Jenny was beginning to think that all military encampments had a certain feel to them, regardless of the facilities they used for housing and transportation.

Two of Tarafau's people came into the lodge with the rest of them. They all seated themselves at the long dining table.

Lova, stood at the head of the table, beaming at them all.

"Welcome home, Earthlings and honored guests," she thought at them in mindspeech. As Jenny looked around the table, she was startled to see the humongous spider, who had captured Sam, at the other end of the table, antennae waving complacently, her huge many faceted eyes taking it all in. Jenny thought of the spider tattoo on Sam's arms and grinned, although that grin seemed somehow out of place.

"Tarafau, would you please introduce our guests?"

Tarafau stood. *"This is my brother, Moalgi, and my daughter, Elizabeth."* With a start, Jenny realized she hadn't noticed the difference in gender. She assumed Elizabeth had been named after her aunt, so couldn't be more than 60 years old. Her black hair was braided into thin braids which hung to her waist, which was saying something, as she stood nearly as tall as her father. She wore battle armor and her huge eyes were golden, also like her father.

Moalgi was of a height with his brother. They could have been twins, except for the long scar that went from his right eye to the lower lobe of his ear. Both Moalgi and Elizabeth nodded respectfully to the assembly and sat down again on either side of Tarafau.

"I would also present to you, Glitha of Arandi. Her species and mine live in peace on the same planet. She is not a shape changer, but she also has the ability to travel dimensionally without a gate, a common

trait among the intelligent species on our planet, which was why her assistance was so imperative to our mission. She has transferred Sam to our planet, and she is under 24 hour surveillance until we decide what best to do for her. The most Sam could do at this point, is to escape into the Arandi wilderness. No one will aid her and there is none who need fear her. She might as well be a butterfly." And he looked meaningfully at Jenny's arm.

Glitha sent to the group. "*I thank you for your kind hospitality, one and all. And to be clear, unlike your indigenous arachnid species, I, and my kind, are vegetarians.*" This was sent with a mental smile. Jenny sensed kindness in Glitha's somewhat raspy mental voice. She hoped she would get the opportunity to actually get to know her.

"*Jenny, I would appreciate it if you would get Lizziebot out of your MDP. What happens next needs to be recorded into the Alliance cloud.*"

Jenny obeyed, and Bob also got Fidget out. "*Always backup your backup,*" he said cheerfully to Tarafau when he raised his eyebrows.

"*OK, we will proceed to report, now that we are all together again, thankfully with few casualties. Let's start when we were all together, as the battle at the enemy portal began. Gariel, please start us off.*"

"*We launched everything per the original plan. Burt and Bob's initial distractions allowed us to secure the Groga sentry posts. At that point, we launched stage two of the decoys, believe it or not, flying saucers! Burt and Bob had redesigned several of our larger drones to look like the Earth myths you Earthlings are so crazy about. This apparent invasion got the attention of a large part of the enemy force. They even had a shoot-out, which covered our incursion with the five who accompanied me into the portal and we emerged onto a planet that was unfamiliar to me, but the population seemed to be pastoral and non-technical, which is a divergence from the Grogans usual modus operandi.*

These beings were very surprised to see us, but not alarmed. We tried to explain their danger, but try as we might, we couldn't get the concept across of war or conflict. We scanned the area and determined there was indeed a gateway there that wasn't in the network. However, we had come prepared for that. We brought an unassigned link with us. Because we expected the Groga to come through the portal in mere minutes, and, at the risk of contaminating a non-technological culture, we used a hover car to get to the gate which was several miles away.

We hurriedly activated the link and connected it to our staging area. Although it took longer than I would have liked to get our force of several thousand through the gate, when the Groga came pouring through from their portal, we were ready for them. I regret to say, it was a slaughter. Not one Groga survived and unfortunately, there were some casualties among the Troopers. These deaths subjected those poor beings on that planet to bloodshed and violence they had never even imagined before.

Of course, we cleaned up after ourselves and we left healers behind to help them deal with the trauma. I remind myself that this outcome was better than them being slaughtered and enslaved, but I can't help but wonder what their future will be like now that they have been exposed to this.

We realized that we had no way, at this point, to completely shut down the Groga portal in that dimension. So, as a stopgap measure, we put up a shield that will no longer allow anyone to come more than a millimeter through that portal without dire consequences. If they try, they will only try once. The natives of that planet won't even notice the shield is there.

We sent word through the Alliance to do the same with the Earth portal and then clean up the area and restore it, as possible. So far, on this mission we have lost relatively few Troopers.

The one thing I can tell you is that these attacks were neither planned by the Groga nor do they have the intelligence to pursue it."

Tarafau nodded. As the Guide to the Gatekeeper, Tarafau had always been the highest ranking among them, beside Jenny. He generally acceded to Lova when in Sanglarka, but here and now, in these circumstances, he was in charge.

"*Burt, please report. The last we knew of you, was in the jungle cave.*"

"*When you and Jenny disappeared, we decided to take a peek out of the cave. There we found your tracks heading back toward the encampment. We also found that the bots had gotten in range. We all got Miriha's message, Tarafau, so we didn't follow you. Instead we had the bots reconnoiter for us.*

The little village where Sam had imprisoned us had burned to the ground. We couldn't tell if there had been any casualties, but the little Shaman was giving orders like a foreman as they cleaned up. We retrieved a boat from an MDP and retraced our path up-river until we could use the hovercars without being spotted by the natives. We figured we had already contaminated the indigenous people in that area enough.

We got to the airstrip and shuttled off to the Puerto Rico gate. Juan and Luz let us rest up for a day and here we are. Nothing exciting from our end, really."

Jenny snorted. "*Nothing but making such amazing distractions and decoys that it allowed Gariel to get his Troopers through the enemy portal in the confusion and to capture the remaining troops they left behind. Spaceships? Really? And SYRUP???*"

A chuckle went around the table at that.

Bob ducked his head. "*I always wanted to try that. Can you imagine a whole fleet of flying saucers over L.A.? Anyway, we wanted to be sure the Groga were looking the other way when Gariel and his Troopers went through the portal.*"

Tarafau was still chuckling. "*Well obviously you got the desired results. I'll be having a talk with the Council about you, Mr. Bob. Something tells me they're going to need minds like yours. The third stage of distractions was brilliant. Gariel tells me they still haven't got that syrup completely off of the Groga they captured.*"

Turning to Mynn and Nona, he said, "*And the two of you? Where did you get off to?*"

Mynn rolled her eyes and Nona looked abashed. "*When the Groga attacked the command post, we were on guard with you, Tarafau. We got off a few shots, but in the meantime, you got hit with darts and one of the Groga hurled a smoke bomb of some kind,*" Nona said. "We hopped into one of the hover cars under the cover of the smoke and hunkered down. We were pretty sure it was more than smoke, since Tarafau went down like a felled sequoia and the Groga were wearing masks as well as the little native guys. The Groga must have thought they could pick up our tech later. They never even looked at the hover cars. We heard them rustling about for a bit and then peeked out to see them carrying all of you off in the direction of their camp. It took four of them to heft Tarafau. They didn't look very happy about it."

Mynn broke in. "*We thought our best chance to rescue you was to follow the mission plan which said to hop into a hover car and get a message to headquarters. Since it looked like everyone else was either engaged in battle at the portal or captured by the Groga, we figured we were the only ones left to do that.*"

"*You did exactly right,*" Lova said. "*Following orders is nothing to be ashamed of. What could the two of you have done under the circumstances, other than get yourselves captured as well, or even worse?*"

Tarafau agreed. "*You followed the plan when everything fell apart.*"

Neither Nona nor Mynn seemed to be buying it, though. They hung their heads and Mynn's face colored. Jenny decided that her very next step would be to sit those two down and make sure they knew, in no uncertain terms, that they were not in disrepute for their actions.

He turned to Juan. "*Do we hear anything that would indicate that anyone in the Brazilian or Peruvian governments are aware of a battle anywhere in the basin?*"

Juan shook his head. "*There is nothing on the news and I can't imagine there wouldn't have been if anyone had noticed. I feel fairly certain we pulled it off and once we clean up the clearings, I doubt anyone will ever realize what happened. We have sent a few agents, disguised as natives to also help the little village with some goods and labor, nothing that they wouldn't ordinarily find in the jungle. In a short time, this will all just be another story about how the shaman once accidentally burned down the village and the mysterious strangers who stayed with them for awhile.*"

"*Lova, what do you have for us?*"

"*We have been keeping the Alliance up to date as more information comes in. They have identified several new priorities, now that stage one is complete.*

> *First: Locate the Insenium and discover what kind of beings they are, what abilities they may have and how their portal system works. The blocking of two of the three gates we are familiar with will not be enough. They are hopeful that Tarafau's people will be able to also block the Fleistian portal, to break that link, but we shouldn't do it until we have discovered how to access the Insenium.*
>
> *Second: Our scientists need to determine how the portal devices work. They have expressed a desire to have Bob work with them on this, as he has proven himself innovative and nimble of mind.*
>
> *Third, we must destroy the ability of the Insenium to access any of the dimensions, which may be difficult, as they may have created the technology in the first place, and you can't unlearn something. Since we know nothing about the beings that inhabit that dimension, we don't have any idea if our mind altering technology would work on them and, even if it did, to alter the minds of an entire planet or maybe even an entire dimension might be beyond us.*

I think that's enough to be going on with, don't you?"

This last was said almost flippantly, but Jenny gasped and looking around she saw jaws drop, eyebrows shoot up and Glitha's pincers clacked, almost like someone tapping their fingers nervously. No one on the team took this news casually.

"*All of us knew when we took on the responsibility of Guardians, that there might be times like these. I for one, will not back down from the threat. Our allegiance to Earth and the Alliance hasn't changed,*" Lova said, taking the time to look into every face, including Gariel, Jenny's Guards, Glitha and Tarafau's brother and daughter. "*I would like to say that I would trust any one of you with my life and all that I have and all that I stand for. But for the purposes of solidarity, I would like each of us to stand in agreement."*

They all stood, which was somewhat alarming, as when Glitha stood fully on her eight legs, her head nearly brushed the 14 foot ceiling. Lova continued, "*Swear with me, that we will not quit or falter as we undertake to accomplish the three missions I have just announced. That we will remain true to the Alliance as we have agreed and give all we have, and hope to have, to this cause.*"

There were variations on "I so swear, I do, or I will," but every single being in their company agreed solemnly to this oath.

"*Jenny, do you have some words for us?*" Tarafau asked as they all sat again.

Jenny nodded and stood again, although unsure what she could add. "*It hardly seems possible that not so many months ago I was a kid out of college, with a tiny little apartment and a comfy little life, using my skills to get along in a world that seemed relatively safe to me. I am not sorry that my life has changed, but I would hate to see the lives of those in our world or any others subjected to the mentality that drives this force against us.*

Now that we have secured Earth, we are not finished, and I have no intention of quitting and letting the rest of the multiverse get along as best they can. I come from a family who believes in serving the cause of freedom and I know what my dad would say if he knew about this. He'd say, 'Where do I sign up?' I am his daughter through and through. If these beings would leave others alone, I would gladly leave them alone. But we don't ignore a threat, just because it isn't directed at us personally.

Our home world isn't perfect, by any means, and it definitely isn't ready for this kind of technology at this point. I would say we can say the same for the Groga, the Fleistians, the Insenium and any other entity that feels that they can excuse their actions of brutality under the cover of it being for the best good of those they seek to enslave.

I'm not as experienced as any of you here today. Every one of you has better skills and knows more about what we're doing than I do, but since I have been given this responsibility, I will not back down, not as long as there is a single person to stand by me and I will die fighting, regardless. This is the pact we just made. This is the cause we undertake, and we will do it together."

Jenny sat down and suddenly the rest were back on their feet, not applauding, not speaking, but shoulders back, heads held high, looking directly into Jenny's eyes.

"Come on then, folks. We've a war to fight and a lot to do to win it," Tarafau said, finally.

Chapter 38: Full Circle

Jenny stood in the middle of her living room, watching Tidbit sunning in his favorite spot. The voices of Burt, Bob, Lyra, Nona and Mynn drifted in from the patio through the open French doors. The repair crew, courtesy of the Alliance, had done a beautiful job restoring her house, including a redwood picnic table on the patio meant to seat eight and beautiful furnishings. She even had a new overstuffed reading chair next to a bookshelf full of books and a little table and stand lamp in the usual place.

Over the fireplace, there was finally a painting, a large portrait of Jenny holding Tidbit on her lap. She wasn't sure how they managed that, considering she had never had the time to pose even for a photograph since taking up this amazing adventure and huge responsibility, but it looked homey and finished up the living room nicely.

They had all agreed to take a deep breath before the plunge. After all, none of them would have the leisure for what might be a very long time to spend any real time in their homes, with the exception of Lova, who would continue to host the Earth Guardian headquarters and be the go-between with the Alliance. So, for the next couple of weeks they would all be battening down the hatches in their various residences.

Tarafau had agreed to take her to his home to meet his family and get to know more about his people as part of getting her training back on track. They planned to do that in about a week.

Lizziebot came through the dining room from the kitchen. "Do you want Spaghetti or Lasagna for supper?" she asked. "I'm feeling Italian tonight."

"Either one sounds fine to me. Why don't you check with the folks out on the patio? Majority rules."

Lizziebot had taken to cooking and cleaning, although Jenny told her it was a waste of all that tech. Lizziebot then informed Jenny that she had enough to be going on with and she didn't mind. Jenny couldn't stop marveling about the hidden talents Bob had programmed into her. She almost never opened the tablet anymore.

She got very used to the convenience of having Lizzie's memories, experience and sense of humor on tap and she knew, when and if everything finally settled down that Lizziebot would continue to be a great asset to her as The Gatekeeper.

Lova had told Jenny that she would continue to get more training once they had everything in hand with the Insenium and Fleist, but until then, it would still be "on-the-job" training by necessity. Strictly speaking, other than leading her team in this struggle, she wasn't doing much in her role as The Gatekeeper, but Lova had assured her that it would all come sooner than she realized.

They had all made a trip to the Dimensional Alliance Council Chamber, in the beautiful atrium, to report on the completion of stage one of the mission. Jenny had been invited with Tarafau to sit on the dais with the three Chief Counselors. After playing the recording of the debriefing at Sanglarka, Ingot opened it up for questions and comments. For a bit there was just stunned silence and then slowly different ones stood and spoke. Although, a lot of what was said was way over Jenny's head, as they referred to precedents from Alliance history and other conflicts Jenny was not aware of, she was impressed with the courtesy and respect each of them treated the various thoughts and opinions among those assembled there.

What it boiled down to was that they agreed that the three step plan was reasonable, that they would support its implementation and that they appreciated the efforts and accomplishments of Jenny's team. There were even words of encouragement for Jenny herself, which stirred her heart in ways she had never felt before.

Afterwards there had been a reception, the first official event of this sort Jenny had attended as "The Gatekeeper". She began to realize what had been meant when various team members had implied that her experience as Gatekeeper and Guardian would teach her much about the myths of earth. She recognized a Minotaur, a Gorgon (complete with veil), a Unicorn and even a group of tall slender beings with pointed ears that could be nothing more or less than Elves.

The different beings mixed not much differently than a cocktail party or ambassadorial reception on earth, conversing in groups, eating and even laughing together (Or at least Jenny hoped it was laughter.

With some of them it was hard to tell.). It kind of felt like some kind of formal cosplay at a fantasy convention.

Jenny stood in a kind of reception line with Ingot, Liliath, Myla and Tarafau. Her head swam with all of the introductions and she knew she would never remember all of the names and titles. However, her title, as Gatekeeper, meant that all of those she met were respectful and interested in meeting her. They asked polite questions about Earth and wanted to know more about her story, of how she became Gatekeeper, although, she suspected most of them already knew. It wasn't exactly a state secret.

All in all, her visit at the Alliance was heady stuff, but the best part was when Ingot, Myla and Liliath had them retire to the private council room and each of them congratulated Jenny and her team on their excellent work. "*We'd have never gotten even close to this far without the courage, ingenuity and persistence of the Earth Guardians their Agents and our new Gatekeeper.*" Liliath said.

"*And we feel confident that when you are able to join forces with some of the other Guardians throughout the network that we can create a stratagem to accomplish our priorities,*" continued Ingot.

Myla held out his hands to her. "*There is so much more in you than you have yet discovered, Jenny. I know this is very daunting. It would be, even to any of the experienced agents among us, but you have the resources to do amazing things and the will to accomplish them.*" He wrapped his arms and wings around her in a gentle hug.

And then they had come to her house and found all well there.

That evening they had Lasagna out on the patio and then the guys headed over to Bob's place.

Jenny and her three Guards who were now also her friends, all got ready for bed and settled in after letting Tidbit out. Now that Jenny knew what he was really doing all of those nights, it made her smile. Tarafau would visit his family and then return. His nightly forays probably explained why he got a nap in on the window seat every day, she thought, amused.

Lizziebot was repowering. She was tied in to the extremely sensitive high tech security system and would wake immediately, if there was anything to worry about, so Jenny turned out the light and went to sleep, knowing that they had a lot of work ahead, but it would wait until morning while she slept in her little house on Infinity Loop.

If you loved The House on Infinity Loop, please take a moment and do a review:

If you bought the book on Amazon, please review it on Amazon.com and any of the other review places suggested below:

Bookbub.com

Goodreads.com

...Or any social media book clubs you may participate in. This helps me know how best to continue to provide good reading for you, my audience and will be greatly appreciated.

For news about upcoming books, audio books, contests, giveaways and fan gear, join my fan group on Facebook: The Dimensional Alliance – Fan Gate

Cast of Characters:

Jenny Japhet: 20 something young woman, professional ghost-writer, avid hiker. She is young, but not flippant, extremely intelligent, but not stuffy. She is committed and a hard worker as shown by her success in the ghost-blogging industry which is highly competitive and requires a great deal of discipline and assertiveness when getting and keeping clients. By this point in our story she is the Guardian of the Los Angeles gate and officially the Gatekeeper of the Dimensional Alliance, a position of overwhelming responsibility.

Lizzie Japhet: Aunt of Jenny, was a Guardian of the Los Angeles gate before Jenny working for the Alliance since she was a young adult. Independent and sometimes a bit acerbic; she never thought of herself as old. She had a strong mind, a sense of adventure and a dry sense of humor. She also had great affection for her niece, who she had secretly observed for many years by the use of alien tech. She is highly respected by all who knew her.

Sam aka Engoza: Had been Jenny's best friend during college. Unfortunately, she turns out to be one of the major villains of this story. She can be snide and snippy, but when we first meet her, she is just a bit of a party girl who works at a local television station. Jenny had no idea she's being set up and when Sam finally reveals the truly evil side of her nature it is a great shock to Jenny.

Bob Reid: Jenny's across the street neighbor. Bob identifies himself as a "tinkerer" He is a middle aged man, an engineer and inventor. He's smart and despite his involvement in advanced technology and multiple PHDs, he is friendly and a bit countrified. He's a simple guy, a widower with one son. He loves animals and loves Tidbit, the cat. He owns a Hyacinth McCaw named Ignatius

Tidbit: Big black tabby cat. He is a cat with attitude, pretty much the king of the neighborhood, lording it over the other pets and/or pests. In reality, he is the alter ego of Tarafau Bane.

Tarafau Bane: Jenny's Alliance Guide, is a Daringi one of several races on a planet in a dimension outside of the Dimensional Alliance. His race has an ability that allows them to transport from any dimension to any other dimension without a gate as long as they know where it is.

Miriha: The original Gatekeeper at the beginning of The House on Infinity Loop. Miriha is gentle, soft-spoken and a loving and extremely kind and wise person. She appears only a few times in the book, but she is a major staple character throughout the series.

Lova Norstrom: Guardian of the Sanglarka gate. A military background, she is a friend and mentor to Jenny and the leader of the Earth division of the Dimensional Alliance.

Arvid Longhammer : Uncle of Ingot and trainer of Earth Guardians. An alien of a dwarvish race. A bit of a curmudgeon on the outside, but with a heart of gold. Arvid is a bit of a drill sergeant as far as the other characters are concerned, but he also loves to cook and has a wry sense of humor. Fiercely loyal to his friends and wholly committed to the cause of the Dimensional Alliance in guarding the Gate Network.

Fidget: AI robot created by Bob. Fidget is developing new abilities and will play a key role in the story as pertains to Bob and the Alliance.

Ingot: Dwarf with a gnomish face, Chief Councilor of the Dimensional Alliance. Seems a little gruff, is related to Arvid. Very business-like, but that hides a gentle and caring heart.

Liliath: Dragon (Alani race) 2nd to Ingot. Advanced mental abilities and strong leadership skills. She is straightforward and doesn't mince words, but she has a mothering heart, especially where Jenny is concerned.

Myla: Calix, humanoid with wings, 3rd to Ingot, birdlike but not soft. Not quite parrotlike either. He is very tender hearted, but not afraid to make hard decisions. Ingot depends a lot on his counsel and support.

Juan Roman: Puerto Rico Gate Guardian. A bit soft spoken, but not shy or retiring. He has a military background. He knows how to lead and how to follow. He is a warm person, but also exacting.

Adelle Becker: Switzerland Gate Guardian. Adelle is a scientist with the heart of a farmer's daughter. She loves animals and the outdoors and cherishes the observatory that houses the Switzerland Gate for its isolation and natural wonders.

Mustapha Kashani: Pakistan Gate Guardian. Very matter of fact and maybe a bit grumpy. Not really a team player by nature, he still plays the part he's been given. He has technical experience and tends to be precise in his communications.

Brendan Lisle: Australia Gate Guardian. An Aussie with a bit of swagger. Bush pilot and ex Australian Air Force military. He has a good sense of humor and is somewhat casual in his speech and attitude. Gets enthusiastic about anything related to flying.

Xao Ting: China Gate Guardian. Bei Shaolin Grandmaster and an herbalist. Stoic, somewhat inscrutable and wise.

Leonora Svoboda: Czechoslovakia Gate Guardian. Stolid and straightforward and nearly no sense of humor. She says her piece and does her job. Not someone you would hang out with or go shopping with.

Dhakirah Jalani: Ghana Gate Guardian. She is gentle and not at all warlike. She deplores violence and is the ultimate peacemaker. Her beautiful spirit is reflected in her thoughtful words and the grace of her body.

Aliki Malala: Samoan Gate Guardian. Bouncy, describes this Samoan man. Over-the-top optimistic and ready to do whatever needs to be done. A consummate sailor and a gentle soul. He doesn't dance, sing or play the ukulele by his own admission.

Leland O'Flaherty: Ireland Gate Guardian. This guy is soooo Irish. He loves people and is quick to act when he knows where he needs to be and what he needs to do.

Guaray Verma: India Gate Guardian. Quiet and soft-spoken. Doesn't put himself forward and a little mysterious. Ultimately it turns out he is a traitor to the cause, because his family has been threatened. Now that his family is safe he works as an agent for the Alliance, but no longer is a Gate Guardian.

Megan Smythe: Canada Gate Guardian. A total shrinking violet. Much more comfortable with animals than people. She is a Canadian Park Ranger by trade although she has a degree in zoology.

Luz Roman: Juan's wife and Guide. Warm, Puerto Rican woman with a welcoming and optimistic personality. She has some hidden talents, but she is who she is, very open and friendly.

King Laman: King of the Fleistians and father of Engoza (Sam).

Queen Ohaz: Queen of the Fleistians (and of the Groga), mother of Engoza (Sam)

Mynah: The instructor who is to teach Jenny Fleistian ways and induct her into he plan of the Insenium for domination of the multiverse.

Wellis, Gras and Cheb: Jenny's lady's maids while in imprisoned by the Fleistians.

Glitha: Giant female arachnid originating on the same planet and dimension as Tarafau and the Daringi. She is the leader of the arachnid race on that planet and takes custody of Sam after her capture by the Daringi.

About the author:

Bonnie K.T. Dillabough

To write or not to write has never been the question...
She wrote her first 26 line poem at age 8, entitled "My Christmas ABCs". She then memorized it and performed it for the church Christmas party. This wasn't terribly surprising.

She started reading before Kindergarten and Dr. Seuss was one of her favorite authors, so rhyme came very naturally to her. She has been writing all of her life, as long as she can remember. A lot of poetry, short stories and, of course, the usual school reports. she always got high grades on her writing assignments, even when she didn't in other classes, simply because she loved to write.

Then, adulthood set in. Always a voracious reader, she dreamt of writing a novel, but got gloriously side-tracked with a wonderful husband and six amazing children. During that time, she still wrote: Musical plays for her kids at church and school, songs, poetry and even an occasional newspaper article streamed from her pen. Then, she got involved in jobs that required clear concise writing and a lot of marketing copy. She put up her first website in 1996 and made her living on the internet for over 20 years, writing everything from blog posts to sales copy to scripts for online videos, not to mention copy for the websites she built for her clients.

Now, at age 65 she finally published the first novel in an ongoing series, The Dimensional Alliance

When she is not writing, she likes to read, crochet hats for the homeless and gifts for friends and family, is active in her church and looks forward to being very involved with the fans of her books from her website:

DimensionalAllianceHeadquarters.com.

CPSIA information can be obtained
at www.ICGtesting.com
Printed in the USA
LVHW010325190720
661024LV00001B/29